THE KILLING STONES

By Ann Cleeves

The Vera Stanhope series
The Crow Trap   Telling Tales   Hidden Depths
Silent Voices   The Glass Room   Harbour Street
The Moth Catcher   The Seagull   The Darkest Evening
The Rising Tide   The Dark Wives

The Shetland Island series
Raven Black   White Nights   Red Bones
Blue Lightning   Dead Water   Thin Air
Cold Earth   Wild Fire

The Detective Matthew Venn series
The Long Call   The Heron's Cry
The Raging Storm

The George & Molly Palmer-Jones series
A Bird in the Hand   Come Death and High Water
Murder in Paradise   A Prey to Murder
Another Man's Poison   Sea Fever
The Mill on the Shore   High Island Blues

The Inspector Ramsay series
A Lesson in Dying   Murder in My Backyard
A Day in the Death of Dorothea Cassidy
Killjoy   The Healers   The Baby Snatcher

The Sleeping and the Dead
Burial of Ghosts

Ann Cleeves

THE KILLING STONES

MINOTAUR BOOKS
NEW YORK

This is a work of fiction. All of the characters, organizations, and events portrayed in this novel are either products of the author's imagination or are used fictitiously.

First published in the United States by Minotaur Books, an imprint of
St. Martin's Publishing Group

EU Representative: Macmillan Publishers Ireland Ltd, 1st Floor, The Liffey Trust Centre, 117–126 Sheriff Street Upper, Dublin 1, DO1 YC43

THE KILLING STONES. Copyright © 2025 by Ann Cleeves. All rights reserved. Printed in the United States of America. For information, address St. Martin's Publishing Group, 120 Broadway, New York, NY 10271.

www.minotaurbooks.com

Map artwork by ML Design Ltd

The Library of Congress Cataloging-in-Publication Data is available upon request.

ISBN 978-1-250-35728-1 (hardcover)
ISBN 978-1-250-35729-8 (ebook)

The publisher of this book does not authorize the use or reproduction of any part of this book in any manner for the purpose of training artificial intelligence technologies or systems. The publisher of this book expressly reserves this book from the Text and Data Mining exception in accordance with Article 4(3) of the European Union Digital Single Market Directive 2019/790.

Our books may be purchased in bulk for specialty retail/wholesale, literacy, corporate/premium, educational, and subscription box use. Please contact MacmillanSpecialMarkets@macmillan.com.

Originally published in Great Britain by Macmillan, an imprint of Pan Macmillan

First U.S. Edition: 2025

10 9 8 7 6 5 4 3 2 1

For Stewart Bain: Orcadian, reader and friend.

Dear Reader,

It's been twenty years since I wrote the first Jimmy Perez book, inspired by a brief midwinter trip to Shetland to catch up with old friends. The anniversary of its publication will be next year. *Raven Black* was planned as a stand-alone novel, a brief foray into the islands that had been special to me since I'd worked there in my early twenties.

In the end, there were eight books. The last, *Wild Fire*, showed Perez settled, about to become a father and ready to leave Shetland. I'd met my husband on Fair Isle, one of the more remote islands, during my first year of working there, and the publication of the final book so soon after his death seemed fitting. It was time, I thought, to move on to new projects.

More recently, I felt an itch to move north again, to experience once more the constant views of the sea and the big skies. I'd visited Orkney on my first trip to Shetland, and I've been back many times since. It's gentler than Shetland, more fertile, and it had become Jimmy Perez's home. It occurred to me that it would be interesting to catch up with Jimmy and Willow and to explore a new setting. The result is *The Killing Stones*.

Like *Raven Black*, this is a midwinter book. It explores the history of the place and the more modern Orcadian traditions. But really, this is a domestic story, about families and the secrets that can pull them apart. I hope you enjoy catching up with Jimmy and Willow as much as I enjoyed writing about them – and thank you for supporting your local independent bookshop by purchasing this special hardcover edition.

Ann Cleeves

Acknowledgements

I loved writing this book and having time to explore Orkney. Thanks to everyone in Westray who made me welcome – especially the knowledgeable volunteers at the heritage centre, Mabel Kent of the Pierowall Hotel and Tom and May Bain. Stewart Bain was my driver and fixer throughout my research, and through him I learned about cold beans and fatty-cutties. I'm grateful to Orkney Islands archaeologist Paul Sharman for sharing information about the Noltland dig; to Sandra Miller and her team for organizing the trip to Maeshowe; and to Neil Stevenson for checking that I didn't stray too far from the reality of the Ba'. Of course, all mistakes are mine.

My friend Dr James Grieve appears again as himself in the novel, and I'm pleased that he continues to work in fiction, even if he might eventually retire in fact. Thanks to the relatives of Rosalie Greeman, who donated a considerable sum to charity at Bouchercon San Diego for her name to be remembered in this novel.

While writing is a solitary occupation, it takes a team to get the book to readers. Thanks to the support team at Pan

Macmillan – Alex, Lucy, Fran, Ellah, Charlotte, Natasha, Stuart, Rosa, Mary and all the reps who spread the word. In the US, I'm grateful to Kelley, Catherine, Kelly, Martin and Sarah; in Australia to Praveen and Candice; and in Canada to all at PGC and especially to Jen. Huge thanks to my agent, Moses; to all the overseas co-agents and publishers; and to Rebecca of VHA. I'm grateful as always to Jean and Roger of Cornwell Internet for their friendship and for managing my website. A special shout-out to Emma, fabulous publicist and fun travelling companion. Also, touring wouldn't be the same without Steve and Geoff of Benchmark.

I've had a great time working with the Reading for Wellbeing and Woodyard projects. I don't do much of the actual graft, so I'm thankful to the people who do – my assistant, Jane, all the staff in libraries, the NHS and voluntary organizations for Reading for Wellbeing in the North-East, and the Woodyard committee members striving to turn our community centre plan into reality in North Devon. Special thanks go to Naomi, who had that idea, and my best friend, Sue, for agreeing to be a part of it.

Finally, thanks to all the booksellers and library staff who share the magic of reading, and to the readers themselves who allow me the joy of telling stories.

THE KILLING STONES

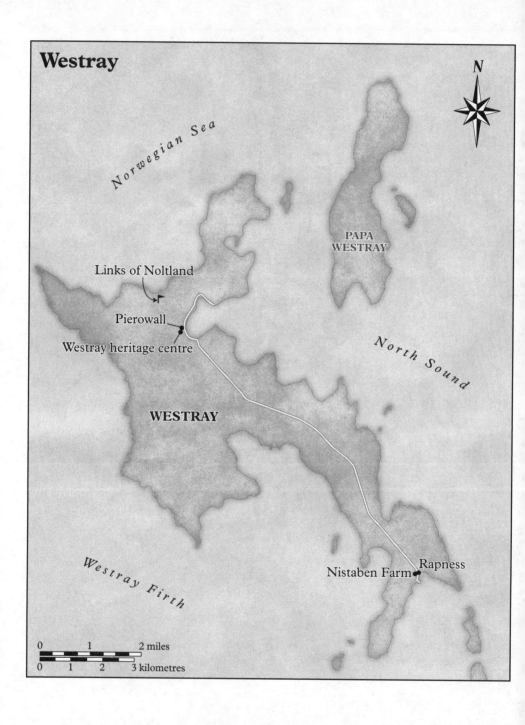

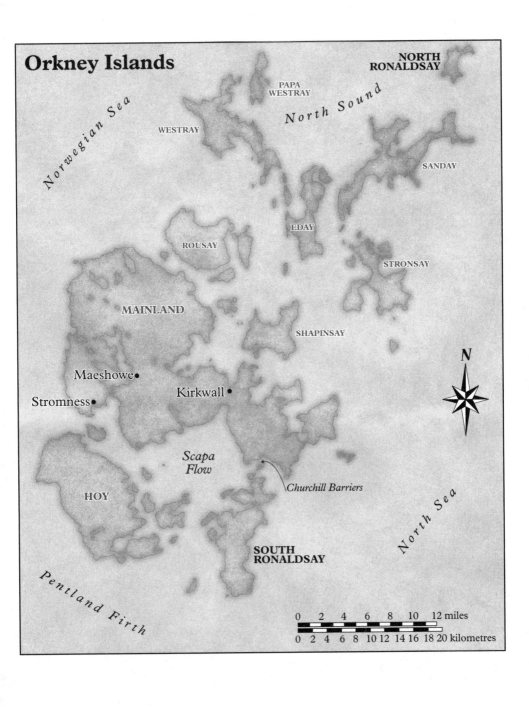

Prologue

ARCHIE STOUT SCREAMED INTO THE STORM. His voice was as loud and echoing as a foghorn, but the noise of the wind blew the words away, scattered them like spindrift over the water. Incoherent and pointless. The person they were aimed at couldn't have heard them anyway. The torchlight had already disappeared, swallowed up by the midwinter darkness, and Archie was alone.

He was Orcadian, a Westray man born and raised. He loved a good gale, the power and the drama of it, and there was a trace of childish pleasure in his fury now. An exhilaration. He loved a good argument too, especially when he knew he was in the right.

That moment passed. He was dressed for the weather, but there was no joy in standing here, ancient bones and rocks under his feet, when the Pierowall Hotel bar was waiting for him, and his friends had been expecting him an hour ago. He imagined the warmth of the fire and the laughter when he arrived, soaking, his hair sleeked to his head and his beard still dripping. Their words: 'Where have you been, man? What the hell have you been doing out in this kind of weather?'

There was still that problem that had been troubling him all day. Archie wasn't sure how that could best be dealt with. It wasn't something to discuss with Vaila, certainly. If his father had still been alive, he might have known the right thing to do. For the island and the family.

Then it came to Archie that he could talk to Jimmy Perez. Jimmy was his oldest and closest friend, a relative of a kind. Jimmy was a wise man. He could tell what other folk were thinking and feeling. Archie would phone him first thing in the morning. That decision made, it felt as if a weight had been lifted from him, and he shone his torch away from the sea and towards the path to his car.

The light coming his way almost seemed like a reflection of his own torchlight at first, wavering through the gloom. Archie stood where he was, curious, waiting for it to reach him. He saw a figure appear before him, shapeless, wrapped in a waterproof that reached to the boots. Anonymous until Archie shone his torch into the face.

'Ah,' he said. 'So it's you.'

Chapter One

WILLOW LOVED GETTING TO THE ISLANDS by ferry, even now with a baby in her belly, and a four-year-old to care for, and the boat already late because of the earlier storm. Winter in Orkney stirred her like no other season. It was the exhilaration of wild, windy days and the chance of exploring the islands' secrets alone for a while, until the tourists came again. Digging in. Rooting herself and her family in this place. Because she and her man, Jimmy Perez, had already decided that they would never leave here.

She'd treated herself to a Magnus Lounge pass, and sat on one of the comfortable sofas, with James lying sleeping on her lap, staring out at the darkness and then at the approaching lights of home, thinking that if she weren't pregnant, she'd be raising a glass of Highland Park malt whisky to this place and her life here. She'd been south to visit an elderly relative in Aberdeen while she could still travel, and now she was glad to be coming home again. The child was due in six weeks' time. She'd be giving birth to a winter baby and that thrilled her too.

The lounge was almost empty. There weren't many visitors

at this time of year, and most of the locals were in their cabins. She'd never been seasick, and James seemed to have inherited her resistance to the affliction. The boat would move on to Shetland once they'd stopped in Kirkwall. Shetland would always be special to her – Jimmy Perez had been born in Fair Isle, the southernmost island in the group, and Shetland was where they'd met – but gentler, more fertile Orkney was the home they'd made together.

It was midnight when they arrived. She carried the child, still sleeping, to the car deck and strapped him into his seat, then drove out with the handful of other vehicles onto the dock, with its shadowy industrial buildings, out of Kirkwall and into the country.

She'd been expecting Perez to be up, waiting for her, the fire still lit. She'd texted when they'd come close to shore and phone signal had been restored. There'd been no response, but Jimmy was as taciturn in text as he was in speech. There were lights in the downstairs windows of the old manse when she drove up. She could see them seeping through gaps in the curtains that had been drawn against the cold. But when she let herself in, she could tell at once that the house had been empty for a while, although there were still embers in the grate and the heating had been left on. If he'd been in, Jimmy would have heard the car pulling up outside and come into the hall to greet them, reaching out for his son, insisting that he be the person to put James to bed. His adopted fourteen-year-old daughter, Cassie, was part of the family too, of course, but she was in Shetland for the school holidays, staying with Duncan, her birth father and Celia his partner. Over Christmas, it would just be the three of them. And the child waiting to be born.

Now, Willow climbed the stairs and put James to bed. He'd

already been changed into his pyjamas. She wasn't anxious about Jimmy's absence. It would be a work matter. He'd always cared too much about work, and now she was on maternity leave, he was more conscientious than he'd ever been. His patch included Shetland and Orkney and he was often pulled away. Perez had married when he was young, but the marriage hadn't lasted. His wife couldn't cope with the time and energy he'd given to his work. She'd called him 'emotionally incontinent', and it was true that all his sympathy seemed to be channelled towards the victims, the relatives and even the perpetrators of crime. Sometimes Willow wondered how he had anything left to give to his family. But she was passionate about her work too, and she understood.

She pushed the kettle onto the hotplate of the Rayburn to make tea, before seeing the note in Jimmy's handwriting propped on the kitchen table.

Archie Stout is missing and Vaila is frantic. I've managed to get a boat to Westray. I'll phone in the morning. So sorry. I miss you and love you.

She didn't try to phone him. He'd be busy and anyway there'd probably be no signal. She wondered how he'd managed to get to Westray. It got dark so early at this time of year, and the weather had been so wild, though the wind was dropping now. Perhaps the lifeboat crew had taken Jimmy over there. It was possible that Archie had been out in his little creel boat and got into difficulties. He was a farmer more than a fisherman. The storm had come on suddenly, and its ferocity hadn't been forecast. There was a niggle of anxiety at the back of her mind, but she knew it was pointless to guess what might have happened and tried to close it down. She'd taken up with Jimmy Perez knowing who he was, and she'd been determined not to try to change him.

Besides, she understood his desperate attempt to get to the island of Westray. Archie Stout was a friend. The closest friend he had in Orkney. Perhaps his closest friend ever. They were relatives of a kind. A grandfather, or a great-grandfather, or uncle had moved to Orkney from Fair Isle, and Archie had spent many of his holidays on the Perez croft. Archie farmed on the island of Westray, living in Nistaben with his wife and two boys, and now the families were close too.

Willow drank her tea and went to bed. It was too late to phone Archie's wife, Vaila, and in any case the man was probably safe at home. They might well be sitting in the farm kitchen eating a late supper, drinking in celebration at his return. He was a sociable man, a grand fiddle player. He liked a party, and any excuse would do. Willow was tired.

She woke in the morning to the quiet. No wind at all. It was still dark and there was no sound from James in the next room. She wondered for an instant what could have woken her and realized it was the humming of her phone. She'd switched it to silent, but she was a light sleeper and the buzzing had penetrated her sleep.

She reached for it before it stopped, saw it was from Perez, and allowed the relief to swirl round her stomach. Until then, she hadn't realized that she'd woken with a sense of anxiety. There'd been a troubling dream, perhaps, though she couldn't remember the detail.

'Hello. You still in Westray with Archie and Vaila?' The image she'd conjured the night before of the three of them drinking into the early hours, Archie playing his tunes, returned to her.

Then she realized that Perez was gasping and could hardly speak. It was as if he was struggling for breath.

'Jimmy! What is it?'

'It's Archie.' The words seemed to be forced out of his mouth. 'He's dead.'

'How?' She might be on maternity leave, but she was a detective. Not quite Jimmy's boss, and with a wider brief, covering all the Scottish islands, but still with an instinct to be in charge. Her brain was already firing with the procedures that would have to be followed.

There was a long pause. 'It looks like murder.' Another pause. 'It must be murder.'

'Is there a doctor on the island who can certify death?'

'Oh, he's certainly dead.' Jimmy was sobbing now. He was no longer holding it together. That excess of emotion again.

'But you know the procedure, Jimmy. You know how it has to work.'

'Sure. Yes, there's a doctor.'

'Where was he found?' Now, Willow had the bedside light on and had found her notepad and a pencil.

'On the Links of Noltland, just inland from Grobust beach. Close to the old archaeological dig.'

'Any sign of cause of death?'

'Blunt force trauma to the head. The weapon is still next to the body.'

'We'll get Dr Grieve from Aberdeen onto the next plane. You'll make sure nobody else can get into the site.'

'Of course.' His voice was already calmer.

'Who found the body?'

'Me,' he said, almost in a whisper. 'It was me.'

Chapter Two

IT WAS COLD, THE FIRST FROST of the winter, shocking after an autumn of mild, windy days, and after the previous night's storm. Jimmy Perez stood on a narrow dune, keeping guard over his friend's body. When it was properly light, he'd have a view of the long beach. There was a footpath where dog-walkers came, a bench looking out to the sea. He'd asked Vaila's mother to stay with Archie's wife and bairns and was glad to be here alone until colleagues arrived from Orkney mainland on the early ferry into Westray. He looked north into the first light of dawn, everything shadowy and blurred, and not quite real. There was still a pale moon.

The fact of Archie's death wasn't real either. The man had always been very much alive, even larger than life, a risk-taker, fearless as a boy, leading the quiet Jimmy into mischief and adventure that he'd never have had the guts to face on his own. Perez had loved him for that. Perhaps it was Archie who'd given him the courage to move south to Aberdeen to join the police service, and Archie who'd pulled him back to the Northern Isles when his first marriage had failed. They'd been opposite in every way. Perez had inherited the dark looks of his Spanish ancestors and Archie was Viking through and through. Sandy-haired and icy-eyed, impulsive and quick to laughter and to anger. Tamed by Vaila, his childhood sweetheart, but not entirely. There'd still been an edge of danger to him.

Archie had been overjoyed when Perez had told him he was bringing his family to Orkney. He'd wrapped Jimmy in his arms and repeated over and over again: 'What splendid news! Just splendid! The old team together again.' The *j* in 'just' pronounced *ch* in the Orcadian way.

He'd helped them to find their new home in Harray, unloaded boxes and bags and drunk to their health. Archie was one reason why Perez had decided he never wanted to move again.

Perez looked at his phone to check the time. The ferry from Kirkwall would be arriving soon. It was a roll-on, roll-off and the officers would have a car with them. When they got here, he'd have to drive back to Nistaben and face Vaila. After he'd been dropped off at Rapness pier by the lifeboat crew, Perez had called in at the farm and asked to borrow a car. Westray was a big island, three times bigger than his original home of Fair Isle, and he'd known he'd need transport. He dreaded meeting Vaila this morning. She would be full of questions, and he knew that he had no answers to give.

He'd spoken to Willow. She'd manage matters with her usual quiet efficiency. He was overcome suddenly with a wave of gratitude for the woman who always had his back. She might look like a hippy with her long tangle of hair and charity shop clothes, but she was the best detective he knew. The best woman, wise and totally reliable. *His* woman. Despite his grief, he smiled at his good fortune.

He heard them before he saw them: Phil Bain and Ellie

Shearer. Ellie was older, apparently happy to be in uniform and to stay a sergeant, policing their patch. Solid and sensible. She'd grown up in the north of England, had come to Orkney on holiday, fallen for an Orcadian and never returned. Phil was new and raw and innocent, and still looked like the student he'd recently been. He'd gone south to Teesside to do the policing course at the university there, but the pull of the islands had been too strong, and he'd returned. Their words were indistinct, but Perez could make out the tone, a mix of shock and excitement. They might have been aware of Archie as a musician and farmer, but they wouldn't have known him well.

It was properly light now. The pair were walking down the path from the golf course, following Perez's instructions, taking the route he'd used when he'd found Archie. They'd left their vehicle in the golf club car park. It always made Willow chuckle that Westray was sufficiently wealthy to have a golf club. There was a driveable track from the village, but Perez wanted to keep that clear in case of tyre marks. The rain of the previous night had left it a boggy quagmire though and he wasn't hopeful that they'd find much of use. Now he called out to his colleagues to stay where they were. He didn't want them stumbling over the body. Then he moved down the slope to greet them, only aware of how chilled he'd become as he started moving. He circled a good distance from the locus and joined them.

'I'm sorry, Jimmy.' Ellie spoke first. 'I know you were good mates.' She looked towards the body. It lay between patches of heavy black plastic, which was held down by dead tyres. 'What's this place? Some kind of dump?'

'It was an archaeological dig. When they'd finished on it, they covered it for any other team that might want to come back to excavate again.'

Perez remembered one summer when the diggers were on the island. He'd been staying at Nistaben with Archie and his parents. He and Archie had been young then – eight or nine – and the students had seemed exciting, creatures from a different world. The archaeologists had been staying in a holiday rental owned by Archie's parents. It was close to Nistaben Farm, and the team had held parties on the beach that went on late into the night. Perez and Archie had peered out of their bedroom window to see the dancing shapes in the firelight, to hear the strains of music.

'Will you wait here,' Perez said, 'while I go and talk to Archie's widow? I'll need you to keep an eye on things until the pathologist arrives. Willow has arranged for Doc Grieve to come in on the early plane, and I'm hoping he'll have the crime scene team with him too.'

'Is he still working? I thought he'd retired.'

'Nah, he can't keep away.' Perez wasn't sure why the forensic pathologist was back in post, but he was glad he'd be dealing with someone whose respect for the dead and their relatives only matched his skill.

Nistaben was solid and squat, built against the weather, but substantial, surrounded by byres and outbuildings. Orcadians were real farmers, not subsistence crofters. The place had been in the Stout family for generations, and for Perez it had become almost a second home. He took off his boots in the porch and padded into the kitchen in stockinged feet. He didn't knock. That would have felt odd, yet he was here officially, so perhaps he should have done. There would be senior officers from Glasgow arriving to take over the case, but until that happened, he was in charge of the investigation, and he'd have to walk the tightrope between friend and cop. An ambiguous role wasn't unusual in these small island communities, but he'd find it tricky.

Vaila and her mother were sitting at the table. There was a pot of tea and two mugs, but he couldn't see that they'd been used.

He sat with them. 'Where are the boys?'

'Upstairs.' Vaila looked up at him. 'They don't know yet. I couldn't find the words to tell them. They know that their father's missing, but not the full horror. I thought I could give them a couple of hours more of not knowing.'

'They haven't had their breakfast and they'll be starving. Why don't I take them to my house to feed them?' Evelyn, Vaila's mother, had been crying, but she hadn't fallen apart. She came from a generation to whom the experience of sudden death wasn't so unusual. Her elderly relatives might have died in a storm at sea or through untreated illness when the islands were more isolated. 'You can chat to Jimmy and then come over and we can explain to them together. You might have more to tell them then.'

Vaila nodded as if the movement took all her effort. Her mother went off to round up the boys. Perez heard subdued voices, the clatter of feet on the stairs, then suddenly the house was quiet again, apart from the pull of the tide on the shingle outside. A constant background.

'Is it true, Jimmy? He's really dead?'

'Aye.' Perez paused for a beat. 'He's been murdered, Vaila. Not an accident. He had a violent blow to the head. The weapon's still there.'

He nearly added: *And such a strange weapon.* But this wasn't the time. He had to remind himself that Vaila was a potential suspect. He tried to gauge what she was thinking, but she only seemed lost and numb.

'There'll be an investigation,' he said. 'Questions.'

'But who would want to kill Archie?'

He looked across the table at her. 'I thought you might have more idea than me.' Because Archie had made enemies almost as easily as he made friends. Nothing that lasted very long. He never held a grudge. But he'd been known to lash out. With fists and words. Not so much recently though. Not since he'd settled down with Vaila.

She didn't reply immediately. Instead, she stood up to make more tea. The inevitable compulsory hospitality of island women. Perez didn't try to stop her, and besides, just in that moment, he longed for tea, hot and strong. She set the pot on the table, and he poured it out into one of the unused mugs.

'Honestly,' she said. 'I have no idea at all. He's been a bit calmer lately. And everyone here knows him. Even the new islanders, the folk who've come in more recently. If he were to lose his temper, they'd just laugh at him and tell him to cool down.'

Perez thought that was right. 'Tell me everything about yesterday. I know we went through it all when I got here last night. But the detail is more important now. You do understand?'

'Not really. I can't take it in. It's like a nightmare or a gruesome fairy tale.' She looked up at him. She was slight and dark. As a young woman she'd always looked older than she really was, but she hadn't changed at all in nearly twenty years. She'd look the same at sixty. There were Fair Isle relatives who were just like her. 'And I'm so very tired.'

He wondered how he'd respond to any other wife of a

murder victim, a man with a temper. He'd be kind, of course, but he'd press her for answers.

'I'm sorry. We have to do this now. You'll start to forget as time passes. Or you'll make things up, without realizing, jumping to conclusions and turning them into facts. Then it *will* become a story.'

'Yes,' she said. 'I see. And perhaps best to do it now while the shock makes things unreal. Before it starts to hurt too much.'

He put his phone on the table. 'I'll record the conversation, because I'm in shock too. I might get things wrong. Is that okay?' A long pause. 'I loved him.'

She looked up, shocked by the words. 'Of course. You know what you're doing, Jimmy.'

'Yesterday. It was an ordinary day?'

'Sure. The boys were off school for the Christmas holidays, and I let them sleep in. Usually, we have them up to help on the farm when they're home. But you know how it is, the last week of term, all treats and parties and the bairns getting more and more wound up. They might be older now – Lawrie's almost a man and Iain started in the hostel in Kirkwall for school in September – but they still get excited for Christmas.'

He nodded.

'It was already windy, and the forecast was for a storm, so straight after breakfast, Archie went out to feed the beasts in the byre and then check that everything was all tied down and secure before the wind started. He came back in for coffee.' A pause. 'He'd already been out to meet the morning ferry from Kirkwall.'

'And that was normal. All as you'd expect?'

Vaila paused for a moment, and he thought how seriously

she was taking this. She was running the events of the previous day in her head, like a film.

'It took him a bit longer than I'd expected to come in for coffee. I was just going to go out to see what was holding him up. In case he needed a hand with anything. But then he walked in.' A pause. 'He was putting his phone in his jacket pocket when he came through the door. It seemed that he'd been taking a call.'

'Did you ask him about it?'

She shook her head, and he sensed a moment of awkwardness, but thought this wasn't the time to push it. They'd be able to trace the call.

'How did he seem?'

'I'm not sure.' She hesitated, choosing her words carefully. 'Maybe a bit unsettled. Restless. The wind always got to him like that. It was like the kids. Have you noticed them in the playground when it's windy? They become kind of frisky. Wild. Like the kye when they're let out in the spring after being in the byre all winter.'

'And that was Archie yesterday morning. A bit wild?'

'Aye,' she said. 'Maybe.' There was a sudden smile. 'But no more than usual! You knew him, Jimmy.'

He nodded. 'And then what happened?'

'We had coffee together here. The boys were up by then and they had their breakfast.' A pause. 'But maybe you don't need to know stuff like this.'

'I do! You're doing fine.'

'I went out then. I help with the old folks' club, and it was their Christmas lunch in the Pierowall Hotel. I left Archie doing paperwork in his office and Lawrie was chilling, playing some computer game he's obsessed with. Iain had arranged to spend the afternoon with a pal in the village – Fiona the teacher's boy – so I dropped him off there.'

'What time did you get home?'

'It was three o'clock by the time we'd cleared up.'

'You came straight home?'

Vaila shook her head. 'Our Christmas decorations were looking a bit tired, and I dropped in to Lizza and picked up some new baubles there. She has lovely new ones in the shop.' For a moment, it seemed, Vaila had forgotten Archie's death, and a bonny Christmas tree was all that mattered to her. 'We talked for a while. You know how Lizza loves to chat. Then I picked up Iain from his friend's house and there was a bit more talk there.'

Perez nodded.

Vaila was still speaking. 'When I got home, I'd expected Archie still to be here with Lawrie, but there was no sign of him, and his car had gone. I'd left soup for their lunch, and that had been eaten. There were two bowls on the draining board and a whole loaf demolished.' A pause. 'Lawrie was still in his room. He'd never leave his computer if you let him.' She gave a little smile. 'We were hoping he'd find a nice lassie, someone to spend his time with, but he's so shy. I called him down and asked where Archie was, and he just said he'd gone out. You know fifteen-year-olds. Not the most communicative.'

'Archie hadn't told him where he was going?'

'Lawrie said not, but he might well have done. Boys that age, they don't really listen when adults talk to them. They seem wrapped up in a dream world of their own.'

'That's true enough.' He had no experience of teenage boys, other than having been one himself, but he wanted to reassure her somehow, and to encourage her to continue speaking. 'But that wasn't the last you saw of Archie?'

'No! He was in for dinner. He was later than I'd expected, and it was already dark. I was starting to worry – the wind was really fierce by then. He said he'd been delivering wood. He took down a long fence last week and cut up the posts and bagged them. There was more than we need here and some of the old folk are grateful for it. This close to Christmas, wherever he went he was invited in for tea and homebakes.' She hesitated. 'Or a dram.'

'He was drunk when he got home?'

'Not stupid drunk,' she said, 'but he'd been drinking. This time of year, you know how it is.'

He nodded. He knew how it was. And he knew how Archie had been: never one to refuse a dram. 'Would you be able to give me a list of everyone he visited?'

'Of course.' She turned away from him for a moment and he thought these details were bringing her man's death home to her. But it was hard to tell and when she faced him again, her face was still stony and unmoving. 'We had an early supper, all of us together around the table. It was Iain's first term away at the hostel in Kirkwall, and it's been good to get him home for a few weeks, at least.'

Most of the Westray kids boarded during the week in Kirkwall once they'd been through the junior high in Pierowall. It had been the same for Perez growing up in Fair Isle and moving out to the Anderson High in Lerwick, though he'd had to leave home even earlier, at eleven. It was a rite of transition that some children found more difficult than others.

'How's he been doing?'

'He seems fine. And thanks to you and to Willow for keeping an eye on him.'

They'd had the boy out for tea in Harray a few times and

taken him to see a film and some music. Iain was a great musician, something of a show-off. A little young for his age. 'It was nothing. He's a lovely boy.'

'Aye well, Lawrie's the quiet one, but Iain can be a bit wild.' Perez knew in different circumstances she might have added: *Just like his father* with an affectionate smile. Now she was very close to tears.

'How was Archie at the meal? Did you notice anything unusual about him?'

There was a moment of silence broken by the sound of a small plane circling over the island. If Dr Grieve had managed to catch the early flight from Aberdeen into Orkney mainland, he'd be on it. Ellie would know to meet it from the airstrip.

'Archie was restless,' Vaila said. 'But he'd been like that all day. It was the wind and being nearly Christmas. He was like a bairn about Christmas. He loved every minute of the preparations. With the weather as it was, I'd thought we'd stay in, leave the boys to their gaming and watch a film of our own in front of the fire, maybe share a bottle of wine. A bit of adult time.'

'But he decided to go out again?'

'Yeah, he said he'd arranged to meet some of the boys in the Pierowall bar, but he'd not be more than an hour or two. His mind was made up. I didn't like the thought of him driving home after more drinking, but you know how it is in the smaller isles, Jimmy, with no police stationed here any more.' There was the quick flash of a smile, a glimpse of the old Vaila.

'Was there a row? Because he'd rather be drinking with his pals than staying in with you and the boys?'

'No!' She looked at him, horrified. 'What are you thinking, Jimmy? That I followed him out to wherever he was going, and I killed him? Leaving me a widow and my children without a father. Do you really think me capable of that?'

Perez looked away. 'I'm sorry,' he said. 'I told you that there'd be questions.' A pause. 'I hate having to ask them. You do know that?'

She gave a little nod, but he couldn't be sure that she really understood.

'Go on. What happened then?'

'Once I'd cleared up the supper things, I was a bit restless too. Of course, the boys are old enough to leave now, so I thought I'd go and meet him in the bar. I could have one drink with them and drive him home.'

And make sure he didn't get silly drunk and stay out all night, Perez thought. Or end up driving into a dyke. He said nothing and waited for her to continue.

'But he wasn't there.' Now Vaila was struggling to hold things together. She stuck to the facts, her voice flat and cold. 'His friends had been expecting him, but he hadn't arrived.'

'Where was his car?'

'I didn't notice when I first got there. When I looked later, I saw it was parked in Pierowall, close to the hotel. Nobody in the bar had seen him. I tried his mobile, but reception can be tricky, so I phoned everywhere he might be. Annie and Bill at the hotel helped and between us we called all the houses on the island in the end. That took quite a while. And then I phoned you.'

Perez knew what had happened after that. He'd left a note for Willow and banked up the fire, and arrived in to Westray on the lifeboat after the storm had reached its peak. The cox had seen it as a practice run but had just dropped him off at the Rapness pier and scurried back to Orkney mainland. Vaila had met him, waiting outside the car despite the weather. She'd been wearing a bright yellow oilskin that reached the top of her wellington boots, standing just under one of the street lamps at the pier, downlit, crazy with anxiety.

'The whole island has been out looking, Jimmy, but it's as if he's disappeared into thin air.'

He hadn't known what to say, or how to reassure her. 'It's a huge island,' he'd said in the end. 'Just at the north end, there are lots of places he might be sheltering.'

The wind had dropped quite suddenly, magically, as they were standing on the quayside. The cold front from the northwest had moved through, and the clouds had parted suddenly and dramatically to give sight of the moon. Perez had seen the sweep of the white beach and the cottage where the students had partied all those years ago. Everything sharp and clean after the rain, monochrome like a moody black-and-white photo.

He'd told Vaila to go home to stay with the boys. 'Archie might come back after all, with some tale of adventure, and you need to be there for him. I'll join the search.'

He'd travelled at random then, through the strange landscape, as much to escape Vaila's panic, the fraught tension she generated like sparks, as in any hope of finding Archie. He'd started off in Pierowall, where Archie's car had been left, and followed the footpath until he'd reached Grobust Bay. The sky was completely clear now and filled with stars, the moon huge and not quite full. He'd stopped for a minute, admiring its beauty despite himself, and had looked inland towards the old dig site to see Archie, lying on the plastic, a pale shadowy shape in the sea of black, caught in the soft light. Beside the shape a square stone, almost exactly rectangular, quarried. Not much bigger than a modern house brick, but obviously not some random rock lifted from the beach.

He'd run towards Archie, stumbling over the uneven ground, with a mixture of fear and relief, hoping to see some sign of life. Then, horrified because the man was clearly dead, he'd looked more closely at the stone in the torchlight. He saw the markings, exact spirals, picked not chiselled. He'd seen the stone before in the Westray heritage centre. A Neolithic find, one of a pair. This was one of the Westray story stones.

Chapter Three

After that first almost-interview with Vaila, Perez drove back to the golf course car park and walked to the locus. It wasn't a long walk from Pierowall, Westray's biggest settlement, to Grobust, but in the storm why hadn't Archie taken his car? Suddenly, Perez had an image in his head of Archie, strong, marching across Ward Hill on Fair Isle, impervious as he was dive-bombed by bonxies. That had been after a mutual relative's funeral, a woman Archie had cared for. The man had always walked when he was troubled. He'd said it helped him to clear his head. It occurred to Perez that no other investigating officer would know that or understand it. After all, despite their friendship, perhaps he was the right person to be working this case.

A skein of greylag geese flew overhead and landed in the flat field behind him. In the distance he saw the ruins of Noltland Castle, romantic, the stuff of adventure stories. As he'd expected, Dr Grieve was crouching beside the body. This adventure was Gothic too, but far too close to home.

'You're back then, Doc? You've had more retirement bashes than I've had arrests.' Perez was keeping it light. Not wanting the pathologist to know how closely involved he'd been with the man, how deeply the death had hit him.

The words were muffled by his crime suit mask, but the doctor must have heard them. He just pretended that he hadn't, and Perez continued: 'I hoped it would be you.'

'There's nobody else, Jimmy.' He paused. 'This is a strange kind of do. Where would anyone get a stone with all that fancy carving?'

Perez could answer that question at least. 'From the heritage centre. It's known as the Westray story stone, one of a pair.' He made a sweeping gesture with his arm. 'This land has been extensively excavated by archaeologists, and once, it was part of a Neolithic settlement.' A pause. 'That suggests planning, doesn't it? If there was an argument, leading to a fight, you'd grab the nearest thing to hand. You wouldn't wait to steal an ancient stone from the island museum.'

'Maybe.' Grieve was unwilling to commit himself to anything beyond the body. 'But I'd say he was killed here. This is the crime scene. The body wasn't moved any distance.' Another pause. 'There aren't many rocks in the immediate vicinity that would cause that kind of damage. Besides, look at the blood.'

Perez thought that was even more reason to suggest that the crime had been planned, but the whole death was mystifying. Archie had been a huge personality, given to occasional outbreaks of temper, but here on Westray he was truly loved. He'd gone out of his way to help people – the afternoon of his death he'd been delivering firewood. Here, they'd forgive him anything for the warmth of his smile and his generosity. It occurred to Perez then that he should check who else had been staying on the island. This might not be peak tourist season, but the Pierowall Hotel had rooms. Islanders might have guests with them too: friends and family visiting for the holidays. Though the island had a population of five hundred and it wouldn't be easy to check out all the visitors, the thought that Archie could have been killed by an outsider was strangely reassuring.

'I don't suppose you can give me anything approaching a time of death.'

The pathologist straightened. 'By now, you should know better than to ask me that.' He returned to his work.

Phil and Ellie were standing some distance away, listening and watching.

'How's the victim's wife?' Ellie asked. 'Vaila, is it?'

'Just about holding it together. She's gone to her mother's place to tell her teenage sons that their father is dead.' Perez paused, wondering if Vaila had told the boys yet, how that was going. 'Can you look after them all when she gets home? She's in shock now, but this doesn't look like the work of an islander to me. If it had been in the bar, some fight that had got out of hand, I might have been able to understand it. But not this. This is theatrical. Odd.'

'And only incomers are odd?'

He gave a little laugh. 'I don't think of you as an incomer.'

'All the same . . .'

'You're right, of course. I'll make an effort to keep an open mind.'

'Well, you're an incomer yourself! Fair Isle might be close enough as the crow flies, and there are connections, I know, but Shetlanders and Orcadians are a different kind of breed.'

'Yes,' he said. 'I suppose they are.' The trite saying was that Orcadians were farmers with a boat, and Shetlanders were fishermen with a croft. It held some truth. Orkney was less bleak, more wooded, more fertile. Rounder and softer, despite some dramatic cliffs. Willow said that the landscape here was less macho than Shetland and Perez thought she was right. If islands could be gendered, Orkney would be feminine.

'You want me to find out from Vaila if Archie had any contact this week with visitors?'

'Aye.' Perez laughed again more awkwardly. 'Something like that.'

Perez drove to the hotel. Archie's car was still parked there and Perez thought that was something else he should do. The crime scene team were due in on the lunchtime ferry, and he'd need to keep it uncontaminated until they arrived. He suspected it wouldn't be locked – only visitors locked their cars here – and he was tempted to have a thorough look inside. Instead, he used gloves to take the keys from the ignition and clicked it shut. It was the best he could do until the team could take over.

The hotel looked out over the water. It was welcoming in the low winter sunlight, and there was a fire in the bar inside. He realized how hungry he was; he'd not had a meal the night before and it wouldn't have been right eating in front of Vaila. The landlord was preparing for any lunchtime customers and recognized him.

'What a terrible business this is, Jimmy!'

Naturally, everyone on the island would know of Archie's death by now. 'Can you do me a strong coffee and a bacon sandwich?'

'Of course I can. Anything you need, just say.' Bill was a new islander. He'd arrived originally from Belfast and there was still the accent to set him apart. He'd been running the hotel with his Orcadian wife for thirty years, but the awareness of difference was there, all the same. 'Annie will sort you out.' Annie was his wife, a quiet, nimble woman, who kept things running smoothly in the background. She'd looked middle-aged when she was twenty, and now, approaching her sixties, she didn't look any different. Bill was a joker. He could have the whole bar in fits, smooth over any tension by turning it into laughter. Despite the difference in ages, he and Archie had been close friends.

'This was Archie's second home,' Bill said now. 'I can't imagine the place without him.'

'You were expecting him in last night?'

'His pals were expecting him, sure enough.'

'They were surprised when he didn't turn up?' Perez was distracted briefly by the smell of bacon frying from the kitchen beyond the bar. Annie MacBride was working her magic.

'I don't know if there was a definite arrangement, but aye, there was some comment at his not being here.' A pause. 'They thought Vaila was cracking the whip. There's a lot to do this close to Christmas if you have a family.'

'And then Vaila turned up looking for him?'

'Yes, she braved the storm and drove down the road to collect him. At first, we thought she was getting her own back for all the times she'd stayed at home with the bairns, that she'd left him in the house with the lads and was in the bar for a bit of craic herself.' A pause. 'There was a kind of cheer when she came in. Ironic, you know.'

Perez nodded. He could picture the scene.

'Then it turned out she'd been expecting him here.' Bill looked out at Perez. He was a big man, with shaggy white hair. His large head always reminded Perez of an animal. Maybe an old English sheepdog. 'At first there was no panic. We thought he'd be in one of the houses drinking, keeping one of the old boys company on a wild, winter night. It was the sort of thing he might do. He was a kind man.'

'He was.'

And I loved him, Perez thought again.

'But Vaila had seemed certain that he'd be *here*,' MacBride went on. 'She said he'd been out visiting in the afternoon. So she used her mobile to get in touch with all their friends, and we got on the landline to go through the Westray directory to speak to everyone else on the island and nobody had seen him.'

'How did Vaila seem when she arrived in the bar?' Perez hated asking the question. 'Did she look as if she'd spent any time out in the gale?'

Bill looked at him sharply. 'No! Nothing like that. A bit damp maybe, but it was raining so hard that she'd get wet just running from the car.'

There was an awkward silence before Perez asked the next question. 'Do you have any guests staying?'

'Not many just now. A middle-aged couple who met here in Westray and are celebrating some kind of anniversary. The Johnsons. He's a professor, a bit of a celebrity because he's appeared on the telly. An expert in the history of the island, apparently. He brought a film crew in a while ago. We were hoping they'd stay here, but they were in and out in a day. She's something arty. And Godfrey Lansdown, who's an elderly guy, a regular. A kind of naturalist writing a book about the island.' A pause. 'We're expecting more visitors in tomorrow and the day after. Mostly folk who used to live here or relatives of islanders. Will that be okay, Jimmy?'

Perez nodded. 'There'll still be areas cordoned off, but I don't see why not.'

'I'd hate to turn customers away. This time of year, we're grateful for all the business we can get.'

'Where are your guests now?'

Bill shrugged. 'They all went out straight after breakfast. The prof and his wife were getting the ferry to Papay, I think. Godfrey said he wanted to make the most of the light for a walk.'

'Did they know Archie's dead?'

'They knew he was missing last night. They all went out this morning before the news came through that you'd found the body.'

They'll know by now, Perez thought. Even on Papay the news will be out. Papa Westray was a small island with a great community spirit, linked to Westray by ferry and history.

'I'll need the full names and contacts of your visitors.'

Bill paused and then nodded. 'Of course. But I'm not sure how well they'd have known Archie, apart from meeting him in here. Why would they want to have killed him?' There was a hopeful edge to the question. It seemed to Perez that Bill too would much rather one of the ferry-loupers was the killer than an islander.

Annie appeared before Perez could reply. She looked grey and tired. Nobody had managed much sleep the night before. She set a plate with the sandwich and a mug of coffee in front of Perez.

'This is a terrible business, Jimmy. You'll clear it up soon.' She looked out at the room decorated with a tree and lights and strings of paper lanterns. He knew what she was saying: *Clear it up by Christmas. Please bring things back to normal by then.*

It hadn't quite been a question and he didn't answer. He wasn't one for giving false promises.

'Why don't you get a coffee for yourselves? I'd like to talk to you both before folk start coming in. I need to know who was here last night. When people left.' He paused, wondering how much of Archie's death he should give away, then he thought that news would get out soon enough and he needed information more than secrecy.

Annie sat beside him without bothering to get herself a drink. Bill came out from the bar and took a seat next to her.

'I'm interested in the story stones,' he said. 'They're kept in the heritage centre, aren't they?'

'Aye. Apparently, the prof is an expert. He went in to look at them when he first arrived. We arranged for the centre to be open for him.' She shot him a look across the table but didn't ask why he wanted to know. Maybe listening to other folk's tales in the bar had made her incurious.

'Would you mind having a look this morning? See if they're both still there.'

'Sure.' Still, she didn't ask why he wanted to know, but she had a question of her own.

'When did Archie die?'

Jimmy knew what Doc Grieve would say. 'Vaila last saw him after having had supper with the boys. I found him at nearly seven o'clock this morning. So between those times. It's not like in the films. Impossible to be more precise.'

'It could have been anyone then?' Annie sounded distraught.

Perez nodded. 'But maybe more likely soon after he left Nistaben. Otherwise, surely, he'd have turned up here where everyone was expecting him.' Nistaben was at the other end of the island, close to the Rapness ferry terminal, but no more than fifteen minutes' drive away.

His car is here though. So what does that mean?

Bill shot a glance at Annie.

'What?' Perez said. 'You think he might have been somewhere else?'

'He was always a ladies' man. You know that, Jimmy.'

'Aye, when he was younger. Not now!'

Silence.

'Tell me.'

'There's a young Englishwoman who's renting Quoybrae, the big house just out of Pierowall. She makes jewellery from silver and sea glass. Bonny stuff. Sells it in Kirkwall but mostly online. Rumours are he's fallen for her.'

'Were his feelings reciprocated?' Perez knew better than to ask if the rumours were true. Bill wouldn't have spoken about them otherwise. Besides, Archie had a history of making a fool of himself over women.

'Not at first,' Annie said. 'But I had a feeling she was warming to him.'

'Tell me about her.'

'Her name is Rosalie Greeman. She's in her thirties. She arrived in the late spring, and we thought she'd just be here for a couple of months while the weather was good, and the nights were light. You know what it's like, Jimmy. These arty folk fall for the dream but they can't cope with the dark days and the lack of facilities.'

'Is she single?'

Annie nodded. 'It seems so. She doesn't speak much of her life before she came to the island, but there are stories of course. I heard that her man died young. An accident or illness maybe. There was a lot of sympathy for her.'

Perez nodded. He could understand that. He'd lost Fran, the love of his life, when he was a relatively young man too.

After his divorce, he thought he'd never get close to another woman, and then one snowy midwinter he'd met and fallen head over heels with Fran, a single mother. She'd left him Cassie, her child. A gift and a responsibility.

Annie was still speaking. 'But then people's attitude changed a bit when they thought she was having an affair with Archie.' A pause. 'I hoped that the rumours wouldn't chase her away.'

Perez hadn't heard any of these rumours. Westray was quite a different place from Orkney mainland and news didn't always travel. Archie wouldn't have mentioned it. He thought Perez was strait-laced and would have known that he'd disapprove.

'But Rosalie's staying through the winter?'

'Aye. It seems she'll make this her permanent home. She's become a part of island life now: she helps out with art classes at the school, trained to join the fire crew and takes her turn up to the airstrip with the fender when the planes are due in. In the summer she volunteered in the heritage centre.'

'She's liked?'

This time the answer came immediately: 'Yes, generally.' A pause. 'Perhaps I was more worried that *Archie* would have chased her away, rather than the gossip of Westray folk.'

'He was making a nuisance of himself?'

'Not exactly a nuisance, but he was kind of flirty. At first, I thought there was no harm in it if he was making her feel good about herself. In the last month or two, I've wondered if there might be something more serious between them.' Annie looked up at Perez. 'A couple of times he was seen coming out of her house, when he had no real reason to be there.' She shrugged. 'It could have been nothing, but you know how people talk.'

Perez knew. 'Vaila must have been aware of the gossip.'

'This is Westray, Jimmy. There are things we don't speak of to the people concerned, but we're all aware of the gossip.'

'Was Miss Greeman in here last night?'

They shook their heads in unison, sad, it seemed, that they couldn't provide the woman with any kind of alibi.

'Can you give me a list of everyone who was in last night?'

'Of course.'

There were six of them. Most of the names were familiar to Perez. He'd met them in here on his visits to Archie and Vaila. He'd eaten meals in many of the houses and listened to their music. Perez made a note of the names, finished his sandwich and coffee and stood up.

'I might need a room for the night. Have you got one free?'

'Sure. There's a lovely double and I'll reserve that for you. And a couple of singles in case Phil and Ellie need to stay over.'

Perez nodded his thanks and walked outside.

Chapter Four

PEREZ MADE HIS WAY BACK TO Nistaben. It was seven miles away, and he drove slowly through the fertile farmland, still frosty in the shade of walls and houses. He wasn't looking forward to this. He parked outside the byre and heard the cows moving inside as he made his way to the house. He paused there for a moment and looked in through the window at Vaila and Ellie. It was only early afternoon, but already the sun was low in the sky and the women were caught in a deep red glow. They were both sitting at the kitchen table. Vaila must be back from her parents' house and Ellie had joined her as he'd asked. He supposed Phil Bain was still with the pathologist, helping. Or getting in the way.

There was more tea in the pot on the table in front of the window. He thought they'd all be swimming in the stuff by the end of the day. Perez wondered suddenly, with a sharp longing, if he'd get home to Orkney mainland that night to see Willow and his son. Probably not. It was just as well he'd booked himself into the hotel. There might be press turning up once word of the murder got out. They'd see a killing on a remote island where nobody bothered locking their doors as a great story. Especially just before Christmas. It would be like one of those old-fashioned mystery stories set between the wars. He pulled out his phone, planning to call his woman, but Ellie glanced up, saw him and waved. He slipped the phone back into his pocket and went inside.

Vaila had been crying. The initial shock seemed to have passed and the grieving had begun. Perez felt a stab of sympathy and had to remind himself again that she wasn't a friend and a bereaved wife now, but a potential suspect. If Archie had been playing away with the arty Englishwoman at Quoybrae, Vaila had motive as well as opportunity. He couldn't believe that she'd killed her husband, but he had to train his thoughts to consider the possibility.

He sat beside Ellie at the table, then wished he'd chosen a different seat. This felt too much like an interview, with Vaila sitting opposite to them.

'I'm sorry,' he said. 'I have more questions.'

Vaila didn't respond directly. 'Is Archie still there?' she asked. 'Behind Grobust beach at the old dig site?'

Perez nodded. 'Dr Grieve, the pathologist, is with him.'

'Can I see him? I still can't quite believe he's dead.'

'Not there,' Perez said. 'It's a crime scene. We have to be careful about contamination. You understand. But when he's in Kirkwall. Before he goes south to Aberdeen for the post-mortem. I'm sure we can arrange something then.' He thought Grieve would be open to that. He was the most compassionate medic Perez knew. He'd said once that his patient wasn't the body on the table, but the grieving relative, and that his door was always open to them.

He thought she might protest, insist on driving off and

walking along the beach to see Archie at his last resting place in Westray, but she seemed overwhelmed by a kind of lethargy. 'So,' she said. 'What questions do you have for me now?' He sensed a bitterness in her voice and wondered if she'd guessed what was coming.

'There have been rumours,' Perez said, 'about Archie's relationship with a woman on the island. Rosalie Greeman.'

'You know Orkney.' Her face was grey with exhaustion. 'There are always rumours.'

'Sometimes, they have some basis in truth.'

'You knew Archie too. He was given to wild infatuations.'

That word again, Perez thought. Wild. That surely was the best word to describe Archie. He said nothing and waited for her to continue.

'I knew it would pass,' she said.

'Did you talk to him about the woman?'

She shook her head. 'He would have lied. I could tolerate his flings, but not the lies.'

'I didn't know,' Perez said, 'that Archie had flings.' Then he wondered if that was true. There had been times when the two of them had met for a drink in Kirkwall, and Archie had been high, not with drink or drugs, but some kind of excitement that had made him talk too much and laugh too much. Perez had suspected then that Archie might have come straight from a woman. But like Vaila he hadn't asked. Not afraid of lies, but the truth. Archie was the sort of man who might have boasted about his conquests. To his best friend at least, and Perez would have hated that.

Vaila leaned forward across the table. 'It wasn't the most important thing about him,' she said. 'His sordid encounters with women, I mean. He wasn't at it all the time.' She shook her head, as if the words hadn't come out as she wanted, as if they were too crass. 'He was easily bored, you know.'

'What was the most important thing about him?'

She looked up, straight into his eyes. 'Us. Me and the boys. Whatever else was going on in his life, he loved us best and for ever.'

Perez wanted to ask if Archie had loved any of his other women, if he'd loved Rosalie Greeman for example, but he couldn't bring himself to do it and asked the question differently.

'Was the relationship with the woman at Quoybrae just a fling too? Like all the others. Something that would pass?'

There was a moment of silence, broken by the sound of sheep on the in-bye land next to the house and a plane coming in to land. Perez wondered if it were bringing reinforcements. Maybe some of his crime scene officers.

'I don't know,' Vaila said. 'Like I said he was infatuated. Less cautious. Probably because she didn't fall for him straight away. He had to woo her, and he was always up for a challenge.'

'If you didn't talk about it, how do you know all these things?'

'I'm his wife!' It came out as a scream. 'I've looked after him all these years, sorted out his scrapes. I knew him as well as I know myself.'

'But this time,' Perez said, almost to himself, 'you couldn't fix it.'

'No. I wasn't sure I could fix it. All I could do was wait. And hope that it would fizzle out like all the others. Or that she would tire of the island and him and move back to where she belonged.'

Again, there was a silence. Perez could sense Ellie beside

him, uncomfortable, because this wasn't the way interviews should be conducted. This was too intense. Too personal. She shifted a little in her seat, and he was worried that she might intervene.

'Tell me about the heritage centre,' he said. His voice was normal now. More detective than priest. 'Is it kept locked?'

'Of course.' Vaila seemed surprised by the change in tone, but grateful too. 'There are valuable artefacts. The Westray Wife is famous. The oldest representation of a woman in Britain. We're all fascinated by what the archaeologists found when they did their exploration.'

'And there's the Westray story stone.'

'Stones,' she said. 'There are two of them – stones with a spiral carving. Why are you asking, Jimmy?'

Because one of those stones killed Archie. It's lying beside him, smeared with his blood and fragments of his scalp.

But he didn't answer. Instead, he asked: 'Who has a key?'

'All the committee members. I have one.' She looked up at him. 'Why?'

The response, honest and open, made his heart sing. She couldn't be guilty, could she? Then he thought of all the suspects he'd known who were liars. Brilliant liars.

'You know I'll have to talk to Miss Greeman.'

'Mrs,' Vaila said. 'She took her husband's name. They married just before he died.' She paused for a moment before continuing: 'We were friends when she first came. I was pleased. Someone of about my age bringing in a breath of the outside world. We got on so well. I loved art when I was at school. And history. There was a time when I thought I might go south to study. I was offered a place in the art school in Glasgow. We shared ideas. She took me seriously.' Vaila was nearly in tears again. 'I was almost angrier about Archie spoiling that friendship than about what he was doing with her. The cheating.'

Perez nodded. He thought he understood. In a small community, it was often hard to find a soulmate.

She looked at him. 'What will happen now?'

He was already on his feet and looked down at her. 'We'll investigate. And find out who killed Archie.'

'I'll need that.' Her voice was desperate. 'It's not about revenge or justice, but I'll need some sort of explanation to give the boys. And for me. I need to understand.'

He thought again that he was crazy even to suspect Vaila of killing Archie Stout.

'Are the boys back here? I'll have to talk to them too.'

'Lawrie's out on the tractor. It's as if he thinks he's got to look after us all now and run the farm as Archie would have done. He's grieving, Jimmy. He hasn't cried since he was a toddler, but he was sobbing. He went outside so I couldn't see. Iain's upstairs, curled up and asleep. Maybe hoping it's all a dream. Can it wait for another day?'

Perez thought for a moment. 'Sure,' he said. 'It can wait.'

Out in the yard, his phone rang. It was Annie from the hotel.

'I've been in to the heritage centre, Jimmy. Both the story stones have disappeared.' She rang off before he could thank her.

He parked back in Pierowall and began walking up the road towards Quoybrae, curious now to meet the woman who had captivated both Archie and Vaila. He was lost in thought and the figure coming in the opposite direction towards him seemed to appear out of nowhere. The low sun was behind her, so he had to squint, and she was just a silhouette, but he knew her at once and broke into a run, excited as a boy. When he drew level with her, he took her in his arms and held her for a moment.

'What are you doing here?'

'Well, that's a nice way to talk to the mother of your children!'

They still weren't married. He liked the idea, but Willow had grown up on a commune in the Western Isles and he thought of her as a free spirit. He was worried that she'd laugh at him if he asked. Even after all this time together, he still didn't feel that he entirely knew her.

'I'm all there is,' she went on. 'There's a technical fault on the plane that was going to bring the team from Glasgow, and besides, none of them fancy being stranded here just before Christmas if the weather closes in. The forecast isn't great and they're all city boys. I suspect they'll make excuses until after the holiday.' She laughed and his mood improved again. 'James was very happy to stay with his Aunty Alison, who will of course fill him with sugar and let him stay up for most of the night, so here I am, on the scheduled flight from Kirkwall. Not really in an official capacity, but to provide a bit of oversight and feedback to Glasgow. I dropped my bag at the hotel. Bill said you had a room. And then I needed a bit of a walk to get a feel for the place again. You know how I work, Jimmy. It's all about the place.'

He nodded. He knew how she worked. 'James will have a fine time.'

Alison wasn't a real aunt, but a friend and occasional childminder. James adored her.

'Are you sure you'll be okay?' Perez put a hand on her belly, then quickly pulled it away. Willow hated any kind of sentiment.

'Of course! I'll leave the strenuous stuff like running after dangerous criminals and car chases to other people. My role is to listen in. And drink tea.'

'Are you okay to sit in on an interview now?'

'Of course. The old team. Back in action.' She turned to him. 'I'm so sorry about Archie, but it feels good to be back in the field again and not stuck behind a desk.'

They walked slowly up the road, and he brought her up to speed. He sensed the intensity of her listening.

'Tell me about the murder weapon.'

'I recognized it,' he said. 'It came from the heritage centre, one of a pair of Neolithic stones. It had Norse writing on it. Apparently, that was added later. A kind of Viking graffiti.' He paused. 'I asked Annie to check. Both the stones have disappeared.'

'So what does that mean?' She stood still in the road. 'A message? Premeditation?'

He shook his head. He had no answer for her.

Rosalie Greeman was sitting outside her house on a white bench, looking out over a small cove of sand and shingle. Perez had never been to this part of the island before, but he'd heard Archie speak of the house. Once Quoybrae would have been the grandest property on Westray, home to the laird. It had two storeys and thick stone walls. Since Perez had been visiting Westray, it had been rented out as a holiday let or short-term rental. He thought it was owned by a Shetlander, bought perhaps as some kind of investment.

The woman was wrapped in a long fleecy coat and had her hands around a brown pottery mug. Perez could smell the coffee above the notes of salt and seaweed. She had cropped dark hair and big dark eyes.

'I've just been for a dip,' she said. 'Sit here with me until I stop shivering, and then I'll get you a drink.'

'You've been in the sea?' Perez was horrified. He might have grown up next to the water, but he thought of it as a dangerous place, full of treacherous tides and currents, not somewhere to play. Especially in the winter.

'You get used to it. It's become a habit. Good for the mental health, they say, and I was depressed, I think, when I first arrived in Westray. Usually, I get in early in the morning – it sets me up for the day – but today nothing is quite as usual.'

Perez started to introduce himself, but she interrupted. 'I know who you are. You're just as Archie described you. Dark hair, he said, and olive skin. Descended from Spanish sailors rescued from an Armada shipwreck. Just like the Dons here in Westray. They were saved from another Armada ship that went badly astray. The Spaniards must have been crap navigators to get it wrong so often.' She turned to Willow. 'And you are?'

'Willow Reeves. Jimmy's boss. Kind of. On maternity leave at the moment, but here to keep an eye.'

'Of course.' Rosalie nodded and gave a little smile. Perez thought that Archie must have described Willow too. She'd understand their relationship.

The woman got to her feet. 'Come in. There's still coffee hot and I'm sure you'll have questions.'

Perez wasn't sure what he'd been expecting, but it wasn't this. There was no sign of grief and her response to two detectives turning up on her doorstep was matter-of-fact. She'd not even broken her routine of a daily swim in the sea. It seemed cold and hard-hearted. It came to him that Archie had deserved better, but he pushed away the thought.

Inside, the kitchen was a blast of colour. He thought this was Rosalie's work. A rental landlord would have played it safer. One wall was painted a deep red. There was art on the others, big paintings, abstract splashes of yellow and orange. Autumn colours. Autumn colours if you lived in the south, at least. Perez was reminded of Fran, the artist who had once been the centre of his life. She'd have enjoyed this room. He'd taken Fran to Fair Isle to celebrate their engagement, and she'd died there. It occurred to him in that moment that perhaps he hadn't discussed marriage with Willow out of a strange kind of superstition. If he proposed to her, did he think that she would die too?

Rosalie poured coffee from a filter machine. Willow shook her head at the offer. 'I'm trying to avoid too much caffeine.'

So here they were in another kitchen, talking again about a dead man and who might have killed him, to a woman who might have had a motive for wanting him dead.

Willow had taken a seat in a rocking chair next to the Rayburn, leaving Perez and the woman at the table. It seemed that she expected Perez to lead the conversation.

'We're investigating Archie Stout's death,' he said.

'Of course.' Rosalie had shed her dry robe but her fingers were still a startling red, a response to the icy water. Her hands were flat on the table as if she needed to be steadied. 'You'll have heard that the two of us were friends.'

'Friends? Is that all you were?' It came to Perez that the Archie he'd known had always wanted more than friendship from a woman.

'We weren't even that at first. And perhaps we *were* more than friends at the end, but I never slept with him, despite what all the gossips here think.' She looked straight at Perez, challenging him to doubt her word. He'd never met anyone with such dark eyes, such black eyebrows, such a pale face.

'Vaila thinks you were lovers.' He paused. 'Why didn't you tell her she'd got that wrong?'

Rosalie turned away. 'Archie loved me. Deeply. Better that she should believe we were having some sort of fling than that I tell her that.'

'Yet you didn't have sex with him?'

She shook her head. 'But I was close to it, and that was another reason for not explaining to Vaila. I think it might have happened in the end.' A pause. 'It's rather flattering to be adored.'

'I knew Archie,' Perez said. 'He was never a patient kind of man.'

'You think he was putting pressure on me to have sex, perhaps even that there was some kind of sexual assault, or stalking, and so I killed him?' She gave a bitter little laugh. 'No, it was nothing like that.'

'When did you last see him?' Perez thought it was safer to move on to facts. He found this relationship impossible to fathom. He was glad Willow was in the room. She might understand it better.

'Yesterday afternoon. He was delivering wood and he called in. He wasn't here for long.' She hesitated. 'He seemed troubled.'

'Did he tell you what was troubling him?'

She shook her head. 'Not in any detail.'

Perez was starting to lose patience. 'But you were close. You must have had some idea.'

She shook her head again. 'I don't think it was anything to do with us, with our relationship. Maybe it was an island matter.

He had a sense of responsibility, you know, for Westray. His father had been a community leader, and since he died a couple of years ago, Archie felt he should take over the mantle. They were different men though. Archie was easily bored and couldn't step easily into his father's shoes, so there was a kind of frustration. Yesterday, he seemed weighed down with some problem, but he said he couldn't discuss it with me. I had the sense that it was because I was an outsider and that I wouldn't understand.'

There was a silence, while Perez struggled to process that.

'How about later? Yesterday evening? Did you see him then?' Perez thought Archie might have parked at the hotel to give the impression that he planned to spend the evening there, then walked out to Quoybrae.

She paused for a moment. 'I was expecting him,' she said. 'We'd planned that when he called in earlier. But he didn't turn up. I wasn't surprised. This time of year, the family will always come first.' There was no trace of bitterness in her words. 'At any time of year, I think family would have come first for Archie. I believe that he loved me, but he wouldn't have left his wife for me.' She looked across the table at Perez. 'He might have been unfaithful, but he had a great sense of duty.'

Perez nodded. He would never have described Archie in that way, but he thought it was probably true.

'And that didn't make you angry? That you always had to come second?'

'Not at all,' Rosalie said. 'I wasn't ready for another intense, long-term relationship.'

There was a moment of silence before she continued speaking in a voice so low that it was almost a confession.

'I was lonely when I first came here. So lonely. My husband had just died. I'd spent months of my life knowing that he would die and just trying to make the end as good as it could be. Neither of us wanted company. I was happy to care for him alone. Then he was gone, and I had nothing. No purpose. I've no close family and no kids, and I'd lost touch with most of my friends. Besides, I couldn't stand their sympathy, their pity, when they *did* get in touch. So I ran away here. Just by chance. There'd been a documentary about the place on the radio, and it sounded magnificent. I was only going to stay for a couple of weeks, but it felt like a fresh start. There were new people who made me welcome.'

'Vaila?' Perez asked.

She nodded. 'Vaila and others. But she was lovely and the person I felt most at ease with. We were both readers, and we talked about books and sometimes she'd come for an evening, and we'd drink wine and watch a film. Then Archie started calling. Always with some excuse in the beginning. Vaila had said I had a dripping tap that needed to be fixed. He'd seen that there was a piece of fence that had blown down in the gale.'

She paused for a moment. Perhaps she expected some response from her visitors. When none came, she started speaking again. 'I could tell from the beginning that he wasn't just being helpful, and soon he came along with no excuse at all. At first, I sent him on his way. A flea in his ear. But he was persistent, and I found myself looking forward to his visits. I was missing the company of a man – that physical male presence in the room – and he had such good stories to tell. He made me laugh. He could listen and I had stories of my own to tell. I discovered that I was falling for him, despite how close I was to Vaila.' She looked across at Willow. 'But nothing happened. A hug of welcome when he arrived and a chaste kiss when he left. We talked. I knew how he felt, but he was prepared to wait.'

'Will you stay in Westray now he's gone?'

She considered that for a while. 'I think so. I've always been a maker and the place has inspired my craft. I turned the bedroom upstairs into a studio. I saw my future here. I can sell my jewellery and I've been planning workshops. Working with Bill and Annie at the hotel to run courses in the off-season. They could provide the accommodation and I'd give the tuition in my studio.' She paused. 'In one sense it'll be easier to stay without Archie. Less complicated.' She stared at him, challenging him to be shocked by her words.

'Are you involved with the heritage centre?'

'Sure. I volunteer there when they're busy. It's closed most of the week for the winter, but I still go in occasionally to make sketches of some of the artefacts. I like to incorporate the images in my own designs.'

'You don't have a key?'

'No. I'm not on the committee.'

Perez didn't answer and thought that really, she wasn't that interested in the history of the island. She only cared about how the ancient objects could feed into her work. He thought again that there was something cold and hard about her. He wondered how Archie could have fallen for her. 'You don't seem upset that Archie's dead.'

'Don't I?' Rosalie sounded almost amused. Perhaps this was the response she'd been expecting from him. 'You think I should be in floods of tears and run away back to the mainland, just as I ran away from home when Adam died? Listen,

Inspector, I'd been with my husband since I was sixteen. He was a cameraman working on natural history films, and we travelled the world together. He was older than me and he taught me so much. I worshipped him. I was fond of Archie but not in the way that I loved my husband. This is my home now. I'm sad that Archie's dead, of course I am, but not in the same way. Our relationship was complicated and shaded with guilt. Besides, perhaps I've run out of grief. I have no tears left to weep.'

'Do you know who might have wanted to kill him?'

She shook her head. 'I have no idea at all.'

Chapter Five

Willow and Perez stood outside for a moment. It was still clear and cold, with hardly a whisper of a breeze, the sky pink and grey, the sun gone. Rosalie hadn't switched on a light in the house, and Willow imagined the woman looking at them through the window, waiting for them to move on and leave her to her own devices. Willow touched Perez's arm.

'Maybe you should show me the crime scene.'

'Aye,' he said. 'Sure.'

Willow knew that Perez had been lonely after Fran had died. Had he felt the same kind of intense loneliness as Rosalie, the loneliness that had prompted her to run north? He'd had the support of his colleague Sandy Wilson and his parents in Fair Isle, but he'd been deeply troubled when Willow had first met him in Shetland. She wondered now if he'd ever been tempted to escape, to run away south.

They'd turned a bend in the road and were out of sight of Quoybrae.

'What did you make of her?' Perez asked. 'Did you believe her?'

'That she wasn't having sex with Archie? Yes, I believed *that*. It's hard to know why she never did though. If it was all about moral scruples, why encourage him to visit? That seems a bit cruel, letting him hope that there might be more to the relationship. A betrayal of her friendship with Vaila too. Or maybe she was enjoying the power over them both.'

Perez considered that. 'Rosalie didn't seem the sort to crave power, though she struck me as cold as the water she was swimming in today. But I can't see what motive she might have for killing him.'

Willow thought motive was always tricky. It didn't take much for some people to be submerged by anger, overwhelmed by it. She knew one killer who'd strangled his wife because she laughed at the way he ate his food. That had been about power too, or the lack of it. 'Rosalie had opportunity though. And no alibi. We only have her word that she was expecting him to turn up at Quoybrae last night. If she'd asked him to meet her at Grobust, he'd have done it, wouldn't he? She was always the person pulling the strings.'

'You didn't like her?'

'Not that exactly. I don't quite trust her.'

'What about means? How would she have got hold of that stone from the heritage centre?'

'She said herself that she visited the place to sketch the artefacts. I doubt there's much security or if they do an inventory after a regular's been in.' She looked across at Perez. 'I'm not saying she's our killer, but that we have to keep an open mind.' She knew that sometimes Perez found it hard to maintain a distance. He often had too much compassion, too much empathy. Was he putting himself in Rosalie Greeman's place, because he knew what it was to grieve? If so, wouldn't he find it even more difficult to stay objective when it came to Vaila?

They walked on for a moment in silence, down the path towards the old dig site. It wasn't a long walk from Quoybrae to Noltland. Willow thought that Rosalie was fit and strong. She'd get there in fifteen minutes, probably faster than that.

When they arrived, the pathologist was still working on the body. He preferred to do as much as he could at the locus. The body, he said, was a crime scene too and could be contaminated when it was moved. The CSIs must have arrived from Kirkwall on the mid-afternoon ferry. They'd set up a generator with fierce lights.

Perez recognized the crime scene manager and handed over the key to Archie's car.

'It's parked in Pierowall. Can you check it out? See if anyone other than Archie has driven it?'

'I've nearly done here,' Grieve said. 'The funeral director from Kirkwall will come in on this evening's boat with a vehicle to take Mr Stout to Orkney mainland. I'll not be able to get him to the mortuary in Aberdeen for the post-mortem until tomorrow evening's NorthLink.'

'His wife would like to see him before you take him south,' Perez said. 'Would that be possible?'

'Sure, I'll talk to Balfour Hospital in Kirkwall. We'll arrange for her to see him there.' He straightened and nodded across to Willow. Despite the mask, she could tell he was smiling.

'Lovely to see you, Chief Inspector. Is all going well?' His voice was almost soppy. He was thinking about her pregnancy. Once, after a few drams, he'd told her that if he hadn't become a pathologist, he would have liked to be a midwife.

'All's going fine.'

'Will you be with the victim's wife when she says her goodbyes?'

'No,' Willow said. She came to a sudden decision. It was wrong for Perez to be here in Westray. He was too close. Too involved. 'I'll leave that to Jimmy. He's more sympathetic than I am and besides, he's not seen his son for a while. He can go out on the ferry to Kirkwall with you and have a night at home so they can catch up.'

She could tell that Perez was shocked and probably hurt that she'd not consulted him first. 'Is that a good idea? Leaving you here on your own?'

'I'll not be on my own,' she said. 'I'll hang on to Ellie. But Archie was your friend. A distant relative. If we had more available officers, you'd be off the case altogether. You're too attached, and when we find our killer, the defence will have grounds to pull any of your evidence apart. You could do with some distance, and there's work to be done in Kirkwall. You got in the night of the storm. We don't know yet if a ferry earlier in the day brought in a stranger. Somehow, they might have slipped out this morning. It all needs to be checked.'

This wasn't a conversation they should be having in front of another person, but Doc Grieve was discreet. Besides, it was true. James needed to see his father, and Perez needed to see his son.

Willow continued: 'Take Phil back with you to do some of the legwork. And he can take a formal statement from Vaila in the station after she's said her goodbyes to Archie. You shouldn't be the person to do that either. Give James a big cuddle from me.' She looked across at him and smiled. 'We might have this sorted by the end of tomorrow.'

There was no returning smile, but Perez nodded to show

that, though he might not like it, he could see the sense in his going back to Kirkwall. He turned to the pathologist. 'How much time have we got before they come for the body?'

'A couple of hours. Shall I see you at the pier then?'

'Sure, I'll let Vaila know. She can decide whether she wants to come out with him, or whether she prefers to wait and get the boat tomorrow.'

'Phil's on the beach,' Grieve said. 'Trying to work out which way our victim and killer might have come to get here, if they walked across the sand. It was a high tide though. I think any footwear marks will have been washed away.'

'We'll get some people in first thing tomorrow to do a proper search of the area.' But Willow wasn't sure how much evidence might be left after the wind and the rain of the night before. Traces of fibre would have been blown across the smooth black plastic covering the archaeological site and into the North Sea. The killer might have dropped something heavier, but it seemed unlikely.

Phil Bain was still in his scene suit. When he saw them, he took off his mask. If he was surprised to see Willow, he didn't show it.

'Nothing,' he said. 'Archie Stout could have landed there from outer space, with his skull already split open by the stone.'

'No sign of a boat having landed here?' Perez asked. 'I know it's a long shot, the way the weather was last night, but someone might have come ashore from the water. Maybe in a RIB?'

'No way of telling after a high tide and all that wind and rain.'

Perez explained that Phil would be going with him out on

the Kirkwall ferry with the pathologist. 'The boss thinks there's important stuff we should be doing back at the station. She'll stay here with Ellie.'

The boss. Willow wondered if he was being sarky, but maybe not. It wasn't his style.

Perez continued: 'We're just going to Nistaben to chat with Vaila. She wanted to see her man before he goes south for the post-mortem. I'll check whether she wants to come with us or out on the morning's boat.'

Phil nodded. He seemed relieved to be leaving Westray. He was a town man, born and brought up in Kirkwall. 'It's too dark now to do any more on the shore. I'll see you at the pier.'

Willow had been to Nistaben a few times with Perez. They'd been social, often boozy nights, neighbours turning up with fiddles to make music. James, their son, had been very taken with Lawrie and Iain, and they'd been kind to him, allowing him into their rooms, playing simple board games with him, finding cartoons for him to watch on their computers. Willow thought that was the sign of a good mother – to bring up kind sons in the islands, where the macho was often celebrated.

Ellie was still in the kitchen with Vaila, but this time the boys and Vaila's mother, Evelyn, were there too. Willow let Perez go in on his own. The room was already crowded, and she didn't know Vaila well enough to give her more than token support. She stood at the porch door, unnoticed, and gestured for Ellie to join her.

The light had almost gone now, and the temperature had dropped. They stood outside, shutting the door behind them.

'You okay to stay on for a couple of nights?' Willow explained the plan. 'I've been in touch with Bill and Annie, and they've got rooms for us both.' She nodded back towards the house. 'How are they all getting on?'

'Still in shock, I think. Evelyn, the grandmother, is trying to hold it all together.'

'There are no direct relatives of Archie's still living on the island?'

Ellie shook her head. 'He had one brother who lives in Canada. They've been in touch with him, and he'll come back for the funeral when they've got a date. Archie's parents have both died.'

Willow remembered what Rosalie had said about the father having been a community leader and Archie feeling he had to take over the mantle. She'd remind Perez to chat to Vaila about that when they were together in Kirkwall.

Ellie broke into her thoughts. 'I asked Vaila if Archie had met any visitors to Westray recently, but she couldn't think of anyone.'

Looking through the window at the brightly lit kitchen, Willow could tell that some decision had been made. There was movement. The room emptied apart from Vaila's mother and Perez who remained, talking. Willow told Ellie to go back to the hotel. 'You had an early start and it's been quite a day. I'll catch up with you there. We need to talk to the other guests.'

Ellie nodded and slipped away to her car, a shadowy figure in the dusk. Willow watched the headlights sweep across the frosty field and then she went inside.

'Vaila is coming with me,' Perez said. 'She has friends in Kirkwall she can spend the night with. She's just packing a bag.'

'And the boys will stay with us,' Evelyn said. 'They're doing the same.' A pause. 'I think it'll be good for them all to get out of this house for a while. It holds such memories. It'll be hard for any of us to make sense of it all.' She looked across the table at them both. 'Archie Stout was a very complicated man.'

Willow wanted to ask what the woman meant by that, but the boys came back into the room, carrying a rucksack each, and a smaller bag, trailing wires from chargers and headphones. Willow supposed games would provide some form of escape, and Internet contact with their friends some support. Vaila arrived at the bottom of the stairs with a holdall. Evelyn hugged her and led the boys out to her car.

'We'd best be on our way too,' Perez said to Vaila.

'I'll give you both a lift to the ferry.' Evelyn had turned back and shouted to them across the yard. 'Then Willow can use Vaila's car.'

'That would be great,' Willow said, but the woman hardly seemed to notice she was there. She followed Perez through the door.

'I'll switch everything off and lock up,' Willow said.

'Thanks.' Now Vaila did see her and gave a little smile of recognition. 'Thanks.'

'Is it okay if we have a look round while you're not here? Just in case there's something to tell us who Archie might have been meeting?'

'Yeah. Anything you need.'

When they'd gone, Willow had a quick exploration of the house, motivated more by curiosity than by any real idea that she might find anything useful. She'd come in the following morning with Ellie for a real search.

The home had started off as a classic single-storey farmhouse, but it had been extended and they'd turned the loft into rooms for the boys, with dormer windows looking out over the shore and a little shared shower room. Iain's still felt like that of a child. There were Lego models on a shelf. Lawrie had made an effort to make the space his own, to show that he'd grown up. The walls had been painted purple. There were posters of bands Willow had never heard of, bands who had almost certainly never performed in Orkney. And a photo of Archie, filthy and battered, lifting the ba' after the annual community game, part rugby match, part riot, that took place in Kirkwall on Christmas Day. This felt like hero worship. No wonder Lawrie was grieving.

The Ba' was an Orkney institution, named after the heavy ball at the centre of the game. It was a competition between the uppies – men and boys born or living at the top of Kirkwall – and the doonies who came from the other end of the town. The object was to get the ba' either into the harbour, which meant that the doonies had won, or for the uppies to reach a spot in one of the higher streets. It had always seemed a crazy, lawless sport to Willow. She looked at the photograph a little longer, then moved on to the rest of the house.

Downstairs there was a large kitchen, a comfortable living room with a wood-burner, the parents' bedroom and a bathroom. A corner of the living room had been turned into an office, with a desk and a laptop.

The place was warm and welcoming, not too tidy to be off-putting, but with a sense of design; Willow could see how Vaila and Rosalie had become friends so quickly. There were reminders everywhere that this had been a happy family: a picture of them all pulling silly faces, paintings the boys had done when they were younger, a couple of medals Iain had won for athletics and Lawrie in a photo of a group of young farmers, looking as if they were celebrating at a barbecue. It was hard to believe that this had housed a marriage in crisis.

Willow wondered where the money to extend the house had come from. Small farmers hadn't had it easy in recent years and as far as she knew, Vaila hadn't worked away from the farm. Maybe Archie had inherited land or money or a house when his parents had died. That was something else to ask Jimmy. She locked the door and went outside. It had been warm in the house and the sudden cold shocked her. Instantly, she felt more alive. Perhaps this was how Rosalie felt during her icy dips in the sea. But Willow thought that she was exhilarated too at the prospect of working in the field again. And working almost alone.

Chapter Six

ELLIE WAS WAITING FOR HER IN the lounge reserved for hotel guests. She'd changed into jeans and a big hand-knitted sweater and was flicking through her phone. The room was otherwise empty.

'Where are the other residents?' Willow asked. Because Ellie was experienced. She'd have found that out before coming here to relax.

'The old guy is in the bar with the locals. Maybe wanting the authentic island experience.' Ellie's voice was a little mocking. 'The couple's having dinner in the restaurant.' A pause. 'Do you want to talk to them now?'

Willow shook her head. 'They've had all day to perfect their story, if that was what they wanted to do. And they're not going anywhere. According to Bill, they're here until after Christmas and there are no ferries or planes until mid-morning tomorrow. Let's eat first. And if they're still around, we can always see them later.'

Annie MacBride came in then. Willow wondered if she'd been listening, waiting for a good moment to take their order.

'Can we eat in here, Annie? The veggie special for me.' Willow had rejected most of the commune's weirder ideas, but still couldn't bring herself to eat meat.

Ellie seemed to be relieved about the prospect of food. 'And haddock and chips for me.'

'Of course you can eat in here. I thought you'd want a little privacy.' Annie hesitated. 'Is it right they've taken Archie south for a post-mortem?'

'Not yet,' Willow said. 'Vaila will see him tomorrow and then he'll go to Aberdeen on the NorthLink. Dr Grieve will be looking after him.'

'But he'll be back in Westray to be buried.' That wasn't a question. 'When the time is right. He'll rest in the graveyard next to the shore and his friends will dig the grave for him. The way it was done for his father. The Stouts have always followed the Fair Isle tradition.' Annie nodded towards the bar. 'They've been talking about it.'

'Of course. But I can't tell you yet when the body will be released.'

Annie frowned. 'His brother will want to come from Canada. It would be good for him to have a date.'

Willow nodded but said nothing.

After they'd eaten, she led Ellie into the bar, curious to listen in to the talk there, and to meet the older visitor, though she didn't have the energy or concentration for even an informal interview. She ordered drinks from Bill and took them to the table in the corner where Ellie was sitting. With their backs to the wall, they had a view of the whole room. The conversation had paused briefly when they came in and everyone stared, but then continued, the voices lower and a little self-conscious.

The hotel resident was obvious. He sat separately at a table furthest away from the fire. He was writing in a notebook. His binoculars stood on the table beside him, although it had been dark for hours. Willow had spent time in Jimmy Perez's home of Fair Isle, a magnet for birders, and had come to understand the passion.

The heat and the background buzz made her feel very tired. She'd been late off the ferry the night before and it had been a long day. She wanted to talk to Jimmy and check that their son was well and asleep.

She got to her feet and went to the table where the man, Godfrey Lansdown, was sitting. She introduced herself, aware that the locals were eavesdropping and would already know, fine well, who she was and what she was doing there.

'You'll have heard that a local man was killed here, either in the early hours of today or yesterday evening. You'll understand that we need to talk to everyone. As you're staying in the hotel, and we are too, would it be convenient if we spoke in the morning?'

'Of course.' Lansdown was grey and wiry, his voice a little anxious. Perhaps that was his nature. He must wear boots when out on the island, but now he was in highly polished brogues. Willow thought there was something of the tortoise about him. It was the way his face was thrust forward, the wrinkled neck. 'I breakfast early. The days are so short that I like to be out as soon as it gets light.'

Willow arranged to meet him in the residents' lounge in the morning once he'd eaten, and he made his apologies and left. The exit seemed unplanned. The conversation appeared to have thrown him. He moved deliberately across the room, looking down at his feet, and the image of the tortoise returned.

She left the bar then and made her way through the restaurant on her way to the stairs and her room. A couple was still sitting at a table, the only diners left. They'd finished eating, but some coffee cups and glasses remained. An empty bottle of wine was upturned in a bucket. It appeared that they'd moved on to whisky to go with the coffee. In contrast to Lansdown, the couple seemed entirely relaxed. They too were English, but of the confident, educated variety. They would feel no need to scuttle away to their room.

They sat opposite each other, and for a while seemed not to notice she was there. They were speaking very quietly, something intimate that she couldn't hear. She felt that she was intruding. The woman gave a throaty chuckle, then looked up and saw Willow.

'Oh hello, we're quite finished if you'd like to clear the table.'

'I'm afraid I don't work here. I suspect all the staff have gone home and Annie will be busy in the bar.'

Amused, Willow introduced herself. The woman laughed again. 'Oh dear, now I feel like a terrible fool.' There was no sign of embarrassment though and no apology. 'We're the Johnsons, Tony and Barbara.' She didn't ask Willow to sit down.

'I'm investigating the sudden death of one of the islanders. I'll have to ask you some questions. I won't interrupt you now, but if you could be free after breakfast. Perhaps at nine o'clock.'

'Could you make it a *little* later?' This was the man. He had a voice like some of the politicians with whom Willow was forced to work, charming but entitled. 'We are on holiday after all.'

Willow agreed to make it nine-thirty and left them still talking across the cluttered table.

In her room, she opened the curtains and looked out at the

night. When she phoned Jimmy, he answered at once. They spoke of their son, and then a little about work and their plans for the following day.

'I looked round Nistaben this evening,' Willow said. 'They've had lots of work done on the farm. Any idea where the money came from to do all the upgrades?'

'Magnus, Archie's father, was a grafter, full of ideas for the island. He had his own creel boat and bought into a couple of Westray ventures. He came across as a gentle, dreamy soul, but he was a good businessman too. Archie would have inherited much of that. Money was never a problem for the family.' Perez paused. 'I have a feeling that Archie owned a part-share of the Pierowall Hotel too. Magnus bought into it when it was struggling after the financial crash.'

'Something else to check out tomorrow.' Money had never meant much to Willow, but she knew it could be a powerful motive.

They said goodnight. There were no declarations of love. Perez might be emotionally incontinent, but there was nothing showy about him. Unlike Archie Stout, his feelings were deep and hidden, and for that, Willow was grateful.

Chapter Seven

Perez ended the call from Willow and went into his boy's room to check that James was still covered by the quilt. It was a cold night. He stood for a moment looking down at the child, listening to the breathing, and felt the weight of paternal responsibility. Willow had taken to motherhood easily, almost recklessly. She'd teased him for his anxiety and told stories of her childhood in the commune. She described it as benign neglect. Or freedom. Children were resilient, she said. They usually survived. He should worry less. He could hear her words in his head and found himself grinning. Really, he knew, she was as protective of their son as he was.

James had been born in this house. Perez and Cassie had moved in with Willow at the same stage of pregnancy as she was now. She'd opted for a home birth despite his anxieties, and Perez had been astounded by the whole loud and messy and joyous process. The exuberant physicality of it.

'Let's have lots of bairns!' he'd said, caught up with the excitement of the experience, when the midwives had left and they were lying together, quiet now, the baby suckling.

Willow had rolled her eyes. 'You *are* joking. I'm not going through that again anytime soon.'

Downstairs Perez made coffee, poured himself a dram and took it into the living room to sit again by the fire. This was the most comfortable place he'd ever lived. While occasionally he missed his house in Lerwick, the Lodeberrie, with its roots in the water, this substantial former manse felt like home. It was odd, he thought, that they'd chosen to live in the only land-locked parish in Orkney. They'd both grown up close to the sea and perhaps this was another way of making a start that was new to them both.

They'd shared parenting of James from the beginning. Willow's work, supervising policing throughout the Scottish islands, took her away for extended periods. He was Orkney based and had loved getting to know his new patch. Cassie had settled well into the grammar school and her accent was already morphing into Orcadian. So far, she was riding out her teenage years without too much drama. The hop north to Shetland to visit her biological father on the ferry or the twin prop plane was no longer an adventure. She loved her new brother and was looking forward to another sibling. All seemed calm and well. Perez had climbed out of the depression that had sucked him in after Fran had been killed.

But now Archie was dead, and he could sense his mood starting to shift again. There was the old fear of incompetence, the old image of a wave of disaster on a watery horizon, waiting to swamp him.

Furiously, he began to plan work for the following day, but he couldn't focus and in the end, he took himself to bed.

He slept better than he expected and woke next morning to another clear and unusually still day. James was awake and playing with his toys in the adjoining room, not yet bored enough to rouse his father. Perez got up and went in.

'Time for us both to get ready. Let's show Mum we can manage by ourselves.'

They made their way downstairs to the kitchen. It was a nursery day. Since she'd started maternity leave, Willow had taken on full responsibility for James, and it took Perez a moment to remember the routine of breakfast and then to find the boy's outdoor clothes.

'Where *is* Mum?'

'She'll be home soon,' Perez said, and hoped that was true. 'Or we'll go and find her, eh?'

How things had changed since he was a boy! He suspected his father had never changed a nappy in his life, though his mother had been fully involved with life on the croft, and on top of that had baked and cleaned and knitted. Some years her Fair Isle patterned jerseys and gloves and scarves, sold to fancy shops in London, had contributed more to the family's income than the lambs sent for slaughter.

In the police station, after safely delivering James to the nursery, he tried again to focus on work, on the detail that might lead to a successful outcome of the investigation. It was easier here, but half of his mind was on Westray with Willow. His first call was to Orkney's archaeologist, a man called Paul Rutherford. Perez had met him occasionally, when members of the public came across ancient bones and believed them to be more modern, sinister. Paul could call on the right people to date them. Sometimes, Perez thought, Orkney was founded on the bones of the long dead. He made an appointment to call on the man later in the day.

He met Vaila outside the new Balfour Hospital. She looked out of place here in the town, with cars going past on the main road out of Kirkwall, and the bustle of people heading into the building. He wondered if she'd stay on Westray. It would be hard work farming Nistaben on her own, even with Lawrie to help and her parents to support her. Perhaps she'd move in to the Orkney mainland, where the boys could come home every night from school, and she could find a different kind of job. A new life. Something artistic and fulfilling. He and Willow could help her settle.

Immediately, he heard Willow's words in his head, exasperated and affectionate: 'Jimmy man, you can't fix the problems of the world. Who do you think you are?'

Dr Grieve was waiting for them inside the hospital. Nobody else was there. Thoughtful as ever, perhaps he'd sent the mortuary assistant out for a break. Perez wasn't sure whether Vaila would want him in the room with her, but at the door she clung to his arm, and he walked in with her, more friend now, he supposed, than cop. The pathologist pulled back the sheet, so only the face was visible, then retreated to a corner of the room.

For a moment, Perez didn't look down at the body. It seemed like an intrusion, almost self-indulgent. They were here for Vaila, not for him to say his goodbyes to his friend, but the hold on his arm tightened and he didn't feel he could pull away. So he looked down at the man, and saw him motionless for perhaps the first time. Archie had never been still even as a child. He'd pulled faces and every emotion had shown on his face. Of course, this looked like Archie – there were the generous features, a little too big, and the sandy Viking hair and beard – but there was no sense of the man he knew. Little sign either, because of the way the doctor had placed him, of the trauma to his skull. He had certainly been hit from behind.

Vaila was crying now. Perez didn't hear any sound, but he could feel the convulsions as little tensions on his arm. He turned to look at her and saw the tears on her face. Grieve came forward with a box of tissues. She wiped her eyes, pulled away from Perez and bent to kiss her husband's forehead.

'Would you like some time alone with him?'

She nodded 'Just a couple of minutes.' The men left the room, and stood awkwardly waiting, the door open so they could see inside.

'We have his clothes, and everything that was on him.' Grieves spoke in a whisper. 'They're with the crime scene team.'

'Did you see anything unusual?'

The pathologist was about to speak, but Vaila turned away from the body to join them.

'We'll look after him,' Grieve said, 'and get him back to you as soon as we can.'

Perez took Vaila for coffee. There was a place that he and Willow liked, which would be quiet on a winter's morning even this close to Christmas. But the decorated tree in the corner and the cheery seasonal background music seemed to mock them. After asking her what she'd like, and if she needed anything to eat, he waited for her to speak.

'I didn't sleep,' she said at last. 'I'm not sure I'll ever be able to sleep again.'

'Is there anything I can do? Anything you or the boys need?'

'Just find out what happened, Jimmy. I go over and over the possibilities in my head, and I can't tell what's true. It's like a story on a loop, small details flying around in my head. It's driving me crazy.'

'I'll have to ask you to tell the story again. And the small details will be important. We'll need to take a formal statement in the police station. Phil Bain will do that. I'm too close.' A pause. 'And I'm grieving too.'

She nodded to show she understood.

'Did Archie still own a share in the Pierowall Hotel?' Perez was remembering his conversation with Willow the night before. It seemed a safe topic of conversation, not too emotional for Vaila or for him.

But Vaila tensed. 'Why? What have folk been saying?'

'Nothing at all. It's just me being a cop. Being curious.'

'I'm sorry, Jimmy. I'm sensitive about everything just now.' She drank the last of her coffee. 'Bill and Annie wanted to buy Archie out, but he wasn't having any of it. You know how stubborn he could be.'

'Like a mule when the mood took him.'

'Bill said they were working all the hours God sent and Archie was contributing nothing.' Vaila stared at the shoppers on the pavement outside. 'Archie said they'd have lost the place altogether if Magnus hadn't stepped in. It would have sorted itself out in the end, but it had caused some bad feeling.'

'Why wasn't Archie prepared to sell?'

Vaila shrugged. 'He said it was for the boys. Lawrie was a natural-born farmer, but he couldn't imagine Iain driving a tractor all day. He might make a good landlord though and would be full of ideas to pull in more visitors.'

'And now the share in the hotel comes to you?'

'Aye,' she said. 'I suppose it does. But it hardly seems important now.' She looked across the table at Perez. 'Let's do that statement now, shall we? Get it over with, so I can go home to my boys.'

Perez had phoned Phil Bain and told him to be ready, so there'd be no hanging around for her. While the interview was taking place, he sat at his desk, unable to concentrate on the work in front of him, then phoned Willow. She didn't answer and he left her a message about the MacBrides wanting to buy out Archie's share of the hotel.

He heard voices in the corridor outside his office. Phil Bain and Vaila must have finished. It seemed to have taken such a short time. He worried that Phil might not have asked the right questions or listened carefully enough to Vaila's answers. He wished he'd taken the statement himself, and the control freak in him wanted to read it before letting her leave the station in case there were gaps or inconsistencies. But she was keen to get back to Westray, and that wouldn't be fair to her or to Phil. Instead, he saw Vaila out of the building, and stood there with her. She hesitated for a moment before heading off.

'I'm not sure I want to go home now,' she said. 'Archie and I had known each other since we were kids in the little school there. The whole place is full of him.' She looked up at him. 'How did you manage after Fran died?'

'I didn't very well. I had to hold everything together for Cassie, I suppose. Or at least to pretend that I was holding it together. It took a lot of time. It's trite, but grief can't be hurried. And even now I get swamped by it. It's like a wave with the tide behind it breaking over my head. I sometimes feel that I'm drowning.'

She took his hands in both of hers and then turned away. He watched until she walked around a corner and was lost from view.

Back in his office, he looked at Vaila's statement. There was nothing new – a list of facts and times, apparently accurate and precise. Perez supposed Phil had got what was needed, but now he regretted not talking informally to Vaila about the case when they'd been in the cafe. He could have asked about any of the conflicts within the island, the power struggles that Rosalie Greeman had mentioned. He wondered if he should have told Vaila that Archie hadn't been having an affair with the woman, but he suspected she would have found her husband's restraint harder to handle than any fling. Looking back, the whole encounter with Vaila had been unsatisfactory. He thought that Willow would have handled it much better.

He phoned Willow again, but still there was no reply.

Chapter Eight

GODFREY LANSDOWN WAS WAITING FOR WILLOW in the residents' lounge when she went downstairs. He still seemed nervous, but perhaps anticipating a meeting with the police could do that to you. The fire was already lit there. Annie looked in and asked if she'd like breakfast, but Willow shook her head. She'd stopped throwing up every morning months ago, but still couldn't quite stomach anything but tea until later in the day.

Lansdown stood up when she came in. She thought the gesture was an automatic response to a woman, not respect for her position. He seemed to belong not just to a different generation, but a different age. Willow suspected he'd be shocked that a pregnant woman was heading up the inquiry.

He was still neat, but dressed now for outdoors in cord trousers, a jersey and thick socks. His boots and jacket would be in the flagstoned porch waiting for him. His binoculars were round his neck. Everything about him was tense. Perhaps he was shy, thrown by any contact with strangers. It occurred to her that birdwatching might attract loners.

'Thanks for giving up your time. I know you just want to be out on the island.'

'Of course I want to help. It's such a tragedy. He was so young.' There was a pause and he seemed to feel the need to explain. 'My wife died three years ago. She was a little older than me and suffered a heart attack. Terrible for me – we'd been married for fifty years and had scarcely spent a night apart. We never had children and were everything to each other, but Mr Stout still had his life ahead of him, and a family depending on him.'

'Did you know him?'

The man shook his head. 'Not really. I'd seen him in the bar. It would be hard to miss him. He'd be the life and soul of every party, I think.'

'But you're a regular here in Westray. You must have come to know the locals.'

The challenge to his answer seemed to throw the man. He was silent for a moment, before speaking again. Upstairs there was the distant buzz of a vacuum cleaner.

'My wife and I took early retirement. We were both civil servants with a decent pension, the mortgage all paid, and as I said, no dependants. We came to Orkney first on an island cruise. A retirement present to ourselves. There was just one day in Orkney, and that was on the mainland. We took the classic coach tour taking in the tourist sites, Brodgar, Stenness and Maeshowe. But we fell in love with the place and returned independently. Westray was our favourite island. We loved the beauty and the history of course, but more than that, we found it very friendly.' He looked up at Willow, struggling to explain in more detail. 'It's such an optimistic and positive place. The people here seem open to new ideas, to starting new enterprises.

Edith was a very positive woman, and she loved the islanders' attitude. Her ashes were scattered into the sea at Grobust, close to where Mr Stout's body was found. His murder feels somehow like a personal insult. A desecration.'

Willow stayed silent. Through the window she saw a young mother walk past with a toddler in a pushchair. Godfrey still hadn't answered her question. He hesitated for a moment, but then he continued, pleased perhaps to have the opportunity to talk about his wife.

'Edith was much more outgoing than me. She loved a party too. People took to her. She was interested in them, and she made them laugh. One of the reasons we returned every year was because we felt the islanders had become friends. Some of them, at least. We knew Archie's parents well enough to invite them to have dinner with us here, and we went to their house for a meal. The last night of each holiday. It had become a kind of ritual.' He looked up again and there was a ghost of a smile. 'We always boarded the ferry next morning with a terrible hangover. We weren't big drinkers. But no, we didn't really know Archie. He'd married and moved away from the family home by the time we first visited, though of course he's back there now. He was of a different generation.'

'Archie's parents died too.'

'Within a year of each other,' Godfrey said. 'Magnus first and then May. They were older than us and of course they'd had a harder life. Farming isn't easy. Edith passed away soon after. I didn't think I'd ever come back, but she'd always said that she'd like her ashes brought here, to the place where she'd been so happy. I couldn't refuse her that last gift.'

'And you kept coming back?'

Lansdown nodded. 'I'm an anxious man. Not brave like

Edith. I couldn't imagine travelling somewhere strange, but I needed to get away from my house occasionally. Birdwatching had always been a hobby, but it became something of an obsession. A distraction, I suppose. Something to take my mind off my loss. I'm writing a natural history of the island. It won't be a book. Nothing so grand. A pamphlet for people who might be interested. It's nearly completed. The heritage centre will take it and sell it. I don't need to make any money from it, so they'll keep the profit.'

'You know the people who run the heritage centre?'

'It's run by a committee of islanders, I think. Annie, who owns the hotel, is a leading light. She's my main contact.'

Willow made a note of that, but she already knew that Annie and Bill had access to a key, and so to the stone that was the murder weapon. She turned back to the man.

'I need to ask you your movements the evening that Archie Stout disappeared. You do understand. It's routine. We'll be asking everyone.'

'Of course, Inspector.' His voice was formal again, a little distant. Perhaps he regretted having told her so much about his personal life. 'I was out on the island until it got dark. My work is almost finished, but I wanted to take photos so I could add some illustrations. The weather was wild and stormy, and there were some breathtaking waves breaking over the jetty. In the fading light, the scene was dramatic. Just what I wanted.' A pause. 'Edith always loved a good gale.'

'And once it got dark?'

'I came back here to the hotel. I had a shower and changed before coming down to dinner. I eat early these days. Then I went into the bar for a last drink, just as Vaila Stout came in looking for her husband. At first there was a lot of joking about where he might be. Now, that seems in rather poor taste. Later, I understand, everyone went out to look for him. I wasn't a part of the search team. I'd already gone to bed.'

'Did you have any contact with the other hotel guests, the Johnsons? Were you with them the evening before? The night Archie went missing?'

'Ah, they've been very kind to me. They don't like to see me sitting on my own and always join me if we're in the bar together.' He looked up at Willow and the smile returned briefly. 'Honestly, I'd rather be left to read in peace. As I explained, I'm not a very sociable man, and we have so very little in common, but it would be churlish to ask them to leave me alone. I didn't see them the night Archie went missing though. I'm sure they have more pleasurable things to do on a dark winter's evening than making small talk to an elderly gent.'

Willow smiled back at him. She found herself warming to him. There was something brave about his honesty and his determination to face the reality of his loneliness. The lack of self-pity. 'That's been very helpful,' she said. 'Did you see Archie at all on this visit? If you were close to his parents, you must have known him by sight.'

'Only to wave to if I saw him on his farm or out on the tractor. A brief word when we bumped into each other in here.' A pause. 'I'm not sure that he and his parents entirely saw eye to eye about island affairs. I never quite understood the details. Magnus represented Westray on the island council, and there was an expectation that Archie might take over the role, but it never happened. Vaila's father Tom was voted in instead. I suspect that May might have had something to do with that. Magnus died first.'

Willow understood something of the complication of island politics. She'd grown up with them at home in the Hebrides. 'Thank you,' she said again. 'I'll know where you are, if I need to speak to you again.'

'Oh yes. I'll be here for another couple of weeks, until after New Year. I come every year now.' He paused. 'It sounds ridiculous but it's a way of spending Christmas with Edith.'

Although it was already nine-thirty, she found the Johnsons still in the dining room. They hadn't even ordered breakfast, though there was tea and coffee on the table. Annie was hovering waiting for them.

'Oh, sorry! We slept in. And then we saw you were still chatting to Godfrey, so we thought we'd have something to eat before Annie stopped serving.' Barbara smiled, as if she was sure Willow would understand. 'The full breakfast for us both please, Annie.'

'Would you like your baked beans hot or cold?'

'Hot of course. Who on earth eats cold beans?'

'Westray folk.' Annie turned sharply away.

Willow couldn't help smiling to herself. Vaila had served her cold beans when she'd stayed over at Nistaben after a party, and she'd been about to comment when Perez had explained. Cold beans was a Westray thing. Almost a statement of identity and pride. An odd form of patriotism.

Now, they were alone in the place and Willow thought this would do as well for a talk as anywhere. Tony Johnson was looking at his phone and had barely looked up.

'Would you like tea or coffee?' Barbara said. 'We can always ask for more.'

'Tea, please.' She found a cup and saucer on a sideboard

under the window and pulled up a seat to join them. 'Tell me what you're doing in Westray.'

'We came first as part of a university project.' Again, Barbara spoke for them both, though Tony did stop looking at his phone to help himself to more coffee and seemed to be listening.

'We were volunteering on a dig,' he said. 'Both university students, looking for adventure. I was at Durham and Barbara was at Bangor, so it was this place that brought us together. It's forty years since we met here as youngsters, so we thought we'd come back to celebrate the anniversary.'

'You were digging over Christmas?' Willow thought that with frosty ground or torrential rain it would be hard going.

Barbara laughed. 'No! It was hard enough work in the summer. But our kids wanted to do their own thing this year, so we thought why not? Neither of us is really into the traditional Christmas nonsense. The anniversary year gave us an excuse to escape.'

Annie appeared with the breakfasts. Willow waited until the couple had started eating before she continued with her questions.

'And that was the last time you visited the island? When you were students in the 1980s?'

'No.' The man spoke now. 'We came back in 2006 when the Noltland site was opened up again. I brought a couple of PhD students for the whole summer. Barbara visited a few times. We got more friendly with the islanders then, perhaps because we were older and less wrapped up in our own group.'

'Do you both still work in archaeology?'

'Tony does,' Barbara said. 'He's back in Durham but now he's a prof. It was never my true passion and I moved on to arts management. I look after a little community arts centre in Gateshead. A bit of a nightmare with all the funding cuts but great fun.'

Willow couldn't imagine either of these people experiencing any kind of bad dream. It seemed to her that they'd float through life cushioned by a regular income, the prospect of a decent pension, and a mortgage paid off years ago. There was a smugness about them, a complacency. But she knew that was probably unfair. How could she judge their lives on one meeting?

'Are you still involved in the archaeology here in Westray?'

Tony shook his head. 'Not since the dig in 2006.' He had his hand over his phone and Willow could tell that he was itching to look at it again. What could be so important? 'Since then, I moved on from the Neolithic to quite a different field. I'm interested in the Nordic influence on our culture. The people popularly known as the Vikings.'

'Can you tell me anything about the story stones? If you were here in the eighties, that must have been around the time that they were found.'

'We were here as students when they were discovered.' Barbara sounded excited. 'Not by us unfortunately, but it was the beach party celebrating the find of the stones that brought Tony and me together. A lot of Spanish wine followed by cheap whisky can do that to you.' She looked across at her husband with a smile. 'And that influenced your later research, didn't it, Tony? The runes carved into the stones intrigued you from the beginning.'

Willow directed her attention back to the man. 'Could you explain?'

Now Tony turned into lecturer mode. 'The stones are certainly Neolithic. They're made of Caithness flagstone like much of Maeshowe.' He looked at her to see if she understood the reference to the burial mound on Orkney mainland. She nodded and he continued. 'Our stones were part of a similar chamber here in Westray. We think at least part of that structure was still standing when the Vikings came to Orkney. One side of each stone has picked traditional Neolithic spirals. The other was carved much later with runes. Viking graffiti.'

'And you can tell what those runes say?'

'Well, I couldn't then, but I can now after nearly twenty years of research. We can't tell the exact date of the carving, because of course carbon dating would only give us the age of the stone, which we already know is Neolithic. One says: "I am Olaf, teller of tales." The other: "Hear my stories and know death."'

'So that's why they're called the story stones?' Despite her antipathy to the man, Willow was fascinated.

Johnson nodded.

'Were they one stone originally, and split into two later?'

'No. We think they always were two separate stones, and that they were chosen for the later Viking decoration because they were so evenly matched. They're each larger and squarer than a modern house brick. We believed that they were used originally as part of the entrance to a Neolithic burial chamber, then stolen by the Vikings to form part of a building for communal feasting.'

'And now the stones stand in the heritage centre?'

Or they did, until someone used one of them to kill Archie Stout. And the other has disappeared.

That was a piece of information they had so far managed to keep secret.

Johnson nodded again. 'They were held in the museum in

Kirkwall until the centre was built and then they were brought back here.'

'Did you know Archie Stout?'

'We knew his parents better,' Barbara said. 'May and Magnus. A few of us stayed in their holiday rental on that first visit in the eighties. They were so kind and did seem very interested in everything to do with the dig. May would come along to volunteer sometimes. Magnus would drop off crab if he'd been out with his creel boat and we'd invite them to our parties. They were farming Nistaben then and Archie was just a lad. Mischievous, into everything.'

'They died,' Willow said.

'They must have been quite elderly,' Barbara said. 'I think Archie was a late child. The first son was already away to school in Kirkwall when we were here as students. They were still alive in 2006 and I got to know them better then. Because I wasn't officially working, I had more time for visiting islanders. They were always up for tea, homebakes and chatting.'

'When did you last see Archie?'

'The afternoon before he disappeared,' Barbara said. Now that Tony wasn't talking about the stones, he seemed to have lost interest again in the conversation, and his hand twitched back towards the phone on the table. 'We were here in Pierowall walking down the street past the shop, and he was just coming out. We stopped for a moment to chat.'

'How did he seem?'

Barbara looked at her husband. 'I'm not sure. A bit distracted? We've been talking about it since we heard he was dead. Because we know what happened later, we wondered if we've been reading too much into it.'

'I know what you mean. We all make up stories in our heads

after any kind of drama. I'm interested in your impression though.'

'Usually, he was very friendly,' Barbara said. 'He'd take time to chat. Reminiscences of when we were staying in his parents' cottage. He remembered that summer with great fondness, I think. He was the sort of man who wanted to be liked, a big character. We've met him in here in the hotel a few times, and he could switch on his personality like a light as soon as he had any sort of audience. He became more alive. But that afternoon, it was as if he hardly saw us. I wondered if he'd had bad news and called after him to ask after Vaila and the boys, in case one of them was ill. He just muttered a response and turned his back on us. It was almost rude.'

'It *was* rude.' Now the temptation became too strong, and Tony picked up his phone. 'I'm sorry, there are some work calls I need to make.'

'I won't be much longer,' Willow said, her voice mild. 'This *is* a murder inquiry and I'm sure you want to help. Where did Archie go after he left you?'

'He was walking, and he came this way. Towards the hotel,' Barbara said.

'Did you see a vehicle?'

The woman shook her head. 'We were walking in the opposite direction though. It might have been parked here.'

'What were you doing later that evening? Godfrey Lansdown said he hadn't seen you in the bar.'

'We'd been invited out to an early supper, and then we went straight to our room. We skipped the bar. We fancied a night to ourselves.'

'Where did you go for supper?'

'To Hillhead, with Tom and Evelyn.'

'Vaila's parents.' Willow was surprised. She wasn't sure what the couples might have in common. 'Are you friends?'

'We knew them when we were here that summer in the eighties, and then again in 2006. I've kept in touch. Nothing formal. Christmas cards. They let me know when Magnus and May died, and they came to stay with us once when they were on their way south for a wedding. Islanders are remarkably hospitable, Inspector.'

I know, Willow thought. *I grew up on an island. And I'm married to an islander.* She found herself resenting the woman's tone. There was something annoying about tourists who felt they absolutely understood a place's culture and sensibilities because they'd visited a few times.

'Did you mention that you'd seen Archie? Or that he'd been behaving a little strangely?'

'No! It wouldn't have been appropriate to gossip about their son-in-law, would it?' Barbara seemed amused. 'Besides, it only became more significant once he'd died.'

'What did you talk about?'

'I'm not sure. It turned into a strange evening, cut short when Vaila phoned to say that Archie was missing. We thought maybe there'd been some domestic problem, a row between them before Archie had stormed off. I'd have thought he might be given to dramatic gestures. It seemed tactful just to make our excuses and leave.'

Chapter Nine

ELLIE HAD BEEN OUT AFTER AN early breakfast, liaising with the crime scene team at the Noltland site. The investigators had gone back to Kirkwall the evening before, taking Archie's car with them, and arrived in again on the first ferry. Willow met Ellie in the lobby, just as she'd finished talking to Tony and Barbara Johnson. The sergeant was red-faced from the cold, wrapped up in her bulky down coat.

'It's freezing out there. And I always thought that Yorkshire was Baltic.'

'Have the CSIs got anything?' Willow wasn't optimistic, but something real, concrete, would be helpful. At the moment, all she had were impressions.

Ellie shook her head. 'Nothing from the scene. It's so exposed, and there was a gale that night. There might be trace evidence snagged in the long grass on the dunes, but nothing so far. They reckon they'll be done there today. They found a few spots of blood in Archie's car, but they reckon that might be coincidental. He could have cut himself on a quite different occasion. They'll test the DNA to check that it was his. They have Archie's clothes and any possessions that were on him back in Kirkwall, and they'll work on that.' A pause. 'Are we heading back to town too?'

'Not yet.'

Willow couldn't decide what Ellie made of the decision to stay. Did she want to be home with her family, or was she enjoying the break in routine?

'Won't the team from Glasgow want to take over?' There was a reflex sneer in Ellie's voice. In Orcadians' experience Glasgow always wanted to interfere in island affairs.

'Nah. Apparently, there's freezing fog all over the mainland and there's no way the flights would get north. I think they're more worried about being stuck here for Christmas.' Willow grinned. 'So let's show them how it's done, shall we? I'd like to chat to the Angels, before Vaila gets back from Kirkwall. And Jimmy has asked me to talk to the boys. They were too upset to face any questions yesterday.'

'Angels?'

'That's Vaila's parents' family name. A ship was wrecked here years ago. There was a little lad still alive inside. He was adopted by an island family. They wanted to give him their own name, but the ship was called the *Archangel*, so the island called the lad Archie Angel. He married an island woman later and the name persists. And I presume Archie has become a traditional Westray name too.'

Another tale, Willow thought. Another story that might or might not be true.

She nodded towards the dining room, where the Johnsons were lingering over a second pot of coffee. 'Those visitors had supper at Hillhead, Tom and Evelyn Angel's place, the night Archie disappeared. They had the impression that he and Vaila had some sort of domestic before he stormed off into the night. That's a slightly different tale from the one we got from Vaila. I'd like to check before she gets back this afternoon.'

Hillhead was another traditional Westray farm – solid and surrounded by barns and outbuildings. Some land low and green for grazing, other fields cut for silage. These were very different from the smaller crofts Willow knew from Shetland and her home island in the Hebrides. Despite the name, it stood in the lee of a curve of hills, which ran down the west of the island, and this time of year, with the low winter sun, it must almost always be in shadow. Willow felt shut in.

Vaila's boys must be helping their grandfather to feed the cows, because she could hear their voices, coming from the byre, when she and Ellie got out of the car. She knocked at the back door and Evelyn shouted them into the kitchen, which was shiny, rather grand, like something out of a design magazine. Evelyn was baking. On the table in front of her there was a mixing bowl, pale yellow like one Willow's mother had used, and bags of flour and sugar.

'I don't feel much like it, but we still have to eat.' Evelyn looked up at them. 'And the boys do love a chocolate cake. Anything to cheer them up, eh?' She slid the kettle onto the hotplate of the range. 'You'll have some tea? Tom's trying to keep the boys busy. We don't think it's healthy for them to be cooped up in their rooms on their screens all day.'

Willow thought this was a complaint that Evelyn had aired long before Archie's death – grandparents thinking they knew best – but the woman added: 'You never know what they might read about their daddy on social media.'

'Of course.' And that was something else they'd have to check: crazy theories that probably had no substance, but which should be monitored. She'd get Phil onto it. He was great with anything tech.

More tea. They sat not at the table where Evelyn was baking but at a marble breakfast bar. There was a view east through the window of a spit of beach, backed by shingle. A sliver of sunlight lit it, but soon even that would be in shadow.

'They're very lucky growing up here in Westray,' Willow said. 'With all this space.'

'Aye, we think so, though some kids can't wait to get away. Iain loves being in the hostel in Kirkwall and he's thinking already of a university in the south. Lawrie's not academic. I think he'll leave school as soon as he can. We always thought he'd work with his father, but I'm not sure what'll happen to Nistaben now.'

'Vaila never fancied a different path?' Willow was taking the lead in the conversation. Ellie sat to one side, listening. She was a great listener and had a memory for detail. 'She seems very interested in the history of the islands and she's made a beautiful home. You could imagine her as a designer.' She looked around the room. 'She must take after you.'

'Aye, maybe.' Evelyn was dismissive. 'We'd have encouraged her if she'd really wanted to go. She had a fancy for art school at one time.'

It seemed to Willow that any encouragement had been theoretical rather than practical. 'But she fell for Archie and stayed in Westray?'

'Something like that.' Evelyn's mouth snapped shut. Perhaps she'd been even less enthusiastic about the marriage than the idea that Vaila might go south to study.

'It seems as if they were a lovely family, Archie, Vaila and the boys.'

This time Evelyn didn't reply. She emptied the kettle into a pot before turning back to the table.

'We're checking where everyone was on the night Archie disappeared,' Willow said. 'Can you confirm that the Johnsons spent the evening with you?'

'The prof and Barbara? They did. We've known them for years.'

'But they've only been in Westray twice, once when they were students and then again when Tony came back in 2006 to work on the dig.'

'They were different from most of the visitors who come. Westray was special for them because this is where they met, and they weren't just here for a week at a time. They kept in touch with us. And then they put us up when we went south last year. The least we could do was offer them a meal.' Evelyn's voice was defensive.

'What time did they arrive?'

'You can't think they had anything to do with Archie's death? Respectable people like that! Tony's famous in his field. Besides, they barely knew him.'

'We have to ask,' Willow said gently. 'Routine, you know. It's what makes for good policing and how we'll find out what happened.'

Evelyn rubbed her cheek with her hand and left behind a smudge of cocoa powder.

'I'm sorry,' she said. 'I know.' There was a pause. 'We always eat early, especially in the winter. And that night there was such a storm although it passed through quickly enough. They arrived at about six, and I had the meal on the table by half past. I had some stewing beef in the freezer from the last cow we killed. Some animals can be a peedie bit tough, but I made a casserole, tarted it up with lots of wine and shallots and called it beef bourguignon. They liked it fine. And we had crab for starters. There's never any shortage of shellfish.'

She stopped abruptly. 'I'm sorry. You don't need to know all that. I'm rambling.'

'Not at all. The more detail the better.'

'I was a bit nervous about the meal. I thought they'd be used to what they call fine dining. The prof's famous, you know. He's written a book about the runes on the story stones, and like I said, we've seen him a few times on the television. He had his own show last year. Something serious on BBC Two.'

'I didn't realize that.' Willow glanced across at Ellie, who gave a little nod to say that she'd check the details when they were back in the hotel. Willow wondered if that explained the man's arrogance: he was something of a celebrity in his field, and he was used to being recognized. 'What time did you hear that Archie was missing?'

'We'd finished eating and we'd moved into the living room with coffee and drinks.' She looked apologetically at Willow. 'We don't have a resident police officer here in Westray, and we're not as careful as we should be about drinking and driving.'

Willow smiled back. She understood even if she didn't condone, and this certainly wasn't the time to comment.

'It was just before eight when Vaila phoned. Maybe a little bit earlier. At first, I wasn't anxious at all. We knew they'd been going through a bad patch recently and Archie wasn't the easiest of men. I thought he'd be in some house down the island with a pal, whining about the life that he had.' A pause. 'He was given to self-pity and didn't realize at times how lucky he was.'

'And the Johnsons left at about that time?'

'Yes. It was a bit awkward. They could see that something was wrong, and I'd had a few drinks myself so maybe I was a wee bit indiscreet, talking about Vaila's marriage. They probably thought they were being tactful to leave us to it. Or that one of us might want to go to Vaila.'

'But you didn't?'

'No. She was in the bar at the Pierowall Hotel, and I thought one of the guys there would track down Archie soon enough.' A pause, then her voice bitter, the crudeness shocking: 'You can't fart in Westray without everyone knowing.' She stared out of the window before adding: 'I thought Vaila was making a fuss over nothing. No marriage is perfect. We were here in the warm, a fire going and a good meal inside us. The last thing we wanted was a wasted journey up the island. Of course, I feel guilty now.'

'You'd heard rumours that Archie had been having an affair with Rosalie Greeman?'

Evelyn didn't answer directly. 'Like I said. No marriage is perfect. We all have to work at it.'

'Someone must have checked that Archie wasn't with Rosalie at Quoybrae.'

'Of course they did. Bill o' the hotel phoned her first. He didn't want one of the lads going up there. They'd have loved catching Archie with his trousers down while his wife was making a scene in the pub. That would give them something to gossip over through to the New Year.'

'According to Rosalie, they weren't having an affair,' Willow said gently. 'They were just friends.'

'Aye well, she would say that.' Evelyn shot her a look that suggested Willow would be a naive fool to believe such a thing.

There was a moment's silence.

'Archie's position on the island,' Willow said. 'Was he respected? His father represented the north isles on Orkney council, but Archie never took on the role. I think Tom took over once Magnus died?'

Evelyn was dismissive. 'Archie would never have been interested. He'd have been bored stupid after the first meeting. There was something of the hyperactive child about him. He could never sit still.'

'Yet it seemed something was worrying him that day. Something close to home.'

Evelyn looked up sharply. 'Who told you that?'

Willow shrugged and didn't reply. 'Had you heard any rumours? As you said, you can't fart in Westray without everyone knowing.'

Evelyn shook her head. 'No. I never heard anything like that.' But the reply came so quickly that Willow didn't quite believe her.

'I'm sorry,' she said, 'but I need to talk to the boys. Could you call them in? Or I could go out to them?' She thought that Evelyn would protest, but she must have realized that Willow was determined.

'Wait there. I'll fetch them in.'

Willow watched the woman cross the yard to call in her grandsons. Evelyn had pushed her feet into wellingtons but hadn't put on a coat over her apron and she wrapped her arms around her body to fend off the cold. She stood at the door of the byre and shouted inside. Willow couldn't hear what she said, but it didn't take long for Tom and the two boys to appear.

Tom led them through to the overheated living room. The carpet had recently been hoovered. There were lines in the pile like an English lawn that has just been cut. The grandfather stayed there with the boys throughout the interview. He sent Evelyn away before it started. 'You need to finish off in the kitchen, get that cake in the oven,' he said to his wife when she tried to join them. His voice was firm, and reluctantly Evelyn left them to it.

Lawrie had grown since Willow had seen him last and looked very like his father, sandy-haired, blue-eyed. She thought he could be descended from the writer of the runes on the story stones. Iain was small and slight and took after his mother.

'I need to ask you some questions,' Willow said. 'I know this is painful, but it might help us find out who killed your father.'

They stared back at her.

'I'd kill the bastard,' Lawrie said, 'if I got my hands on him.'

Willow only realized then that anger had overtaken grief. It must be his way of dealing with the loss. He'd clenched his fists, and his whole body was tense. His grandfather reached out and put a hand on his shoulder. Iain started crying.

'I'm sorry.' Willow looked up at the grandfather. 'Let's get this over as soon as we can. Your mother's in Kirkwall now, with Jimmy, but she'll be home soon. We have to think of her too.'

There was a moment of silence, then Tom spoke. 'We'll help in any way we can, won't we, boys?'

They stared at him, and then they both nodded.

Willow continued: 'Lawrie, you were at home with your dad while your mum was helping with the old folks' lunch, and Iain was at his friend's house. How did your father seem?'

'Fine.'

Willow had interviewed lots of teenage lads in her time as a cop. Most were monosyllabic. She knew not to take it personally.

'What did you talk about?'

'The farm. Christmas. The Ba'. It's my last year in the Boys' Ba' so we're hoping for a doonies win. We were all going into Kirkwall for it.'

'We'll still go in for it,' Tom said. 'Whatever your grandmother says. It's all planned, and your dad would want it. He was a great one for the Ba' although it's such a Kirkwall tradition. It'll be a celebration for your father.'

'I saw a photo of him in your room at Nistaben,' Willow said. 'He must have been a great player.'

'Fearless.' Tom put his arm around his grandson's shoulder. 'Just like this one.'

'What else did you talk about?'

'He told me what he'd got Mum for a Christmas present.' The boy was talking more freely now. 'Some fancy perfume he'd had to send away for. He'd asked the purser on the ferry to bring it in from Kirkwall so she wouldn't see it arriving in the post. He got me to hide it in my room.'

'That's why he was at the pier when the ferry came in?'

'Aye. John, the purser, is a Westray man.'

'Your dad didn't seem upset about anything? Disturbed in any way?'

Lawrie shook his head. 'He was just Dad.'

'Did he tell you where he was going when he went out after lunch?'

'He was taking bags of firewood to some people. I helped him load it in the trailer.'

'And both you boys were here when he came back for dinner later.'

'I was in my room,' Lawrie said, moody again. 'Headphones on. Listening to my music. I don't know when any of them came back.'

'I had to go and get Lawrie when it was time to eat,' Iain said. 'He can never hear even when we shout. Sometimes we have to text him.'

'And you didn't notice anything unusual about him when you were eating that evening?'

'Not really.' Iain looked across at his brother. Asking for permission to speak or perhaps needing support before he went on. 'He was a bit quiet maybe. Like there was something on his mind.'

'Did you notice that, Lawrie?'

The elder boy shook his head. 'Like I said. He was just Dad.'

Chapter Ten

KIRKWALL WAS LOOKING FESTIVE, BUT THERE was nothing cheery about the police station, from the outside at least. It was a square, stained concrete block, which Perez supposed had been put up very quickly in the sixties, with no thought to any aesthetic appeal. He loved being in Orkney, but there were times when he missed the police station in Shetland's biggest town, Lerwick, with its traditional stone and its view over the town to the playpark, where the Up Helly Aa galley was burned every year.

Phil wandered into Perez's office. After taking Vaila's statement, the constable had been on the phone, checking the records of the ferry to Westray on the day of Archie's murder and back to the Orkney mainland on the first sailing the following morning, the day Archie's body had been found. He was good at chatting and getting better at listening, and his local connections made him valuable to the team.

'There was only one crossing the day that Archie went missing. The early one, with the others cancelled because of the gale. It was mostly trucks and one new tractor. Eight cars. They booked and paid online, and I have their details. All but two have Westray addresses. The others come from Kirkwall.' Phil paused. 'There were half a dozen foot passengers, but if they pay in cash once they're on board, and a couple of them did, then there's no record.'

'Can I have a list of the drivers and the details of the passengers who paid by card?'

'Sure, I've printed it off.'

'Might be an idea to talk to the purser and see if he recognized the ones who paid cash.'

'Yeah, I'll head down to the pier when the ferry comes in this afternoon. I was at school with some of the crew.'

Perez looked at the list. The Westray names meant nothing to him, but one of the Kirkwall drivers stood out. Perez pointed at it on the list. 'You'll recognize him?'

'I do! He taught me history. Some character him.'

Everyone in Orkney knew George Riley. He was an Englishman with unruly red hair and a voice that would have commanded attention on the battlefield. He was flamboyant, charismatic, a leading member of the Kirkwall Musical Theatre Society. He directed all the grammar school productions and occasionally took a leading role himself. He sang in the cathedral choir. He taught Cassie history too. Perez had bumped into him at parents' evenings and found him a little intimidating. 'Do we know when he left Westray?'

'The first boat yesterday. He probably wouldn't have known anything about Archie's death when he went.'

He will now though. Perez was surprised that the teacher hadn't been in touch. He'd know the Stout boys from school. Besides, he was the kind of man who might enjoy the drama of a murder investigation, and they'd asked everyone who visited the island that day to come forward.

'You've checked if any of the other passengers has come to our attention?'

'This foot passenger – Nat Wilkinson – was done for possession, but that was more than ten years ago and there's been nothing since. I'm guessing he's settled down. He'd be in his thirties now. A bit old for partying.'

Perez smiled at the thought that the thirties were a bit old for anything. 'Maybe.'

'There is an earlier note in his record though,' Phil went on. 'He was questioned about the death by drowning of his father. Nat was fourteen, still at the grammar school, and home from the hostel for the summer holidays. His father slipped off the pier and the lad was the only witness.'

'Any indication that the death was more than an accident?'

'Nothing here to suggest it. The father was known as a boozer apparently, and often unsteady on his feet.'

Perez thought about that. It was hard to see how a tragic accident so many years earlier could be connected to Archie's death, but he'd let Willow have the information in case she wanted to follow it up. 'We'll get Willow and Ellie to chat to all the Westray folk on the list this afternoon.' He looked at his watch. 'Could you phone Willow and fill her in? I have to go. I've arranged a meeting with Paul Rutherford, the local authority archaeologist in the college, and I'm already running late. It might be a waste of time, but I want to find out a bit more about the Westray story stones.'

The college was on a hill outside the town. Waiting in reception and looking down over the water, it seemed to Perez that there could be no other academic institution in the UK with a better view. Then he thought that Orkney was all views: water and land and more water stretching to a low horizon and a changing sky.

Rutherford was English, a proud Geordie, middle-aged. He was wearing a Newcastle United T-shirt under his jacket and had kept the accent. He looked more like a trucker than an academic and Perez liked him immediately. They sat in his office.

'You're interested in the story stones?'

Perez nodded. 'They could play a part in the Westray murder.'

'Of course. Everyone in Kirkwall is full of it. You were friends, weren't you? It must be hard, dealing with all this.' He looked up at the detective but didn't expect an answer. Perez liked him even more. 'There are rumours that one of the stones was the murder weapon.'

'Where did you hear that?' So, Perez thought, word had got out.

'The lass on reception has an aunty whose man comes from one of the Westray fishing families.'

They shared a grin.

Perez didn't think Annie would have gossiped, but Bill was a storyteller in his own right. He'd have been tempted to entertain the bar and any information about the murder would spread like wildfire. There'd probably be a Facebook page dedicated to it, WhatsApp groups sharing weird theories.

'One of the stones was the murder weapon,' Perez said. 'The other is missing. I just wondered if they could have any significance to Archie and his death.'

'As far as I know, Archie never showed any interest in the stones themselves. Vaila was an important part of the heritage centre committee. I don't know her well, but she's been along to every meeting I've held there.'

'Tell me about the stones.'

'They're a matching pair. We don't think they were split as part of the excavation. They're both smaller versions of the famous Westray stone and were found a little later during an excavation of one of the Noltland sites. We believe they were part of a chambered tomb, much like Maeshowe here in Orkney mainland, but much later the stones were incorporated into a communal feasting structure, probably in the ninth century.'

'The time of the Vikings?'

Rutherford smiled and nodded. 'We can tell that because of the runes, carved into the back of the stones.'

'And you can tell what those runes mean?'

'Yes, they were first translated when the stone was found in the eighties, then Prof Johnson looked at them again when he was in for the later dig in 2006 and confirmed the original translation. He's an expert in the field now.'

'And what *did* they say?'

'The first one reads: "I am Olaf, teller of tales," and the other: "Hear my stories and know death." It's clear that they were meant to be read together. Olaf sounds like a show-off, a ninth-century vandal.'

'You think he raided the original burial mound of the stones?'

Rutherford laughed. 'No, but I think he wanted to make his mark on them once they were incorporated into the feasting structure. You can imagine him holding court there with his stories of Nordic death and destruction.' His voice became more serious. 'These are important pieces, both for the original picked carvings on the front and the runes on the back. We need to retrieve them.'

Perez took a while to reply. 'The stone that killed Archie is evidence. We'll have to hang on to it until after the trial. I have no idea yet where the other is, but of course we're looking for it.'

And if we find it, he thought, *we'll know who killed my friend, who hit him so hard that his skull is all over the stone.*

Perez got out his phone and showed Rutherford a photograph of the murder weapon with the runes. 'Which inscription is on this one?'

'Is that blood?' Rutherford looked away for a moment. Perez wondered if the man might throw up, and then why *he* had so little physical response to the image. *Because this is work,* he thought, *and I need a level of detachment.*

'I'm sorry, yes. It was used to kill Archie Stout. But I'd like to know which inscription is on this particular stone.'

'It's not really my field, but I understand the stones well enough to know that this one says: "Hear my stories and know death."' Rutherford was still pale. 'Do you think there was a reason this was used? That it was some kind of message?'

Perez shook his head. 'I don't know anything yet.'

On impulse, when he left the college, he drove out of Kirkwall towards Finstown and stopped at the house where the teacher George Riley lived. It had been built in the Scottish baronial Gothic style as a hunting lodge for the grand people who came to the islands to shoot with the laird. It had a tower in one corner with a conical roof, leaded windows and an arched front door. Perez had always thought it would be a draughty, gloomy place for one person to live, but maybe it suited George Riley with his taste for the theatrical. The rumour was that he was the son of landed gentry, something of a laird himself. Certainly, the man didn't seem short of money. There was a Range Rover parked on the gravel drive.

Because the car was there, Perez assumed that Riley would be in. There was an iron bell pull and he could hear the ringing, loud despite the thickness of the door. Perez waited for a while and tried again. When there was still no response he wandered to the back of the building. Even in the grandest houses, most Orcadians used the rear entrance.

The back garden was walled, and a flagged courtyard lay between the back of the house and the wall. A latched door led into the garden and Perez could hear a noise inside, a gentle scratching. Riley must be working there, though it was hard to imagine him as much of a gardener. That seemed too gentle a hobby for someone so flamboyant. Perez lifted the latch and went through.

The garden was magnificent; it could have belonged to a grand English country house. There was a greenhouse against one of the walls, tall enough to contain fruit trees in pots. Half of the rest was separated into beds with paved paths running between. In the other half, there were a couple of rows of vegetables – leeks and sprouts, already frosted. Then there was a large patch ready to be dug over for planting in the spring. Something about this winter garden suited his mood.

The light was already beginning to fade, but in the far corner a figure was raking dead leaves into a pile. The house backed onto a shelter belt of established deciduous trees, and the leaves must have blown across in the recent gale. The gardener was preoccupied with his task and seemed not to have heard Perez come in. He was wearing a knitted cap that covered his head, but even without seeing the hair colour, Perez could tell at once that this wasn't Riley. This man was slighter, a little older. The inspector walked towards him, and now the gardener did look up.

'I'm sorry to disturb you,' Perez said. 'I'm looking for George.'

The worker straightened. 'I'm afraid he's not here.'

Perez had been expecting an island voice. He'd assumed that this was a local man, employed to tidy the garden for winter, or maybe a regular employee. But this voice could have come from a radio announcer of the 1950s or a member of the royal family. It was clipped and very formal.

'Do you know when he'll be back?'

'Tomorrow evening if the weather holds. He flew to Inverness this morning and he was only expecting to be away for a night, but there's freezing fog apparently. He's not sure when he'll be home.'

'Would you have a phone number for him? It is rather important that I speak to him.' Perez was annoyed to find that his voice had become as formal as the stranger's. He felt he'd been sucked into a strange piece of period drama. It was the fading light and this grand garden, the Gothic house as a backdrop. What could this place have to do with the Archie he'd known?

'I'm sorry, but may I ask who you are?' The man didn't sound sorry at all. He was using the politeness as a weapon.

Perez introduced himself. 'I'm investigating a murder. It took place in Westray and George was there the night that a local man was killed. We're speaking to all potential witnesses.'

'Ah, I see.' The man stood for a moment staring at him. 'Well, I suppose you'd better come to the house. I'll see if I can find his number for you.'

They walked back through the door in the wall and across the flagged yard. Perez looked into a large kitchen with a range at one end. He waited outside while the man took off his boots at the door. He felt awkward and wondered whether to follow and if he should remove his shoes, although they were quite clean.

'Come on in.' The man was impatient now. 'Do shut the door. It'll be freezing again soon, and this place is impossible to keep warm.'

'Who are you?' Perez was curious, but he also wanted to stamp a little authority on the encounter.

'My name's Chambers. Miles Chambers. I'm a friend of George's.'

'You're staying here?'

The man looked at Perez as if he were an impertinent schoolboy. 'I am. For a while.'

'What is George doing in Inverness?'

'I didn't ask. None of my business. It'll be something to do with his work, I suppose. But the flight was booked weeks ago. George told me that he'd be away again soon after his visit to Westray. Though he wasn't expecting to be stranded overnight on the island. It was planned as a day trip.' Miles was looking through a bowl of assorted objects – keys, batteries and scraps of paper – which stood on a shelf close to the range 'I think there's a card in here with his number.'

'You wouldn't have the number on your phone?' Now it was Perez's turn to be impatient.

'I don't own a mobile phone. Not any more. I don't hold with the things. A terrible invasion of privacy.' With a gesture of triumph, Miles pulled out a card and passed it across to Perez.

'Were you in Westray with George when he went into the island?' Phil Bain's list hadn't included any car passengers, but perhaps he hadn't asked the purser for that information.

The strange man looked up sharply. 'No. I believe that trip

was for work too. I stayed here.' A pause. 'I try not to interfere in George's life.'

'Did George discuss his visit with you?'

'He didn't get a chance. He came in for a shower, then he went out to school. Some meeting. Yesterday evening he had a pantomime rehearsal.' His tone made it clear that he despised the idea of pantomime. 'We didn't even eat together. This morning, he went out to catch his plane. He left before I was up.' Another pause. 'I'm not a morning person.'

'Did you know Archie Stout, the man who died?'

'I know the name, but I never met him.' Miles's tone was impatient. It was almost dusk and freezing outside, the first faint stars appearing, but still he went to the door and put his boots back on. 'So I'm afraid I can't help you any further.'

'Where did George stay in Westray?' Perez had followed Miles to the door. 'The ferries were cancelled once he got in and he didn't take a room in the hotel.'

'I think one of the islanders was kind enough to give him a bed. But really, Inspector, you should ask him.' Chambers stamped off towards the garden.

As Perez walked round to the front of the house and to his car, the sun had already set.

Chapter Eleven

WILLOW WAS BACK IN HER HOTEL room when Perez phoned. She'd felt suddenly tired and in the need for a quiet space to think through the investigation. Ellie was still canvassing the islanders who'd been visited by Archie on the afternoon of his death. She might not be local, but Willow knew she'd be good at that – easy, patient, genuinely interested.

Because they both travelled so much for work, she and Perez had become accustomed to communicating by phone, and as soon as he spoke, Willow could tell that he was both excited and frustrated.

'I've found out more about the story stones,' he said.

'And me. Apparently Johnson, the English professor staying here, is a leading expert in the runes. He gave me a lecture.'

'So you know what they say?'

'Yeah.' They quoted the legend on the stones at almost exactly the same time and then laughed.

'Important, do you think?' she asked.

'It'd be an odd coincidence. The bit on one of them about

knowing death. That was the stone that killed Archie. I showed Paul Rutherford a photo of the inscription.'

There was a comfortable silence while she thought about that. 'Coincidences do happen. I can't see any of the islanders going for anything so elaborate though. They'd know about the stones, and what was written there, but it seems too much like a cheap horror movie to be a Westray person's style.'

'I've found out that there was someone staying in Westray that night who definitely had a flair for the dramatic.'

'Oh, who?'

'George Riley.'

Willow listened while Perez told his own story – about his visit to Riley's home and his encounter with the strange visitor who was working in the garden there.

'And George must have stayed on the island overnight,' Perez said, 'because there were no ferries running. According to Riley's pal, someone there gave him a bed.'

'What was the friend like?'

'Strange. Uncommunicative. You can't imagine they'd have much in common.'

'In a relationship, do you think?'

There was a moment's silence on the other end of the phone. Perez was usually good at working out what was going on between people, so she was happy to wait. At last he spoke. 'Perhaps.'

'I'll try to find out where he stayed.' Willow paused for a moment. 'He's not a man who you'd miss. Someone will know.'

'I'd be interested to know what brought him to Westray. Miles said it was work, but term ended nearly a week ago.'

'You know George. He has fingers in lots of local history and community arts pies.' A thought occurred to her. 'That's what Barbara Johnson does for work now – she runs a community arts centre.' A pause. 'Another coincidence?'

'Maybe. But Miles wasn't very helpful. I'm not sure if he was being deliberately difficult or if he really didn't have anything to tell me. He could be one of those people who is kind of awkward and shy. Miles told me that as soon as Riley got back from Westray, he went into school to catch up on some work, later there was a panto rehearsal, and he got the early flight south this morning. George isn't answering his phone either. He's not due back until tomorrow. I'll talk to him as soon as he's home.'

'That is interesting. You think it'll wait until then? We could get one of the Inverness guys to track him down and do a quick interview.'

'Nah, this is George! George Riley, with his passion for all things Orkney. Famous for his panto appearances and for writing the definitive history of the Ba'. What reason could he have to kill Archie Stout?'

Willow was thinking about a logical answer to that, when Perez continued talking: 'Can you check out a guy called Nat Wilkinson? He was a foot passenger on the ferry early that morning. He has an address in Westray, so he was probably just coming home after a trip into town, but he's worth talking to. He's the only one on the boat who has any kind of criminal record. It's a long shot. He was done for possession ten years ago.' Perez read out the address and she noted it down, recognized it.

'Isn't that the cottage on Nistaben land?'

'Of course it is! So he'd have been close to Archie, geographically at least.' There was a moment of silence before Perez continued: 'Wilkinson was also questioned as a witness to an accidental death when he was a juvenile. Before our time in Orkney. His father drowned. They were living on North Ronaldsay.'

'You think that might be significant?'

'I can't see how. Not after all this time.'

'Interesting though.' At this stage in an investigation, Willow thought, everything was interesting. 'We'll do a visit this evening.'

'You'll not be back tonight then?' Perez sounded wistful and she couldn't help smiling.

'No. But we should have the initial interviews done by tomorrow evening. I'll book onto the last ferry back to Kirkwall.'

'James will be very pleased to see you.' A pause. 'And so will I.'

Willow waited in the bar for Ellie to return. It was quiet this early. Annie was preparing the dining room for a couple of parties, people who'd be coming along for their works' Christmas dinners, but Bill was there, polishing glasses, trying not to ask questions about the investigation. Willow had questions of her own to ask and didn't mind chatting.

'I understand that Archie owned a share of this place.'

Bill looked up warily. 'Aye. Well, his father bailed us out when we were going through a sticky time. We were grateful. It was a kind of loan and Magnus said we could pay him back whenever we liked.'

'But Archie didn't see it like that?'

'No. We've been paying him a percentage of the profits since the old man died, and we'd rather be in sole charge of the place. With Archie, you could never tell what he'd come up with next. We found it kind of unsettling.'

Willow thought about that. 'Will Archie's share pass on to Vaila now?'

Bill shrugged, an attempt to make the matter seem unimportant. 'I suppose that it will.'

'She'll be a lot easier to deal with than Archie,' Willow said. 'She'll have so much to cope with now, she might be glad to sell.'

'We won't be pushing the matter.' Bill's voice was harder. 'Not with a woman who's just lost her man.'

'Of course.' Willow held up her hands, a gesture that she meant nothing by the questions. 'Perhaps you could help me with something else.'

'Aye?' The landlord was still suspicious.

'George Riley, the teacher at the grammar school, came into Westray the morning of the day that Archie went missing. Any idea what he was doing here?'

'No! I didn't even know he was on the island.' Bill sounded affronted. He *should* have known.

'Do you know where he might have stayed? Anyone else doing B&B?'

The landlord shook his head. 'Not at this time of year. Everyone knows George though. He taught most of the young folk on the island. And he's a kind of showman. Always performing. But he's a good teacher. At least he *likes* kids. Our two got on great with him.'

'He teaches history, doesn't he? Did he have anything to do with the archaeology here?'

'Aye, he comes in occasionally to give a lecture in the heritage centre. He's always a draw because he's so entertaining.' A pause. 'I think he was planning a book for bairns on all the Neolithic history here. Something all the primary and junior highs in Orkney could use. Perhaps that's why he was coming to Westray, to do some research.'

Willow thought that was possible, but Ellie had talked to the volunteers at the centre asking about access and keys and none of them had mentioned meeting Riley.

It occurred to her that the children's book might provide Riley with a tentative link to all the outsiders staying in the hotel – Godfrey Lansdown was writing something too, there was the historical connection with Tony Johnson, and the teacher was involved with community arts like Barbara. It was all very weak though, forced. If she tried hard enough, Willow was sure she could find connections with other residents too. They needed something stronger.

Ellie came in through the main door of the hotel then. Willow waved across at her. Ellie waved back and pointed to show she needed to go up to her room before they caught up.

Willow nodded and turned back to Bill. 'I want to chat to Nat Wilkinson. Just because he came in on the ferry too that day.' She wanted to make it clear that the man wasn't any sort of suspect. The last thing she needed was other islanders accusing him of murder and maybe taking things into their own hands after too many drinks in the Pierowall Hotel. 'He lives down by the beach at Nistaben. You know him?'

'Of course. He's in the cottage that used to be the Stouts' holiday let. It was where the archaeology students stayed all that time ago. When Magnus and May got too old to manage the weekly turnarounds, they let him have it as a long-stay rental. He used to help them out on the farm before Archie took the place over. He still does a bit of casual labouring around the place.'

'That was the cottage where the Johnsons stayed during the first dig when they were undergraduates?'

'Aye.' He smiled. 'If the walls could talk, eh? The parties they had in that wee house.'

Ellie appeared at the door of the bar. She'd changed into her indoor clothes. Willow grinned at her. 'Sorry, we're off out again. Can you save us a table for dinner, Bill? Even if it's just here in the bar.'

'Sure,' he said. 'Sure.'

The house was small and low, so close to the shore that the sound of the sea seemed to surround them when they got out of the car. It sucked on the shingle bank, rattling the smoothed pebbles as it drew back with every wave. The air was icy and took away their breath. All the curtains were drawn, but someone was home. There was a chink of light showing where they weren't quite closed, and when they approached, they could hear music, something classical and restful. Willow knocked at the door. It was opened by a very tall man. The light in the house wasn't very bright and that was all they could make out at first.

'Yes?' He sounded anxious, his voice almost trembling, as if the knock had woken him from a deep sleep.

Willow introduced herself and Ellie. 'We just want a chat. It's nothing scary.' She felt the need to reassure him, as if he were a small child.

'Ah, come in.'

The place couldn't have changed much since the Johnsons

had stayed here as students, though Willow suspected it was very much tidier now. The students she knew would be more messy. There was a small range stove and beside it a frayed wicker basket of chopped wood, which might once have been fence posts. A table covered by oilcloth. A couple of easy chairs and a small sofa with a plaid throw. In the eighties, Willow thought, there might not have been mains electricity, and the students would have the rumble of a generator in the background, but even today the lamp on the table threw out very little light. No television, but a laptop playing the music, which Willow decided was Radio 3. So Nat Wilkinson must have an Internet connection of some kind.

Now they were inside, she could see him properly. He was so thin that she wondered if he was suffering some kind of disease, if a cancer was eating away at his body. His clothes – jeans and a jersey – seemed too big for him.

'Sit down,' he said. 'I'm sorry, I don't have very many visitors. Should I make you some tea?' The thought seemed to make him anxious again.

'No, but thank you.' Willow sat in one of the chairs. 'We won't be long.' Then, when he didn't respond, she repeated: 'It's just a chat.'

He folded himself onto one of the hard chairs by the table. 'It'll be about Archie Stout, of course.'

She nodded. 'We're talking to everyone on the island. You do understand?'

'I do.'

'You came in on the ferry from Kirkwall the day that he disappeared.'

He nodded.

'What were you doing in Kirkwall?'

There was a pause. 'I'm not very well. I was in to meet the team who look after me.'

So I was right. 'I hope it's not too serious.' Because what else could she say?

He shook his head. 'I have underlying mental health issues. Depression. Anxiety.' A pause. 'Addiction in the past though that's not so much of a problem these days. There's a community nurse who keeps an eye on me. The appointment was the day before and I stopped the night with a recovery pal in Kirkwall, then got the early ferry back.'

'Did you see Archie that day? He must be your nearest neighbour.'

'Aye, he dropped in some wood for me soon after the ferry got in. He was waiting at the pier for a delivery, saw that I was home, and came along not long after.'

'You were friends?'

Nat had to think about that. 'Kind of. I'd like to think so. My parents were English, but they moved to Orkney before I was born. They ran the shop in North Ronaldsay before my mother retired and moved south again. I never fitted in. When I was eleven, I had to move into the hostel in Kirkwall for school. It was terrifying. There was a lot of bullying. Archie was there too, but he was older than me, in his final year. He saw I was struggling and became a kind of protector. He was popular, you know, confident. It made a difference to have him on my side.'

Willow was working out how to bring up the drowning on North Ronaldsay. The man seemed so emotionally frail that she wanted to be tactful. In the end though, he mentioned it himself. 'I saw my father die. We were fishing together, and he slipped on the pier. I was only a lad, too young to know death. It took me a long time to get over it.'

The words shocked her. *To know death* seemed a strange way of describing his reaction to what had happened. And mimicked almost exactly the words on the stone that had killed Archie. She didn't follow it up though. Now wasn't the time. If he'd been involved in the murder, she didn't want to spook him.

'How did you come to be living here in Westray?'

'When I left school, I got a bit lost. Drink. Drugs. I was in a real mess. Archie saw me in a bar in Kirkwall, when I was so blootered I could hardly stand. I guess that he kind of rescued me again. He said I could work for him. It was winter and there were no holidaymakers to stay in the cottage, so I got a place to live too. His parents were getting older and not wanting the hassle of new people coming in every week, and they were happy enough with a little bit of rent. Then Archie took over the farm from them. That was more than six years ago and I'm still here. I do some casual work on the farm, help out where I can.' A pause. 'I've taken up painting and turn some of my work into greetings cards and postcards. They sell in the shops in the village. I make enough to live. I don't need much.' He stopped for a moment, then looked across at his visitors. Suddenly there was pride in his voice. 'Archie showed them to Rosalie at Quoybrae. She's a real artist and she rated them.'

'How did Archie seem when he called in to drop off the wood?'

Wilkinson shrugged. 'He was busy. It's that time of year, isn't it, if you have a family? We didn't really have a chance to chat. He dropped off a bit of wood and drove north.'

The man had turned down the sound on the computer when they came in, but the music was still there, very faint in the background. A piano piece that Willow didn't recognize.

'You came to Westray on the ferry with George Riley, the teacher. Did you speak at all?'

'We did! He taught me in the grammar school, and I always got on fine with him. I think he liked the strange and troubled kids better than the swots. He thought we were more interesting.'

'Did he tell you why he was coming into the island?'

'He was a bit vague. I know he was planning a kids' book about Orkney's Neolithic archaeology. He was going to do something on Maeshowe and the stones of Stenness, and he wanted to include the Westray digs too, so I assumed he was here to do a bit more research on that.'

'Are you interested in the island's archaeology?' Willow looked across at him, hoping for some reaction, but he only shrugged.

'Not much.'

'Do you know where George planned to stay that night?'

'He hadn't planned to stay over at all. It was going to be a day trip. Then, when we were halfway across, the captain announced that it would be the last boat of the day. They do that sometimes. Cancel the boats without warning. The wind was already getting up and you could see the clouds building from the west, and they said the more recent forecast was for storm force winds.'

'So where did he stay in the end?'

'He stayed here.' The pride was back in his voice. 'I have a spare room, and it's so close to the pier that he knew he wouldn't have to get up too early in the morning.'

'Was he with you that evening?'

'Aye. He turned up here late afternoon. I don't know exactly what time it was, but just as it was getting dark. We ate a meal together. I cooked for us. I had some monk in the freezer, and I'd got that out when I came in from the ferry.' A pause. 'He did go out for about an hour after we'd eaten. He said he had someone he needed to speak to, but he wasn't late back here. He was probably back in the house by eight-thirty.'

'Did he say where he'd been?'

'No, and I didn't ask.' Another pause. 'He'd been my teacher. You don't pry into a teacher's doings. I thought maybe he'd fancied a drink and he'd know I don't keep alcohol in the house.'

'Had you been told that Archie was missing before he came in?'

Nat shook his head. 'Vaila phoned just after nine to ask if I'd seen him, but Mr Riley was already in his room by then. He said he had work to catch up with and he'd have to be up sharpish to get the first boat out the next day. By the time I knew Archie was dead, George had already left on the ferry.'

'How did George seem when he got back here from the island?'

Nat shrugged. 'A bit quiet maybe. I thought he might stay up with me for a while. I had a few bits in for Christmas. Good cheese, fatty-cutties, mince pies. I was going to make some coffee and bring those out. Have a bit of a celebration, you know. I spend a lot of time on my own and I'd have enjoyed the company. But I could tell as soon as George walked through the door that his heart wouldn't be in it. He seemed low when he got in, quiet, and he wasn't usually that sort of man.'

Willow thought that anyone would be a little low if they'd just battered the head of a former pupil with a large piece of Caithness flagstone. She thanked Nat for his help, and she and Ellie walked out into the still, frosty night.

Chapter Twelve

When the police officers returned to the hotel, a table had been laid for them in the residents' lounge again and the fire had been lit. Willow looked through to the bar where Godfrey, the elderly birder, was sitting at a table writing in his notebook. There was no sign of the Johnsons but there was laughter coming from the dining room, and they could be there.

She made her way into the bar, and again Godfrey stood up when he saw her approaching.

'Just a quick question,' she said. 'Do you know a teacher called George Riley?'

The older man was still standing. He shook his head. 'I'm sorry, I don't know anyone by that name.'

'Ah well, thanks anyway. I'll let you get back to your book.'

He seemed almost disappointed when she returned to Ellie. Perhaps he was just choosy about his companions.

Annie took their order almost immediately and left them to talk. Willow wondered if Bill had told her of their previous discussion about the ownership of the hotel.

'Do you really think George Riley could be a killer?' Ellie

sounded sceptical, and Willow thought it *was* hard to believe that the man who every year performed with the Kirkwall Players as a perfect pantomime dame dressed in an outlandish wig and corsets was the sort to hit a Westray farmer so hard that his skull was smashed into thin fragments of bone.

'I'd like to know what he was doing here and who he met. None of the people we've spoken to has mentioned him. And then to disappear off in a plane to Inverness, without giving any real reason, is a bit odd.' A pause. 'Jimmy has tried to speak to him, but he's not answering his phone.'

Annie appeared to say that their food wouldn't be long, apologizing because the kitchen was busy.

'Did you know that George Riley was in Westray the day that Archie went missing?' Willow asked.

'I'd heard that he was here.' Annie smiled. 'What a lovely man he is! I was expecting him to call in, asking for a room when the boats were cancelled, but I didn't see him that evening at all.'

'Not even for a drink in the bar?'

She shook her head. 'I didn't see him at all that day.'

'Had he asked anyone for a key to the heritage centre? He might have wanted to be in there to do his research.'

'He didn't contact me, but I can ring round the committee and find out for you.'

'Thanks.'

The woman left.

'So,' Ellie said, 'what was the man doing all day?'

Annie came back in with more information. 'George Riley got the heritage centre key from Vaila, but she didn't see him. She gave it to Archie to pass on at the pier when the ferry got in. Archie had to be there anyway, waiting for some delivery.

Then George dropped it back at Nistaben later in the afternoon, while she was still at the old folks' lunch here. It was waiting for her in the porch when she got home.'

'The boys didn't see him when he dropped it in?'

'Apparently not. She says George didn't even knock. He left the key in the porch without speaking to them.'

Willow nodded. She supposed that explained Riley's presence in Westray. The story seemed to be hanging together, but something about it struck her as unusual. He was a sociable man. He'd surely have enjoyed an evening in the hotel, catching up with former students, playing the entertainer, more than an alcohol-free, solitary night in Nat Wilkinson's place. She hoped that Perez would be in touch with the teacher soon.

Annie returned with their food and more apologies for the delay. In the restaurant, the diners were becoming even more rowdy, and she left the women to talk.

'How did you get on chatting to the islanders who'd been visited by Archie the afternoon he went missing?' Willow had finished eating. She was tired now and wanted her bed and her last chat with Jimmy, but she hadn't had a chance to catch up with Ellie before they'd headed out to talk to Nat.

'It was all just as we thought. Archie turned up with his bagged wood. He refused to take any money for it, so in most places, he got invited in for tea or a dram instead. A lot of the folk he called on were elderly and maybe a bit lonely. I've drunk more tea this afternoon than I have in years. Archie didn't stay long in one place, and really, I don't think he'd had so much to drink that he wouldn't notice if someone came up to him and hit him over the head with an ancient rock.'

'There's not much more we can do here at the moment.'

Willow was turning over the logistics in her head. Suddenly, she felt a longing for home. 'Let's book ourselves out on the ferry to Kirkwall tomorrow. We can bring Phil in to be a presence on the island, because folk here will still be anxious.' She looked up at Ellie. 'It's Christmas in a few days, but he doesn't have kids and he'll be glad of the overtime. We can always come back if anything crops up.' A pause. 'I'd like to talk to Vaila again before we go, but we can do that on our way to the ferry. And I still haven't quite got a handle on Rosalie Greeman. It might be flimsy, but her entanglement with Archie does give her a motive of a kind, and she certainly had means and opportunity. Let's visit her in the morning. We might catch her just as she's doing her swim, if you fancy joining her for a dip.'

Ellie pulled a face and nodded towards the bar. 'I'm having one last drink before bed. Shall I go and disturb Godfrey Lansdown again? Just for a chat?'

'Sure. Have a drink for me!'

Willow thought she should find the Johnsons to ask if they'd had any dealings with Riley, but the noise from the restaurant was even louder, and she thought it would wait for another day. She couldn't face the educated English tonight.

In her room, Willow opened her curtains wide so she could see the stars. Perez answered the phone as soon as it started ringing.

'How are you?' His voice was concerned without being patronizing.

'I'm fine. Both of us are fine.' Meaning her and the baby. 'I'm planning to head back tomorrow on the afternoon ferry. Ellie will come too. I want to talk to Rosalie and Vaila before we leave. We need a presence here though, so let's bring Phil back in. He's a local – Orcadian at least – and if anyone has any concerns, they'll feel they can talk to him. He's bright enough to know that he has to pass on everything he hears, even if it doesn't seem to be immediately important.'

'That makes sense.'

'I think we've found out what George Riley was doing here, and we know where he stayed last night.' Willow explained about the children's book on the Neolithic history of the islands.

'So he had a key to the heritage centre?'

'He did, and as far as I've been able to tell, nobody was in there after him, so he could have taken the story stones. And Wilkinson told me he seemed quiet and preoccupied when he got back that evening. We still don't know where George went after he'd eaten there. According to Bill, he wasn't in the bar. He'd dropped the heritage centre key back to Vaila in Nistaben, so he couldn't have been in there still working on his book.'

'Isn't the old guy, Godfrey Lansdown, writing a book too? There must be more written about Westray than anywhere else in the UK.'

Willow laughed. 'That's more of a pamphlet, I think, and he claims never to have met Riley.'

'What did you make of Nat Wilkinson?'

Willow could imagine Perez in the living room of the old manse, a notebook on his knee, a pen in his hand, waiting for her answer. She was tempted to tell him how much she was missing him, that she wanted to be there too, but instead, she played the professional and answered his question.

'Honestly, he seems like a reformed character. Sober and clean. And I know that addicts make the best liars, but I believed him when he said he was no longer using. He brought up the fact that he'd witnessed his father's drowning and said that it had screwed him up.'

'I suppose it would.'

'Yeah, but the words he used resonated a bit. He said he was just a lad. *Too young to know death.* That last phrase made me think of the inscription on the story stone.'

'Another coincidence?'

Willow had been thinking about that herself. 'Maybe. Worth checking out though. It might be useful to speak to the cop who went in to look at the accidental death. And I wonder if Doc Grieve did a post-mortem.'

'I'll ask him.'

There was a moment's silence then. Willow imagined that she could hear slightly damp wood spitting in the fire in their living room. She wished that she was there already. But when she spoke, she was calm.

'Nat's still living in the cottage on the Nistaben farm, earning a living with his art – he makes cards and gifts for the tourists – and helping out as a casual labourer there. I'll ask Vaila about him tomorrow.'

'I've been trying to phone George all day,' Perez said. 'He's still not answering. I'll be at the airport to meet the Inverness plane in the morning if the flight goes ahead. The weather's still not looking good on the mainland though. It's beautifully clear here, but there's still a blanket of freezing fog grounding the planes across the central belt and into the highlands.'

Willow thought at least that meant they were keeping Glasgow off their backs. She couldn't imagine that they'd want to make the trek on the boat. Not until after Christmas. She hoped she and Perez and the team would have things tied up by then. If only for Vaila and the boys.

'Maybe you should get in touch with the head teacher of the grammar school,' she said. 'Lucy Martindale. If Riley is away with work, she'll know what he's doing.'

'I've set up an appointment with her. I'm going to see her first thing in the morning.'

Willow stopped talking about work then, and asked about James, and nursery festivities and all the Harray gossip. That was what kept her grounded. Kept her sane.

Chapter Thirteen

They arrived at Quoybrae while Rosalie was still in the water. They saw her swimming in the small bay below her house, her hair black and sleek so she looked like an otter or a seal.

'Is it safe?' Ellie sounded concerned. 'Surely she shouldn't be out there alone. There's still frost on the ground and ice on the shore. Aren't there rules about it?'

Willow shrugged. She knew what it was to take risks and she'd been brought up by hippy parents to have a disregard for rules, even the sensible ones. 'She looks as if she knows what she's doing.'

It seemed the woman had had enough, because she turned towards the shore, and walked out of the water, shaking her head like an animal. Willow saw she wasn't even wearing a wetsuit. The skin of her arms and legs was glowing red, contrasting with the white face and black hair. She wrapped herself in her dry robe and headed for the house, grinning. It seemed to Willow that she was high or light-headed with the cold and the freedom. Again, there was no sign of grief at the death of her friend. She caught sight of them and waved.

'Inspector,' she called. 'You should have come a bit sooner, then you could have joined me.'

'Not for me! Though, if I weren't pregnant . . .'

'Ah, excuses. Come on into the house. I'll just change and then I'll join you, make us all some coffee.'

They sat in the kitchen where Willow had been with Perez. She looked at the paintings on the walls. A recent addition was a piece of driftwood, which had once been part of a tree. Now it was white as bone, and Rosalie had planted it in a green ceramic pot and tied red glass balls to the upper limb. Rosalie came into the room. 'My own concession to Christmas,' she said. 'White, green and red, the colours of the season.' She switched on the kettle. 'I suppose you have more questions.'

She'd changed into jeans and a big Norwegian sweater.

'A few. This is Ellie, a sergeant from Kirkwall.'

'Hi, Ellie!'

'We're heading back to Orkney mainland later today, so I thought I'd bring you up to date.'

'That's kind.'

Rosalie scooped coffee into a jug and poured over the water. She waited before pushing the plunger.

'Do you know a man called George Riley?'

'He's a teacher at the grammar school. He's writing a children's book about the islands' history.' She looked up from the coffee. 'Vaila told me about it before the rumours about Archie and me began and she stopped visiting. She encouraged me to talk to George about doing the illustrations.'

'And did you?'

'Yeah, I phoned him. He said he hadn't reached that stage, but he'd keep me in mind.'

'He came into Westray on the morning Archie disappeared. Apparently, Archie gave him Vaila's key to the heritage centre. Did you meet George to discuss his book when he was here?'

She shook her head. 'I didn't even know he'd come into the island.'

She poured the coffee. Willow was about to refuse a mug, but the smell was so tempting that she took it.

'Have you had any more thoughts about what might have disturbed Archie that afternoon? A number of people say that he was quiet and preoccupied, but so far, we have no explanation for his change in mood.'

'No, but perhaps there is no explanation. His mood could change like the Orkney weather, triggered by some comment or slight. He came across as thick-skinned and jovial, but in reality, he was remarkably sensitive. He needed everyone to love him.' For the first time since their arrival, Rosalie seemed sad. She stared out at the water. 'He was a very complicated man.'

Willow remembered that, according to Perez, Evelyn Angel had said the same thing.

'You didn't say anything that might have troubled him while he was here?'

Rosalie frowned. 'What sort of thing?'

'You might have broken off the friendship that was developing between you.'

'I've already explained, Inspector, there wasn't that sort of friendship to break. We might have ended up having a fling – he had a kind of teenage crush, and I was flattered – but I knew he would never leave his family. They'd always be the most important part of his life.' She looked up at Willow. 'You asked when you were last here why I seemed not to be grieving his loss. I'll miss him, of course I will. I'll miss his fun and the laughter and feeling attractive again. But in a lot of ways, my life here will be easier, less complicated without him. I'm not a sentimental woman. Now I'll be accepted by the island again. I can be my own person and grieve for the real love of my life in my own time.'

'Did you say any of that when you last saw him?'

Rosalie shook her head again. 'I had a vague plan that I would explain to him just how I felt, but he seemed so down that I ended up holding him, and reassuring him that all would be well, that he'd come through whatever was worrying him.' She glanced up at them. 'I'm not sure that I convinced him.'

They left Rosalie and drove south down the island to Nistaben, where Vaila and the boys were living. To talk to another of Archie's women. Ellie was driving and Willow looked out on hills flooded with light, stretches of water, and deserted buildings falling into ruin. This end of the island was almost empty. She asked Ellie about her conversation with Godfrey Lansdown in the hotel bar the night before.

'Did he have anything useful to add?'

'Nah, I asked if he'd seen George Riley on his wandering around the island, but he didn't even know who the man was.'

'He said the same to me.'

Turning into the track to the farm, they almost bumped into a small tractor carefully driven by Lawrie. He'd be doing his best, Willow thought, to keep the farm running, to take his father's place. He raised his hand in a kind of greeting – almost exactly mimicking the gesture Archie would have made – and pulled in to let them past. She hoped that Iain would be out too. She wanted to speak to Vaila alone.

They walked past the barn where the cows were in for the winter, the rolls of silage, a smaller shed holding the chainsaw Archie had used to cut up wood for his neighbours, a sawhorse and a shiny new quad bike. They glimpsed Vaila through the living room window. She was sitting in the corner that she'd turned into an office, staring at a computer screen, apparently lost in thought. Her hands weren't moving across the keyboard. Willow tapped on the window and the woman turned and waved for them to come in. By the time they were in the room, the screen was dark, and she was on her feet to greet them.

'Willow, Ellie.' This time there was no offer of tea. She still seemed preoccupied. 'I was trying to keep things straight for the farm, but I just can't focus.'

'Of course not. It's too soon.'

She nodded for them to sit down. There were still ashes from the night before in the grate and the house felt a little cold.

'How can I help you *now*?' She was doing her best to be civil, but Willow could sense that she resented the interruption, the demands on her, the inevitable questions.

'We've just come from Rosalie.'

'Oh?' Vaila pretended not to care, but Willow picked up a spark of interest.

'She said that she and Archie weren't in any sort of sexual relationship, that she was flattered by his attention, but there was nothing more to it than that. And honestly, I think I believe her.'

There was a silence. They could hear the rumble of the tractor coming back into the yard.

'This island,' Vaila said at last. 'It's just full of stories. Stories of the past, of shipwrecks and heroes and lost children. And if that wasn't enough, we make up more stories to explain the present.' She looked straight at Willow. 'Are you saying that's all this was – a story?'

'I think that Archie might have been attracted to Rosalie, but that nothing happened.'

'And that story ripped a hole in our marriage. The last months were all bicker and mistrust. The last things Archie would have known of me was as a shrew of a wife.' Now Vaila started to cry. She pulled a tissue from a pocket and scrubbed at her face with it.

'Rosalie told me that the most important thing to Archie was his family.'

Vaila didn't answer. 'I'm taking the boys into Kirkwall tomorrow morning. We need to escape. Our memories and all the talk here. It's like a poison, seeping into your system. You find yourself not being sure of anything. My parents will look after the farm and this time of year, there's not much to do. My dad will manage fine on his own, and Nat Wilkinson will always help if he's needed.'

'How do you get on with Nat?'

'He's a gentle soul. A perfect tenant, since he straightened himself out. He worshipped Archie and would do anything for us.'

'Did you know George Riley was staying with him the night that Archie disappeared?'

'No, I didn't know that.'

'But you knew that George came into the island that day?'

'Yes, he wanted access to the heritage centre, so I sent Archie down to the ferry to pass on the key. George dropped it off later that afternoon. I wasn't in, but it was in the porch when I got back from the old folks' lunch.'

'The boys would have seen him though?'

'No, Iain was in Pierowall at a friend's house. Lawrie was in, but he'd have been upstairs in his room.' Her voice tailed away. 'He's a good lad, a great worker, but he still needs time for himself. He'll take over the farm when he's old enough. That was always the plan. If I can hold on to it long enough now.'

'Of course.' Willow tried to choose her words carefully. As Vaila had said, stories could be fabricated out of nothing here. 'George was out that evening, and nobody seems to know exactly where he went. Would you have any idea?'

'None at all. He wasn't in the hotel when I went there looking for Archie. You'll have to ask him.'

'We're struggling to get in touch with him. He flew south and he's not answering his phone. We're hoping he'll be back today.' Willow paused. 'How did George and Archie get on? I assume they knew each other.'

'What are you saying?' Vaila looked horrified. 'That George Riley killed my husband? Why on earth would he do that?'

'We have to ask these questions,' Willow said, 'if we're going to find out how Archie died. George might be an important witness if he met up with Archie that evening. Were they friends?'

'I wouldn't say they were friends. George taught Lawrie throughout the grammar school. The boy's never been particularly academic, but George was good at bringing subjects to life. We were grateful for the effort he made. Some of the teachers didn't seem to care, because everyone knew he'd probably leave as soon as he could and come back to work here on the island. Folk think of Westray as a wealthy place, where the kids just fall into a job. Iain's only been there for a term, but George has been great with him too. We had George in for drinks and a meal a couple of times when he was here researching his book — a way to thank him for being such a good teacher — but we've never been into his home. It wasn't that sort of friendship.'

'And there was never any animosity between them?'

'No! Nothing like that.' Vaila looked at Willow. 'You have to be close, don't you, before you can really fall out?'

'Like you and Rosalie?'

Vaila seemed shocked by the question. 'Aye, just like us.'

'Ellie and I are leaving today. Phil Bain will be in to keep an eye on things here.'

'You're giving up looking for Archie's killer?' Vaila was scathing. 'Just so you can be home for Christmas?'

'Of course not. The team from Glasgow will be in soon. They have the manpower and the skills to do the real investigation. And Jimmy and our team will be working from Kirkwall. We can be here in an hour if we need to be. You know that.' Mentally she crossed her fingers behind her back. She wasn't sure when the Glasgow officers would get here. 'And Jimmy will be talking to George as soon as his flight gets in. He might well have important information for us.'

'I'm sorry.' Vaila paused. 'I know you'll both be doing your best. I've booked us into the Kirkwall Hotel until the New Year. There are friends who've offered us rooms, but I wanted somewhere more anonymous. I don't want to have to talk about any of this. Lawrie thinks he has a good chance of getting the Boys' Ba' this year. His father was a staunch doonie and he sees it as a way of honouring him. It's all he thinks about.

After that, we'll take time to think about our future and where we want it to be.'

'That makes sense. You know where we are. You'll be welcome in Harray any time. And we'll be there in the town on Christmas morning to cheer Lawrie on.'

They went back to Pierowall to collect their things and texted Vaila to let her know her car was at Rapness ferry terminal. Willow left the keys in the ignition. Someone would give Vaila a lift to fetch it. They'd arrived at the pier early enough to watch the ferry come in; the water was as still as a mirror and reflected the distant islands, the creel boats out working. They waited for the trucks and cars to drive onto the ferry, and walked on once the vehicles were loaded. As they made their way to the passenger lounge, Willow recognized Bill MacBride climbing out of his car. They sat in the stuffy little cafeteria together. Ellie ordered a bacon roll and Willow drank weak tea.

'Are you out for a bit of Christmas shopping?' Willow asked Bill.

'Aye. And sometimes I just need to get away for a few days. I'm a city boy at heart. Annie was brought up to Westray, but she understands how I feel. Sometimes the claustrophobia gets to me. If I don't get into the town every month or so, I feel as if I'm going mad.'

Chapter Fourteen

As soon as he woke up that morning, Perez checked the airport website. All the flights from the Scottish mainland had been cancelled again, and Riley still wasn't answering his phone. But Willow would be home later in the day, and the inspector's mood lifted a little just because of that. It would be splendid to have her safely home.

When they'd started their new roles in Orkney for Police Scotland, Perez had been anxious about how it would work. In Shetland, she'd been his boss, flying in to bring a new perspective to a troubling investigation. He'd still been grieving over the death of his fiancée, awkward, spiky. Then he'd been riddled with guilt when it seemed he might find happiness again. Here in Orkney, Willow had been given a wider remit, more political. A woman who'd grown up in the Outer Hebrides was overseeing policing throughout the Scottish islands. In his more cynical moments, he'd thought it was a ploy, a way of persuading people living far from the Central Belt that under the reorganization of Police Scotland their needs were still being met.

His role was more traditional, and his focus was tighter. He was a police inspector, a detective, but overseeing a small, uniformed team, and much of his work was routine, more mundane. He and Willow had been based in the same police station, but since moving to Orkney, they'd never before worked on the same case. In Westray, she was live policing again, and though he'd never admit it to Willow, he'd been worried about her.

Perez dropped James at the nursery and went straight to visit the grammar school head teacher. She'd invited him to her home and not to the school.

'I've got a plumber coming to the house this morning, Inspector. I've been waiting an age to get my boiler fixed and I don't want to miss him.'

Lucy Martindale lived in an Edwardian villa on the outskirts of Kirkwall on the road leading to the airport. It was separated from the street by a small front garden. There were bare sycamores and a holly bush bright with berries. She seemed a little disappointed when she opened the door to him. She must have hoped that it would be the plumber.

'Inspector Perez, come into the kitchen. It's the only warm room in the house.'

He saw that was true. There was still ice on the outside of the front room window.

Perez knew, because her appointment had been recorded in the *Orcadian*, that Martindale was new to the post, that she was single, and that she'd arrived from a large comprehensive school in southern England.

'I'm here because of the Westray murder.' It *was* warm in the kitchen. A solid fuel range was belting out the heat, and almost every surface held tropical plants that were thriving. It felt like being in a greenhouse. He took the seat that she indicated close to the table.

'Of course. The victim was the father of two of our students. I've been there such a short time that I don't know them well, but the whole community is in shock. Of course, we'll make sure that the boys have all the support they need once school starts again.' A pause. 'Is there anything I can do to help them before then? Is that why you're here?' She was in her forties, tidy, composed. The only indication of personality long, colourful earrings that might have been made by Rosalie Greeman. He thought she'd be efficient. After all, she'd come straight to the point as soon as he'd entered the room.

'That's not why I'm here. One of your members of staff was on Westray that day. George Riley. He could be an important witness. He's not in Orkney and he's not answering his phone. I wondered if you might know where he is.'

'George, yes. I arranged for all senior members of staff to attend a short conference on school leadership. They weren't entirely enthusiastic.' She gave a brief little smile that made him think she might be rather fun if she weren't in work mode. 'There are a number throughout the year, but George drew the short straw and agreed to do his session this close to Christmas. It's taking place in Inverness. I can give you the telephone number of the hotel if that's any help.'

Perez said that indeed it would be a great help. He'd never thought of Riley as a potential murderer, but he was pleased that there was a logical reason for his disappearance. The doorbell rang and this time it was the plumber. Perez thanked Miss Martindale and took his leave.

★ ★ ★

He made his way back to the Kirkwall police station. A member of the public had brought in a box of home-made mince pies. He ate one while he emailed the team in Glasgow. It was a full report, though he thought it would be hard for city officers to understand life on a small island, the preoccupations and concerns of the community.

There was a one-line reply: *'You'd better talk to that teacher and find out what he knows.'* Which was all very well, Perez thought, but easier said than done. He'd phoned the number given to him by Lucy Martindale. A receptionist told him that the education conference was over, and all the delegates had left. Perez didn't want to go public with an invitation through the media for Riley to contact him. If he was the dedicated teacher he'd always seemed, the last thing he'd need would be his photo on the Scottish television news in connection with a brutal murder.

He tried to talk to James Grieve about the Wilkinson drowning in North Ronaldsay, but his secretary said the pathologist was tied up in the university. She'd ask him to get in touch when he was free. Perez's frustration only increased. He'd always thought of himself as a patient man, but this lack of progress was eating away at him. He felt he was letting down Vaila and the lads. Archie had *never* been patient, and he could hear his friend's voice in his head: *Will you just get on with it, man.*

Back in the station, he had a meeting with Phil Bain, briefing him on his role in Westray. 'You're Orcadian. The only one of the team that is. They'll speak more freely in front of you than to any of the others. There are five hundred residents, and we haven't had the chance to talk to them all. Visit them. Listen to the gossip. Chat up the lonely, elderly women and see what they have to say about Archie Stout. These are the questions we need to be covered: What was going on there that could have made him so worried? Had he plans for some development on his farm that might have upset folk? Or has anyone else done something that might have changed the nature of the island? Archie was always a traditionalist when it came to Westray.'

Phil nodded and scribbled more notes. He looked like an eager schoolboy.

'You said George Riley taught you. How did you get on with him?'

'I liked him fine. In some ways he was like a kid himself. Not much time for rules. Full of enthusiasms. He was there every Christmas Day at the Ba' cheering on the uppies who'd been at the school. He had time for everyone.'

'Well, if you can find anyone in Westray who saw him on the night Archie went missing, or who knows where he is now, I'd be very grateful. You'd get a bottle of the best malt to put in your Christmas stocking.'

Phil pulled a face. 'I'm not really a whisky drinker, sir, but a good Burgundy would go down a treat.'

They drove in Phil's car to the pier. The constable would need to take it to Westray with him, and Willow, on the same ferry coming into the harbour, travelled light. She could walk back to the station with Perez. He'd be glad to carry her bag. Phil sat in his car in the queue while the ferry unloaded. Then Willow was there, striding to meet him, a rucksack on one shoulder, a knitted hat over her hair. With her outsized anorak hiding her belly, she could have been a student, home after a backpacking trip to the wilds. Perez thought this was crazy; he was feeling like a teenager again, giddy at the sight of her.

She kissed him. He was the one to pull away, feeling awkward and shy, aware that Phil Bain would be watching, but he took her bag and her hand, and they walked together like that into the town. For once, he wasn't embarrassed by the public show of affection. In the police station, Willow made straight for her office.

'Hey, you're supposed to be on maternity leave. Why don't you go and get James early? Surprise him.'

'I just want to make a few notes. While things are still fresh in my mind. Then we'll go to the nursery together, shall we, at the end of play.'

When they collected James, he had paint on his sleeve and glitter in his hair. Willow swung him into her arms, and all the way home in the car they listened to his chatter about his day.

I know I'm a soppy git, Perez thought, *but I want nothing more than this.*

The call came just as they were thinking of going to bed. They'd fed James early and Willow had pulled something veggie and home-made from the freezer. He'd drunk several glasses of wine to celebrate her return. They'd lit a fire and eaten chocolates for pudding.

Perez recognized the voice at once, loud and confident and English.

'Hello, Inspector. Miles said you'd been trying to get hold of me.'

'George, where are you?' Now that he could hear the man, Perez thought that his suspicions about Riley must surely be groundless. Someone with this cheerful disposition and standing in the community couldn't be a killer. 'I'm glad your friend passed on my message. I wasn't sure that he would.'

There was a throaty chuckle on the other end of the line. 'Miles is rather more than a friend, Inspector. We've been together on and off since he taught me at university. But he's a private man and he persuaded me to be discreet.' A pause. 'I'm home. I got a lift to Scrabster and then the ferry back to Stromness.'

'Why haven't you been in touch?'

'I've been stuck just outside Inverness at a conference in some soulless hotel. The new head stamping her mark. All about training for school leadership. A load of bollocks, especially when we're supposed to be on leave, but sometimes you have to play the game.'

'I've been phoning, leaving messages.' Perez thought he sounded like a jealous and suspicious lover, checking up on a partner.

'I dropped my phone somewhere in Inverness airport on the way out. Bloody nightmare.'

'I need to talk to you.'

'About Archie Stout. Yes, Miles explained.'

'You must have heard about his death when you were away.' Again, Perez tried to keep the suspicion from his voice.

'I didn't! Honest. It was nose to the grindstone all day. You wouldn't believe the boredom! All targets and budgets and bugger all about the poor bastards we're supposed to be teaching. Then getting pissed in the evenings with my teaching mates to let off steam. I didn't know anything about it until I got home to Miles. Then of course I checked the news.' A pause. 'Those poor lads. I taught them both.'

'When can I come to see you?'

There was a hesitation on the other end of the line. 'I'm rather tied up for most of the day tomorrow.'

'This is urgent, George. More important than admin meetings at the school. It's a murder investigation.'

'I know. Look, I've got special access to Maeshowe in the afternoon. They're keeping the visitors away for one day, so I can spend a bit of time there to myself. Research for my kids' book. It's all rather wonderful – I've been taken on by a mainstream publisher down in London.' Riley sounded so excited that Perez suspected that *he* might have been drinking too, celebrating his return to Miles and his book deal. 'Why don't you meet me there? About three o'clock. If it stays this clear, we might even see the solstice light on the back of the burial chamber. A once-in-a-lifetime experience.'

'You really can't make it before that?'

'Sorry, no. I have something rather urgent myself that I need to get sorted. I can't do it later because I'm singing in the cathedral for the carol service. And then of course, there's Miles . . .'

Before Perez could press him again to meet in the morning, the line went dead.

Chapter Fifteen

THE NEXT DAY, WILLOW DECIDED TO keep James at home. They could put up a few decorations and perhaps she'd try some baking. She could pretend to be one of those women she saw in the magazines at this time of year. Perfect mothers. Domestic goddesses. Besides, she didn't want to cramp Perez's style. He was in charge of the Kirkwall police station. He didn't need her breathing down his neck.

Perez headed out to work, grumbling about entitled Englishmen. Willow presumed he was talking about George Riley, who'd refused to see him until the afternoon, and then only on his own terms and in a place of his choosing. She listened to Radio Orkney and was told that this would be the longest cold, clear spell that the islands had endured for years.

'We're not expecting the temperature to rise above freezing for the next few days. But there'll be no snow for the big day, unlike in the central belt of Scotland which experienced a blizzard overnight, with more forecast over the next few days.' Then a list of the major road and motorway closures. Willow thought they'd definitely not see the Glasgow team until the New Year.

Her interest in local news started to wander at about the same time as James's. She put CBeebies on the TV, gave him his advent calendar chocolate to keep him quiet and devoted her attention to Archie Stout and his death. She trusted Rosalie's evidence that the man had been anxious about more than their relationship. Willow had got on with Archie well enough, but she'd never liked his attitude to women. He'd always been charming, but a bit flirty in an old-fashioned rather lecherous kind of way.

His relationship with Rosalie had seemed different, more serious. Willow could see how he might imagine himself in love with someone like the artist – strong, intelligent, a little exotic because she was an outsider. It was likely though that the infatuation would soon have passed. What mattered most to Archie was his family, and then Westray and the community where he'd grown up. She knew he was fiercely proud of the place's forward thinking, its courage in starting new ventures. He would be an awkward adversary to anyone who challenged Westray's integrity.

She took James into the kitchen to make gingerbread men. The smell of spices always made her think of Christmas and the boy loved baking. But while she was helping him roll the dough and cut out the figures, she was pondering the investigation, Archie's relationship with the artistic Rosalie and Vaila's bitterness and jealousy.

She'd just lifted the baking tray from the oven when her ruminations were disturbed by her phone. Phil Bain was calling in as she'd asked him to.

'How's it going?'

'Okay, but I'm not able to speak to that many people today. It seems there was a mass exodus on the ferry this morning. Lots of islanders have gone in for the carol service at the cathedral. Most are planning to come back this evening on the last ferry. I'll get to the folk who are still here today and catch up with the others tomorrow.'

'That's fine. Nothing else you can do. I know Vaila was planning to bring the boys out. Who else have you lost?'

'Bill was already out. The three residents at the hotel – Godfrey Lansdown and Prof and Mrs Johnson. Apparently, Godfrey goes to the service every year. It's something he used to do with his wife. I think the Johnsons made a last-minute decision to join him.' A pause. 'They might rave about island living but I get the feeling they were getting a bit bored and the idea of the bright lights of Kirkwall and a fancy lunch attracted them.'

'Ah well, island life isn't for everyone.' Willow had left the commune on North Uist as soon as she was old enough to run away. Though now she was back on another island, and she had no wish to escape from this one.

Phil was still talking. 'They said something about wanting to explore some of the archaeological sites as it's close to the winter solstice.'

'Did they say which ones?'

'Nah, they don't really think I'm worth talking to. I'm definitely seen as their intellectual inferior.'

She laughed. 'Yeah, right! Any news on George Riley and where he might have gone the night Archie died?'

'Yes. I caught up with Fiona, one of the Westray teachers.'

'I know who you mean. Her son is best pals with Iain Stout, and he spent the afternoon of Archie's disappearance there.'

'Aye. I tried her because I thought she might know George professionally, and she might even recognize his car.'

'And?' James was starting to fidget. Willow fed him half a gingerbread man to keep him quiet. So much for being the perfect mother.

'Fiona went out that night to check on her mother, who's been a bit poorly, and she saw George's car parked outside the Pierowall Hotel.'

Willow thought that was odd. Everyone said that Riley hadn't been into the hotel.

'Did she see George?'

'Not then. But when she was on her way home later, George was just driving away.'

'What time was that?'

'About eight-thirty, so that fits in with the time he got back to Nat's.'

Willow was sorting through the details in her mind. 'Well, I guess that's interesting, but it doesn't help much. Jimmy's meeting up with George later today, so he should be able to give us more useful information. He's back in Orkney at last.'

But still playing hard to get, she thought. *What's that all about?*

'There is something else,' Phil said.

'Yes?'

'Fiona noticed that the light was on in the heritage centre when she was on her way to her mother's.'

'That couldn't have been George,' Willow said. 'He'd already dropped the key off at Nistaben in the afternoon.'

'He might have left the place unlocked, so he could get in again later.'

'You're thinking he might have gone back to pick up the story stones?'

'Maybe.'

'Aye, so he could.'

Again, her mind was racing, trying out different possibilities, different scenarios, but she could tell that Phil was waiting for further instructions. 'Can you ask around and see if anyone else was in the heritage centre that evening? There might have been a volunteers' meeting, or some sort of party for them this close to Christmas. Annie might know, though I think she would already have mentioned it.'

'Sure,' he said. 'What are your plans for the rest of the day?'

'I think we'll wrap up and go out. It's too sunny to be at home all day. James might enjoy the carol service at St Magnus Cathedral.'

'That sounds like a grand thing to do. They hold it in the early evening, just after it's dark, so all the kids can take part.'

'Perfect!'

Besides, she thought, *I've had enough of being stuck in the house with a four-year-old. It'll be interesting to see who turns up at the service from Westray. There might be the opportunity for an informal chat.* So much for not wanting to cramp Jimmy's style.

Outside, the chill took her breath away, and she had to clear the ice from the windscreen of her car, which was parked in the shadow of the house.

In the market square outside St Magnus, a crowd had gathered. Old friends stood chatting before going into the magnificent cathedral. The sun was already low and the lights on the tree shone in the early dusk. The sandstone of the building glowed red. Shoppers wandered down the street. The people at the front of the queue were already making their way into the building. Willow hadn't seen any of the Westray visitors, but they could already be inside.

She'd never been religious. Her father had been a scientist before he dropped out to set up the commune in the Western Isles, and if her mother had believed in anything, it was a vaguely pagan celebration of the living world. At first, she was scanning the crowd, looking for people she recognized, the Westray visitors and any of the island residents. It had occurred to her that Vaila might have brought the boys, that being together in this space might have provided some comfort for them. But Vaila had come to Kirkwall wanting anonymity and she wouldn't have found that here.

Just before entering the cathedral, Willow looked out again at the busy street. A woman in a coat made of brightly coloured patchwork drifted past, carried it seemed by the tide of people. It was the coat that had caught Willow's attention – she would have worn it herself – but then she realized she knew the woman. It was Rosalie Greeman with her pale face and her dark eyes. She too, it seemed, had taken advantage of the convenient ferries to come to Kirkwall. Willow would have liked to speak to her here, away from her home territory, but by now, she and James were at the head of the queue, and they were swept inside.

Inside the cathedral, Willow caught a glimpse of Godfrey Lansdown sitting near the front of the nave, smart and serious, focused on his carol sheet, remembering, she thought, his beloved wife. She couldn't imagine this quiet, dignified man as a killer. But as the service progressed, the investigation became less important, and she found herself moved by the music and the readings. The story of the virgin birth. This building. The child beside her and the child in her belly.

When her thoughts did return to the investigation, it was to ponder the old communities that seemed to have infiltrated the case. The Neolithic Orcadians and the Vikings who came later. They'd all needed faith that the seasons would shift, and the light would return. Like Olaf, they'd needed their tales of horror and of wonder.

James was getting bored. He started kicking the chair in front of him, and annoying an elderly woman who turned and frowned. Willow put his favourite video – about a dog with magical powers – on silent on her phone and handed it to him. He was soon quiet and engrossed. That, she told herself, was just a story told in another form. Nothing to beat herself up about. She wasn't a terrible mother, whatever the woman in the chair in front might think.

When the service was over and they went outside, it was already dark, and the people in the street were finishing their shopping and making for the bars. She thought she saw Bill MacBride, already a little unsteady on his feet, heading away from her.

'Inspector!'

She turned and saw Tony and Barbara Johnson, arm in arm, part of the crowd behind her.

'What a lovely service!' Barbara said. 'So moving and of course it's a magnificent building.'

'You were there? I didn't see you.' Willow couldn't work out why she disliked the couple so much, why she was so eager to distrust them.

'Oh, we were there. Right at the back though. It's really a celebration for the locals, isn't it? We didn't want to intrude.' Barbara smiled. 'We're just going to sample one of the local whiskies before we get the ferry back to the island.'

They wandered away.

Only then did Willow look at her phone and see that there were a number of missed calls from Perez. She thought that George Riley must have passed on a piece of very useful information. Perhaps this was what they needed to find out who had killed Archie Stout.

Chapter Sixteen

PEREZ HAD BEEN RESTLESS ALL MORNING, annoyed with himself for not insisting that George Riley should make himself immediately available. He should have stood up to the man. Why had he allowed himself to be intimidated by an Englishman with a loud voice and a sense of entitlement? He wondered if Willow would have been more assertive, then thought this wasn't a competition.

He was tempted to head to Finstown to see if Riley was there, hiding away in his Gothic pile, but his first encounter with Miles had been less than productive, and after all, Perez *had* agreed to the meeting in Maeshowe.

He tried James Grieve again and this time the pathologist was free to speak to him.

'There was an accidental death on North Ronaldsay.' Perez had already tried to work out the time frame. 'Midsummer twenty years ago. A fourteen-year-old lad witnessed his father drowning. I wondered if there'd been a post-mortem.'

'That's a long time ago, Jimmy.'

'Aye, but you have a better memory than anyone else I know.'

There was a moment of silence. 'Was the man's name Wilkinson? Trevor Wilkinson?'

'It was!'

'If you're thinking suspicious death, then I'd say that was highly unlikely. The man had so much alcohol in his blood that I was astonished he could stand. It was hardly surprising that he slipped on an uneven pier.' There was a moment's pause. 'His son was with him. He jumped in and tried to save him, but he was a skinny little thing, and the father was heavy, clinically obese. He had no chance.'

'Thanks.' So it was a coincidence, Perez thought. Odd though that Nat had used almost the same words as those on the story stone, when he'd said he had no interest in the archaeology of the island. It must have been a coincidental turn of phrase.

Just before midday he had a Zoom call with the team in Glasgow. The chief inspector was working from home.

'It's a nightmare,' the man said. 'Nothing's moving. I can't even get into the city. Anyone not living within walking distance is working remotely. So you finally tracked down your teacher?'

'Aye, he came in on the ferry yesterday evening. I'm just about to meet him.' Perez passed on the latest information from Phil Bain about Riley's car having been seen outside the Pierowall Hotel and the light having been on in the heritage centre.

'And that's the nearest you've got to a suspect? It seems a bit thin.' The DCI was less than impressed.

'I don't see him as a suspect at this stage. He might have had access to the weapon, and he had the opportunity, but there's no motive at all and no evidence to connect him to the scene.'

'It seems that there's no evidence of *anyone* at the scene.'

'We're a very small team here.' Perez was losing patience. 'We could have done with more officers. As I said, Riley managed to get back here . . .'

The implication was that the Glasgow officers could have taken the ferry too. But Glasgow seemed to see the islands, as the Romans saw northern Britain, as a wild and uncivilized place best avoided. That was why they'd appointed Willow to manage all the Scottish islands on their behalf.

'Aye well, he was coming from Inverness. It's a bit different down here.' The man was defensive, but immediately became more placatory. 'Orkney's a small place, Jimmy, and you know it well. With your experience we thought you'd have it all wrapped up in a couple of days. No need to stretch the budget with overtime and travel at this time of the year. And as the weather's turned out, it seems we made the right call.'

'I see George Riley as an important witness rather than a suspect,' Perez said. 'I'll get back to you when I've talked to him.' As he spoke, he wondered if that was true. There was something odd about the teacher's lack of communication, his insistence on meeting Perez at a tourist site instead of agreeing to come to the police station.

'Sure, Jimmy. We'll leave it in your capable hands.'

Behind the DCI, a woman appeared on the screen. She was carrying a mug of coffee and a slice of cake. Suddenly, the Zoom call ended. For the Glaswegian, it seemed, the holidays had already begun.

★ ★ ★

Riley had arranged to meet the inspector at two-forty-five in Maeshowe.

'If it stays as clear as this, we might even see what our ancestors saw, the very reason for building the burial chamber in that position.' The man had sounded as excited as one of his pupils. 'I'll be there before you, Inspector. I'll be inside. Waiting for you and for the magic to happen.'

Perez parked outside the old mill, which had been turned into a visitor centre. There was nobody there now – it would open again in the summer. In the far corner there was an old Land Rover, and closer to the road there was another car, belonging, Perez supposed, to George Riley.

He crossed the main road, waiting for the bus to Kirkwall to pass, and made his way along the footpath towards the rounded mound of Maeshowe, stopping on the way to look out over the standing stones of Stenness, with the Ring of Brodgar in the distance. These were Orkney's answer to Stonehenge, and the area was flooded with visitors in the summer, the car park full of tour coaches from the cruise ships. In the distance there were the twin hills on the island of Hoy. They seemed visible from every point on Orkney mainland. Now, everything was still and quiet, the flatland leading down to the loch still frosty, the water covered in ice.

At the entrance to the burial chamber, he waited for a moment. There was a metal cage on the wall next to the tunnel, which Perez thought had held the key to the entrance. The cage had needed to be unlocked too, and George Riley must have been given *that* key. He'd be inside as he'd promised. Perez paused for a moment and looked out once again to Hoy. The sun was lower, approaching the rim of the left-hand hill. Perez felt something of the teacher's excitement. He knew people who'd visited

Maeshowe many times in midwinter, only for clouds to appear at the last moment to cover the sun. Today the sky was still completely clear. He bent double and almost crawled through the low entrance into the chamber itself, determined not to miss the spectacle that was only apparent at the time of the solstice.

Inside, it was dark. Electricity had been connected to the monument, but with his sense of the theatrical, George must have switched off the lights. Perez saw that he was just in time to see the magic of the solstice, but at the same time felt a frisson of danger. The teacher was a murder suspect, and Perez could be walking into a trap. Then he remembered the man that he knew and thought he was being ridiculous.

A thin light ran along the floor of the chamber. Not silver, but gold. A very rich gold. Perez called out to the teacher.

'George, where are you?'

The chamber was small – it would hold only a dozen people in comfort – and there was no sign of the man. Perez was torn between a desire to see the full impact of the rays of the sun filling the place with its light, and a sense that he should go back outside to look for the teacher, his star witness, his possible suspect.

The earlier anxiety returned, with the idea that this could be a trap. But the light was increasing and Perez stood mesmerized, astounded at the knowledge of the ancient builders who had built this place in exactly the right place for the sun to come through this narrow entrance and fill it with light in midwinter. George must be playing silly buggers. Or perhaps, with a teacher's desire to thrill his students, he wanted Perez to have this almost mystical experience alone. In any event, Perez waited, sharing some of the wonder and awe felt by the early builders. He had never felt so close to the ancient world.

The gold path was widening. Perez started to make out the scratched runes on the walls. There had been Viking graffiti artists here too, it seemed. The light appeared liquid now, more like a stream than a path. Perez saw the shadowy circles in the curved wall on each side of him, mini-chambers for the dead. Then the golden stream seemed to defy nature and gravity and to flow up the wall ahead of it, lighting the whole building, pouring into the small cavity opposite the entrance, which had been in darkness until now.

George had been a big man, and it must have taken some force to squeeze him into that small circular chamber, carved into the wall. He was bent double and one of his legs hung out, limp, making him look like a giant puppet. His face was turned out towards Perez. His eyes were open, astonished. Lying on the floor at the foot of the chamber, behind a large rock, was a rectangular stone picked with spirals. Perez knew that on the other side there would be carved Viking runes. Translated, they would read: 'I am Olaf, teller of tales.' Even in this fading light, Perez could see that it was covered in blood and shards of bone.

The flood of light was withdrawing, like an ebbing tide. The sun would be sinking behind the hills of Hoy. Perez pulled on gloves and felt for a switch to turn on the electricity. Suddenly everything was normal, prosaic. With the discovery of George Riley, the magic had disappeared. Perez went outside to check that he had phone signal. His first call was to Willow, but there was no answer. Then he rang the police station to set the new murder investigation in motion.

Standing, freezing, waiting for his uniformed colleagues as the colour drained from the surrounding landscape, Perez tried to work out what Archie Stout and George Riley might have in common. They were both big personalities, well known by their communities. George had been on the northern isle on the night that Archie had been killed. They'd known each other, but there was no indication that they'd been close friends. And they'd both been killed by an ancient stone from the island of Westray.

Chapter Seventeen

WHEN PEREZ GOT THROUGH TO WILLOW, she was at home with James.

'Sorry to miss your calls. I was at the cathedral carol service with James. And then he was a bit fidgety in the car, so I thought I'd get him home before calling you back.' A pause. 'Well, what did George Riley have to say?' She sounded eager. She obviously thought that there'd been a breakthrough in the case.

'Nothing.'

Perez was about to explain, but Willow broke in. 'Are you saying he wasn't there?'

'He was there, but he was dead. Like some sort of ancient sacrifice. Stashed just where the light would catch the body as it came into the chamber for the solstice.' A pause. 'He'd been hit over the head with the other story stone.'

There was a silence for a moment. Perez could almost sense Willow's thoughts racing through the phone. 'The murders are obviously linked then,' she said. 'And Archie was found close to a Neolithic site on Westray.' Another silence. 'Do we think our killer is a history buff? Or someone with stories of their own to tell?'

Perez was thinking too. 'It's all so contrived. Definitely not some random killing. I have to go and inform Miles, George's partner, of his death now. I'm not sure what time I'll get home. Dr Grieve has agreed to come in on this evening's ferry. He's already checked in. I've said he can stay with us. I'll pick him up at the terminal, and I might not be home before then. That *is* okay?'

'Sure,' she said. 'Of course.'

Perez thought then that nothing would ever throw her. She was *his* rock, the calm centre of his world.

It was dark. The Range Rover was still parked in front of the grand and slightly ridiculous house outside Finstown. It must belong to Miles. Perez had confirmed that the car he'd seen outside the Maeshowe visitor centre had belonged to George Riley. It should already have been brought into Kirkwall on a low loader. Now he stood on the steps, his breath coming in clouds, and rang the bell. It echoed inside. There were footsteps and the door opened.

'Oh, it's you. I was expecting George. He's always losing his key, or he can't be arsed to look for it. What do you want? I thought he was meeting you this afternoon.' The man was frowning as if this was an invasion too far.

'He was.'

Miles stood blocking the door.

'Can I come in?' Perez said. 'We need to talk.'

George's partner must have picked up something from the tone of the inspector's voice, because he stood aside, and instead of taking Perez to the kitchen, he led him into a grand living room, which had a piano in one corner and long windows covered by red velvet curtains. They wouldn't have been out of place in a Victorian theatre. The fireplace was elaborately tiled, and radiated heat – it was banked with coal. Miles sat on a plush plum-coloured sofa.

'What's happened?' His voice was very quiet.

'George is dead.' Perez hated euphemisms. In this situation, it was better to be honest and straight.

'How?' Miles was very tight, very tense, as if that was the only way he could hold himself together. It seemed to Perez that every muscle in his body was working just to keep him upright. But he thought too that Miles Chambers was a man used to the unexpected, used even to news of other people's tragedies.

'He was murdered,' Perez said. 'In a situation very similar to Archie Stout in Westray. We have to assume that they were killed by the same person, though we can't rule anything out at this stage.'

'So he was hit,' Miles said. 'Battered. It must have been quick?'

'Yes, it would have been quick.' Perez didn't know how true that was, but in this case, honesty was less important than kindness.

Then the control that had been holding Miles in place failed him. He sagged, his back curled, and he covered his face with his hands. When he straightened, he looked, dry-eyed, out at Perez. 'You'll have questions. I'll try to answer them.'

'Can I get you something? A drink?'

He shook his head. 'Not yet. Later, when I'm on my own, I suspect I'll get very, very drunk. But not now. Now, I need to help you with your investigation.'

'Do you know what George was doing this morning? I know he got back from Inverness on the ferry yesterday evening.'

'I think that he went into school. He said there was something he had to do. But I'm not sure. I'd hoped we'd have the morning together. I've only recently retired from a rather demanding job in the Foreign Office, and we spent so much time apart over my Whitehall years. Snatched moments. He loved Orkney, this house, and couldn't contemplate moving to London. I couldn't imagine giving up work. I have always had an inflated sense of duty, and I felt that I had a valuable role there. Then I reached a point where I needed to be with George more than I needed to be in charge of my department. But when I arrived here, it seemed that George was still wrapped up with island affairs. I almost felt that I was getting in the way, that he resented my presence.' He stared out at Perez. 'We argued this morning. Nothing major. A niggle because he wouldn't change his plans to spend the morning with me.'

'I'm sorry.' Perez wasn't sure how to go on. He added: 'George told me that you were lovers.'

'Did he?' The man's face lightened. 'I always felt the need for discretion. I hated the idea that people should know our business, but I find that very comforting. A kind of acknowledgement. A validation.'

'So this morning,' Perez prompted, 'you think he went into school? Was there a meeting?'

Miles shook his head. 'Nothing like that. I could have accepted that he'd have to attend an organized meeting. No, he said it was research, something he needed to check. Then he would head out to Maeshowe to see the sun in the chamber. I asked if I could come too, but he told me he'd arranged to meet you there. And there was something else he needed to sort out. A problem that was troubling him rather. Nothing much troubled him, so I could tell that it was important. I sulked like a teenage boy, like one of his pupils denied a treat, but I didn't make a fuss.'

'Did he come home at lunchtime?'

'No. He said he'd grab something in town. Once the sun had thawed out the soil a bit, I did some more work in the garden. That's my project. It keeps me sane. Almost.' Miles looked directly at Perez again. 'I haven't been entirely truthful. I retired from the Civil Service on medical grounds. I was forced out. Stress. Burnout.'

'I can think,' Perez said, 'of no better place to recuperate.'

Miles was continuing to speak. 'The anxiety makes me a little paranoid. I scroll through possible scenarios in my head: that George had run away to Westray because I was annoying him, that he had another lover, that I'd misinterpreted the whole relationship.'

Perez shook his head. 'He spoke of you so fondly. I don't think any of that was true. Do you know exactly why he went into Westray?'

'He said it was to research his book. He'd just be there and back in a day. But I wasn't sure that I entirely believed him. I thought there was more to it than that.' He gave a little smile. 'That worm of doubt crawling inside my head once more, especially when George said he had to stay over because of the storm and that he was spending the night with one of his former students.'

'We've investigated that,' Perez said. 'The two of them met by chance on the ferry. It was an act of hospitality, nothing more than that.'

Though how can I know? How can I be sure? Am I just being kind again?

'Did he have any enemies? My working theory is that George was killed because he knew something about Archie Stout's death, but we have to explore all the possibilities. You will understand that.'

Miles nodded. 'You're right. He wasn't the sort of man to make enemies. He was usually a warm person, open, good at everything he did.'

There was a silence, deep and intense. The house was too far from the road for there to be any traffic noise. Perez waited. He thought that Miles had more to say. The man spoke at last. 'He was preoccupied. Even before Archie Stout died, before he went to Westray, there was something on his mind. I asked him what was bothering him, if I could help in any way. "This is nothing to do with us," he said. "This is something I need to sort out for myself." I wonder if he was protecting me, if he thought I wasn't mentally strong enough to help him.'

Perez thought that was another coincidence because Archie Stout had been preoccupied too.

'Did he talk to you about what he did on Westray, who he met? Anything that seemed strange to him?'

'He wouldn't talk about his Westray stay at all, and that wasn't like George. He'd be sad that someone had died of course but he'd usually be rather enjoying the drama of a murder. I'd told him about your visit and thought he'd come back from Inverness full of theories and suspicions, playing the big detective, creating an exciting narrative. It wasn't as if he and the dead man were close. The man was the father of two of his students. But he just shut down the conversation.'

Perez wouldn't have expected that sort of response from

the teacher either. Reticence wouldn't have been the man's default position. It occurred to him that the couple's relationship had been less perfect than he'd first supposed. The silence could have been the result of a deeper conflict, a crack or a split. Sometimes a long-distance partnership was easier to maintain than close, day-to-day living. It was a big step though to believe that Miles was a murderer. His response to George's death had felt totally authentic, and besides, the man had no reason to kill Archie Stout. He hadn't even been on Westray when the farmer had died.

'Is there anyone I can contact? Someone who might stay with you?'

Miles shook his head. 'I've been rather a recluse since I moved here permanently. George said it was his mission to find me some friends.'

'Will you stay on in Orkney?'

'Oh yes!' As if the question was almost ridiculous. 'This is where George was happy. The house is mine. George fell in love with it when it first came on the market, so I bought it. He insisted that it should always stay in my name. We never married, you see, so there'd have been legal complications if he'd been the owner. If he'd died first.' Miles stared bleakly into space. 'He asked me to marry him, but I hated the idea of any fuss. He wouldn't have contemplated a wedding without a party. Besides, I have to stay. There's my garden to consider. I have so many plans for the garden.'

There was another silence, and again Miles was the first to speak. 'If you don't mind, Inspector, I think you should leave now. I do need that drink rather badly, and I think I might weep. For George and for me.' He smiled again. 'I can't blub in front of anyone, you see. My public-school upbringing. So perhaps you could go now. Come back tomorrow if you like. Not too early because of the hangover. I've enjoyed speaking with you. But now, I do insist that you go.'

Sitting in his car, the heater blasting, waiting for the windscreen to de-ice again, Perez imagined Miles in the big, theatrical house, with a bottle of very good malt whisky, howling alone.

The ferry from Aberdeen arrived in to Kirkwall a little early. Dr Grieve hadn't managed to book his car onto the boat. The vessel was already full of people returning home for Christmas, and there'd been no room left on the vehicle deck. Perez waited for him in the terminal building and watched the students with their rucksacks being greeted by parents, the older couples being met by children.

The pathologist was as smart as ever, his shoes highly polished. 'This is a bad do, Jimmy.' His only comment on the second murder while they walked to Perez's car and put his bags in the boot. 'Are you sure you want to put me up? I can easily find a hotel.'

'We'd like it. Really. Willow insisted.' Grieve had always had a soft spot for Willow. 'She might already be in bed when we get in though.'

When they reached the house, however, Willow was waiting for them, dressed in pyjamas and dressing gown, the fire still alight, and a platter of local cheese ready in the kitchen in case they were hungry. But not just, it seemed, playing the dutiful little wife. 'I don't want to miss anything. I can sleep in tomorrow, while you two are out working.'

It was, Perez thought, an odd debriefing. Willow was still, in one sense, in overall charge, and she led the conversation. If it were anyone else, he thought, he'd resent it.

'Have you had a chance to carry out the post-mortem on Archie Stout?'

'Yes, there was nothing unexpected. He was a fit man, healthy for his age. He'd been drinking, but at the point of his death he wouldn't have been drunk. He was hit from behind, and the murder weapon was at the scene. It was all as we surmised when I first saw him.'

'Could you tell if the assailant was left- or right-handed?' Willow again asked the question. Perez was feeling very tired now. He was willing to let her take the lead.

'I'd guess right-handed, but I wouldn't swear to that on oath.'

'I think the assault on George Riley was almost identical to that on Archie,' Perez said. 'It's difficult to tell though, because he was stuffed into the smaller chamber facing the entrance to Maeshowe, and I couldn't see the back of his head. The stone has the same traces of blood and bone. We've left him where I found him, Doc. You can see for yourself. I'll take you first thing tomorrow.'

Chapter Eighteen

DESPITE WHAT SHE'D SAID ABOUT LYING in, Willow was up before the men. She'd left Jimmy sleeping. Sleep never came easily to him, and he'd been restless the night before, troubled. An investigation would never just be work for him. It was a personal crusade, even if he'd never met the victim. He'd be troubled by guilt too. She knew that he'd be feeling responsible for Riley's death, believing that he should have gone to more effort to meet the man earlier.

She made coffee and laid the table for breakfast, then went to get her son dressed and ready for the day. She heard Perez stirring, and the sound of the shower. Both he and Dr Grieve were up when she returned to the kitchen with the boy, who was already in his coat, ready to go out.

'I'm dropping James with Alison. She said she'd feed him and take him to nursery. I'd like to come with you to Maeshowe.' This wasn't a question. She wasn't asking permission. She might officially be on maternity leave, but she was the senior officer. 'I'll see you there, shall I? Can you wait for me in the car park? I won't be long behind you.' And she left them there and drove off into the darkness, wondering why she was such a control freak, why she found it so hard to let go. She knew that it wouldn't help Perez's state of mind, his confidence, if she continued to interfere, but she thought too that she could contribute to the outcome.

It was still dark when she arrived at the car park by the old mill, but the men were already there, waiting for her. There were other vehicles, all related to the investigation. Some of their people had been there all night. She pulled on her big coat and her knitted hat and allowed Perez to take her arm as they crossed to the main road. The ground was icy underfoot, and she wasn't so proud that she'd risk her baby with a fall.

Maeshowe was lit up. The spotlights that had so recently flooded the Noltland crime scene on Westray were here now, making the place look like a film set. There was an officer near the entrance to the footpath who recognized them and let them through the cordon.

'You'll be freezing,' she said. 'When does the next shift start?'

'Half an hour. Ellie was here earlier with flasks and bacon sandwiches. A lifesaver!'

She made a mental note to thank Ellie. She should have thought of that herself.

'We need extra people on the ground.' She was talking to Perez now, her scene mask already in place. The pathologist was walking ahead of them. She could hear the crunch of his boots, with their covers, on the path. 'We're seriously stretched. Glasgow can't pretend that this is a little local incident now. Two killings. They'll have to take it more seriously. They can drive to Scrabster, get the ferry and be here this afternoon.' She realized how angry she was. Did headquarters only care about their own patch? 'I know I'm officially on mat leave, but do you want me to contact their chief? Get them to shift their arses?'

She sensed that Perez was smiling. 'You can try if you like. But really do you think it would help? Three days before Christmas and a carload of resentful Glaswegians who have no understanding of a small community moving in.'

He paused. 'They're already blaming me for not speaking to Riley earlier. I can understand why. I blame myself too. But I'm a useful scapegoat. They'd rather not get involved because then they might have to take some responsibility.'

'They're not all like that, Jimmy!'

'No,' he conceded. 'Not all of them. I'd like us to deal with it ourselves though if I can. For Archie and for George. Let's have Glasgow on standby to come in straight after Christmas if we haven't had things wrapped up by then. We know the islands. Their officers are mostly city folk and people are more likely to talk to us without outsiders throwing their weight around.'

'I spoke to Phil yesterday evening and explained about the second murder.' In her mind, Willow relived the phone conversation they'd had, or rather the silences as her colleague had tried to process the news of Riley's death. Phil had liked George Riley, admired him. He was another Kirkwall man who'd been influenced by the teacher. She'd been able to guess at Phil's distress by what had been left unsaid. As news was getting out, she thought, the whole town would be horrified and seeking justice. Or revenge.

'Did he have anything useful for us?'

'He spoke to as many folk as he could, people who Ellie couldn't get round to when we were there, but it seems half of Westray was on Orkney mainland yesterday afternoon. There was a late sailing of the ferry, and folk either came in for the service at the cathedral, or for last-minute shopping. Or just for a change of scene. Phil knows the purser and I've asked him to get the passenger details through to me.'

'We'll go through them when we've finished here,' Perez said. 'It would be a start, wouldn't it? Just having a list of the people who had the opportunity to be at both scenes.'

As they reached Maeshowe, the sky was lightening, a pale grey line shot with streaks of pink over the eastern horizon. Willow and Perez stayed outside the burial chamber. They had no reason to go in to contaminate the scene further, and there was little enough space for Dr Grieve to work. Willow was curious though and crouched to look through the low, tunnel-like entrance to see inside. Grieve was still setting up and out of her line of sight, so she could see straight through to the back of the domed space. The place was brightly lit by the electric lights installed by Heritage Scotland. George Riley's body was there, just as Perez had described, forced into his own burial chamber. He seemed to be staring straight out at her.

'Why do that?' She was speaking to herself now, rather than Perez. 'He must have been killed in the main body of the place. Why take the time to put him in the smaller chamber? It wasn't as if the body was properly hidden from view. It wouldn't stop him being identified. It almost suggests a kind of revulsion. A need to dispose of the body with some violence, to push it away.' She straightened and shook her head, not coming up with any real answer to the question. 'It's almost personal.'

'Let's go,' Perez said. 'We're not helping by being here. You didn't have any breakfast and you should be eating for two.'

★ ★ ★

Perez agreed to come back to the house with her – the team knew where he'd be and that they could contact him. Willow scrambled eggs and broke her caffeine rule to drink the coffee Perez had made as soon as they'd got home. They sat at the kitchen table and went through Phil Bain's list of people who were away from Westray on the day of Riley's death.

'Vaila and the boys are here on the mainland,' she said. 'They're staying until after the Ba' on Christmas Day. I didn't see them at the cathedral and Vaila came out with a car. She could easily have met up with George before you turned up.' She put down her fork. 'I'm assuming he was killed not long before you got to the place. We only have Miles's word that he had lunch in town, or even that he went into school that morning. He could have met his killer much earlier.'

Perez shook his head. 'I don't think so. It was so cold yesterday that my windscreen iced up when I left the car for an hour outside Riley's house to inform his partner of the death. I noticed that the windscreen on George's car was quite clear when I saw it at the mill. It was earlier in the day, but the temperature was already dropping. If he'd been there very much sooner, it would have frozen.'

'Did you see anyone then? Anyone driving away from the mill when you arrived?'

He shook his head. 'Certainly not from the car park. But I was quite preoccupied, wondering what George might have to tell me. And you know how busy that road can get, even at this time of the year.'

'You would have noticed if someone was on foot though. They could have parked at some distance from Maeshowe. It wouldn't have been too far to walk even from the public space down at the Stones of Stenness.' Willow tried not to sound impatient.

'Yes,' he said. 'I would have noticed that.' She saw again how deflated he was and reached out to touch his hand.

'All three of the Pierowall Hotel residents were in Kirkwall. Godfrey Lansdown was in the cathedral, but if he came out with his car, he might just have had time to kill George at Maeshowe and be back for the service. He's an elderly man though and a gentle soul. I'm not sure he'd have the strength for those attacks. Besides, I can't see that he'd have any motive for either murder.'

'Wouldn't he only need a motive for killing Archie?' Perez was writing notes on a large sheet of plain paper. That was always his way of ordering his thoughts. 'My assumption is that George saw something while he was out that night on Westray, and he was killed to stop him talking to me.'

'If George was suspicious of any individual, I don't think he'd arrange a meeting with them, would he? And the killer can't have bumped into him in Maeshowe by chance.' Willow paused. 'But you're right. It's too much of a coincidence to assume that the murders aren't connected. The fact that the story stones were used in both cases means we're only looking at one killer.'

Perez stood to refill his mug with coffee. 'Who else did you see in Kirkwall yesterday?'

'The Johnsons, the professor and his wife. They claimed to have been at the service, but I didn't see them inside the building, just when we got outside. That doesn't mean anything. It was packed with people. I couldn't see everyone. Besides, I think they might have claimed to be in the cathedral just to show they've really become part of the island community. Not common-or-garden tourists.'

'That's a bit harsh!'

'Maybe.' Willow tried to put her mistrust of the couple into words. 'They seem so respectable and above suspicion, but they've been involved with Westray and the story stones since they were students. The man's professional reputation is founded on his work on them. He has a lot to lose. I've been thinking about how Archie might have threatened that. For example, if he'd worked out that Tony Johnson's research was unreliable, or that he was guilty of plagiarism, that might be a motive.'

She looked across the table at Perez and saw that he was taking the theory seriously.

'It would matter to Archie,' Perez said, 'if it seemed that Westray's famous archaeology was based on a lie. The island's reputation was important to him. And Rosalie told us that he was worried before he died. She thought it had something to do with the place, the community. I'll talk to Paul Rutherford again. He might have picked up some rumours in academic circles, that Johnson's work wasn't entirely safe.'

'It's possible that George came across something that didn't quite hang together when he was researching his kids' book. He read history at Cambridge. He'd have the background knowledge.'

'It's not much, but at least it gives us a thread of a motive that works for both murders.' Perez sounded a little brighter.

'Rosalie was in Kirkwall yesterday too.' Willow remembered the brightly coloured coat worn by the woman. The artist certainly hadn't been trying to make herself look inconspicuous. 'I didn't speak to her, but I saw her wander past when James and I were going into the cathedral.'

Perez added another name to his list.

'And Bill MacBride came out on the ferry with me the day before. He said he needed to escape Westray for a while, that the island was driving him crazy. I saw him when I came out of the cathedral too.'

'Phil was right,' Perez said. 'It seems that most of our suspects were on Orkney mainland yesterday.'

His phone rang. 'Phil!' He looked across at Willow and smiled at the coincidence of the DC calling just as they were speaking of him. 'What have you got for us? Where are all our Westray residents now?'

Willow watched him take another sheet of paper and start scribbling on it. She'd never been able to read his writing, certainly not when it was upside down, and had to wait until the call ended to find out what was going on.

'He's spoken to the purser,' Perez said. 'Vaila and the boys are still in Kirkwall, as we knew they would be. Everyone else on our list took the last boat home last night.'

'I'll pack a bag.' Of course, Perez would want to come with her, but again Willow knew that his involvement would cloud any trial that followed. They would be handing a gift to the defence. 'There's a plane in an hour. If you give me a lift to the airport, I should be able to make it, and I'll get Phil to meet me at the airstrip. I might even get home on the last ferry tonight.'

'I'll talk to Rutherford again and check out Tony Johnson's research. Find out if there have ever been any suspicions that he's not quite the reputable academic that he seems.'

'Great. Yeah, that makes perfect sense.'

Willow got the last seat on the plane – it only held eight passengers and she had to sit next to the pilot. She was a neighbour of theirs, and her daughter was at nursery with James. She didn't need to ask why Willow was going in to the island. She just grinned a welcome and talked through the safety procedure over a crackly mic. Willow didn't recognize anyone else, but gathered as they boarded that the elderly couple were from Westray and heading home to visit family for Christmas and the others were a group who wanted to do the shortest scheduled flight in Europe. The plane would fly on from Westray to Papa Westray. She and Perez had done it once, just for the craic. As soon as the plane took off, it had come into land. It had been something of an anticlimax.

It was another cold and sunny day. The weather was forecast to be like this almost until Christmas. Orcadians and Shetlanders were smug, watching the chaos the freezing fog and the snow were causing further south. The flight was as smooth as any Willow could remember and she had a magnificent view of the islands scattered beneath them, a living map of water and land. She could hear the tourists behind her gasping at the beauty and felt again the privilege of living in this place.

Phil was waiting for her at the airstrip. 'Where do you want to start?'

She thought about that. 'Let's leave the hotel residents until later. We're not far from Rosalie. We'll go there first, shall we?'

They found Rosalie at work. It took her a while to come down from her studio on the first floor.

'I thought you'd be here. I heard about George Riley. I didn't really know him, but everyone said he was a lovely man and a brilliant teacher.' She looked out at Willow. 'What's going on, Inspector? Everyone's scared. We thought this was a safe place where the kids could play out and we didn't have to lock our doors or our cars. And now people are hiding away indoors. The snake's slithered its way into our paradise. I didn't even swim this morning. My imagination was running wild.'

'We're talking to everyone from Westray who was on the mainland yesterday.'

'Of course. You have to do that. I saw you with your little boy outside the cathedral. Do you want to come upstairs? I've had the heating on in the studio because I'll be there all day.'

It was a large, light room with windows looking out across the bay where she did her ritual swim. Under the windows a large trestle table held scraps of sea glass and coils of silver wire. 'I just need to put the lid back on this glue.'

There was a battered sofa against the opposite wall and Willow lowered herself onto that. Phil took a bentwood chair and Rosalie leaned against the table.

'What were you doing in Kirkwall?' Willow asked. 'I didn't see you at the carol service.'

Rosalie shook her head. 'I was there on business. The craft shop that takes my work had run out of my jewellery. I know there are only a few days until Christmas, but I didn't want to miss out on sales, so I brought in a load more stuff for them.'

That made sense. 'I'll need the name of the owner. You understand that we'll have to check.'

'Of course.' Despite her comment about the snake and paradise, Rosalie seemed entirely at ease now. These questions weren't shaking her.

'Did you spend the whole time in Kirkwall? We can see from the passenger list that you had your car with you. Why would you do that if you only intended to stay in town?'

'I had boxes of merchandise. I'd have to drive down to the pier at Rapness anyway, so it made sense to take the car. I booked it in a while ago.'

'Of course. But did you head anywhere else? Take time to do a bit of sightseeing while you were out on the mainland?'

There was a brief hesitation before Rosalie answered. 'I went to Stromness, to the gallery there, to see if they would take any of my stuff.'

'The main road from Kirkwall to Stromness would take you through Stenness and past the footpath to Maeshowe. Did you stop at all? You're into the islands' archaeology. You might have been tempted on a clear day on the solstice.'

There was a flash of anger. 'Are you accusing me of killing a schoolteacher I barely knew?'

'No.' Willow kept her voice calm. 'But if you did stop that afternoon, you could be an important witness. You might have seen somebody you knew or a car that you recognized.'

Rosalie shook her head. 'I was tempted to stop. But I wasn't sure what time the gallery would close.'

'Did you manage to sell any of your goods?'

'No. When I got there, the manager had already left and the lad at the desk didn't have the responsibility to make a decision. I left a few samples. You can check. It was my fault – I was starving when I arrived in Stromness and went for lunch in the cafe in the street before going to the gallery. But it felt like a wasted afternoon. I'd just arrived back in Kirkwall when you saw me outside the cathedral. I was looking for somewhere I wouldn't feel awkward on my own to have a glass of wine.'

Chapter Nineteen

Perez had phoned Lucy Martindale, George's head teacher, the evening before and had arranged to meet her in Kirkwall Grammar School that morning. She'd been stunned by the news of Riley's death.

Perez had heard the catch in her voice on the phone and imagined silent tears. When he'd talked to her in her home, she'd been cool, matter-of-fact. Archie's death hadn't moved her. She might not have known George for long, but it seemed he'd made a strong impression on her.

'I can hardly believe it. I've never met anyone so full of life.' Perez was thinking that he'd had exactly the same impression of Archie. Martindale was still speaking. 'Such a huge personality. Of course, I'll need to let the parents and students know. I'll be in school all morning, Inspector, making arrangements. Some of our students might want to come later to be with their friends, to mourn together. And a skeleton office staff will be in. They'll look out for you in reception.' She was still efficient despite the emotion.

Since meeting Martindale, Perez had put out feelers, asking

what people had made of the new head. The response had been mixed. There were grumbles about a new crackdown on behaviour, rules rigidly upheld. *This isn't an inner city. She could be a peedie bit more flexible.* Other parents liked the change. The old head teacher had been a soft touch, they said, and academic standards had been slipping. The kids had been allowed to get away with anything.

The building was relatively new, a comprehensive school, despite the name and the history — it had been going since the twelfth century. Most of the island children would go there, at least to finish their education. Cassie had settled in well, and Perez supposed that James would go there too when he was old enough.

There was, as Martindale had said, a woman in reception and she was expecting him.

'I'll just phone the head to let her know that you're here.' Then, as if she couldn't help herself: 'I can't believe that George won't be coming back after Christmas. We'll all miss him so much.'

Lucy Martindale's office was large and airy, immaculately tidy as he'd imagined it would be. She sat behind her large, pale wood desk and he felt like one of her students, called in to be questioned about some misdemeanour.

'Is it true that he was murdered? Like the Stout boys' father? I find that almost impossible to believe. I came here from an inner-city school. Even there, the death of a teacher seemed unimaginable. But here . . .' Her voice tailed off.

'Tell me about George.' Details of his work and movements, Perez thought, could come later. He wanted her impression of the man. This woman would be clear-eyed about anyone working with her.

'We didn't always get on, but – and I never told him this – I think he was one of the best teachers I've ever worked with.'

'Why didn't you get on?'

She paused for a moment and when she spoke, she chose her words carefully. 'The former head teacher was here for years. I have a feeling that for a while he'd been coasting towards retirement. Exam results weren't as good as they could have been. We were letting down some of our brightest students. I was brought in to make changes. When you're new to a school, or even to a class, I've always thought it important to go in tough. It's possible to relax later, but it's almost impossible to start off as if the rules don't matter and then try to tighten up.' She looked up at him. 'I'm guessing that's the same in any institution.'

Perez thought about that. Willow wasn't exactly his boss now, but she was his superior. She'd never been one for sticking to protocol, even at the start. They were a small team though and she understood every different personality. It would be much harder trying to treat nine hundred pupils and nearly a hundred staff members as individuals.

'Perhaps,' he conceded. 'And George didn't understand your approach?'

She gave the mischievous smile that had attracted him in her home. 'He understood it perfectly well in theory, but then he was always asking me to make exceptions. He came to me with kids he felt should be treated more leniently, cases where he thought we should bend the rules. I explained that we couldn't work like that. Not at first.'

'Yet you still thought he was a good teacher.'

She nodded. 'A great teacher. Sometimes his approach was

unorthodox, but he had a charisma that hooked the students in. Actually, I never saw any problem with discipline in his lessons, but he cared about every one of them. Recognized them as individuals. That's why he came to me to battle on their behalf.'

'Were there other ways that his approach was unorthodox?'

'He despised the box-ticking that has become so much a part of education. He was, perhaps, a little lax when it came to risk assessment.' She looked up and smiled again. 'He would have taken his history group to one of the out-isles to look at the archaeology and had them camping out in a bothy, without doing any safety checks or completing parental consent forms, if I'd let him, so we didn't always see eye to eye. But he understood the students. He listened to them. I started at the school in September and at half-term I created a new post for him – head of pastoral care. I could tell that he'd be perfect in the role.'

'What did that involve?'

'If our kids were struggling emotionally, if they were being bullied, or there were troubles at home, they knew that they could go to George.' She looked across the desk. 'Even here we can't escape some of the problems adolescents face everywhere, especially since Covid: eating disorders, cyber-bullying, self-harming. Of course there was a female staff member on his team, but George took the lead.'

'Did the Stout lads have any troubles at home?' This, Perez thought, might be another line of inquiry.

'Not that I was aware of,' Martindale said, 'but then I might not have been aware of them. Unless there was a safeguarding issue, the conversations that the students had with George were confidential. Lawrie and Iain both stayed in the hostel, of course, and some students find that daunting, but they went home at weekends, and when I did meet them, they seemed happy enough.'

'According to his partner, George came into school yesterday morning. Do you know why that was?'

'I knew that he was here, but I only saw him briefly. He was just back from that conference in Inverness. So he could have been updating colleagues about that, or breaking the habit of a lifetime and doing some routine admin. He asked if I'd be free for coffee and a catch-up, but I was busy all morning and he said he had a meeting off-site in the afternoon.'

That could have been with me, Perez thought, or he might have meant a meeting at Maeshowe with his killer.

'Did he tell you who the meeting was with, what it was about?'

He held his breath, waiting for the woman to reply, but she shook her head. 'As I said, I only bumped into him briefly. It probably wasn't anything to do with school. He had an active life in the community. I don't know where he found the energy. I was anxious that he might burn out.' She paused for a moment, before adding bitterly: 'No chance of that now.'

Chapter Twenty

PEREZ DROVE FROM THE GRAMMAR SCHOOL straight to the college at the top of the town where he'd agreed to meet the Geordie archaeologist Paul Rutherford. Term had finished for the students and the place was almost empty, quiet, with a slightly chaotic air. It was as if all the staff were waiting to set off for an office party or were getting over one that had happened the night before. It seemed that very little work was being done.

Rutherford took Perez to his office again. His face was grave. 'I heard about George. What's happening to us, Inspector? Things like this don't happen here in the islands. Not to good men like Archie and George.'

'You knew him well?'

'We were friends,' Rutherford said simply. 'Good friends.' A pause. 'This isn't bias because we were close, but he was one of the brightest people I know. He could have had a senior academic post in a university, but he chose to come here and to teach our kids. He loved the place and its history. He loved the people.'

'You'd met his partner, Miles?' This wasn't the conversation Perez had expected to have, but he knew Rutherford's insight would be useful. This was a lucky encounter.

'A few times.' Rutherford smiled. 'Miles isn't the most sociable of people and gives very little of himself away. They were a strange couple, but the relationship seemed to work all the same. George once told me, after far too many glasses of wine, that he was deeply and madly in love still, after all the years that they'd been together.'

Perez thought about that. It was a truism that the intensity of emotion in love and hate could become tangled and twisted.

'You hadn't been aware of any crack in the relationship?'

Rutherford shook his head. 'I'm sure it wasn't all smooth sailing – George loved a drama and a good argument – but they seemed very strong to me.'

'I had to inform Miles of George's death.' Perez paused for a moment. 'He could use a friend now. He might seem reserved, even offhand when you make the approach, but I think he'd really be glad to see you.'

'I found him fascinating when I met him. His apparent need for secrecy intrigued me. I once asked George if Miles was a spy.'

'What did George say?' Perez was intrigued too.

'He laughed and said that Miles could turn his hand to anything he wanted, but that his life was full of secrets. Which left me none the wiser. George did love a mystery though. He could have been joking at my expense, not expecting me to believe a word of it.'

'I'm here to pick your brains,' Perez said, 'about one of the people staying in Westray. He's not under suspicion at all, but because the story stones were used as murder weapons, I'm interested to know more about him. He's a professor of archaeology and he was on the island as a student when the stones were first discovered.'

'You're talking about Tony Johnson?'

'Yes, do you know him?'

There was a moment's hesitation. 'Not personally. I know *of* him. I'd heard he was in Westray.'

'Who told you he was there?'

Rutherford looked across his desk at Perez. 'George Riley. He phoned me from the island, early on the evening that Archie Stout died. Just for a gossip, he said.'

'You didn't mention that when I spoke to you last.'

'Didn't I? Of course I should have done. I suppose we were just talking about the story stones then. As I explained, George and I were friends. When he phoned, he told me he was stranded by the weather. He was bored, I think, though maybe he had other things on his mind.'

'Any idea what?'

Rutherford shook his head. 'Maybe he was just pissed off because he'd had to change his plans. His idea had been to spend half a day in Westray checking a few details for the kids' book he was writing and then be home for an evening with Miles. A decent meal and several glasses of very fine wine was more his notion of a good time than roughing it in the home of a former student.' Rutherford looked apologetic. 'Those are his words not mine.'

'Why didn't he stay at the Pierowall Hotel? They would have had rooms free, and he could have eaten there.'

'I asked him that. That was when he told me about Johnson. "The fraudster is there and the last thing I need is to spend time with him. At least Nat Wilkinson is a reformed character these days."'

'Do you know what he meant by that, "the fraudster"?'

There was a long silence. 'Within academic circles, I understand that there have been rumours. I come from the north-east of England, and I still have contacts in the region. Johnson is a professor at Durham. I did my master's degree there.'

Another silence. 'What sort of rumours?'

'That the paper he wrote on the story stone runes wasn't completely his own work. The feeling was that his sudden change of research focus meant that he couldn't have had the depth of understanding to produce the findings. At best he must have had help which he never credited – at worst all his ideas came entirely from someone else.'

'Did you pass on these rumours?'

Rutherford shook his head. 'It's a big step to accuse another man of plagiarism. His career would have been ruined, and I had no proof.'

'But George found out anyway?'

'He suspected that Johnson's work was appropriated from a local man, someone he'd got to know, an amateur with an obsession with Viking culture, who had hardly any formal education. Someone who'd lived and breathed the subject since he was a boy, who'd travelled to Scandinavia to follow up his studies and research the carvings there.'

'And the name of the man?' But Perez thought he knew. He'd seen the books and the maps in Nistaben when he'd stayed there as a boy. He remembered Archie's father as a calm, grey-haired man, a voracious reader during the dark winter evenings when there was little to do on the farm. Now it seemed he'd been a businessman too, buying a stake in the

Pierowall Hotel when it was in danger of closing. But, Perez thought, Magnus been more attracted to the tradition of the island than making money. His research into the history of Westray and his desire to keep the hotel, a valuable community hub, open had probably come from the same impulse.

'Magnus Stout, Archie's father.' Rutherford paused for breath, but his anger carried him on. 'Johnson didn't name Stout as a joint author or even acknowledge his help when the paper was published. He took all the credit for himself.'

'And Magnus didn't go public about being left out of the picture?'

Rutherford shook his head. 'I don't think he viewed it as a big deal. He was a Westray farmer who loved what he did, living on the island and bringing up his boys. He was grateful that Johnson had put the island on the archaeological map and glad that he'd contributed to its historical fame.'

'They stayed friends,' Perez said. 'Right until the end.' He looked across the desk at Rutherford. 'And nobody else challenged Johnson's findings?'

Rutherford shrugged. 'Who would have believed us? There's still so much intellectual snobbery in academia. Who would believe that an ill-educated farmer from Orkney could have made such a breakthrough?' There was another pause. Perez thought that Rutherford was choosing his words carefully. 'George was going to turn the intellectual theft into a story for his kids' book. Magnus was going to be the hero of the tale. The whole story would be told from his point of view. He said that Johnson would find it impossible to challenge the content of the book – after all, George could say it was only a story, or a theory – but at least local people would realize what had really happened.'

'Would an alternative narrative about the discovery of the translation of the runes in a children's book really damage Johnson's reputation?' Perez was sceptical.

Now Rutherford grinned. 'George had plans. Nothing he liked better than making mischief. He'd made a list of important academics, broadcasters, journalists – he had a lot of media friends away from the islands, he'd grown up in those sorts of circles – and he was going to send them all a proof copy. He'd already found a mainstream publisher willing to take on the book. Along with the proof, he planned to send a little note explaining the background. Johnson is something of celebrity now, with his television appearances and books, and journalists love a scandal. I think there might have been quite a stir among historians, but the story could well have spilled over more widely.'

'Had George made Johnson aware of those plans?'

Rutherford shrugged. 'That I don't know. But he was never particularly discreet. It's possible that word would have come out before the book was published. In fact, I think he was planning to send out proofs before it was available for sale.'

'At the very least,' Perez said, 'George might have discussed the idea with Archie?'

'Oh, I think so. He'd need Archie's blessing, wouldn't he, before stirring up such a hornets' nest? George was an honourable man. I don't think he'd have gone ahead without talking to Archie first.'

'You didn't mention this to me when we last met.' Perez tried to keep any element of judgement out of his voice. The last thing he needed was to guilt-trip Rutherford when he was being so helpful.

'Of course I should have done!' The guilt, it seemed, was

there without any help from Perez. 'It never occurred to me that a wrangle over intellectual copyright might cause the murder of a Westray farmer. It only seems relevant now with George Riley's murder.'

'Perhaps Johnson and Archie met that night.' Perez was running through possible scenarios. 'George didn't mention anything like that when he phoned? He hadn't seen them together?'

He thought that investigation was all about *what if*. Perhaps Archie realized for the first time just how much Johnson had stolen from his father – he and George would have met at the pier when the ferry came in. Archie was proud of the island's heritage, and he'd had a very short fuse. He'd been drinking all day and the resentment on his father's behalf could have grown until he'd demanded a meeting with Johnson. It was possible that *Archie* had removed the story stones from the heritage centre, a dramatic way of making his point, and that Johnson had grabbed one of them to kill his accuser.

'Sorry, no.' Rutherford was apologetic. 'It was just a chat. And I was cooking supper at the time. There was all sorts of noise going on with my kids in the background. I didn't realize that it might be important.'

'It probably isn't important, just something that I need to follow up. Can you give me a shout if anything else occurs to you?'

'Sure.' More than anything, Perez would like to be sitting with Willow in the old manse in Harray, throwing out ideas, reaching some sort of viable conclusion. But Willow was in Westray. And so was the man he suspected might have killed twice.

Chapter Twenty-One

WILLOW SAT ON THE HARBOUR WALL at Pierowall and listened with fascination to Perez's account of his conversation with Paul Rutherford. But she couldn't allow herself to be swept along by his enthusiasm, his certainty that he'd found a probable suspect. She knew that her antipathy to the professor was in danger of colouring her attitude to the man, triggering an unconscious bias, and she needed, above all things, to keep an open mind.

She and Phil had just arrived at the hotel after speaking to Rosalie Greeman. When the call came through from Perez, she waved at her colleague to carry on inside, mouthed: *See you in a bit* and stayed where she was, her back to the hotel, looking out over the still sea.

A creel boat was making its way slowly towards the jetty. Its outline was reflected in the water, every line clearly etched, a mirror image. It was so quiet that she could hear the cries of the gulls that followed it.

'I'm sorry, Jimmy, I just don't see it,' she said at last. 'Johnson and his wife were at Evelyn and Tom Angel's house that evening, weren't they? According to Evelyn they arrived at about six and stayed until the call came through from Vaila telling them that Archie had disappeared. I don't see how the man could have made it to the excavation and back without the Angels noticing. And James Grieve said there would have been blood on the killer's clothing. Tom and Evelyn would have noticed that.'

Willow could understand Perez's excitement, and she wished she could accept his theory. For the first time, he'd come up with something like a credible motive. Besides, she'd disliked the Johnsons on first meeting them and wouldn't have minded at all if they turned out to be involved in the murders. Better them than one of Perez's friends on the island. But policing wasn't about personal preference and practically she couldn't see how they might make this work.

Perez wasn't swayed by her argument. She could tell he was committed to his idea. Maybe dangerously committed. It wasn't like him to be so wedded to a notion that he might twist the facts to fit the story he'd created in his head.

'I've arranged to talk to Vaila,' he went on. 'Archie might have mentioned something about Johnson to her. Really, it's one of the few theories we have that explains both men's deaths.'

'But that doesn't get over the problem of opportunity.' She was almost shouting now, trying to get through to him. 'Johnson has an alibi.'

'Can you talk to Evelyn and Tom this afternoon? See if they might have made a mistake about what time the Johnsons arrived there.'

'Sure.' A pause. 'But they were certain. And what reason would they have to lie?'

Perez continued talking, his words only just catching up with his thoughts. He was usually considered, cautious, and the ideas tumbling straight from his brain surprised her. But of course, this was personal. Archie had been as close as a brother. 'Besides, I've been thinking about that. Even though Vaila might have *thought* Archie was missing when she first went into the bar, that doesn't mean he was already dead then, does it? He could have met up with George to get more details of the professor's scam and then accosted the Johnsons later. Or summoned the man to meet him. He'd have liked the drama of a meeting at the old excavation site. We know that Dr Grieve couldn't be precise about the time of Archie's death.'

'That's true!' For the first time, Willow felt a spark of optimism. This might work out. Perez had thought this through carefully after all. 'It would be interesting to know if the Johnsons received a phone call from Archie while they were at the Angels' for dinner. I'll talk to Evelyn and Tom before speaking to the Johnsons, just to see how it all might have worked out.'

Chapter Twenty-Two

After leaving the college, Perez had phoned Vaila's mobile. When she'd answered she'd sounded wary. She knew about George Riley's death – he'd asked Ellie to tell her what had happened soon after the body had been found – but it had been clear that she'd wanted to distance herself from the investigation.

'I'm sorry, Jimmy. I can't cope with this. Not now. I can't help you.'

'You wanted me to find out who had killed Archie. For the sake of the boys.'

'And have you?' The question had been blunt, forceful.

'There's a new line of inquiry. I think you'll be able to help us.'

'I don't know Jimmy. I'm at the stage where I just want to pretend none of this has happened. Lawrie is focused on the Ba' – that's all he talks about, strategies and plans, his way of coping, I guess – and Iain loses himself in the fantasies on his screen, and I just want to sleep and weep.'

'I'll come to you,' he'd said. 'To the hotel. Is that where you are?'

'Aye, that's where I am.'

'Let's have a late lunch. I doubt you've eaten. Just you and me. The boys will be okay?'

'Oh, the boys will be okay. Not in the long term of course, but for now.'

He phoned Willow to bring her up to date, drove back from the college into town and parked at the police station, then walked along the harbour front to the red-brick Victorian hotel. Vaila was waiting for him in reception, small and neat, inconspicuous. She seemed to have shrunk since he'd seen her last on Westray. It was very late to eat – service for lunch was nearly over – and the restaurant was cold and almost empty. They had a table by the window. She ordered without looking at the menu.

'Soup of the day and then haddock and chips.'

He'd expected her to choose something less hearty. She must have sensed his surprise because she gave a little smile and, once he'd ordered the same and the waitress had left, she continued. 'That's what I always had when Archie and I came in to Orkney mainland for some do or other and spent the night here. It's beyond me to come up with anything new. My brain won't function.'

He nodded to show he understood.

'What's all this about, Jimmy?'

'Do you know a man called Anthony Johnson?'

'The historian? Archie's dad knew him better than we did. You know how passionate Magnus was when it came to local history, and Tony stayed in their cottage when he was a student.'

'That's where Nat Wilkinson lives now?'

'Aye. Magnus took a kind of pleasure in seeing the professor become a bit of a celebrity.'

'It seems that Magnus did much of the work that made Anthony Johnson famous.'

'Oh, he'd have loved to hear that. I think he always considered himself a collaborator. Tony's assistant.'

'He wouldn't have been angry that Johnson took the credit for much of *his* original work?'

'Honestly, I don't think he would.' She paused while a young waitress brought the soup. 'Magnus wasn't a man with any sort of ego. He was self-taught. He watched Open University lectures on the television in the middle of the night when it first started, but never bothered taking the degree. He wanted the pleasure of knowledge, not any sort of recognition.'

'Would Archie have been angry on his behalf?'

There was a moment of silence. Vaila was an intelligent woman. Perez thought she'd be working through the implications of the question.

'You knew Archie, Jimmy. You probably knew him better than I did. He never minded having an excuse for his fury. I think he felt most alive when he could lose himself in righteous anger. And he loved his father, admired him more than anyone else in the world. Yes, he'd have been furious to think that Magnus hadn't been given proper recognition. I don't think he knew what had happened though. Certainly, he'd not given it any importance. He hadn't mentioned it to me.'

'It seems that George Riley intended to make all this public, by putting it into the children's book he was writing. Magnus would have been the hero of the story.' Perez set down his spoon and looked across at Vaila, but she said nothing and waited for him to continue. 'They would have met at the pier that morning,' he said. 'It's possible that George explained his suspicions about the stolen research to Archie. You said that he was in a strange mood when he came in. He didn't mention anything of George's theory?'

She shook her head. 'I was in a rush to get out. Besides, he might not have done, even if they'd had that conversation. Archie and me, we'd reached a point where we weren't speaking much. Or I wasn't listening to what he had to say. My mind was clouded with jealousy.' A pause. 'It's a terrible thing. The worst kind of sin.'

Perez didn't know how to respond to that. He didn't think there was anything he could say to make her feel better. Instead, he continued talking about his friend's last day:

'Everyone says that Archie's mood changed that morning. It's possible that he brooded over the slight to his family. And to the island. He'd discovered that it wasn't an outsider who made sense of the story stones, but a Westray man. His own father. I think he'd have found the deception unforgivable.'

Now Vaila did respond. 'He wasn't a man who found forgiveness easy.'

The comment sounded personal, about more than academic plagiarism, but Vaila didn't expand. Perez wondered if he should probe the matter further to find out if Vaila had behaved in a way that required forgiveness from her husband. He couldn't quite push the point though, because the woman was so emotionally frail now. He didn't want to scare her away, back to her room and her sons. Instead, he returned to his earlier point, realizing that this was a form of cowardice.

'You're quite sure that he didn't mention any of this to you?

You had dinner together that evening. He didn't tell you what he'd learned?'

Vaila shook her head. 'I knew that something was troubling him. He was so preoccupied. But I didn't ask. I thought it might have to do with Rosalie, and the boys were at the table with us. I didn't want a row about the woman in front of them.'

Perez nodded.

The waitress appeared to take the bowls and bring the fish. She had blue hair and a very short skirt and seemed full of joy and vigour. She stood for a moment chatting about the food, but their mood must have dampened hers, because she wandered back to the kitchen disheartened.

'What will you do now?' Vaila asked.

'Willow flew into Westray this morning. I've spoken to her about this. She'll talk to the man, see what he has to say for himself. We have no evidence, you see, and Johnson had very little opportunity to have committed the crime. Your parents have provided him with an alibi. He and his wife had supper with them at Hillhead that night. We need to look into that. See if the timings are remotely possible. But I wanted to ask if Archie had mentioned this at all, and to let you know how things are going.'

She'd been poking at her food, pulling back the batter to pick at the fish. 'That was kind, Jimmy. You always were a kind man. Too kind maybe for your own good. I'm glad you and Willow are so happy.' There was a wistful note to her voice.

He was thinking that she was still young and that she had a chance of happiness too, but he knew from his own experience after losing Fran that it was far too soon for her to consider something like that.

★ ★ ★

After the meal, Vaila refused the offer of coffee. 'I need to check on the boys.' He could tell that this was an excuse and that she wanted to escape again into her own space, her own memories, her own grief.

Perez walked back to the station along the icy pavements, but when he arrived there, he couldn't face going inside. Some of Vaila's depression had descended on him too. There would be the same end-of-term atmosphere as he'd found in the college. Someone would have brought cake. They'd be opening Secret Santa gifts and talking of family Christmases. Suddenly, he was missing Archie again more powerfully than ever and a wave of sadness washed over him. After Fran's death, Archie had flown in to Shetland to be with him. They'd sat together in the house by the shore, talking for hours. And later, he'd always been there, at the end of a phone to listen to Perez's pain. Perez thought he should be providing the same sort of comfort to Archie's wife, but his position was compromised. He couldn't just be her friend.

Instead of heading into the police station, Perez sat in his car until the windscreen had cleared and then drove back towards Finstown and Miles. The man had invited him to return, and George might have shared something of his plans for the Westray book with his lover.

Chapter Twenty-Three

WILLOW WENT ON HER OWN TO the Angels' farm. This wasn't a formal interview – in Scotland the police needed two officers to do that – and she didn't want the pair to feel awkward or on their guard, protective of their daughter. This should feel like a chat between friends.

She found Tom and Evelyn together in the smart Hillhead kitchen. The sun was already low behind the hill beyond the farm and the place was in shadow. Willow glimpsed the couple as she walked past the window. They seemed to be having an earnest conversation, heads almost together. They must have heard her footsteps, or sensed that she was there, because she saw them break apart suddenly, as if they'd been caught in a shameful or inappropriate activity. It occurred to her briefly that they might be in some form of collusion with the Johnsons, or that they had been asked to provide an alibi, but they'd both seemed so distressed by Vaila's loss of her husband, and their daughter's grief, that she couldn't believe they would do anything to protect a potential killer. It wasn't as if they were close friends of the professor and his wife.

Evelyn had opened the back door into the kitchen before Willow had a chance to knock.

'We saw you go past. You'd best come in.' It was hardly a welcome.

'I thought I should bring you up to date with the investigation.'

'We'd heard that George Riley had died. You know how news spreads. There was no need for you to traipse out here just to tell us that.'

Willow was surprised at the antagonism. The woman, who had seemed strong and competent, holding the family together after Archie's death, now seemed so tense and brittle that she might snap at any moment. Willow bent to take off her boots before going into the immaculate kitchen. Grief hadn't stopped Evelyn cleaning. 'Is everything okay?'

'I'm sorry.' Evelyn rubbed her face with her hand, as if she could wipe away the exhaustion. 'Neither of us have been sleeping. I know Vaila thought it was the right thing to do, to take the boys in to Kirkwall, but I'd rather she was here in Westray, where I can keep an eye on her. I imagine how low she must be. Maybe she thought they'd be safer there. Now there's been another death, and out in the mainland . . .' She stared at Willow, her face bleak. 'Things like this don't happen in Orkney.' Expressing horror and disbelief.

Oh, believe me, Willow thought, *things like this happen everywhere.*

They were standing just inside the door, and Evelyn remembered the island woman's duty of hospitality. 'Come along through and get warm. You have to look after yourself, with a bairn on the way.' Then there was the inevitable offer of tea, and a plate of beremeal shortbread appeared on the breakfast bar.

'How can we help you?' Tom Angel's words were polite enough, but the tone was wary, suspicious.

'How well do you know the Johnsons?'

'We explained all that when you were last here.' Now Tom sounded even more prickly. Willow thought stress would do that to you. She couldn't jump to conclusions.

'Had you ever heard rumours about how much Magnus Stout contributed to the professor's research?'

'Magnus was a history nerd, always with his head in some book or another. Tony Johnson was kind to him and made him feel he was useful. I thought he was pandering to his ego.' Tom was dismissive. Willow sensed there'd been rivalry between the two older men, or at least some jealousy on Tom's part if Magnus had been the acknowledged leader of the island. That happened sometimes in small communities.

'Some experts believe that Johnson took credit for research that had actually been done by Magnus.' Willow paused. 'Archie would have been angry if he'd thought his father hadn't been sufficiently recognized, that another man had got all the glory for discoveries that had been made by Magnus.'

'What are you implying?' Evelyn had been standing ready to take the kettle from the hotplate. She turned to face Willow, her eyes on fire, her voice shrill.

'Nothing.' Willow kept her voice even. She couldn't understand the couple's overreaction. Even though they were stressed and tired, it seemed out of all proportion. 'I'm asking questions, looking for a reason why two men might be dead. Accusations have been made and I have to follow them up. I was hoping that you might help me to get the facts straight.'

'Who's been making accusations?' Evelyn spat out the words.

'You know I can't tell you that.' Willow paused, wondered

how much she could give away. 'But George Riley had his suspicions about Johnson's research too, so you can see why I must follow this up. It links the two murders. I can't ignore that.'

'George Riley. He always seemed a strange sort of teacher to me. All that prancing around on the stage. Dressing up in women's clothes. Everyone says he's a fine man, but I'm not sure you could take anything he said too seriously.' Evelyn poured the hot water into a pot, her voice calmer now and her hands hardly shaking at all.

The woman was doing her best to appear reasonable, Willow thought, to regain control. And she was almost succeeding.

'Johnson can't have killed Archie,' Tom said. 'He was here with us all evening, until Vaila phoned to say that her man was missing. And I thought that Riley was found in Maeshowe?' A pause. 'The Johnsons have been staying here in Westray, in the Pierowall Hotel.' He spoke slowly and clearly as if stating the obvious to a small child.

'The Johnsons took the ferry out to Kirkwall the day that George Riley was murdered.' Willow was used to being patronized. It would take more than that to upset her. 'And of course I'd like to check the timings for the Johnsons' evening with you.' She made sure he was listening. 'We won't ever have an accurate time of death for Archie. It's not as it is in TV cop shows. Just because Archie wasn't in the bar of the hotel when Vaila arrived there, it doesn't mean that he was already dead.'

Now both Evelyn and Tom were sitting opposite her. She looked at each of them in turn, checking that they were taking in the implication of what she was saying.

'So I can't rule the Johnsons out as suspects.' Now she spoke clearly too. She had a right, she thought, to be a little patronizing herself. 'That's why I need to speak to you.'

Almost simultaneously, they nodded reluctantly. They understood why she was asking the questions, but they didn't like the premise.

'I know you told us what happened before, but I'd be very grateful if you could take me through that evening again. Evelyn, you start. You'd cooked a special meal. What time did the Johnsons arrive?'

'They were dead on time. Six o'clock, just as we'd said.'

Archie was still alive then, having supper with Vaila and the boys, so the Johnsons couldn't have killed him before they arrived.

'And what time did they leave?'

The pair looked at each other. 'Soon after Vaila called,' Tom said.

'Did she call your landline or mobile?'

'The mobile.' This time Evelyn answered. 'Through WhatsApp. We have terrible mobile phone reception here, but the broadband is fine, so people know to use that.'

'So you'll have a record of the exact time of the call on your phone. Would you mind checking for me? Whose phone did Vaila call?'

'Mine,' Evelyn said. 'I'll get it for you. It's just charging in the other room.'

She returned with a smartphone that was much more modern and flash than Willow's, opened it with her thumbprint and scrolled back to check the calls. Then she handed it to Willow. 'Five minutes to eight.'

'And they left almost immediately?'

Evelyn nodded. 'It was a wild night, so it took them a wee while to put on their outdoor clothes and say goodbye, but surely not more than ten minutes.'

'Thanks.'

George Riley's car would have been outside the hotel then. Had he changed his mind and decided that he should confront the Johnsons? Everything was confusing.

'Is that all?' Tom was becoming tense and resentful again.

'Just one question. Did either Tony or Barbara receive a phone call while they were with you?'

'Aye, Tony did.'

'I presume that was on his mobile. So it would have come through WhatsApp too, if your phone reception is poor.' Which, Willow thought, would be harder to trace, unless the professor decided to be cooperative.

'No,' Evelyn said. 'It came through as an ordinary call, and he struggled for a while to make out what the other person was saying. We told him to take it in the front bedroom because there's usually some reception there.'

'Did he tell you who the caller was?'

'No! And we wouldn't be cheeky enough to ask. Not our business.'

'He made me think that it was a work call,' Tom said. At last, the couple had thawed a little and now seemed willing to answer Willow's questions. 'When he came back downstairs, he said something like: "No rest for the wicked. And they make out it's an easy life in academia."' He looked across at the detective. 'That was the impression he wanted to give, that it was to do with the university.'

Willow stood up, aware of the baby and how much heavier she was feeling. She felt a moment of resentment at having to hoist herself down from the high stool. 'I'm sorry to have disturbed you. That's all been very helpful.' She stayed where she was for a moment. 'I'd be grateful if you'd keep this conversation confidential. Until I've talked to the Johnsons, and everything's been sorted out. In island communities it's so easy for stories to spread. I'd hate to ruin a good man's reputation.'

Evelyn answered almost immediately. 'Oh, we're used to keeping secrets in this house. It's the one thing we're good at.'

Willow wanted to ask the woman what she meant, but Evelyn had turned away to show her out, and when she stood by the door, waiting for Willow to put on her boots, her face was hard and blank. It was clear that she already regretted those words and intended to give nothing more away.

Chapter Twenty-Four

When Miles opened the door to Perez, he looked rough. The hangover he'd predicted must have lasted all day. It was late afternoon, but the man was still in pyjamas and a frayed tartan dressing gown, with slippers on his feet. He hadn't shaved and his face was grey.

'Ah, Inspector, to what do I owe the pleasure?' The words were still formal, but today he seemed glad to see Perez. If the detective hadn't appeared, perhaps he knew he would start drinking again. 'I'm afraid you don't find me at my very best, but do come in.'

He led Perez through the house and into the kitchen. It was uncluttered and tidy. Perez suspected he'd been drinking in the grand living room where they'd talked the day before, and the debris of empty bottles and snack wrappers would be there. He'd probably fallen asleep on the comfortable sofa. Perez would have behaved in exactly the same way after Fran had died if he hadn't had her daughter Cassie to look after, to hold him together.

'I've just made coffee,' Miles said. 'Do help yourself while I go and make myself respectable.'

The man was gone for longer than Perez had expected. It was quite dark outside by the time he returned. He'd showered and shaved and was wearing corduroy trousers, a flannel shirt and a hand-knitted sweater. The country gentleman in mufti. He went to the range where the coffee pot had been standing and poured himself a cup.

'I suppose you have more questions. But do you have any information?'

'A little information, which has led to more questions.'

'Go ahead!' The man must have spoken like this, Perez thought, to his subordinates. He could have been an army officer demanding information. The shower seemed to have cleared his head. He was sharp. Focused.

'A professor of history called Anthony Johnson is staying on Westray. I wonder if George ever mentioned him.'

'Oh, he did, especially recently, and never in a complimentary way. Most of his comments are unrepeatable. George had a wide and varied vocabulary when it comes to insults. A good university education can do that for you.'

'George thought that Johnson had stolen much of his research from Archie Stout's father, Magnus,' Perez said.

'Ah, that's why I recognized your other victim's name! I thought it was familiar when you first came looking for George. I knew about Magnus of course. He was the main player in the story. And I knew he had a son, but I don't think George mentioned what he was called.'

'George did suspect that Johnson was a plagiarist?' Perez kept his voice even. He didn't want to influence his witness.

'He didn't just suspect. He *knew*.'

'George had proof?' Again, Perez tried to keep the urgency from his voice.

'Magnus's son came to see him in school a couple of months ago. That was how George referred to him. Always as Magnus's son.'

Perez nodded to show that he didn't blame Miles for not making the connection to Archie earlier. Miles continued talking.

'In fact, it was a little longer ago than that, because it was at the beginning of the school term. The new head had just started, and George was finding life a little less easy-going than under the last one. It was parents' evening, so officially Stout was there to talk about *his* sons, but he'd brought a box of notebooks and papers that he'd found at the back of a cupboard. His father's research. The notebooks were all dated, so it was clear to George that the initial translation of the runes on the story stones had come from Magnus. He'd done all the research about the presence of Vikings in the islands, before Johnson had shown any interest in the topic.'

'George didn't confront Johnson then?'

Miles shook his head. 'He wanted to get his facts straight before accusing a prominent academic of stealing another man's research. But then, in October, a television documentary aired to a lot of publicity. It was a history of the Northern Isles – Orkney and Shetland – fronted by Johnson. There he was, looking out from the screen being smug and professorial, with the beautiful island landscapes behind him. All the material he used to confirm his theories about the Westray archaeology had been taken directly from Magnus Stout, but the Westray man's name wasn't mentioned once. In fact, the islanders came across as ignorant farmers who hadn't realized the importance of the excavations on their land.' Miles looked out at Perez. 'I've never known George so furious.'

'Even though he wasn't personally involved?' Perez thought it was unusual to feel such anger on another person's behalf. This seemed too abstract a subject to be worked up about.

'But he *felt* involved.' Miles paused, pulling together the words so he could explain. 'It *felt* personal. History mattered to him. George might have appeared flippant and carefree, and in lots of ways he was, but he thought history was about truth. How could we understand the world if our knowledge of it was based on lies? He felt Johnson's rewriting of history like a kick in the gut. He said it wasn't just about the past, but about the way Westray people were regarded in the present. Political decisions were made on the basis of facts provided by historians.' Miles was becoming more and more animated. He stopped and pulled a little face. 'I'm sorry to sound so passionate. It's not my default setting and it feels a little odd to become so emotional. But now he's dead, I suppose I feel I should take on George's mantle. Protect his legacy.'

He got to his feet, stood with his hands resting on the edge of the deep, old-fashioned sink, and looked out of the window into the darkness, towards the garden where he spent so much of his time. Perez thought he needed a moment to gather his thoughts. Or once again perhaps he wanted to hide the fact that he was crying. When he turned back into the room, though, he was dry-eyed.

'Did George tell you that the Johnsons were staying in Westray the day that Archie Stout was killed?' Because he'd told Rutherford and explained that was why he'd spent the night with Nat Wilkinson.

'No!' Miles Chambers seemed genuinely shocked.

'I'd have thought he might have mentioned it.'

'I told you, Inspector, George and I hardly spoke to each other once he returned from the island. I was sulking. And George would have waited until we had time to talk it through properly. He'd know I'd find the story entertaining. He could make anything entertaining, and he loved an attentive audience.' Miles looked across at Perez. 'Do you think Johnson killed George? To stop him publishing his book?'

'It's one theory. The one thing that links Archie and George is that they believed Johnson was a fraud. But we have no proof.'

'I'll publish the book on George's behalf,' Miles said suddenly. 'You can tell Johnson that.'

'I'm not sure that would be a sensible idea.'

'You think Johnson would kill me too?' Miles gave a little laugh that was more sinister than the question. 'I'd like to see him try.' There was a moment of silence before he repeated, with more venom: 'I'd *really* like to see him try. That would give me a legitimate excuse to hurt him.'

'As I said, we have no proof that Johnson was involved in George's murder at all, so please don't do anything foolish.' Perez wondered if he'd made a terrible mistake talking like this to Miles, if Archie's death had coloured his judgement. The conversation had run into a direction he regretted now, and there was something frightening in the man's anger. Perez believed that Miles had the ability to be entirely ruthless. Violent even. 'Besides, if you confront the professor, you might frighten him off. He could get rid of all the evidence we need to get a conviction.'

Miles held up his hands, a gesture of surrender. 'I'm not a foolish man, Inspector. I promise that.'

'Would you be able to recreate the book? Do you have the box of Magnus's notes, which Archie gave to George?'

Miles shook his head. 'I don't have them. I'm pretty sure he planned to take the originals to Westray with him on that last trip. He thought they belonged in the heritage centre there. That was their true home.'

Perez made a mental note to tell Willow that, as soon as he was alone. They knew George had been given a key to the heritage centre by Vaila, but surely he'd have told someone that the notes were there. He wouldn't just have dropped them at an unmanned reception desk. They were too valuable for that.

Miles interrupted Perez's thoughts. 'He made copies though. He scanned them all. They're on his computer in the study upstairs. The book is almost finished. He just wanted a few more details from people in Westray. He'd sent a first draft to his publisher. I'm his executor, he left everything to me. I've seen the will. I can give permission for publication to go ahead.'

'Can you email the notes across to me? I'd like Orkney's archaeologist to take a look at them.'

'Of course.' A pause. 'I met Paul Rutherford a few times through George. They were friends. He seems a decent chap.'

'Did George know that Anthony Johnson was staying on Westray before he set out? I know that he found out once he was on the island.'

Miles shook his head. 'I don't think so. He'd have prepared for battle if he had. As I remember, the visit was more routine than that. He was there as a teacher, working on his kids' book, not to champion the name of Magnus Stout. That was how it seemed to me, at least. Giving Magnus the credit he deserved would come later. George wanted the heritage centre to have the notebooks, and he might have discussed his ideas with Archie, but I don't think he was expecting a confrontation with Johnson. Not yet.'

Miles was still standing. Perez got to his feet too. 'Thanks for all your help.'

'Not at all, Inspector.' There was a pause. 'It's been a welcome distraction.'

They walked together into the hall, with its curved staircase, and faded paintings in tarnished gilt frames. 'Paul Rutherford might come to visit you,' Perez said. 'Would you mind that?'

Miles shook his head. 'He might be willing to help form a plan to tell the truth about the Westray story stones. Another documentary perhaps, putting the record straight. George would have loved that. Besides, a visit from Rutherford would be a kind of distraction too.'

Perez nodded and left the house. Outside, the air smelled a little different. It had lost the scent of iron and ice that came from extreme cold, carried by winds from Siberia. It was softer, gentler and his windscreen was clear.

He drove to Alison's house to pick up his son. The pair were curled together on the sofa, and she was reading a story to him. There was a decorated tree in the corner and a fire had been lit. When Perez got home, the house felt empty and cold.

Chapter Twenty-Five

Willow listened to Perez's account of his conversation with Miles. If the CSIs had found anything at all to place Johnson at the crime scene, she felt they'd have more than enough for a formal charge, but because of the storm on the night of the murder there was no trace evidence.

'I'm not going to get back to Harray this evening,' she said. 'You do realize that we have to speak to the Johnsons about this before I leave.'

She could sense Perez's disappointment, but he said nothing. He'd know she was right. Johnson's motive might be strong, but there was nothing to convict him. In her room in the hotel she was running through possibilities. To make a charge stick, they'd need a witness or a confession. Barbara could be a witness if she decided to cooperate. She must have had knowledge of what happened that night. But why *would* she cooperate? She had almost as much to lose as her husband if he were to fall from grace, and Willow suspected that Barbara would be harder to break down. She was a performer. She worked with actors and storytellers, and she did all the publicity for the community arts centre that she ran. Her job was to manage the narrative, to portray the place in the best possible light.

Willow was convinced that the next meeting with the Johnsons would be crucial, and she didn't rush into arranging to speak to them. She discussed her plans with Phil Bain, as they sat waiting for their evening meal. It was still early, but she'd had a long day, and she found her focus shifting, sliding from one possible approach to another.

'I'm not sharp enough to talk to them tonight. Let's arrange to do it in the morning. Not here though. Somewhere more formal.'

'Where were you thinking?'

'How about the heritage centre? It's only open at weekends in the winter, so we won't be disturbed. Annie can give us a key, and make sure the heating's on. And I'd like to talk to them separately. Tony first, I think. They're both arrogant. They'll underestimate us and think they can bluff their way through.'

'Shall we see them this evening though? Just to make an appointment to talk to them?'

'Why not? Let's rattle them a bit. I'll sort it.' Willow got to her feet. She was finding the hotel claustrophobic now. The darkness outside seemed to be closing in, and she was feeling restless, uneasy. Even a wander to the bar would provide some movement and a brief change of scene. When she pushed open the door, she didn't recognize any of the locals there, though Perez would probably know most of them. There was no sign of the professor and his wife. Godfrey, the elderly widower, was sitting in his usual corner, his back to the room, repelling any overtures of company. His half-pint of bitter sat, almost untouched, on the table in front of him. He turned when he heard her approach, smiled and seemed almost glad to see her.

'Inspector. I saw you were at the cathedral. That must have been your little boy. What a wonderful service! Edith and I always loved it.'

'Yes.' Willow pulled across a chair and sat beside him. 'It's rather terrible to think that George Riley was being killed that afternoon too.' She looked straight at him. 'Did you come across George while you were here? You were working on similar projects.'

'I did meet him once. It was on the morning that poor Archie Stout died. He'd come over on the ferry. It was just before the storm hit. I was taking a photo of the links. The beach there is a great place for sanderling, the little wading birds.' Godfrey smiled. 'Such comical little creatures. They run like clockwork toys.'

'And George was there too?' Willow tried not to sound impatient.

'He was. Staring at the former dig site. It looks so ugly. All that black plastic weighed down with old tyres. Like a dump or an abandoned building site. He was taking photos too. We talked for a while.'

'What about?'

'The island and what a special place it is. He explained that he was a teacher, and he loved what he did, that it was a privilege to shape young minds.' Godfrey paused for a moment. 'After a while, he seemed a little troubled. I asked if anything was wrong, and he became jolly again. "Nothing that can't be put right," he said. We walked together for a way along the beach. He told me stories of the Neolithic people who'd lived on the site and then the Vikings who arrived centuries later. I was entranced. I could see that he'd be a magnificent teacher and I told him so.'

'What happened then?'

'George said he was meeting someone, and he peeled away. He'd brought his car with him, and I suppose he'd parked it somewhere close by. I walked back to Pierowall to the cafe for a bite of lunch. I'd asked if he was staying at the hotel – I would have been glad to hear more about his work – but he said he'd met a former student on the ferry, and he was staying with him.'

Willow nodded. All this confirmed the theory that Riley was planning to expose Tony Johnson. She was about to offer to buy Godfrey a drink – although his glass was still half full – when the Johnsons came in. The locals all recognized them now and shouted their greetings. The couple seemed to bask in the recognition. Willow imagined them back at home, boasting to their friends.

Oh yes, we're part of the island now. We're not treated like visitors at all.

None of us like to admit that we're tourists, Willow thought. We're all travellers these days.

Johnson saw Willow and waved across to her. 'Inspector, so you're back.'

She got close enough to him so the other drinkers couldn't quite listen in.

'Perhaps you've heard,' she said. 'There's been another murder, so I'm afraid there will be more questions.'

'Of course! George Riley, the teacher. But naturally we hardly knew him.' There was a tight, impatient smile.

'I'm talking to everyone.' Willow didn't respond to the words. 'I'd like to see you in the heritage centre at nine-thirty. You too, Mrs Johnson. Though perhaps you could come along a little later. We'll have a word with you after we've spoken to your husband.' A pause. 'Please don't be late.'

Johnson was about to protest, to make an excuse, but Willow jumped in before he could speak. 'I'm investigating two deaths and I believe that you can both help me with my inquiries. I'll either talk to you here in Westray, or I'll require you to come in to Kirkwall for a more formal interview in the police station there. It's entirely your decision.'

She waited a moment for an answer and when none came, she nodded and turned away.

After they'd eaten, Willow looked for Annie. Bill was serving behind the bar.

'I've sent her home to rest,' he said. 'The lasses can manage fine by themselves in the restaurant, and it's been manic all week. She needs a bit of a break.' A pause. 'Pop in to see her though, if it's important. We're just a couple of doors away.'

Willow pulled on her jacket and went outside. There was a milkiness to the sky, which meant she saw the stars as if through a filter. It seemed that the weather was changing at last. The air wasn't so sharp that it took her breath away. The MacBrides' house was a small cottage, one of a terrace. It still wasn't late, but she hoped that Annie hadn't taken herself to bed for a very early night.

It seemed though that Annie was expecting her. 'Bill texted to say you were on your way.'

'It seems a pity to interrupt you on your one night off, but I need your help.'

'Ah, come away in. I'm not much good at resting and there's nothing at all on the television.'

The room was small and warm. There were photographs of beaming grandchildren on the walls. Annie had already made tea and in the little time it had taken Willow to get there, she'd set out a plate with oatcakes and local cheese. 'The tea's decaff,' she said. 'I can never drink the real stuff after lunchtime, and I know you prefer it.'

'I hadn't realized that Archie had a share in the hotel.' Willow wasn't sure if that was at all significant to the investigation, but the fact had lurked at the back of her mind, troubling. 'Did it cause any problems?'

At first, she thought there would be a tactful, anodyne response, but here alone in her own home, Annie felt more able to speak freely.

'He never let us forget that he was part owner. And he never paid for a single drink after Magnus died.' A pause. 'There was a kind of entitlement, you know, and it rankled. Bill could shrug it off, but I couldna. It felt disrespectful to Bill. Archie wouldn't have tried it on if we'd both been born and raised here, but because Bill's a new islander, somehow Archie felt he had the right. I wouldn't have minded so much if he'd offered to help behind the bar when we were rushed off our feet, but he just sat there, playing the fool, entertaining his audience.' She looked up and smiled. 'And now I feel bad for speaking ill of the dead.'

'Really . . .' Willow sipped at the tea and took an oatcake. 'I'm here about George Riley.'

'Aye, I thought you might be.' Annie shook her head. 'He was a lovely man. He taught our three.'

'He was writing a children's book.' Willow paused for a moment. 'Apparently, it wasn't just for kids.'

'Ah, so you know about his great crusade to give old Magnus the credit he's due.'

'I've been told a little. It would be useful to hear what you know about all that.'

'I had George in here about a month ago, sitting where you are, telling me about his plans.'

'What did you think about them?'

'I thought that Magnus wouldn't have wanted all the fuss. He didn't do that research for the glory, but because he loved it. It was an escape into a different world.' She smiled. 'Now, the island bairns escape into fantasy worlds on their computers, but then, in his head, Magnus was living with the Vikings, who came into Westray and discovered the Neolithic mounds, built all those centuries before. Those chambers must have seemed like magic to those people arriving in their longboats from the sea.'

'But George *did* care that Magnus got the credit due to him.'

'He did. I thought it was unhealthy, a bit of an obsession. It felt like revenge, though I'm not quite sure what Johnson might have done to harm him, why he had the urge to hit back. Or maybe it was jealousy, because here was Johnson, who only blew into the islands occasionally, acting as if he understood everything there was to know about the place. George always liked the starring role. It wasn't as if he and Magnus were particularly good friends.'

'Archie Stout found Magnus's notebooks and thought George would be interested. That was what started the whole thing off.'

Annie shot a glance across at Willow. 'So that's the way your mind is working, is it? That this research into ancient stones linked both the dead men.'

'I can't find much else.'

There was a silence, then footsteps on the pavement outside the house. Drinkers perhaps calling it a night and making their way home.

'This isn't to be spread around the island, Annie. I know you understand. It's speculation at this point.'

The woman nodded. 'I'll not even chat to Bill about it. They say women gossip, but . . .' She looked up, caught Willow's eye, and they both grinned.

'You do a great job of servicing the hotel rooms. Your lasses would notice anything unusual.'

Annie nodded again. 'Maybe, though they'd not pry. They don't do a real clean until they're preparing for a new set of guests.'

'I'm wondering about bloodstained clothing. Nobody's asked you to do laundry?'

Annie shook her head. 'We don't offer a service wash, and the girls would have mentioned if they'd seen anything. Like I said, they'd not be prying into wardrobes or drawers.'

'Of course.' And any soiled clothes would be gone by now, put into a bag, weighed down with stones and thrown into the sea. Willow changed tack. 'Did you see George that day? The day Archie disappeared. His friend, Miles, says he intended to bring the notebooks into the heritage centre for safekeeping. Or because that was the place they should be held, where the community could have access to them.'

'Aye, I met him in the centre. It had all been arranged. He wanted a meeting, but I was too busy to spend long with him. We were hosting the old folks' lunch in the hotel, and I wanted everything to be grand for them.'

'You did meet George though?'

Annie nodded. 'He was there before me. He'd picked up a key from Vaila, or I think from Archie, when the ferry arrived at Rapness.'

'He gave you Magnus Stout's notebooks?'

She nodded. 'As if they were the Crown Jewels! He asked if we had a safe. I said they'd be fine in the room where we keep all the archive material, and that the building was kept locked. Who was going to steal a bunch of old notebooks?'

'Were the story stones still there then?'

Annie frowned. 'Do you know, I'm not sure. I was all in a fluster, wanting to get shot of George, who was bursting to tell me a long story of his own. I told him the details would have to wait. He could tell me in the bar later that night. But he said he'd heard Johnson was staying, so he wasn't going to set foot in the place.' She looked up at Willow, who was helping herself to more tea. 'I thought he was making mountains out of molehills.' A little grin. 'Bill always did call him the drama queen.'

'You knew he was gay?'

'Of course. And that's no big deal these days, is it? Bill's idea of a silly joke. No harm meant.'

'You didn't take the key from him?'

'No, he said he'd hang on to it and drop it back to Nistaben when he was finished. He wanted to get some work done and the centre would be a quiet place to do it. I left the heating on for him.'

'And that was the afternoon?' Willow wasn't sure that she could make the timings for this hang together. 'Not later in the evening. His car was seen outside the hotel until gone eight o'clock, and apparently there was a light on in the heritage centre.'

Annie shook her head. 'I suppose he could have left the door unlocked and come back later to work on his project.'

'I suppose he could.'

Willow wondered about that. Perhaps George had been so obsessed with his ideas of providing justice for Magnus that he'd wanted to update his work immediately. Or perhaps he'd wanted to avoid small talk with Nat Wilkinson who might be kind, but not the most entertaining of hosts.

'Did you put the books into the archive room,' she asked, 'or did he do it?'

'He did! At least, I suppose he did. I just left him to get on with it and came back to the hotel.' She set down her cup. 'Should we go and see if they're there?'

Willow shook her head. 'No need for that.' She could tell that the last thing Annie wanted was to go out in the cold again. 'If you can let me have your key though . . . I've arranged to see the Johnsons there in the morning and I can check then.'

But once she was outside, Willow decided she would check the heritage centre now. It would be better to do it alone. Besides, she couldn't quite face going back into the hotel, with the brightly coloured Christmas decorations, the enquiring glances and the laughter spilling from the bar and the dining room. Perez would be putting their son to bed, so it would be too early to talk to him again.

The heritage centre was purpose-built, smart, right next door to the hotel. Willow unlocked the door, switched on the light and went inside. This was more than a collection of the locals' objects and recorded anecdotes, though there were some of those too. She thought it was classic Westray. Anything the island decided to do, it did well. The labelling and information displays were as professional as in any small museum.

THE KILLING STONES

Willow was distracted for a moment by the exhibits: the tiny figure of the Westray Wife, the oldest depiction of a human form in the UK, then the story of the wrecked ship that had given Archie and the Angels their names.

At last, she walked through into the archive centre, a room with shelves on three of the walls, loaded with a collection of books, journals and articles. And there, on one of the shelves, stood a small square box full of notebooks. Each had Magnus Stout's name on the front, and each was dated. Willow stood for a moment, wondering what this could mean. It wasn't what she'd expected. Johnson might have killed Archie and George, but here the evidence of his fraud remained. Johnson wasn't a stupid man. Surely he must realize that even with both men dead, these books meant that his theft of Magnus's research could still come back to haunt him.

There was a noise outside. Willow walked through to the reception desk. Perhaps somebody had seen the lights on and come in to investigate. But nobody appeared and when she'd locked the door and walked back to the street, it was empty.

Chapter Twenty-Six

JAMES'S NURSERY WAS IN THE HARRAY community hall, not very far from the old manse. It was run by a couple of motherly women, helped by some younger lasses. Willow loved it because they got the bairns outside as much as they could, wrapped up against the cold in the winter, scooting around on the trikes and the bikes, climbing on the play equipment.

Each day Perez went there were fewer parents queuing outside the building, fewer excited children; everyone, it seemed, was winding down for Christmas. The school had closed days before and now this was just a service for working parents. When he dropped James off, he felt a little guilty. Perhaps the boy should have been home too.

In the police station, he found Ellie. He'd asked her to go through Archie's phone records again. She was clearly resentful.

'Did he call Johnson's mobile on the night he died?'

'No, he didn't make any calls that night.' She was quite certain and the Yorkshire accent was more pronounced than ever. 'I'd have flagged it up to you if he had.'

'Any way of getting a record of the call Johnson received when they were at the Angels' house?'

'I've contacted his service provider. They're reluctant. We don't have a warrant and we haven't charged him.'

Frustration was digging away at her too, and she thought he was questioning her ability or commitment. Perez softened his tone. It wasn't the woman's fault that they couldn't find a more direct link between Archie and the professor.

'What about from the Nistaben landline? Archie was at home for a few short periods that day, and most Westray folk depend on that because mobile reception's so poor.'

'I've checked that too. Of course.'

'Of course. You will have done.' Perez could sense his theory slipping away. Johnson and Archie *could* have met in person during the day, they *could* have arranged to meet later at the site of the dig, but without any evidence, it would be impossible to move the case forward.

'What do you want me to do now?' Ellie was still feeling truculent.

'Let's see if we can track the movements of all the Westray folk who were on the Orkney mainland on the afternoon that George was killed. We can check the restaurants where they claim to have eaten, the bars where they say they drank. There should be credit card records.' Perez thought his voice sounded as it did when he was trying to jolly James out of a tantrum. Ellie deserved better than that, but he'd promised Vaila that they'd find Archie's killer. Christmas, the day of the Ba' when they'd all be celebrating Archie's life, had felt like a kind of deadline. Now, it seemed certain that he'd fail.

'You take Kirkwall,' he said. 'I'll go to Stromness. See if you can put together a timeline for the Johnsons once they drove off the ferry. We need a gap when they might have gone to Maeshowe. Without that, we have no case at all against them.' He wanted to show Ellie that he had faith in her – this was the more important task after all – but he had his own reasons for choosing to work in Stromness. He felt the need to be somewhere different and alone and to open his mind to the possibility of other suspects. It was dangerous to be too fixed on one theory. Willow was right about that.

Rosalie Greeman had claimed to be in Stromness hoping to sell her crafts to the gallery there and she'd said that she'd called in to the cafe next door for her lunch beforehand. He could check the time. Willow had described her wearing a bright patchwork jacket. That wouldn't be easy to miss. Besides, the drive could have taken Rosalie past the entrance to Maeshowe. There might be regular walkers who parked in the place. Someone might have seen her car. Perez had a strange superstition that just passing the site might trigger some new idea, some other possibility.

His mood lifted a little as he drove out of the town, and the landscape opened out. He drove slowly and pulled in from the busy main road to the Tormiston Mill car park, with its view of the loch and the archaeological sites. An older woman was getting out of a Land Rover. She wore wellingtons, a tweed skirt and a waxed waterproof jacket. A headscarf that gave her the appearance of the late Queen. She opened the back door and a dog jumped out and raced around her, barking.

'Betsy, be quiet!' No Orcadian in the accent, but that meant little. She might be local but educated elsewhere. She had that look about her. Confident. Entitled. Once, maybe, she'd been the daughter of a laird.

Perez approached and the dog jumped up at him. 'Betsy!' The woman had a voice that would have carried all the way to the Stones of Stenness, but the dog took no notice. 'I'm sorry,' she said, the sound gruff as a bark. 'She's still a puppy. Not properly trained yet.'

Perez introduced himself. The woman looked at him sharply. 'You'll be here about poor George Riley's murder.'

'You knew George?' Perez could see that the two people might be friends, or at least that they might move in the same circles.

'We served on some of the same committees.'

Perez nodded. He could tell that she'd be a formidable committee member. He asked for her name.

'Thorne,' she said. 'Belinda Thorne. I was here that afternoon. I saw him drive in. I wanted to talk to him about the local history society agenda, but Betsy was getting impatient for her walk and in the end I just waved.' There was a pause. 'I've been going over it in my mind, that I could have walked with him towards Maeshowe, stayed with him there. Then he'd still be alive, but I wasn't to know, was I?'

She looked at him, suddenly vulnerable, wanting reassurance.

'No,' he said. 'Of course you weren't to know.' He looked across the road towards the burial chamber, his view blocked for a moment by a passing truck. 'Was anyone else here? Other cars? Other walkers?'

She shook her head. 'It was bloody freezing. Anyone in their right mind would have stayed indoors.' She patted the dog's head. 'But we're not quite in our right minds, are we, Betsy?'

'What time was this?'

'About one-thirty. I'd been listening to the radio on my way here. *The World at One*. It was still running.'

Perez thought about that. So George had arrived an hour before he'd arranged *their* meeting. Lucy Martindale had said he'd had to rush out to see someone. Presumably his killer.

'And when you came back from your walk? Was the car park empty then too?'

She shook her head. 'Despite the cold it was a beautiful day, and we were out for an hour and a half. I wanted to tire the rascal out. There was another car parked here when we returned.' She paused, looked across at him and smiled. 'Your car.'

His hopes had been raised for a moment, but he smiled back at her. 'Of course,' he said again.

The dog was tugging at its lead, so desperate to move now that it almost pulled her over. Quickly, he handed her his card. 'If you remember anything, please ring.'

'Of course.' She slipped the card into her pocket and was dragged across the main road, only just missed by a passing van.

He found the Stromness gallery open, and Grace, the manager, in the ground-floor reception area. Perez knew her – she was a friend of Willow's. The women had met in the Kirkwall library reading group and bonded over a passion for translated crime fiction.

'Jimmy! Are you in search of a piece of art for the manse? Feel free to wander around. It's exhibition time and we have some wonderful local pieces.'

He shook his head. 'It's work. I have a few questions if you have time to chat.'

'Sure. I'm hardly rushed off my feet. Lots of people are looking but not so many buying just now.'

'Do you know Rosalie Greeman?'

'The English maker who lives in Westray? Yes, I love her stuff.'

'You'll have heard that George Riley died?'

'Of course! What a miss he'll be. Such energy. And a wonderful teacher. He inspired Orkney kids to look at the place in a different way. He ran a series of lectures for me here in the gallery. I wasn't sure how it would work, but we had a full house every time. The most popular was his history of the Ba' talk. He'd discovered old photos, none of which I had seen before.' Grace shot a glance at Perez, suddenly suspicious. 'You don't think Rosalie had anything to do with his death?'

Perez shook his head. 'No, but we're checking on everyone who was in Westray when Archie Stout died and on mainland when George was killed. The two murders are connected. Rosalie is just one of those people. It's a process of elimination.'

A grandmother holding the hand of a small child came in, followed by a blast of cold air.

Grace waved to them. Perez waited until they'd moved through to the exhibition space before continuing the conversation.

'Rosalie claims that she came here that day, to show you some of her samples, but that you'd already left when she arrived. I need to check where she was, along with all the others. You do understand? It was the day of the St Magnus carol service.'

Grace nodded. 'I *did* leave early that day.' She smiled, pleased that she could confirm Rosalie's story. 'She dropped in a few samples with Robbie at the desk. Some lovely pieces. And she left me a phone message later that day, saying she'd been along, and asking if she could make an appointment for the New

Year so she could discuss her stuff. I phoned her back the next morning.'

'Great, that's all I needed. Thanks.' But really, he knew, this didn't prove Rosalie's innocence. She'd still have had time to kill Riley before driving to the gallery. They only had the jeweller's word that she'd had lunch in Stromness beforehand. Leaving the phone message for Grace just added a little veracity to the narrative. He made his way outside and into the cafe a couple of doors down. If they'd served Rosalie at a time before Belinda the dog woman had met George Riley in the Tormiston Mill car park, close to Maeshowe, that might put the jewellery maker in the clear.

It was busy with the early lunchtime rush. The cafe had laid on a Christmas dinner special – turkey with all the trimmings. He thought it odd that people might want a meal like that so close to the day itself, but they were doing a brisk trade. He waited at the counter, hoping to speak to the manager, but the staff all seemed rushed off their feet, and he felt awkward about disturbing them. They wouldn't be able to focus on his questions while people were becoming impatient, waiting for their meals. Instead, he decided that he'd come back later – if Rosalie had eaten there it would have been early in the afternoon – and walked outside again, feeling guilty because he should be back in Kirkwall. This felt like an escape.

In the distance he could see the car ferry from Scrabster, making its way into the harbour. It was the route that George Riley had taken from his conference on the Scottish mainland when freezing fog closed the airports. Perez tried to open his mind to any other way that he and Archie might have been connected. He'd been so sure that Johnson was involved, and certainty was always dangerous. Perhaps, after all, the obvious reason was most likely: George Riley had witnessed something leading up to Archie's killing and so he'd had to die.

Chapter Twenty-Seven

That morning, Willow went into the heritage centre half an hour early for her appointment with Johnson. She wanted to look through Magnus Stout's notebooks before the professor arrived. But when she went into the archive room to take down the box, there was no sign of it. The low sun slanted through the window, and even with the lights switched off, she couldn't have missed it. She stared at the shelf where it had been, wondering for a brief moment if she was quite sane, if she'd imagined it being there the night before. But she could picture the box vividly: blue cardboard, which might once have held a pair of shoes, with its neat stack of books inside. Somebody must have come in and removed it.

Then she considered who *could* have taken it. She'd locked the door the previous evening. Again, the memory was clear. She heard the click of the lock and pictured herself pulling on the handle to make sure that the door was firmly shut. And with that came another memory, the sense that someone else was close by. So whoever came in must have had a key, unless there was a different entrance. Perhaps the person she'd heard, who'd been waiting for her to leave. She walked briskly around the centre. None of the windows were open and the emergency exit at the back of the building was locked too.

Time was moving on. Soon Tony Johnson would be here, and she needed to prepare herself for the interview. There was a tap on the door. Not Johnson but Phil Bain, whom she'd asked to sit in on the conversation.

She explained what had happened: 'I can't see the disappearance of the notebooks as a game-changer. They've been saved in digital form and can still be used in evidence. Miles told Jimmy that he could retrieve them. Johnson might not know that though. He might think he's in the clear now, and that we have no evidence of his fraud.'

'Show's he's panicking, doesn't it?' Phil said.

'Certainly does.'

Willow arranged the furniture in the space where the archives were kept. She set it up like a classic interview room. A table with a chair at one side and two chairs opposite for her and Phil. She was still angry with herself – she should have taken Magnus Stout's notebooks into safekeeping – but took some breaths to slow her pulse and calm her nerves. Her mother had been a great proponent of meditation, and that was something else that Willow had brought with her from the commune, the power of slow breathing.

She'd expected Johnson to be late. He was arrogant and rude, and he'd see making her wait as a way of asserting his authority, but after fifteen minutes of waiting, she sent Phil Bain to find him.

Phil was back almost immediately. 'They've gone.'

'What do you mean?'

'Bill says they checked out this morning and were on the early ferry.'

'He's not expecting them back?'

Phil shook his head. 'They paid the bill and left, said something unexpected had come up. No details. He charged them until the end of the booked stay, but they coughed up without any fuss. Bill was shocked that they paid without a scene. He said that wasn't like them at all.'

'What time did the ferry leave?'

'Seven a.m.'

She was so shocked that it took her a moment to process the information.

'I guess there's no point in asking Jimmy to meet the boat at the harbour in Kirkwall and pull the couple into the station for questioning then. They'd have arrived at least an hour ago.'

'They could have headed for one of the ferries south to the Scottish mainland,' Phil said. 'Not the NorthLink. That doesn't leave until much later.'

'You're thinking they might be in Stromness? For the big ferry to Scrabster?'

'We can get someone to check. That'd be more likely than going all the way south across Scapa Flow to get the Pentland boat south. As far as I know all the planes to the Scottish mainland are still grounded, so if they're trying to get home it would be by boat, not on a flight.'

She pulled out her phone to talk to Perez, prepared to rattle off instructions, but he was no longer in the police station.

'Sorry.' Ellie's Yorkshire voice sounded very loud over the phone. It filled the heritage centre. 'You've just missed him. He's gone to Stromness to check Rosalie Greeman's alibi for the afternoon of the Riley murder.'

'Can you ask him to look out for passengers boarding the Scrabster ferry? We need to know where the Johnsons are. I must have frightened them off and I think they have the hard copies of Magnus Stout's research with them.'

'Sure. I'll try. And I'll get in touch with all the ferry companies now. There are no planes south because of the Scottish weather.' A pause. 'It doesn't look good for them, does it? The fact that they've done a runner.' Her voice was almost jubilant. She hadn't liked the couple either.

Willow switched off her phone and stood up, feeling again the strain in her back and her legs. She looked across the table at Phil. 'We might as well get back to Kirkwall. There's no point staying here now the Johnsons have disappeared.'

He grinned. 'Fine that. There's a party tonight at my lass's house. Even if we're on the last ferry home I'll be in town in time to catch it.'

Annie was back on duty in the hotel and cooked them a late breakfast.

'The Johnsons have gone then.' She'd delivered their scrambled eggs to the dining room, and looked down at them, still holding the tea towel she'd used to carry the hot plates.

'So it seems.' Willow grinned. 'I don't suppose you're sad to see them go.'

'Not at all, but maybe you're upset that they've left in such a hurry.'

'I went into the heritage centre yesterday after we had our chat. I found those notebooks, just where you said they'd be. They weren't there this morning.'

'You think the Johnsons took them?'

'Somebody did. I left the key with Bill last night.'

'He'd not have handed it over to them.' Annie was certain. 'Not without asking me first.'

'Can you find out if Tom and Evelyn Angel were in the bar last night? And if the Johnsons were in the hotel all evening. They were there when I came to visit you, but that wasn't anywhere near closing time.'

Annie didn't speak. She wasn't a woman to waste words. But she nodded and left them to their breakfast. She returned as Willow was drinking her last cup of tea.

'The Angels were in for an hour before closing.' The information was given with a trace of reluctance. Annie might see this as a form of betrayal – she'd grown up with the Angels and they'd feel like family. 'And Bill very definitely didn't give the key to either Barbara or Anthony Johnson.' She turned and went out before Willow could thank her.

They found Tom and Evelyn Angel at home in Hillhead. It was clearly coffee time, and they were both inside, in the kitchen, exactly as they'd been on Willow's last visit. One sat on each side of the granite breakfast bar. They weren't moving, just staring at each other. It was as if they were mannequins in a fancy department store window, fixed, not quite real and on display. Again, when Willow knocked on the door, it was Evelyn who came to answer.

'What is it now?' She seemed so stressed that she couldn't even summon the energy to pretend at politeness.

'We'll be leaving today.' Willow almost felt sorry for her. She seemed so taut, ready to snap at any moment. But the pair had gone to the Pierowall Hotel late on the previous night. They must have helped the Johnsons to steal the notebooks.

Her sympathy was limited. 'We're just saying goodbye, tying up a few loose ends.'

'I suppose you'd best come in.' This time there was no offer of tea.

Tom seemed anxious to see them too. 'What is it? Have you some news for us?'

Willow shook her head and asked a question of her own. 'Have you heard from Vaila? How is she coping?'

'She's struggling,' Evelyn said. 'We're going out tomorrow. We'll stay with them all in the Kirkwall Hotel and watch the Ba'. A way to remember Archie. The boys might feel a bit more settled when that's done. It's kind of looming on the horizon for them. Having to mourn their father in public. Their mother told them there was no need, but they want to be at the game to celebrate him. When it's over, Vaila should feel able to move them back to Nistaben, to take up their old life. She says she's not sure she wants to stay in Westray, but this isn't a time for rushed decisions.'

Only then did Willow realize that the next day was Christmas Eve. There flashed through her mind a list of the things that needed doing. James's presents to wrap, food to sort out. But what would it matter, she thought, if they ate egg and chips and James pigged out on chocolate all day? If he had to wait for his presents. She'd be home.

'Why did you give the Johnsons your key to the heritage centre?' she asked.

'We never had a key.' Tom's reply shot out without a pause. It was as if he'd been expecting the question and had prepared the answer. There was something of the guilty schoolboy about him. 'We're not on the committee. You can ask anyone.'

'Vaila had a key. You could easily have fetched it from

Nistaben and brought it back to the hotel. You were there last night.'

'We felt the need to get out of the house,' Evelyn said, 'and meet other folks. But we didn't stay long. It was hard, hearing everyone talking about their plans, laughing and joking, when we knew how Vaila is falling apart.'

'And you gave the Johnsons a key to the centre. Why would you do that when I explained how they linked Archie's and George's murders? I took you into my confidence. And now they've gone. They ran away on the early ferry.'

Evelyn looked wretched, but Tom was defiant. 'Tony explained,' he said. 'He'd humoured Magnus, let him help with his work. There was no question of any kind of fraud. They needed our help.' He looked up, shamefaced. 'He could persuade a man to do anything.'

'Did Tony tell you why they needed the key to the heritage centre?'

'For a few last hours of research. That's what he told us.' Now Evelyn was carrying on the tale, desperate to explain. 'He said that the police, that you and Perez, were determined to make them scapegoats. Because they weren't local, they were obvious targets. He thought everyone hoped they'd turn out to be the killers.'

That, Willow thought, was probably true. In her case at least. She carried an entirely conscious bias in her dealings with the pair. But stealing Stout's notebooks and escaping from the island hardly helped in their protestations of innocence.

'The Johnsons stole Magnus Stout's notebooks.' She kept her voice flat. Ranting at the Angels would do no good at all now. 'That was why they wanted the key to the centre.'

They stared at her. 'But the professor was on the television,'

Evelyn said, pleading for understanding. 'He was famous and respectable, and he needed our help. They were so grateful when we said we could get the key to them.'

Willow didn't reply.

Chapter Twenty-Eight

Perez was back, sitting on a bench looking out over Stromness harbour. It might be a little warmer than earlier in the week, but he was still feeling the cold. As soon as he'd heard from Ellie about the Johnsons' sudden escape from Westray, he'd made his way to the ferry terminal. He'd been there when the Scrabster boat came in to watch the passengers disembark. Then he'd stood by the barrier when the vehicles were loaded for the return journey, checking each car, and he'd spoken to the company about foot passengers.

Now he phoned Ellie again. 'I didn't see the Johnsons' car, and they weren't on the passenger list. I checked.'

'I've contacted all the other operators,' she said. 'There are still no flights into Scotland and the space is tight for cars on all the ferries. Lots of folk going south to spend Christmas with their families. The couple haven't booked in anywhere yet. They would need an advance booking, unless they're planning to leave their car behind.'

'They might be staying somewhere on the Orkney mainland. Let's check the hotels and B&Bs.'

'We've already started doing that.'

'Of course you have.' He hoped he hadn't offended her again. 'Great work.'

When he got back to the cafe, it was almost empty, ready to close. He took a seat near to the window, but it was running with condensation and there was no view out. A young waitress came to take his order.

'Were you working the day that George Riley was killed in Maeshowe?' He thought there'd been so much news around that day, that it was the best way to get witnesses to remember. Better than giving a date. He'd already introduced himself. She'd been excited. It was as if she was serving weak milky coffee to a celebrity. Murder had that effect on some folk. They got so caught up with the drama of it that they forgot the sadness and chaos it left in its wake, and for a while the investigating officers became famous.

What an odd thing celebrity was, he thought. It seemed that the Johnsons had taken in people in Westray, because the professor had once hosted a popular television programme.

'I was!' she said. She'd told him her name was Natalie. 'My mother phoned me with the news almost as soon as I got home. It had been on Radio Orkney.' She was a young woman, somehow bonny despite poor skin and a flabby body. It was the lovely smile that made her shine. 'Mr Riley was a wonderful man.'

'Did he teach you?'

'Aye, I work here, but I bide in Kirkwall. I was at the grammar until I left after Highers. I was in the panto the last few years too. Only the chorus, like, but I loved it.' She sounded wistful.

'You won't be in this year's show?' Perez wondered what

the panto would do without George. The first performance was scheduled for Boxing Day. He presumed it would be cancelled, out of respect and because it wouldn't be any kind of show without George as the dame.

The waitress shook her head. 'Some of the kids were kind of mean. I guess I don't have the looks for that sort of performance. There were some pictures on social media of me dancing during rehearsals. The woodland scene. The comments weren't very flattering. It was only a bit of fun, maybe, but not very kind. Mr Riley told me not to be so stupid, and he'd make sure the bullying stopped. The mean kids took no notice of him. I don't think anything would have stopped it, though it was nice of him to try.' She paused, shaking her head to get rid of the unpleasant memory. 'I decided I didn't need the hassle. Besides, there's plenty of overtime going here before Christmas and I could use the money.'

Perez didn't know how to respond to that. It occurred to him that he'd never found anyone yet with a bad word to say about Riley. Was it possible to be so universally admired? Could the man be hiding some secret so dark that he needed to compensate by being pleasant to everyone he knew?

'And then Archie Stout died in Westray just a few days earlier.' Natalie's excitement had returned. She looked straight at Perez, her eyes gleaming. 'The murders must be linked, mustn't they? It couldn't just be a dreadful coincidence.' He had her down now as a viewer of true crime television programmes, a consumer of the gorier podcasts. Perhaps they compensated for the gap in her life, the drama that the pantomime had provided.

'Did you know Archie?'

'A bit. We were kinda related.' Perez could see her searching for the link in her mind, but not quite finding the detail. 'We shared some great-aunt or other. I saw him sometimes at family occasions. Weddings and funerals. But I didn't really *know* him. You ken how it is in the islands.'

Perez nodded. He knew how it was. He supposed that he was probably connected to her in some way too, but he didn't say that. It was unkind, but he imagined her as needy, maybe turning up on his doorstep with some excuse. He could picture her boasting to her pals.

I'm related to that Archie Stout who was killed in Westray. And to the detective fae Fair Isle who's investigating the story stone murders.

Because one of the English tabloids had used the headline **The Story Stone Murders**, and now Radio Orkney had taken up the term. And she'd be hoping for some vicarious drama. That strange idea of celebrity again. Of fame.

'I'm just checking the movements of a few witnesses,' he said. 'Some of the people who knew both Archie and Mr Riley. They're not suspects, not at all, but we just want to eliminate them from our inquiries. I'm sure you understand.'

'You're checking alibis?' Her eyes brightened again, but her voice was serious.

'Something like that. A woman came here for lunch the day Mr Riley died. Her name's Rosalie Greeman. Does that mean anything to you?'

She shook her head. 'But if she's not a regular I'd not know her name.'

'She was wearing a very distinctive coat. Padded, made of brightly coloured patchwork.'

Perez could see that she was trying as hard as she could to remember. She would have loved to give him an answer. But she shook her head again.

'But I might not have seen. It was so cold outside that we cranked up the heating in here. It was steaming, and people took off their coats as soon as they came in.'

'If she paid by card, you'd have a record on the system?'

'I guess so, but you'd have to ask the manager about that.' Natalie sounded disappointed because he'd have to consult the boss, because she wasn't enough for him.

'Can you ask around your colleagues? And if anyone remembers her, give me a ring on this number.' He handed her his card. It had the station general number, not his direct line. Willow would approve. He was learning that he couldn't save the world.

'Sure!' There was that lovely smile again. 'Sure.'

The manager had no record of Rosalie Greeman paying for a lunch by card. 'But that doesn't mean anything.' She was a small shrew of a woman. 'We encourage cash here. Saves us paying the bank fees.'

He walked back to his car, thinking that he'd wasted most of the day.

Chapter Twenty-Nine

IN THE POLICE STATION THE LIGHTS had already been switched on. Ellie was still waiting on news of the Johnsons, and at the same time she was checking sightings of all the Westray folk who'd come in to Kirkwall on the pretext of the cathedral carol service. The A4 notepad in front of her was full of meticulous notes. Like Perez, she preferred paper and a soft lead pencil at work.

'I think better with a pencil,' she'd say when she was mocked by her tech-addicted colleagues. 'The ideas come straight from my brain. I don't need to think what my fingers are doing.'

Perez joined her, perched on her desk. 'Any joy? Have you found the Johnsons for me?'

'Not yet.' She looked up at him. 'I don't think they'd stay here in Kirkwall, would they? And I don't think they'd try to get onto one of the inter-island ferries. They'd stick out as visitors, and I've made sure that all the boats have their details. If I were them, I'd drive south, across the barriers. In South Ronaldsay, they'd be close enough to the Pentland ferry terminal in St Margaret's Hope to get into the Scottish mainland when the heat dies down.'

'Of course. That does make sense.' The four concrete causeways known as the barriers had been commissioned by Winston Churchill at the beginning of the war after a German U-boat had crawled into Scapa Flow and fired torpedoes at a British battleship, the *Royal Oak*. Eight hundred and thirty-four men had lost their lives, and the barriers had been built to prevent a similar tragedy. Orcadian kids were brought up on the story. George Riley had probably taught it in his history class, but the children would already have heard it from grandparents, the tale passed down through the generations, just as the Vikings had passed down their tales of heroes and villains.

Now the barriers linked the four most southerly islands, so there was no need for ferries to cross, and commuting to Kirkwall was much easier.

'I've got the word out to as many hotels and B&Bs as I can,' Ellie said. 'I've contacted Airbnb too. I haven't had much response from their hosts though. From anyone really. Everyone's either very busy or they've shut down their systems for the holidays. I sent a car down to St Margaret's Hope to check out that ferry terminal, but there was no sign of their vehicle there.'

'Sounds as if you've made terrific progress.' Perez had hoped for better news, but he didn't want to upset Ellie again. Not her fault. Nobody could have achieved anything more. 'How are you getting on with the alibis of the Westray people who were on the mainland when George Riley was killed?'

'There's one interesting fact. That's about the Johnsons again.'

'Go on.'

'I went into the Archive cafe this morning.' She looked at him, a quick grin. He nodded; he liked the place too. It had once been part of the old library. 'I fancied a proper coffee to keep me going. I showed Gordon behind the bar Johnson's photo. It was easy enough to get hold of. There are plenty of images of the professor online. Mostly in front of an audience holding forth. Gordon was *sure* he was in at lunchtime the day of the carol service. Johnson paid with a debit card, and he was able to check the name for me.' Ellie paused for a moment. 'It was heaving apparently, but Gordon is absolutely certain that the man was on his own. He could tell me what Johnson ate, and the card record just shows one cover.'

'So no Barbara.' Perez thought about that. 'I suppose she could have been shopping and he just didn't fancy trailing along with her if she was after clothes or local silver.'

'I'd get that if he'd just ordered a coffee,' Ellie said. 'But he had a proper meal. You'd wait for your wife before you ate lunch, wouldn't you?'

'Yeah, I think you would.' Perez paused for a moment. 'Do we have a time for when Johnson was eating?'

'Well, we know when he paid the bill.' Ellie was enjoying herself now. 'A record is kept on the card machine. Professor Johnson paid and left at one-forty-one.'

'I spoke to a witness this morning who saw George Riley parking his car at the Tormiston Mill between one and one-forty-five.' Ideas were racing now. He'd always had Johnson down as the prime suspect, not his wife. 'That might fit. In one way, I guess she had as much to lose in terms of status and income as her man. According to Willow, she loves playing the role of professor's wife. Perhaps they planned the thing together. Much easier to confuse us if they were working as a couple.'

'Would a woman have the strength to bash him on the head and stuff him into the small burial chamber?' Ellie was doubtful.

'I'm not sure. I haven't met her. Lifting him into the chamber would be harder physically than killing him. It would certainly take some nerve to stay there and pose the body. Most people would want to escape from the scene as soon as they could. Barbara works in theatre though – she runs a community arts centre. Perhaps she had a taste for the dramatic.'

Just, Perez thought, *like George Riley.*

Perez called in to the Archive cafe bar before picking up James from the nursery. It was that time when people were switching from coffee to cocktails. For most, it was the last working day before Christmas and people were letting down their hair. At one table there was already singing. At another, a big group of young women were crammed into the bench seats. They wore very little, and their voices were loud, shrill as whistles, piercing the background noise. Gordon was still behind the bar. He was tireless. He'd grown up in North Ronaldsay. Perez had chatted to him about it one day over coffee – North Ronaldsay was the closest Orcadian island to Fair Isle, and they'd compared notes. For Gordon, Kirkwall was the big city, glorious in its variety and attractions. He loved it and had no ambition to move anywhere else.

'I know you spoke to Ellie about this, but why did Professor Johnson stick so clearly in your mind? Because you'd seen him on TV?'

Gordon laughed. 'Nah, I never watch TV. Why would I when there's so much better to do?'

'So why did you remember him so well? Ellie said you were

rushed off your feet that day. All those folk in town before the carol service.'

'Because he was such a tosser. One of those guys who can't help throwing their weight around. You know the sort. Their voices are too loud, they ask too many questions about the menu. Then he complained about the table, even though he was lucky I could squeeze him in at all.'

'That sounds like Johnson.'

But it also, Perez thought, sounded like a man who wanted to be noticed. A man establishing an alibi, while his wife was committing a murder elsewhere.

He looked at his watch. Soon it would be time to collect James from nursery and then Willow would be home. He was about to leave the place when he turned back.

'You must have known Nat Wilkinson when you were growing up. He'd be older than you, but not much.'

'Aye, I knew him. His folk ran the North Ronaldsay shop. Came looking for a better life and found they'd brought all their troubles with them. You'll have met the sort on your fair isle.'

Perez nodded and smiled.

'The father was a boozer,' Gordon went on. 'Secret and steady. He'd disappear out the back of the shop halfway through serving and come back a little calmer and a little brighter. His hand not shaking at all. It was one of those secrets that everyone knew about, but nobody mentioned.'

Perez nodded again. There'd been secrets like that when he'd been growing up too. 'Not surprising then that Nat developed an addiction.'

'I don't think it was his father's drinking that made him an addict. It was his father's death.'

'Oh?' Perez looked at his watch again. He really should be fetching James, but he couldn't ignore a story like this.

'It was just past midsummer. Nat was already at the grammar school then, but he was home for the holidays. He and his father were fishing from the pier. Sometimes you could get sillocks just by throwing over a line and hook.' Gordon paused, building the tension and the drama. 'His dad fell in and drowned. Word was it happened because he was drunk. He must have been kind of wobbly on his feet and he tripped. Nat jumped in and tried to rescue him. Or so he said. There was nobody else with them.'

'You don't believe it was an accident?'

Gordon shrugged. 'The father could be a violent drunk. I've seen the bruises on Nat, and his mother was a timid, peedie thing. She wouldn't have stood up to the man. There was no proof either way, and island folk who knew the family history weren't going to accuse Nat. If he had helped his father into the water, they wouldn't have blamed him.'

'You think that was when his problems started?'

Gordon shrugged. 'Who knows what sends folk into addiction? Maybe he inherited the gene. But he had a bad time after that. In school, the idea got out that he'd killed his dad. There wasn't so much shit then on social media, but kids can be cruel face to face too. His nickname was Murd. Short for murderer. George Riley tried to close it all down. He called out the bullies and threatened to expel them. Told their parents, though some of the parents believed the rumours too and didn't try too hard to stop them. Nat couldn't escape it. But maybe he tried with the booze and whatever else he could get hold of.'

There was a moment of silence and then Gordon walked out from behind the bar to take more orders. His customers were becoming impatient. Perez made his way into the busy street to pick up his son, his thoughts racing. Nat Wilkinson was the one Westray man they'd dismissed from their inquiries, because he'd been on the island when George Riley had been murdered. Now, Perez thought, perhaps they should look at him again. Anyone who held on to a secret was interesting.

He looked at his watch. Willow should be on the ferry on her way in to Kirkwall. Soon she'd be home.

Perez and Willow talked about Nat Wilkinson later that evening, after they'd had a video call with Cassie. Fran, Perez's former lover had, in one sense, bequeathed the girl to him, and he thought of her as his own. The girl was fourteen now, with a mind of her own. She'd decided to spend Christmas with her biological father. Perez had been a little hurt when she'd announced that it was all organized and Duncan, her dad, would come in to Orkney to get her on the last day of term. Now he had to admit to himself, a little guiltily, that he was loving this time just with his new family. But he tried to speak to her every day.

Willow had come home straight off the Westray ferry in time to put James to bed, just as she'd promised. That was when they'd spoken to Cassie, waving at her blurred image on the laptop, listening to her stories of the Shetland family, all the treats that she'd had. It seemed that her father, Duncan Hunter, was enjoying her company and that she was having a splendid time. Perez had grown up in a very traditional family on Fair Isle, and he hadn't been sure how it would work – a lassie with two dads and two step-mums. Would the situation confuse her? What would her school friends make of it? Would there be teasing, or even worse?

But now, it seemed, the blended family was the norm. Cassie would have two celebrations – she'd be back on Orkney for Hogmanay, and they'd celebrate their Christmas then – and two lots of presents. Her only sadness was that she was missing James.

Once the boy was in bed, Perez and Willow started talking about the investigation, catching up over a late meal. Everything seemed easier when they were together: the complicated family, throwing together a dinner, wrapping presents for James. Perez loved that about Willow, the lack of drama. In the rest of the country, people would be panicking about the trivia of Christmas, but Willow just said she'd pop into Asda in Dounby the next day to pick up what they needed. There were only the three of them, and the shops would be open again on Boxing Day. Nothing to get fraught about.

'Are you saying that Nat confided to George Riley that he'd pushed his father off the North Ronaldsay pier, then regretted it and needed to shut him up?'

'Well,' Perez laughed. 'If you put it like that, it doesn't sound very plausible.'

'It doesn't explain Archie's death either. Or the story stones. Besides, we know that Nat wasn't on any of the ferries the day George was killed.' Willow was enjoying the conversation. Perez could tell. Pulling holes in his theories.

'He could have got off on a plane. Or one of his fishing friends could have dropped him in Kirkwall. It was a still day. There were lots of creel boats on the water.'

'He wouldn't have had a car then though. How could he have got to Maeshowe?'

'Public transport? Taxi? A lift with a mate?'

It was Willow's turn to laugh. 'You're clutching at straws. Because you haven't tracked down Johnson or his wife.'

'Maybe, but I'll talk to a few people in North Ronaldsay. Look at any report on the accident.' He set down his fork and changed tack. 'Do you think Barbara could have killed Riley? Would she have been sufficiently strong?'

Willow sat for a moment in silence, quite serious now. 'I think so. I never gave her enough attention. To me, she was just the professor's wife. Ridiculously I'd assumed that our perpetrator must be a man. I should know better. I dismissed her as being loud and silly, and it never occurred to me that *she* could be the killer.' There was another long pause. 'I think she could be strong enough. She's tall and gives the impression of someone who looks after themselves. She cares about her image. Hair professionally dyed, even her outdoor clothes high-end. I can imagine her in the gym, working out, doing resistance training, running.'

'And from what you've told me, Johnson is weak and self-important enough to allow her to kill for him. He has that sense of entitlement.'

The meal was finished, and Perez cleared the plates into the kitchen. He returned with a mug of herbal tea for Willow. She was curled, cat-like, large and sleepy, on the sofa next to the fire. She seemed to be dozing and to wake up again when he came back into the room.

'I think James and I will have a little run out after we've done the Asda shop,' she said. 'It'll get him out of the house, and he'll be high as a kite.'

'What are you thinking?'

'If the weather stays good, and there's room on the plane, I might take a day trip to North Ronaldsay.'

'Are you sure you're okay to fly?'

'Sure,' she said. 'These small planes, it's no more dangerous than taking a bus.'

He nodded. 'So, you think Nat Wilkinson might be involved after all? After dismissing all my theories?' He sat beside her, stroked her hair away from her face. For this brief moment, he didn't care about the case at all.

'Ah, Jimmy,' she said, 'it's a loose end and a bit of a mystery, and you know how I hate loose ends.'

Chapter Thirty

PEREZ'S PHONE WOKE THEM BOTH. It felt to Willow that she'd only just dropped off – sleep came hard to her too in these late days of pregnancy – but when she looked at the clock it was six in the morning. She could only hear Perez's end of the conversation, but worked out that it was the duty officer at the police station. Perez's voice was tight, and the questions clipped, so she couldn't tell exactly what had happened, only that the matter was urgent.

She got out of bed and went to the kitchen to make coffee. It was clear that Perez would need to leave soon.

When he joined her, he was already dressed.

'No need for us to continue with the search for the Johnsons.' His hands were cupped round a favourite coffee mug, blue ceramic, decorated with puffins. Earlier, she'd thought about putting the drink into a travel cup for him to take away, but she'd wanted to keep him here for a few minutes to find out what was happening.

'They've been found?'

'Johnson has. No sign of Barbara or the car.'

'Where did they find him?'

'In the middle of the Stones of Stenness. Some crazy runner training for an ultra race out before work saw him in the light of his head torch.'

Willow knew exactly what would come next, but didn't jump in. Let Perez pass on the news in his own way. He turned to her. 'We were too late. He's dead.'

'How?' She realized that she was repeating exactly the same questions in the same way as Perez had on the phone.

She was thinking too that there were no other story stones, so there must be a different cause of death. A flippant thought flew into her head: perhaps the tabloids would have to change their headline now. They'd been lucky – the weather had kept away most of the reporters from the rest of the UK – but that hadn't stopped the story leading the news for days.

'It looks like a stabbing. I'll let you know more when I've been there.'

She decided that as soon as she decently could, she'd phone Alison to ask if she'd have James for a few hours. There was no nursery today. She also thought that before she dropped off her son, she'd need to hit the Dounby Asda. With any luck it'd be quiet. The organized residents of the parish would already have their freezers full of seasonal treats and their larders crammed. Their presents would have been wrapped months earlier.

Before leaving the house, she made a few more calls. The first was to Nat Wilkinson's phone, but it went straight to voicemail. The next was to the Pierowall Hotel. She spoke to Bill, island gossip and teller of tales.

'I don't suppose you know where Nat is? Still there in Westray?'

'Nah, he went off on the ferry yesterday morning. Something urgent he had to deal with, he said.'

'Any idea what that was?'

'Nope. He was very mysterious about it all. He can get like that sometimes. Apparently, he'll stay out and come back with everyone who'll be at the Ba' tomorrow. We'll be in town for that.'

She thanked him and ended the call, then immediately dialled again. This time to the Loganair office in Kirkwall airport.

'Any chance of getting a flight in and out of North Ronaldsay today?'

She knew that man at the end of the phone. He was older, a former engineer, inclined to be chatty. 'It's urgent, Davie.' Stopping the questions about the welfare of Jimmy and her son.

'You might be lucky. Be here for eleven. There's a charter flight going in. They're bringing old Willie home from the hospital to be with his daughter for Christmas. They have to be sure he's properly settled there before coming back, and that she has all the meds and equipment he'll need.' A pause. 'Myself, I don't think he'll be back. He's gone home to die.' Another pause, before he continued, his voice cheerier. 'So you'll have an hour or so. That do you?'

'Perfectly. You're a total star.' She pressed the button on the phone before he could come up with any more questions.

When she arrived at Stenness it was just getting light. This time of year, daytime was late arriving. The circle of standing stones formed silhouettes against the rising sun, which disappeared occasionally behind low cloud. Willow had been to Stonehenge, but thought this monument was more dramatic, not because of the stones themselves but because of the landscape within which it had been built. The hills of Hoy provided the backdrop, and in the same view, there was the loch and the sea. A breeze had sprung up, and the loch was choppier than it had been for more than a week.

In this light and dressed in scene suits, everyone there looked the same, but she picked up Perez even from a distance. It was something about the way he stood, the space he always managed to create around himself. She'd found an oversized paper suit to reach across her belly. That meant that the arms and legs were too long, and she had to roll them up so she didn't trip and still had use of her gloved hands.

Perez was talking to a group of colleagues, and she stood back, watching, until he'd finished. There was already a cordon around the stones and the road leading to the car park had been blocked. She imagined the locals complaining about the diversion.

The group around him scattered and she approached him. 'You've done well to get all this sorted in such a short time.'

'The team want it over, don't they, so they can get back to their families and prepare for Christmas. And then there's the Ba' tomorrow. We'll need manpower for that.' A pause. 'I was wondering about cancelling the Ba'.'

'Think carefully,' she said. 'There are people who are treating the game as a celebration of Archie's life. George's life too. He might never have participated but you know he wrote the definitive history of the Ba'. So really, it's much *more* than a game to them. There'd be an absolute outcry if you cancel, especially among Kirkwall residents. It's a matter of pride and tradition. You'll be alienating a lot of folk just when you need them on side.'

'Yeah, I know. But it feels like one thing too many.' She could hear the despair in his voice through the mask. He looked through the backlit stones towards the water. 'Do you think his wife could have killed him?' he asked. 'If not, where on earth can she be? How did he get here? I'm feeling swamped by all the questions. Last night, I thought I had a possible answer to it all – Johnson and his wife working together. At least then I had a motive. Now I'm lost and have no idea at all.'

Willow was reminded of the old Jimmy Perez, the Perez she'd first met after the murder of Fran, the love of his life. He'd been drowning then. Lost under a wave of depression. All his confidence gone.

'Nat Wilkinson came out on the ferry yesterday. I tried to call him but he's not answering his phone. According to Bill, he said something urgent had come up. He'd have seen the Johnsons on the boat, so he'd be a witness, even if we don't think of him as a suspect.'

'So that's someone else we need to look for! As I said, it's all too much.'

'Go back to routine policing.' She spoke to him as she would to anyone who came to her, asking her advice. She needed him to focus on detail, the small actions that he could easily achieve. 'Have you organized a search here for Barbara?' She waved an arm, taking in the flat, windswept landscape. 'There might be another body.'

'Aye, that's what I was sorting with the team. They're bringing in the coastguard to help.' He paused. 'Do you really think she might be dead?'

'I'm not thinking anything just now. No facts to work on. But we need to find that car.'

'We've had a watch out for that since they went missing yesterday.'

'Then it'll be found.' She hoped she sounded more positive than she felt. 'Have you come across the murder weapon?'

'Aye, nothing as exotic as a Neolithic stone with Nordic runes. A knife. One you'd find in any workshop or fishing boat. It was left at the scene.'

'A possibility then of prints or DNA.'

'Maybe.' He waited for a moment before speaking again, and now the words came out as a cry, loud even over the sound of the wind. 'But we won't hear about that anytime soon, will we? Not with the holidays. Even without the holidays with the backlog there is, and the time everything takes at the lab. Vaila and her boys are waiting for answers. And Miles is going slowly crazy in that madhouse that he shared with George.'

She wanted to take him into her arms to reassure him. But she was his lover and his colleague, not his mother. Usually, he was the person not to demand comfort but to give it – to friends and colleagues, to witnesses, even to offenders. He was the least needy person she knew.

'They're not your responsibility, Jimmy. You can't stop them from hurting, and at the moment they're just a distraction. You can only do your job.' She paused for a moment. 'I've arranged to go into North Ronaldsay this morning with an ambulance flight. Probably a waste of time, but I'd like to talk to one of the islanders, see if I can dig up a bit more detail on Nat's father's death, and you've got it covered here. I should be back early afternoon.' She looked across at him. In the artificial lights, his face looked gaunt and haunted. His olive skin was grey. 'That *is* okay?'

'Sure,' he said, but he seemed distracted, focused entirely on his own thoughts.

She touched his arm, turned away and started walking back to her car. This was Jimmy's crime scene, and she couldn't interfere. Her presence would only undermine his authority. When she got to the cordon, she gave him a little wave, but she wasn't sure that he'd seen her.

Willow was at the airport half an hour early and the team at the desk were expecting her. She was antsy, uncomfortable, pacing past the display of Orkney crafts, and the posters celebrating the islands' archaeology and natural history. She'd wondered if Nat might be there, trying to get back to a place he thought of as home, but there was no sign of him, and he still wasn't answering his phone.

They were frying bacon in the cafe and the smell made her want to throw up. At last, the ambulance appeared and a frail elderly man was loaded into the plane. Willow knew one of the medics who was with him.

'Thanks for letting me hitch a lift.'

'Ah, no problem at all. We're all seeing the news. Another death! We all want to help as much as we can.'

She knew the man was hoping for information about the investigation but couldn't quite bring himself to ask why she was heading into North Ronaldsay. She was grateful for his tact.

Again she sat in the front, next to the pilot, watching the map of Orkney spread below her, and thought once more how lucky she was to live in this place.

They bounced to a landing on the airstrip. The fire tender and crew were there, and she waved to a couple of islanders she knew. North Ronaldsay always felt remote to her, different and separate. It was flatter, more distant. As in Fair Isle, most of the visitors stayed at the Bird Observatory and came for the natural history. Or the sheep or the knitting.

The person Willow had arranged to meet was there, waiting, with a car that looked as ancient as she was. Willow had met Mima through work. Mima's husband had suffered from early onset Alzheimer's, and in the end, she hadn't been able to care for him at home. He'd had to move out to a residential home in Kirkwall, and away from North Ronaldsay he'd become lost and confused, given to slipping away from the place, even though the door was usually locked. He'd been as wily and invisible as a fox after hens, and Willow had been able to track him down when none of her junior colleagues could. When he'd died a couple of months later, Mima had invited Willow to the funeral.

'You're a kind woman,' Mima had said. 'You saw the man in him. The man that he once was.'

Willow had called Mima on impulse as soon as she'd booked herself onto the flight. 'I'm coming to the island this morning. Any chance I could talk to you?'

'That will be splendid.' No questions. No need for further explanation. 'I'll be there to collect you. I have a parcel coming in on the plane anyway.'

Now Willow gave her a hug. 'I'm sorry to disturb you. Christmas Eve! You'll be busy.'

'Not at all.' The accent was so strong that Willow had to concentrate to understand her. 'I'll be at my daughter's tomorrow. I have nothing to do, and I'm loving every minute of my idleness.'

They drove down the island, past the stone dyke that kept

the wild sheep on the rocky beach, where they ate the seaweed that flavoured their meat.

Mima's house was small and white and close to the pier. Nowhere near as grand as most of the houses on Westray. This wasn't a wealthy island. Her husband had been born here too and had worked on the ferry. In the kitchen there was a solid fuel range, a kettle on the hob, the smell of baking. A view from the window of the little harbour, gulls pecking at a pile of creels, nets waiting to be mended. Mima made tea.

Only when they were sitting at the table did Mima speak.

'Now. How can I help you? You said you were here for work.'

'I have some questions about Nat Wilkinson and his father. I hoped you might be able to help.'

'Not that old story again.' Mima sounded angry. 'Is that what this is about? That cruel and foolish gossip. I'd hoped that had been forgotten years ago.'

'So you don't think Nat killed his father?'

'I never believed it for one minute.'

'How could you be so sure? I understand that the father was abusive. The boy could have lashed out, sent him flying. More an accident maybe than a deliberate killing.'

Mima shook her head. 'Nathaniel was a good boy. Harmless. Nervy. But that's hardly surprising with a family like that. We should have done something about the way his father treated him. Called social services.' There was a pause. 'I nearly called the police once. But you know how it is in a place like this.'

Willow nodded.

The secrets known but not spoken of.

'We suspected that bad things were going on in the family, but we closed our eyes to it. They kept themselves apart, you know. Maybe we thought it wasn't our business. Of course it was our business. It should have been everyone's business.'

'That doesn't mean Nat didn't push his father, you know.' Willow kept her voice low. 'You can't take the blame for what happened.'

'He didn't push his father,' Mima said. 'I saw it all. I was out on that bench in the garden, shelling peas. It was summer, a splendid day. I couldn't hear what they were saying between them, but the lad was nowhere near the man when he tumbled in, and Nat was in the water trying to save him, as soon as he realized that his father had fallen.' She paused for a moment and Willow could tell that she was reliving the afternoon. 'I told the young officer who came asking about it. But that would have been before your time, of course.'

'So what caused all the rumours that the man had been pushed?'

Mima didn't answer immediately. 'Boredom! All those people with nothing else going on in their lives so they had to make up stories. And ignorance. Because the Wilkinsons weren't local, they were fair game.'

'Did you know that Nat was bullied at school?'

Mima nodded. 'He came here once and told me about it. His mother was struggling to keep the shop running and I popped in most days to help her. Not out of charity, you understand, but a place like this, we need a shop to survive. It's not just the convenience. It's a place where folk meet and chat. And who wants to be collecting orders from the boat every time the cupboard looks bare? So I went in, and I helped to keep things straight for her. Nothing formal. No pay.'

'That was kind.'

'Aye well, they could have done with a bit more kindness

in their lives. The woman struggled on for a few more years, but then she gave up the business and moved south. I got to know the lad properly when he was home from the grammar school for the holidays, when his mother was still thinking she could make a go of the shop. I was a sort of nan to him. And he knew he could always come in and chat. I liked the company when my man was out with the ferry.'

'Have you seen Nat recently?'

Mima shook her head. 'When my Alec got sick, I had enough to do taking care of him.'

Willow didn't speak. She let Mima continue.

'One time, Nat came here. It must have been six months after his father died. He sat where you are now and told me he never wanted to go back to school again. "Don't send me back, Mima. You were a teacher once. Why can't I stay here on the island and you can teach me?" I told him that I'd only taught little kids and I'd be no use to him at all. What was so wrong about school? He said that the boys there were so mean to him that he wanted to kill himself. I asked him if there was someone he could tell. A teacher. A houseparent at the hostel. He said he'd already talked to his form teacher, but that had only made things worse. "Now they call me a sneak as well as a murderer," he said. He was almost in tears. It made my heart bleed. He'd told a teacher, who'd had the arrogance to think that he could sort it all out, when what he really needed was professional help for his mental ill health.' She looked up at Willow, who saw that now Mima herself was almost in tears.

'I'm so sorry to bring that time back,' she said. 'You've been very helpful though.'

Mima was still remembering. 'The next time I saw Nathaniel he was in Kirkwall, so drunk he could barely stand, looking as if he hadn't had a bath for a month. He was with a group of other men, and they had that look about them. Edgy. As if it wasn't only the drink that they'd taken.'

She glanced up. 'I just walked past. I didn't do anything to help him. I was scared by them, by a group of lads who could hardly stand. What does that make me? As bad as the teacher Nat confided in, the one who couldn't stop the bullying.'

'Did you ever hear the name of that teacher?'

Mima shook her head. 'If I ever knew it, I forgot it long ago.'

'Could it have been George Riley?'

'Isn't that the man who was killed in Maeshowe?'

'It is.'

'Is that why you're here?' Mima was suddenly upset. Angry. 'You think poor Nathaniel might have killed him after all this time. Is that what folk are saying? That he killed his father, so he must have killed this teacher? More rumours, more people pointing the finger. You do know that's ridiculous.'

'I'm sorry. I'm sure you're right.' Willow couldn't see Nat Wilkinson as a killer either. 'I had to check though. I hope you understand.'

'Aye, I suppose you're only doing your job.'

'Nat's doing well,' Willow said. 'He's living and working in Westray. He's developing his art, selling to visitors. I spoke to him last week. He'd had George Riley to stay when he was stranded in Westray the night of the storm. They were friendly, on good terms.'

'Really? Well, that's good then. He was always a fine artist when he was a boy.' Mima wasn't entirely convinced, but she gave a little smile as she got to her feet. The anger had left her. 'I'd best get you back to the airstrip or you'll be stranded too.'

In the plane on the way home, Willow was relegated to the back seat. One of the medics sat next to the pilot. They were friends it seemed. There was a heated discussion about tactics for the Ba'. Willow stared out of the window and replayed the conversation with Mima. She was quite sure now that Nat's father's death had been an accident. This was another lead then that seemed to be going nowhere, but the meeting had triggered another idea, a connection so tentative that she couldn't quite believe it. She let the thought settle in the back of her mind as they landed into Kirkwall, hoping that it would grow into something more meaningful.

Chapter Thirty-One

PEREZ SPENT ALL MORNING IN STENNESS. He thought Johnson's body would have to stay where it was for a while, perhaps even until after Christmas. When he'd first arrived there, he'd fancied the man looked like an ancient human sacrifice, lying on his back, positioned right in the middle of the stone circle. There must be some significance to the link, he'd thought, between all the crime scenes: the former dig at Noltland, Maeshowe and now the stones at Stenness. All major archaeological sites. The killer must be sending some message.

As it got light and the image of a human sacrifice was corrupted by the scene tent and the lights and the team in their blue suits, hoods and masks, the idea of a killer obsessed with ancient stones seemed fanciful. Barbara Johnson and the couple's vehicle had disappeared. The first priority was to find them. The woman might provide a far more prosaic explanation. If she were still alive. All the same, the connection with the past had been made and he couldn't shake it. He phoned Paul Rutherford, and explained what had happened and where he was.

'Any chance you could come along? I'm going slowly crazy here and I need some expert advice.'

I need more than that, he thought. I need a sounding board, someone to bounce ideas off.

Because Willow had left him to it. In addition, there were still no flights in from the Scottish mainland and it would take hours to bring in reinforcements by ferry, even if he could persuade the Glaswegians to make the trek. It occurred to him then that he should trust his team more. He'd been thrown by the death of a friend, but Ellie was sharp, and she wanted more responsibility. It was a weird kind of arrogance to think he could run the investigation on his own. When this was over, he'd arrange extra training for her, a new, enhanced role. But now the team were busy, and he had to do his best. Alone.

He knew there would be excuses from his colleagues in the south: Orkney was a bugger to get to at the best of times, and even worse in midwinter. It was Christmas Eve. Did he know how much the overtime would cost? Best cover the body up and wait until the weather cleared and the holidays were over. None of that would be said out loud, of course – not to him, at least – but the mood he was in, he imagined it was what his colleagues in Glasgow would be thinking.

Dr Grieve had only just returned home to Aberdeen and Perez couldn't get hold of him. That added to his sense of isolation and his anxiety that the investigation was going nowhere.

He tried to follow Willow's advice and focus on routine policing. He spoke to his blue-suited colleagues:

'Don't contaminate the scene. Make a note of whoever comes through the cordon. Let's try to trace Johnson's movements since he left Westray. And we need to find his wife and their car.' A pause. 'Can we keep a look out for Nat Wilkinson too? He disappeared suddenly from Westray yesterday without any explanation.'

It felt as if he was repeating these instructions as a mantra throughout the morning. That somehow the words were just about keeping him sane. But his mood lifted when Rutherford appeared at the edge of the cordon. A new face and a different perspective. Perez made his way across the cropped grass to join him.

They sat in Rutherford's car. He'd brought a flask of strong black coffee and a plastic tub of home-made mince pies. The sudden blast of caffeine and sugar made Perez jittery, light-headed.

'So Tony Johnson's dead,' Rutherford said. 'There won't be many people in the field who'll mourn him – he loved his celebrity more than his subject – but you wouldn't wish that on anyone. And certainly not on his family.'

'We can't find his wife. As far as we know she's still here in Orkney. We're trying to track down his children too, to notify them of the death, and in the hope that they've heard from Barbara, but according to neighbours they're both abroad for the holidays.'

'I'm not sure how I can help.'

'We think he was killed here.' Perez couldn't be certain about anything just now, but there'd been blood on the grass and no indication that the body had been moved. 'It seems odd that all three bodies were found at sites of archaeological significance.'

'And sites of significance to Johnson.'

'What do you mean?'

'They were all featured in the TV series that he fronted.

There were other places in Shetland, but those were the Orkney sites he visited. I was surprised that he didn't decide to go to Papay, because the Knap of Howar there is so significant. It's thought to be the oldest preserved stone house in Northern Europe. But Maeshowe, Noltland and Stenness were the ones where he stood looking handsome and moody, talking to camera. It could be a coincidence of course.'

'Aye, maybe.' Perez thought this turned his whole perception of the investigation on its head. He'd come to believe that Johnson had killed Archie and George to save his reputation. Now, Rutherford was suggesting that Johnson could have been the intended target all along. If that was the case, why had the other victims been killed? Some warped attempt at misdirection? Or collateral damage? 'According to Miles, it was the television programmes that triggered George Riley's anger and made him determined to expose Johnson.'

'Yeah well, it made me pretty angry too. Seeing the man standing there, posing as the big expert, trotting out his stuff. I suspect that he didn't go to Papay because he didn't know so much about the subject. He had no information to steal.'

'We're still desperate to find the wife. We don't know yet if she's dead or alive. You say there was no other site featured on the television programme?'

Rutherford shook his head. 'Not in Orkney.'

So that didn't help very much.

It seemed though that Rutherford was having second thoughts. 'There was a quick piece about the Ring o' Brodgar, but it was in the same episode as the Stones of Stenness, so it slipped my mind.'

'Did he do a piece to camera from there?'

'Yeah, I think he did.'

The Ring o' Brodgar was very close to where they were now, on the same isthmus between the lochs of Harray and Stenness as the stone circle where Johnson's body had been found. The team had already driven slowly along the road, looking for the Johnsons' vehicle, but Perez wasn't sure that anybody had walked into Brodgar. Not since it was light. If Barbara Johnson was lying anywhere, it might be there.

Rutherford seemed unaware of the impact of his words. 'Is that all? Only I promised I'd get the kids out of the way, so my wife can finish wrapping the presents.'

'Sure.' Perez drew his attention back to the archaeologist. 'It was good of you to come out.'

He watched Rutherford drive away and looked at his phone. There was still no news on Barbara Johnson. He tried to call Willow, but it clicked straight through to voicemail. He wondered briefly if she was wrapping presents too but couldn't quite imagine it. She could have made it to North Ronaldsay. He had to push his way through a line of gawpers to get back inside the cordon. He wanted to shout at them: *Don't you have anything better to do on Christmas Eve?*

At the scene he left a message with one of his team. 'I'm just heading over to Brodgar. Probably a wild goose chase, but that's where I'll be if anyone wants me.'

Then he walked away, along the empty road, with water on both sides of him, glad to be alone for a while and to let the facts of the case churn around his mind.

Brodgar was a completed circle. Massive stones perfectly formed. Tourists came from all over the world to marvel at it. He paused for a moment before leaving the road, aware of the tension in his muscles, his limbs and his face tight and strained. The sun was well up now, the shadows dark and sharp on the grass. He imagined Neolithic people coming to the monument with a sense of wonder and awe. Perhaps they'd been here seeking answers too.

Usually, there'd be traffic moving behind him, but because they'd closed the road, everything was still. He could see the work going on at the crime scene at Stenness, but he was too far away for any noise to reach him. A curlew flew calling across the hill. He followed the footpath, walking slowly, looking for any indication that someone had been here before him. There was nothing. Not even a scrap of litter or an empty beer can.

At the edge of the circle, he paused again. His shadow was thrown in front of him, as if he was one of the stones. He thought he heard a movement behind him, but when he looked there was nothing there. His imagination running wild. The sun was covered by a bank of cloud, so the colours faded, and everything seemed shady, gloomy. He walked into the centre of the ring of stones.

Nothing. An anticlimax. No woman's body. He quartered the space, to be sure that he hadn't missed anything, coming to terms with his shattered theory. In his head he began describing the incident to Willow, turning it into a story, mocking himself for believing in the drama. He walked back to Stenness, guilty because he was a little disappointed that there'd been nothing to find.

Chapter Thirty-Two

BACK IN HARRAY, WILLOW STILL COULDN'T settle. There'd been a missed call from Perez when she was in the plane. She phoned him back and explained about her trip into North Ronaldsay.

'Nat Wilkinson definitely didn't kill his father. I don't know what brought him out of Westray yesterday, but I'm struggling to believe that it was to stick a knife in Tony Johnson. Mima did make an interesting point though . . .'

Even to Willow, the seeds of an idea around Nat Wilkinson's addiction seemed vague and not rooted in reality, but Perez listened intently.

'Important do you think?'

'Aye, maybe.' He paused. 'Definitely.'

'Did you learn anything from Paul Rutherford?'

'Only that all our crime scenes were places featured in Johnson's TV programme,' Perez said.

'That could be significant.'

'Possibly.' Perez sounded unconvinced by the theory. 'Best to keep an open mind at this stage though, I guess.'

Willow felt like cheering. Perez sounded more confident, more like his old self.

She wanted to ask about Barbara Johnson, but he'd have told her if there were any news about the woman.

Instead, she phoned the police station and spoke to Ellie who was coordinating the search from there to get the details. Willow knew she was acting the control freak again but couldn't help herself.

'Anything?'

'Nah.' Ellie sounded defeated. 'No sign yet of the car, or the woman – alive or dead. But we're so thin on the ground. All this space. All these islands. It was hard enough searching even before Johnson's body was found, sucking in all our available manpower.'

'I might just take a drive out,' Willow said. 'I'll be another pair of eyes at least. Maybe I'll head down towards the ferry terminal in South Ronaldsay. As you and Jimmy first thought, that's the most accessible route back to Scotland if you don't want your movements traced.'

Alison had phoned earlier to ask if she could keep James all day – they were having so much fun – and Willow thought that anything would be better than sitting here worrying at a question that had no answer.

She was preparing to leave the house when there was a knock on the door. Tentative. Uncertain. She opened the door to Nat Wilkinson. A van, scratched and dented, was parked in the drive. She supposed it belonged to him and he'd taken it in from Westray with him.

'I'm sorry to trouble you.' He was stumbling over the words. 'You'd left a couple of messages on my phone. Then I heard about the body in Stenness, and I thought I should speak to you. I know I shouldn't have come to your home, but I couldn't face the police station. It has memories. When I was using and in a bad place, I got taken there.'

'Come on in.' Willow wasn't going to make a fuss about his turning up on her doorstep. She wanted to speak to him, after all. Seeing him standing there, looking lost and vulnerable, she could understand why Mima had felt the need to protect him. She didn't ask how he knew where she lived. Of course he would know. It was impossible to keep anything hidden in Orkney. 'What brought you out of Westray in such a rush?'

She took him into her kitchen, settled him into a chair by the table.

'I'm a recovering addict.' He looked up at her. 'But you'll know that. You'll have seen the records. A friend of mine from the fellowship is going through a tough time. He lives in Kirkwall. His woman left him yesterday and took their little boy with her. He was worried he'd relapse. I wanted to be there for him and came out as soon as I could. I spent all day with him and stayed over at his place last night. He has other pals with him now.' A pause. 'You can check if you need to.'

Willow shook her head. 'Did you see the Johnsons on the ferry?'

'Aye, I did. We sat below in the cafeteria. None of us had had breakfast.'

'How did they seem?'

'The wife was quiet. Subdued. Even a bit scared of the guy maybe. He was in a dreadful temper, shouting at the lass behind the counter, making a fuss over some little thing. His wife was trying to calm him down.'

'Did they tell you why they were leaving in such a hurry?'

Nat shook his head. 'I sat at a different table with my back to them, and then I went up on deck. I had enough on my mind about my friend. I didn't need the hassle.' He looked across at her. 'Johnson said he'd sort everything out. The wife just had to trust him. He said he'd make everything right again.'

There was a moment of silence while she tried to process the information.

'Did you see which way they went when they left the ferry?'

'Aye. My van was behind their car. They headed for the town centre.'

After Nat left, she drove south, not into Kirkwall where the Johnsons had first been heading. Even if the Johnsons had gone into the town from the ferry, she thought, if Barbara was still there surely someone would have seen her. Instead, Willow stuck to her original plan to make for South Ronaldsay. She didn't take a direct route, but used the smaller side roads and headed east across the Deerness peninsula before even hitting the Churchill Barriers.

There was a wonderful freedom in driving down the empty tracks. Some routes were entirely new to her, and others took her to remote houses where friends and colleagues lived, places she'd been to dinner or taken James for play dates. She felt a moment of guilt because she was enjoying this meandering road trip so much. Another man had died. She hadn't liked Tony Johnson, but perhaps she should grieve a little at his passing.

Everywhere, she came across spectacular views. She'd grown up on an island, was familiar with the huge skies, but here it was the vista of land and water and more land and more water spreading out to the horizon, that made the landscape so special. The weather had changed. It was mild and breezy, with the knowledge that from now on the days would get a little longer. The distant smell of spring. Gusts of wind blew cloud-shaped shadows across the lochs.

The Johnsons had been driving a blue VW, just a year old. She had the registration number in her memory. She slowed at every smallholding and cottage that might house an Airbnb or take in paying guests. She could have knocked at doors, asked if the Johnsons had stayed the night after they ran away from Westray, but she needed to know where Barbara was *now*, not where she'd been the day before. Besides, she was taking so much pleasure in the drive that she couldn't quite stop. And all the time, her mind was running through information gleaned from Mima, creating possible scenarios. She knew that Perez would be doing the same.

The first barrier took her to the island of Lamb Holm, where Italian prisoners of war had turned two Nissen huts into a beautiful ornate chapel. Willow had visited it, at first on her own, and then taking friends who'd come to stay. All the decorations were hand-painted, and the materials to transform it had been scavenged. It was dedicated to peace, during a time of war. Today she drove on. There were no cars parked outside. Crossing the next barrier, she was aware of the waves from Scapa Flow lapping against the concrete, the westerly breeze behind them. In a gale and with a high tide, sometimes the road was impassable. A flock of geese rose into the air as she passed.

As she arrived in to South Ronaldsay, she looked down to see that the Pentland ferry was moving away from the pier in the attractive village of St Margaret's Hope. This was the first sight many visitors had of Orkney, and many stayed, buying up the pretty houses, inflating prices, only realizing too late that in winter the gales closed the barriers, and that the restaurants and shops that had appealed to them were closed.

So, Willow thought, *if Barbara is on the ferry, I'm too late. I should have driven straight here. She'll be on her way to the mainland.*

But although the crossing to Gill's Bay in Caithness was the quickest route there was, it still took more than an hour, and there would be time to have an officer waiting at the other end. Willow knew she should be regretting her leisurely drive south, but she couldn't quite do it. She'd needed the space and the time to think.

She saw the Volkswagen as soon as she drove into the car park at the pier and thought that Barbara must have got on the ferry as a foot passenger. There would be no photo ID needed and the woman might have paid in cash. A way of slipping south unnoticed. Willow felt a moment of triumph on Perez's behalf. He'd been right. The car hadn't been here when his officers had checked the day before. Barbara must have found somewhere to stay overnight, but this was the route she'd decided to take.

Willow climbed out of her car and made her way towards the terminal and ticket office. Someone there might remember a big Englishwoman. But she took a detour past the VW on her way, and saw that Barbara was still inside, in the driver's seat, with tears streaming down her face. Willow tapped on the window.

Barbara looked up and seemed almost glad to see her. She reached across to open the passenger door, and Willow got in.

Chapter Thirty-Three

It was early afternoon and Perez was back in the police station. He'd needed more coffee and food, and knew he was doing nothing useful at the locus. He sent Ellie there to take his place.

'You're in charge. No reason to get back to me unless you need to.'

She grinned and seemed to blossom in front of him.

He'd downloaded the Johnson television series from iPlayer and was watching it with Phil, drinking takeaway coffee from the Archive cafe and eating a sandwich. He still couldn't quite believe in the coincidence of all three crime scenes appearing in the show, and he wanted to check for himself that Rutherford had been right, and no other ancient site had featured.

He had to admit that the professor had been a convincing performer. The viewers would have believed that he was the expert in the field, and that it was down to his skill that the runes on the story stones had been interpreted. Certainly, it would never occur to them that the man had only stayed on Westray a couple of times before making the film. He spoke fluently, with only a trace of arrogance, and anyone watching would be quite certain that nobody else could have been as knowledgeable as him. He came across as likeable, a bit of a rogue, and he peppered the history with personal stories about his time on the island, first as a student and then as an academic.

'There were some wild parties. I'm not sure we would have got away with anything like that these days.' A little chuckle, as if he regretted the old freedoms.

Perez wondered what Willow would make of that, and again the spark of an idea floated into his head.

Rutherford had been right. The three episodes based on Orkney had featured Westray, Maeshowe and Stenness, including a brief piece shot with Brodgar in the background. Perez didn't bother to watch the films based in Shetland. By then, he'd had enough of Johnson's strutting, the carefully windblown hair and the patronizing air.

'Man,' Phil said, when the screen went blank, 'have you ever seen anyone so sure of himself?'

Perez was about to answer when his phone rang. Willow, her voice a little breathless.

'I've found Barbara.'

For a moment he didn't reply. He could hardly believe what she was telling him. 'Alive?'

'Oh yes, very alive.'

'Where?'

'St Margaret's Hope. You and Ellie guessed she might be there. She was going to get on the two-thirty ferry to Caithness, when she heard on the news that Tony was dead. She was in her car crying her eyes out when I found her – the ferry sailed without her. She's still here. I've just left her in my car for a couple of minutes to make the call. I can see her. She's not going anywhere.'

'Do you believe her? You don't think she killed her husband?'

'Oh, I believe *that*. I'm not sure about anything else. She could have been involved in the other two murders, couldn't she? As Johnson's accomplice. I'll bring her in. Leave their car here, secure. You can send someone down for it.'

Perez was going to tell Willow to take care, to ask if she needed someone to come to South Ronaldsay, so she wouldn't be on her own with the woman who might, despite what Willow had said, have recently killed her husband. But in the end, he thought better of it. The spark of his idea was growing a little brighter – and he trusted Willow's judgement. She knew what she was doing.

He decided, when Barbara walked into the police station, that they'd both been right. He couldn't see this as a woman who'd killed her husband. Not in cold blood. Not leaving him overnight in the middle of a stone circle. She was a mess. Her eyes were red with crying. She was still rubbing them with her knuckles as she came through the door. She'd been wearing make-up when she'd set off for the ferry, but the mascara and shadow had smudged all over her cheeks. The confident extrovert had disappeared, along with the loud voice and the sense of entitlement. She'd clung on to Willow's arm as they made their way from the car park, as if she'd get lost without the detective, as if she wouldn't be able to stand straight without support. Either she was a consummate actor, or she was devastated by her husband's death. Perez knew he could be *too* sympathetic, too easily taken in by a good sob story, but he believed that Barbara was grieving.

While he understood her anger and her pain, now he needed answers quickly. The woman was the best way to find out who'd killed Archie Stout, George Riley and Tony Johnson. And though he knew it shouldn't matter, she was the best way to stop the pressure that was piling up from Glasgow, from the officers who were judging him and his team from the comfort of their offices and homes.

He took her into the room where they interviewed vulnerable victims and witnesses. He wanted to make her as relaxed as possible so she would talk. It had a carpet and soft chairs. A coffee table with a box of tissues on top. A couple of cheesy prints on the wall. He'd taken down the image of the Stones of Stenness at sunset. Willow followed them in.

Barbara pulled her hands away from her face. 'Can I see him?'

Perez remembered that Vaila had asked exactly the same question. Another bereaved woman.

'Not yet,' he said. 'But we can arrange it for you later.'

Willow was sitting next to Barbara. Perez had taken a chair opposite them both.

'Why did you leave Westray in such a rush?' He tried to keep his voice gentle and unhurried as he nodded towards Willow. 'You knew that Chief Inspector Reeves here wanted to talk to you both.'

'We needed to get home quickly. Tony had work commitments.'

'That's not quite true, is it?' Willow could have been chiding a child for an unimportant fib. 'You'd stolen some notebooks from the heritage centre. You were running away before their absence was discovered.'

'But that did relate to Tony's work!'

Perez thought Barbara had convinced herself that they'd done nothing wrong. She'd created a narrative in which she and her husband were the good guys, misunderstood.

And, he thought, *don't we all do that at times?*

Barbara was still speaking now, earnest, desperate to persuade them. 'Tony had used that material for his research paper. He had every right to it.'

'But it wasn't *his* research, was it?' Perez decided it was time to challenge her. 'And he'd failed to credit Magnus Stout for all the work. He took the glory for himself.'

'It wasn't like that!' Barbara leaned forward until her face was so close to Perez's that he could smell the perfume she must have used that morning. Preparing herself for the meeting with her husband. Preparing to run away. 'Tony talked to Magnus and asked his permission. Magnus was delighted that his research had changed the wider world's perception of the archaeology of Orkney and Westray in particular. Tony had asked Magnus if he could have the notebooks, and Magnus had agreed. But he was getting old, and he couldn't find them immediately, and then the promise must have slipped from his mind. Tony reminded him a few times, but Magnus was caught up with other things – the farm and his family – and he never got round to sending them.'

'Perhaps,' Perez suggested gently, 'Magnus wanted the notebooks to stay in Westray. He might not have enjoyed being pressured to hand them over. If he hadn't wanted any kind of fuss, he might just have held on to them.'

'Oh no!' Barbara seemed shocked by the suggestion. 'I don't think that was it at all.'

'Then he died,' Perez went on as if she hadn't spoken, 'and Archie found the notebooks in Nistaben. He showed them to

George Riley. He confronted your husband and accused him of plagiarism and fraud. Riley threatened to make Magnus's role in the story stones translation public, and to accuse your husband of stealing the research.'

'It was ridiculous!' Barbara was almost back to her old self, shrill and certain. The loyal wife fighting for her husband's good name. Or fighting for herself? Knowing, perhaps, that she'd be implicated too, that the lovely arty friends who came to her home for supper or drinks would pick up the scandal on social media and begin to keep their distance. 'It would have ruined Tony's reputation, just as he'd been commissioned to work on a new series for the BBC.'

'So,' Perez said, 'Tony arranged to meet Archie to discuss it all, to persuade him to hand over the notebooks.'

Barbara nodded. She glanced at Willow, as if hoping for her support. 'Magnus had already promised that Tony should have them, you see. Tony wanted to explain. He arranged to meet Archie to discuss it, to set the record straight.'

'Why did they meet at the site at Noltland? It was poor weather for a conversation outdoors.'

Barbara shrugged. 'Tony didn't want other people interfering.' A pause. 'It seemed appropriate to us, and not too far from Pierowall. They met in the golf club car park and walked to the site from there.'

'Did Archie drive there? He didn't walk?'

'No. His car was there before we were. He seemed impatient, as if he'd been waiting for some time.' She paused for a moment, choosing her words so they would understand. 'We'd had the meeting all planned to create the right atmosphere. The storm that night came out of nothing, but Tony decided to go ahead anyway with what we'd arranged.'

It seemed to Perez that the whole set-up had been like a piece of theatre. Maybe the scene-setting had been Barbara's idea. He could imagine her directing the encounter, with Tony imagining himself in front of the camera again. He'd obviously always enjoyed that. The preening. The showing off.

Willow came in with a question then:

'Were you there with them at the meeting? Did you see what happened?'

Barbara shook her head. 'I drove with Tony to the golf club, but I sat in the car, waiting. Tony went out alone.' A pause. 'I left on the headlights for a few minutes and saw them walk away together. Just shadows, blown by the wind, down the path to the sea.'

'That still seems odd to me, to be out there in the wild weather.'

'It hadn't started raining then. That came later.' Barbara paused for a moment. 'Besides, we thought Archie might understand things better if Tony took him to the Noltland site and explained how much it had revealed about Westray's history. The man was a layman, not a historian, not even an amateur like his father. We wanted to capture his imagination and show him how important Westray was to a knowledge of the period.'

'But Archie couldn't be persuaded. He'd spoken to George Riley, who'd already decided that your husband was a plagiarist and was determined to expose him.' Perez was still trying to picture the meeting between the men: Johnson insisting that Archie get out of his car and walk towards the sea, through the storm, in torchlight. Why had Archie gone along with it? Perhaps he was in the mood for a confrontation and Vaila had said he'd always been exhilarated by a storm. He'd gone along with the plan because he was excited by the drama. The evening in the bar with his friends could wait. It fitted the character of the man.

Perez looked across the table at Barbara. He had to push the woman to the truth.

'All afternoon Archie had been around the island, in old folks' houses, having a dram wherever he went,' he said. 'He wasn't drunk or unsteady, but the alcohol would have made him unreasonable, a little aggressive. It could take him that way. I think Tony had already lifted the story stones from the centre. He wanted to prove how much he knew about them, that he was entirely familiar with every mark made on the back of each stone. But Archie wouldn't listen. He didn't give your husband a chance to explain. He was never very interested in detail. He insisted that the work was Magnus's and that he should have proper credit.'

'As you said, Archie had met George Riley earlier in the day.' Barbara was bitter. 'And then I think they met again just before we caught up with Stout at the golf club. They'd wound each other up. Archie wouldn't be reasonable.'

'So,' Perez spoke very quietly now, 'that night at Noltland, your husband lost his temper and killed Archie. Archie must have turned his back on Tony, walked away from him, heading back to his car to drive to Pierowall, the warmth and the craic. Tony would have hated that. He wasn't used to being ignored. He came up behind him and hit him. A moment of rage. Almost understandable.'

'No!' Barbara was beside herself. These tears were of frustration, not grief. 'They argued. But Tony kept his temper. It was Archie who flew into a rage. He set off back to the golf club and his car. He said that he had other more important things on his mind. He couldn't waste time on Tony's lies. I saw him! The rain had started by then, and there was a flash of lightning that lit up the scene. Archie Stout was alive when he left Tony. I saw him run across the car park, his big coat flapping in the wind, and he was still sitting in his car when we drove away.'

'I don't think that's true, is it?' Perez said. 'Archie Stout's vehicle was back outside the hotel the following morning. If he was killed at Noltland after Tony left him, how can it have got there?'

'I don't know!' The woman was almost screaming. 'But I promise that he was still alive when we last saw him.'

'What time did this meeting near the dig take place?' Willow came in again, her voice low, reasonable. 'Was it before or after your dinner with the Angels?'

'Just after.'

'So Vaila had already got to the bar. News was already out that Archie was missing. You and Tony knew that people were looking for him, because you were still at the Angels' when Vaila called them.' Willow paused for a moment. 'When did Tony make this arrangement to meet Archie?' Outside the window the light was fading. She reached back and switched on a lamp on a shelf behind her. There was a soft light that made the space more intimate. A place for therapy not interrogation.

Barbara leaned back in her chair and closed her eyes for a moment. Suddenly the woman seemed overcome with exhaustion. Perez was worried that she might even fall asleep. But she answered, her voice flat. She wanted this over too.

'That was earlier in the day. Tony was anxious. He might have seemed very sure of himself, but it was all a front. That morning, he couldn't settle. I had emails to send for work and, in the end, I suggested that he go out for a walk. He saw Archie go into Rosalie Greeman's house and waited in the road for him to come out. He tried to talk to Archie then, but the man said he was too busy and refused to engage. According to Tony, he seemed upset. That was when Tony suggested meeting at the old excavation. "For old times' sake." I don't think Archie liked it, but he agreed. We planned the detail later in the afternoon.'

'How did you get into the heritage centre to pick up the story stones?'

'Evelyn gave us her key. Tony told her we wanted to do a little research. We pulled the door locked behind us.'

Perez supposed that was when Fiona had seen the light in the heritage centre window. He was trying to make sense of this. He needed to create a real timeline of that day. He'd been given information by so many people that he couldn't keep track.

Barbara was still talking. 'Even if Vaila hadn't phoned the Angels to say she couldn't find Archie, we'd planned to leave Hillhead early. Tony had asked a colleague to phone him, so we'd have an excuse.'

So that was the phone call that Tom and Evelyn Angel had described. Perez and Barbara sat for a moment staring at each other. In the corridor outside someone was whistling 'Silent Night'. It was perfectly in tune.

Willow took up the questions. 'Let's move on to the day of the carol concert in Kirkwall. You came out with the others on the ferry from Westray. I was at the concert, but I didn't see you in the cathedral, though you implied that you had been.'

'No,' Barbara said. 'We just thought we fancied a change, a

trip in to the mainland. It had all got a bit fraught in Westray after Archie died. We wanted a change of scene.' A pause. 'I'm not sure why I lied about having been in the cathedral. I suppose it seemed a bit pathetic to say we'd come to town because we fancied a trip out when everyone else was having a deep and meaningful experience in the service.' There was that sneer in her voice again, as if really, she thought everyone else was pathetic.

'What did you do in Kirkwall?'

'A bit of shopping. A few bits and pieces to take back as gifts for the family. A cocktail or three.'

'A meal?'

'Yes. We managed an early supper at the Storehouse.'

'What about lunch?' Perez asked.

'Oh, I never bother much with lunch and we'd had a full breakfast at the hotel.'

'But Tony *did* have lunch. On his own in the Archive cafe.'

Barbara seemed nearly to lose control again. 'Someone's stabbed my husband and killed him. There have been three murders in your beautiful islands. And you're interested in our eating habits?'

'This was the day that George Riley was killed.' Perez's voice was icy. 'He was hit by the second story stone that you've already admitted was in your husband's possession when he met Archie Stout on Westray. So yes, I'm very interested in your movements that day.'

'Tony didn't have either of the story stones by then!' She was wide awake now, shouting so loudly that her voice sounded hoarse. 'He left them at Noltland with Archie. He'd been upset by the encounter, and anyway why would he bother to carry the stones back with him. He'd had them to set the scene, to make Archie realize how much effort he'd put into making Westray famous. That obviously hadn't worked.'

'Only one stone was there when I found Archie's body,' Perez said. 'It was covered in blood and bone, and it had been used to bludgeon the man to death.'

'That wasn't Tony!'

'Are you sure, Mrs Johnson?' Willow said quietly. 'You weren't there. Can you really be sure?'

Barbara stared at her. 'Of course I'm sure. Tony was pissed off. He'd been out in the cold and the wind, when he could have been in the bar. He'd failed to persuade Stout. His reputation was in danger. But I saw the man come back to his car. Besides, there was no blood on my husband's hands. Literally or metaphorically. And there would have been, wouldn't there, if he'd battered Archie? On his hands and his clothes.'

Neither of them answered.

'Where were you when your husband was having lunch in Kirkwall, Mrs Johnson?' Perez asked at last. 'We know you took your car with you on the ferry that day. Did you go out for a drive? Explore a little?'

She shook her head. 'We did go for a drive – only out to Orphir, it was a beautiful day – but that was just after we first arrived in Kirkwall.'

'What *were* you doing while your husband was eating lunch? You still haven't explained.'

'What is this fixation with Tony's lunch? I was shopping. Tony hates it. Hated it. I love it. So we split up. No big deal. No drama.'

'And then you split up again yesterday,' Willow said. 'According to a witness, you and your husband were arguing in the ferry on the way out of Westray. Is that why you were driving to St Margaret's Hope on your own? You'd decided you couldn't live with him any longer?'

'No!'

'Then perhaps you could explain.'

Barbara didn't answer for a moment.

'Mrs Johnson?'

'Tony thought he'd come up with a plan to get the Stout family on side. All it would take would be for Vaila to explain that he'd collaborated with Magnus. That the notebooks might be in the old man's writing, but that he'd been scribing for Tony. That the work *was* all his.'

'But that wasn't true, was it?'

'No, it wasn't all true, but honestly, I think Tony had come to believe his own story. He was feeling cheated and betrayed.' A pause. 'I wasn't sure about him going to Vaila. She'd just lost her husband. She might see it as the most dreadful intrusion. But Tony thought he had a way to persuade her. I'm not sure why.'

'Your husband had stolen the notebooks the night before you left. I'd been in the centre to look at them, but he came in later. He persuaded Tom and Evelyn to bring their key to the Pierowall Hotel.'

She nodded. 'We had the notebooks, but Tony knew there'd probably be a digital record. Having the books wasn't enough. He wanted Vaila to write him a letter of support.' She looked up at them both. 'He was hoping to persuade George's partner to be on his side too.'

'Did he go to visit Miles?'

'I think so. He got a taxi to Finstown. The last time I spoke to him, the mobile reception was so poor that I wasn't quite clear what he was saying. We'd decided we'd be less likely to be found if we weren't together. We knew that running away from Westray would make us look guilty. So we split up. I found an Airbnb in Deerness. I never met the landlady. She just gave me the code to the key box.' She paused. 'I gathered from that last call that Vaila had refused to talk to Tony, so he was going to try George's partner. George was the person who'd stirred up all the trouble against him.'

'Where was Tony planning to stay last night?'

'I don't know. He said earlier that he'd found somewhere, but the line went dead before he could give me the details. I couldn't get through to him again.' She looked across at Perez, horrified. 'I suppose he was already dead. We'd planned to meet in St Margaret's Hope for the two-thirty ferry. He'd get a taxi down. We'd board separately in case they were looking out for us as a couple. We knew we didn't need photo ID. Then, driving across the barriers, I was listening to the news on my car radio. I heard that he was dead.'

'Didn't you think that running away would only make you look more guilty?' This question came from Perez. He couldn't quite reconcile the attempt to escape with the intelligent couple, who'd believed they could persuade the world that Johnson was an expert and not a plagiarist.

Barbara hesitated before she spoke. 'We panicked,' she said. 'We just wanted to leave it all behind us and go home.'

Chapter Thirty-Four

THEY LET BARBARA GO. IT SEEMED there was nothing more she could tell them. Nothing more, at least, that she was willing to say.

The owner of the Airbnb in Deerness hadn't seen her but had confirmed that someone had been in the place.

'Oh yes, she definitely stayed there. The bed's been slept in, and the kettle was still warm when I got in to clean this morning.'

'Can you tell what time she arrived?'

'I can't do that. I live close by, but I was in Kirkwall with my father all night. A family party. A neighbour might have seen her car.'

Perez sent an officer to check, but even before he reported back, they both agreed that they had no reason to hold on to Barbara any longer.

While they were talking to the woman, Phil had received a call to say that Johnson had booked into the pub in Stenness the night of his death. He passed on the message as soon as the interview was over.

'Ellie went across to the hotel to check the story. Johnson

arrived by taxi, checked in, had a meal, but then he said he was going out again. To see the stones in the moonlight. The landlady thought that was pretty weird, because the sky was a bit cloudy. She didn't come back to the pub until this afternoon, so she didn't connect her absent guest with the body. Johnson had given her a different name.'

Willow rang round to find somewhere for Barbara to stay. After her outburst during the interview, the woman had become calm and compliant. Numb. The only place with vacancies was the Kirkwall Hotel.

'Vaila and her boys are staying there. Will you be okay being in the same place?'

'Why not? I won't see them. I'll be staying in my room. I can't face the world.' Barbara looked up at Willow. 'I just feel exhausted. I want to sleep and pretend that none of this has happened.'

In the hotel lobby, she stood, blank-faced, while Willow made arrangements with reception. The only rooms left were small, not yet renovated, and Willow showed her into the cell-like space, with a single bed and a scratched dark wood wardrobe, a tiny bathroom with a stained sink. Barbara scarcely seemed to notice. She drew the curtains and lay on the bed, her back to Willow, who left without a word.

Willow had phoned Vaila from the police station, saying she wanted to update her on the case, and warning her that Barbara Johnson was staying in the same place too.

'I'm sorry, but we have nowhere else for her to stay. You'll have heard that her husband's dead. I don't think she'll be leaving her room though.'

She called the woman again now to say that she was in the

hotel. It was still early evening, but the bar was already full of Christmas Eve revellers, the noise spilling out into the lobby. Vaila appeared from the lift in a down coat, so big that it seemed to swamp her. She'd always been a small woman, but now she appeared wizened, tiny.

'Do you mind if we go out?' she said. 'This place is starting to feel like a prison.'

'What are your plans? Will you go back to Westray?'

Vaila nodded. 'I wasn't sure that I could face the island and the house again, but now I'm longing for it. For the space and my own bed. Westray folk. Once the Ba' is over, and all the speeches about Archie are finished, we'll head back. I'd go tomorrow evening or on Boxing Day if the ferries were running, but I'll be on the first boat on the twenty-seventh. We'll have done what's expected of us. We've been hiding for long enough.' She looked at Willow. 'I can't wait for tomorrow to be over. The performance.'

'How are the boys?'

'I don't know. I try to speak to them. But teenage boys are bad about talking. In real life anyway. They seem as well as I could hope.'

As they walked out to the street, there was a gust of wind that blew Willow's hair across her face. She pulled it back, tied it in a rough knot. 'Where shall we go?'

'Are you okay if we just walk? It's not so cold now and I need the air.'

'Sure.' Willow waited until they'd crossed the road to the harbour. A group of young women paraded ahead of them. They had tinsel in their hair and wore very short skirts and very tall heels. There was a lot of leopard print. 'You'd already heard about Tony Johnson on the news?'

'Aye. He tried to talk to me yesterday. He came to the hotel.' They stopped to watch a fishing boat pull up to the jetty. 'I wouldn't see him. I thought he might have been the person who killed Archie and George. Besides, he'd cheated Archie's father. It was an outrage that he was bothering me.'

'You should have contacted us. We'd have talked to him.' *And maybe,* Willow thought, *we'd have saved his life.*

Vaila shrugged. 'Aye, perhaps I should. But just now, everything seems too much bother. I just wanted him to go away and leave me in peace.'

'There's a possibility that he *did* kill those men,' Willow said. 'The cause of death in this latest murder is a little different.'

'That would be some coincidence, surely! Two killers in a place like Orkney.'

'I'm not saying the deaths aren't linked. Johnson's death might have been a revenge killing.'

'You think I killed Johnson because he murdered my husband?' Vaila stopped walking and turned towards Willow. The small, pointed face stared out from the billowing hood. She shook her head, very slowly, as if the detective were crazy.

Willow shook her head. 'Not just you. Other people have been bereaved. It's a possibility we have to consider. As a theory.'

'When did he die?'

Willow and Perez had talked about this. 'Late yesterday evening. Certainly after dark.' Because before that there would have been people exploring the Stones of Stenness. And there would have been locals walking their dogs.

'Well then, we were all in last night. We had an early supper in the restaurant, then the boys were in their room. It's a twin and they're in together. We have connecting rooms and I heard them through the wall. They were watching some film on the telly, or maybe playing a game.' Vaila paused for a moment. 'They were still awake at midnight when I shouted at them to go to sleep.'

'Could they hear *you*?'

'You really think that I sneaked out late at night, drove to Stenness to meet a man I disliked and was scared of, and killed him?' Vaila gave a hard little laugh.

'As I said, it doesn't matter what I think. I need to ask these questions. It doesn't mean I don't believe you. It's important that I follow the process. You must understand.'

'I suppose I must, but it's a strange, shitty kind of work you do.'

They'd been walking west away from the bars and the restaurants towards the industrial estate and had reached the little nature reserve on the edge of the town. A loch and wetland. During the day, there'd be geese and swans on the deep water and wading birds at the muddy edges. The ice had all melted and a breeze chopped the reflected street lights into tiny images.

'Did Johnson tell you why he wanted to see you?'

'Oh yes, he was quite open about it, just in that phone call. You'd maybe say that he was desperate. He seemed crazy. Obsessed. He wanted me to write a letter saying that Magnus had given him permission to use his research. In fact, he'd already written the letter. He just wanted me to come down to sign it. He said I'd regret it if I didn't agree. It sounded like a sort of threat. He was still talking but I ended the call. He tried phoning again, but I didn't answer.'

Willow didn't speak for a moment. She was processing the information, wondering how this might be relevant. Why had

Johnson thought Vaila would be so open to persuasion? That overweening arrogance maybe.

'Did he have your mobile number?'

'No, thank God. He was using the hotel phone extension. I called down to reception and told them that I didn't want to speak to him, so they shouldn't put him through if he called or turned up again.' She stood for a moment, looking out at the loch. 'I don't give a shit about all that stuff – the archaeology and the research that Magnus did – but Archie did care. He can't fight any more, so I must fight for him. And if Johnson killed him, then I'm glad that the man's dead. It's what he deserved.'

Willow walked back to the hotel with her, chatted briefly to the lass at reception to check Vaila's story, then went to collect James. It was Christmas Eve and she wanted to spend a little time with her son.

Chapter Thirty-Five

Perez drove to Finstown again, to the grand stone house where George Riley had lived with the love of his life. There was that strange, grey dusk of a midwinter early evening, and the road he knew so well seemed almost unfamiliar. The car's headlights hit shapes that for a moment he failed to recognize: the corners of drystone walls, a looming barn, a sheep wandering along the verge. He could be in a different place altogether.

During the short drive, his mind was racing. He'd already dismissed Miles as the killer of Archie Stout. He had no motive, and there was no evidence that he'd been on Westray the night of the murder. Despite any problems the couple might have had, Perez didn't believe that the man had killed George. He'd been distraught when he'd heard of his partner's death. But if Miles had believed Johnson had murdered George Riley, then it wasn't a struggle to picture him killing the professor out of revenge. A cold kind of fury. The motive was sufficiently strong. Miles had adored George. The men had started a new phase in their lives together, and Miles might feel that he had nothing to lose now, that he hated the thought of life without the man who had adored *him*. Miles would be organized, ruthless. In addition, he'd despised Johnson as a man. He'd thought him a liar and a cheat. Perez couldn't imagine him feeling any sort of sentiment about the professor's death.

Perez had liked Miles, his dignity and his honesty, but now he could see him as a realistic suspect for the professor's murder.

There were no lights on in the house, though the external lamp in its ornate Victorian frame lit up the front of the building. Perez knocked at the door but there was no reply. He looked through the tall window into the grand living room and could see that it was tidy, the piano lid down, the grate cleared of ash. If Miles *had* been drinking there the night after George had died, as Perez had suspected, he'd thrown away all the evidence now. Perez knocked again before walking round to the rear of the house and the kitchen. The back door was unlocked, and he pushed it open, anxious about what he might find.

He anticipated not another murder, but a body all the same. If he'd killed Johnson, Miles might feel that he had nothing left to live for. He would leave his home in good order, and a note explaining his suicide. He was that sort of man.

Perez was about to move further into the house when he remembered his first visit; then he'd been thinking of George as a suspect rather than a victim. Now that the frost had gone, the ground would be easier to work, and he could picture Miles out in the walled kitchen garden, digging obsessively even after the light had faded. He closed the door quickly, not wanting to be caught intruding, and made his way through the arched gate.

He felt a moment of relief, the draining of anxiety, when he realized that Miles was there. It was as Perez had suspected. There were fairy lights strung along the high wall – one of George's fantastical ideas surely – and in their glimmer he saw the man, forking over one of the beds, preparing it for spring planting. He must have been at it for most of the day, working backwards from the wall closest to the house, because there were yards of fine tilth in front of him. He'd taken off his jacket and hung it on one of the apple tree's branches. Even in this shadowy light, Perez could tell that he was sweating.

Miles stuck the fork into the ground and turned away to reach into his jacket pocket for a handkerchief as Perez stood in the archway, but the man must have heard the opening of the gate because he looked round.

'Good timing,' he said. 'I was ready for a break. Besides, it's dark as hell and I can't see what I'm doing. I told myself I should finish the whole bed before I stopped, but now I have an excuse.' He wiped his forehead with the white cloth. 'I hope you'll have a beer with me, even if you are on duty. I've promised myself that I'll not drink alone any more, and I really could do with one now.'

'Maybe just a small one.' Perez thought there were occasions when rules needed to be broken.

'Do you have any information for me?'

They were back at the kitchen table, shoes off. Miles had washed his hands at the large enamel sink. There was a strip of spotlights on the ceiling. They reflected from the work surfaces and seemed very bright, cruel, after the gloom outside. Perez's beer had been opened but he'd only taken a sip from it.

'You haven't heard the news today?'

'No. I've been in the garden since breakfast. It's all that keeps me sane. There's something about the rhythm of digging that's calming. It's not at all demanding, but it takes a little concentration. I hope the physical activity will help me to sleep.' And he *did* seem calm. It was hard to imagine him now as a ruthless killer. But the rumours were that he'd been some sort of spy, and Perez supposed that a spy would be adept at dissembling.

'Did Anthony Johnson get in touch with you yesterday?'

Miles set down his can.

'Yes. He turned up here at the house. No advance phone call. No shame at all about barging in on my grief. No pretended words of condolence. I recognized him. George had made me watch his programme on the television. George swore all the way through it, so I couldn't hear a word, but I could see the images. I couldn't believe it when I opened the door to him.' Miles looked up at Perez. 'It was like the Devil turning up at one's home. A Devil in walking boots, an anorak and a tweed cap. The man was crazy. Obsessed. He was ranting about George and how his lies had ruined Johnson's life. *His* life. All he was in danger of losing was his reputation. I'd lost my partner. My reason for living.'

'What did he want you to do? Precisely.'

'He wanted me to stop George's book from being published. As if I would or could. It's in the hands of the publisher now. Johnson said I should tell the world that George had made a mistake. That his research was his own, that Magnus had done some of the groundwork, but Johnson had made the links, had interpreted all the material, that he *was* the real genius behind the story stones.'

'Why would he think you'd agree to do that?'

Miles shook his head. 'I don't know. As I've said, he was beyond reason. Desperate. It was as if he believed that George had been deliberately vindictive or had some personal grudge, that he'd exaggerated Johnson's fraud for his own purpose. Johnson stood on the doorstep making wild threats, yelling and swearing. He was a bully. He said that if I didn't comply with his demands, he'd ruin *George's* reputation, that the truth would come out in the end.'

'Do you have any idea what he meant by that?'

'Not at all, and he wasn't specific. The fact that George was a teacher in a gay relationship? That might have been a threat fifty years ago, but certainly not now.'

It seemed to Perez that Johnson had been so desperate to clear his name and establish his future that he'd been throwing out random threats to whoever stood in his way. Perhaps his public image, his standing as an academic, was all he had. And as that started to crumble, so did he. He was almost losing his mind; his reason was shredding little by little as the days passed.

'Did you let him into the house?'

Miles had already finished his beer. He crushed it in his fist and threw it into a bin. 'Certainly not! He tried to push his way in, but I'm stronger than he is. I shut the door on him. He might still be there now, yelling all my misdeeds to the wind and the sky, but a visitor turned up. Paul, the island archaeologist. He thought I might need company. Johnson must have recognized Paul, because as soon as he got out of his car, the *professor* left.' There was a mocking emphasis on the word professor. 'Very quickly and quietly.'

Miles went to the fridge and took out another can. 'What

exactly was on the news? Have you arrested Johnson? I'd be happy to make a statement and share all the information about the plagiarism I had from George.'

Perez didn't answer directly. 'What time did Johnson get here yesterday?'

'Early evening. At about this time. It had been dark for a while.'

'How long did Paul stay with you?'

'Most of the evening. I fed him and we had a few drinks together. More than a few. I offered to make up the spare room for him, but he said he had to get back to his family. He got a taxi home and must have arranged a lift to pick up his car early this morning. It had already gone when I woke up. With a monster hangover.'

Perez considered that. It was hardly a cast-iron alibi, and he'd have to check with Rutherford. But after 'more than a few' drinks it hardly seemed likely that Miles would have lured Johnson to an ancient monument, driven there and stuck a knife in his back.

'Johnson hasn't been arrested. His body was found early this morning in the middle of the Stones of Stenness. He'd been murdered.'

There was a moment of silence. Then Miles threw back his head and laughed.

Perez was shocked. It seemed to him in that moment that everyone involved in the investigation was on the verge of insanity. The reaction was embarrassing, almost unhinged, especially from the upright man, with his formality and gentleman's accent. And perhaps Miles was embarrassed too, because the noise stopped as suddenly as it had started. It was as if a switch had been thrown.

'I'm sorry, Inspector. That was unforgivable. But in my head, I'd been willing Johnson's death, imagining how it would be. Knowing I'd never have the courage to do it, you understand, but finding some comfort in the planning. I really believed that he'd murdered George, you see. I still do, though his death complicates matters. When he turned up here, shouting his foul accusations, he convinced me of his guilt. In one of the scenarios I'd created for his demise, he was lying in the middle of the Stones of Stenness. That was where he'd been standing, during that dreadful television documentary. Pretending to the world what an expert he was.'

'How had you killed him? In this fantasy murder?' Perez expressed only mild curiosity.

'Oh, I didn't batter him to death with an ancient artefact. That would have connected him to George and Archie, and he wasn't worthy of that. I stabbed him with a common kitchen knife. Ours are very sharp. George and I both loved to cook.'

Perez took a sip of his beer but said nothing.

It wasn't a kitchen knife, he thought. *But you're pretty close.*

'I suppose,' Miles said at last, 'you have no evidence that Johnson committed murder. Not now. He might have been a victim of the same killer. It might not have been a matter of revenge.' He looked at Perez, his eyes very sharp. Probing.

Perez wondered again what exactly the man had been doing in the Foreign Office. He *could* imagine him as a spy in an alien world, pretending to be a junior diplomat, lying for his country. He might not have killed as part of his work, but he could have ordered another person to. Or turned a blind eye. Perez wondered if there was some way to find out. But he might be creating fantasy scenarios too.

'What are your plans for tomorrow?' he said.

'Tomorrow?' Miles sounded vague. 'Ah, of course, Christmas Day.' He gave a sad smile. 'George was a great fan of Christmas. We made our own traditions. A feast that very definitely didn't include turkey. I might not bother with all the food, but I'll probably excuse myself from the "no drinking alone" rule.'

'Was the Ba' one of those traditions? You do know that George wrote the definitive history of the game.'

'Oh, of course we went along to that. How could we not?' He smiled again, this time self-mocking. 'As you say, George was a leading light, helping with the organization, though he never played. Besides, all those athletic young men, rolling around in the mud, jumping into the water. We wouldn't have missed it for the world.'

Perez couldn't think where there might be mud on the Ba' route, but he understood the sentiment and was relieved that Miles seemed calmer now, brighter, not taking himself so seriously, at least for the moment.

'I understand that there'll be a tribute to Archie and to George before the start.'

'They've asked me to speak,' Miles said. He looked up at Perez again. 'And to throw up the boys' ba'. To honour George's role as a teacher. I agreed in a moment of weakness. Or perhaps in a moment of strength. George would have loved that. Me, standing there in front of all those people, telling the great and the good of Orkney what a wonderful man he was.'

'Have they asked Vaila to speak too?'

'I believe so and hers will be the more important speech of course. She and Archie being old Orcadian, and Archie being so important to the game. I imagine she'll be talking after the main game in the afternoon. Maybe handing over some kind of trophy. That's as it should be. My speech will be very short.

But even just being there will be difficult enough for me. I dislike any form of attention. I'll do it, imagining George laughing at me.' Again, he crushed the beer can and threw it with impressive precision into the bin. 'You should go, Inspector. If you stay, I'll use you as an excuse to drink more. And if I do, my willpower will be weak, and I might continue all night again. Besides, I think you have a family. It's Christmas Eve.'

'Would you like company? I'm sure there are friends of George who would gladly spend some time with you.'

He shook his head. 'I'd rather be on my own tonight. There will be people enough tomorrow. I'll watch an old film and sleep. I might even dream of happier times.'

When Perez got home, it was already past James's bedtime, but his son was still up, sitting beside Willow on a video call to Cassie in Shetland. Perez joined in. In the background, he saw Duncan Hunter's sitting room, and he was reminded vividly of the house where he'd spent time as a boy. Duncan had been his friend, and at weekends, when he might have been stranded in the school hostel in Lerwick, Perez had been invited to the large crumbling house in the north of Shetland mainland, treated almost as Duncan's brother. It was as different from his own ordered and respectable home on Fair Isle as it was possible to be – rambling, cluttered, full of relics of the family's grand past. It had seemed to Perez that there were dusty rooms where the family never ventured.

He'd even stayed there one Christmas Day, when a storm had blown up and the Fair Isle mail boat, the *Good Shepherd*, had failed to make the trip to Grutness, and the small planes had been cancelled for more than a week. They hadn't eaten the

Christmas meal until late in the evening, and Duncan's raffish parents had both been drunk before they'd sat down. They'd all played hide-and-seek in the freezing attics until, exhausted, the boys had taken their own decision that it was bedtime. In the morning, they'd woken to a blizzard and no electricity, because the generator had been allowed to run out of fuel.

Now, behind Cassie's excited face, in the room Perez recognized for its cavernous fireplace, there was an enormous tree, elaborately decorated, with wrapped presents at its foot. Celia's work. Duncan wouldn't have the patience. Perez had worried that the girl might feel abandoned, even though it had been her decision to accept the invitation to stay in Shetland, but she was clearly loving every minute.

'Have an early night,' Perez said. 'Or Santa won't come.'

'Aye, right.' A standing joke. Even when she was a youngster, Cassie had never believed in Santa, had always thought she was being conned. She laughed, blew a kiss at them and the screen went blank.

There was no tree in Willow and Perez's house, but Willow had made some effort after she'd got home from dropping Barbara at the hotel and speaking to Vaila. In a big glass vase there was a huge stem of teasels, sprayed silver. She'd bought baubles from Rosalie Greeman on her visit to Westray, and they hung now from the teasel heads, along with James's gingerbread men. She'd strung decorations made by Cassie in previous years over the mantelpiece.

'Our Christmas weed! We picked it from the garden. James and I decorated it this evening. More eco, we thought, than cutting down a tree.'

'What about the aerosol in the paint?'

She laughed and pretended to hit him. James didn't understand but joined in the mock fight. Willow made hot chocolate for the boy in an attempt to calm him, and then Perez carried him upstairs, with his mushroom-coloured moustache, bathed him, read him stories and put him to bed.

When Perez came down, Willow was in the kitchen. 'I took a veggie chilli from the freezer. From my domestic goddess days. Before Archie got killed.'

'Have we got something to eat for tomorrow?'

'Of course! I bought a chicken from Asda for you and James. And all the trimmings.'

'What about you? No vegetarian treat?'

'Nah, the trimmings will be fine for me.' She turned away from the stove. 'Your work phone rang, I answered it.'

'Oh?' There was always a moment of stress when the phone went off. Tonight, he just hoped it didn't mean going out again. He wanted to be here. To be quiet for what remained of the evening. No bodies. No demands on his time.

'A woman called Belinda. Loud voice. She said she met you at the Maeshowe car park by the old mill.'

Belinda Thorne the dog-walker, who'd seen George Riley just before he'd been killed.

'What did she want?'

'For you to call her back. She'd remembered something. Probably not important but . . . Blah blah blah. You know the sort.' Willow rolled her eyes. She, like him, had been hoping for an evening without interruption.

He nodded. He knew the sort. 'I'll ring her now. Get it over with.'

He went into the sitting room.

'Good evening, Inspector. Sorry to bother you on Christmas Eve. And so late. But better today, I thought, than tomorrow. I won't keep you for long. This is so obvious and I'm sure you've thought of it.' Her voice was so loud that he had to move the phone away from his ear. She was as good as her word. She didn't keep him for long. He imagined that she was hosting a party because he could hear distant voices in the background, one burst of laughter. They'd be people like her who served on committees, ran charities, did good works for the community. When she'd finished speaking, his thoughts were circling, spinning like water moving slowly down a drain. She'd been right. It was obvious, but he hadn't considered its implication. This changed his thinking, and ideas that had seemed isolated and unconnected were gathered together into an almost coherent theory. The spark setting fire. There was no proof though. And proof was what they needed now.

Back in the kitchen he shared his ideas with Willow, who listened with intense concentration. After the meal, Perez went upstairs to fill the stocking that lay on James's bed with tiny gifts. Willow stacked his bigger presents under the Christmas weed. When he returned to the kitchen, Willow had suggestions of her own. A way perhaps to find the proof that they needed. At midnight she had a small glass of wine with him, to see in the day.

Chapter Thirty-Six

They were woken by James, bouncing on the bed. It was early, but not outrageously early. Perez insisted on making coffee first, and herbal tea for Willow, then they sat back in bed, watching their son open the small presents from his stocking. He took the unwrapping slowly and carefully, and lined up the objects – the clockwork train, the sugar mouse, the bag of Shetland puffin poo (an outrageously sugary coconut sweetie that he adored), the wooden jigsaw puzzle, the Lego, the gloves knitted by his Fair Isle grandmother – along the duvet. He was, Willow thought, very like his father. He liked his world ordered. He didn't even start eating the puffin poo until he'd been to the window, lifted a corner of the curtain and looked outside.

They'd left the outside light on, so he could see a circle of the garden, close to the front door. He was shocked and disappointed that there was no snow. There was always snow on Christmas cards and in the films. He'd assumed that everywhere would be white, had imagined snowball fights and building a snowman.

'But those were stories,' Willow said. 'Not real.' She thought it was like this investigation – there was a lot that they'd imagined, tales they'd created. She got him dressed and they went downstairs. It was still Northern Isles midwinter dark.

'Breakfast,' she said. 'A huge breakfast because we don't know when we'll be back from the Ba'.' Soon the kitchen was full of the smell of frying bacon, and she made pancakes too, and scrambled eggs.

'Do we need to be there all day?' Perez said. 'Won't James be bored? We could work it in shifts. One of us could stay here with him. Or we could skip the boys' Ba' altogether and I'll just go myself in the afternoon.'

She thought about Perez's words, wondering how the idea might work. They'd decided that they'd take no action against the killer during the day. They'd watch and wait and let the Ba' run its course. They'd gather their proof. They couldn't believe that anyone else was in danger. But James jumped in, his mouth full of pancake.

'I want to go this morning. Iain and Lawrie will be there.' His chin, sticky with syrup, was thrust forward. He was ready for a battle.

The Stout boys were his heroes. The last time they'd been together, Lawrie had just decided he'd take part in the Ba', his final chance before he was considered an adult – and without really understanding, James had cheered him on. Then he'd worked out how many years it would be before he was old enough to be a part of the game. The Ba' was an Orkney tradition, a legend as potent as anything on the story stones. Some of the locals liked to believe that it dated as far back as that. James, it seemed, was becoming a true Orcadian, and born in the islands, he'd have every right to become a Ba' player.

'What about all those presents under the weed?' Willow said. 'If we stay in this morning, we'd have a chance to open those.'

But James was having none of it. 'One of you could bring me home this afternoon. We can open the presents later before tea.'

'That's true,' Willow said. 'I could do that. Get the meal ready.' She looked at Perez. 'You'll need to be there for the speeches around the adult game, I suppose. Just in case something kicks off. You can bring other officers in for that. Most of them will be there anyway. Phil might even be playing.' She would have liked to be in Kirkwall all day – missing a part of it felt like a sacrifice or a dereliction of duty – but she had James to think about, and the baby. She knew that Perez would handle it fine by himself. It was a kind of presumption to believe she needed to be there with him.

Outside, it was getting light. The air was milder, a little spring-like. The green spears of snowdrop leaves were pushing through the soil. The earth had tipped past the solstice. In the town, families were already gathering for the boys' game. The throw-up would take place at the Merkit Cross on the Kirk Green at ten o'clock, and people wanted a good view, to be seen to support their sons and grandsons.

When they arrived outside the cathedral, Perez carried James on his shoulders, so he'd see what was happening. The boys in the teams were swaggering, full of macho bravado, shouting to their pals. If they were anxious about the fray, they couldn't show it. Willow tried to imagine an older James there, a teenager, surrounded by friends, loud and sweary, and wondered how she'd feel. A mix of anxiety and pride, maybe, though she knew Perez would only be scared for the boy. He might even try to persuade him not to take part. But that would be years away and by then James could be a different lad altogether, quiet, nerdy, uninterested in sport of any kind.

She wondered if women would ever be allowed to take part in the game. After all, they now took their place in the winter Up Helly Aa in Shetland's main town of Lerwick, dressed as Vikings, marching with the Guizer Jarl and his squad. This was different though, a celebration of strength and speed, not only of tradition. Then she thought that island women were strong too. She'd seen Vaila, who seemed so slender and frail, hauling bales, carrying a propane gas cylinder in her arms when they were unloading the boat.

Willow looked up at James, who was twitching with excitement, looking out for Vaila and her sons. He thought he'd got a glimpse of them and wriggled, persuading Perez to lift him down onto the pavement. He didn't want Lawrie and Iain to think he was a baby. As the crowd got bigger, she knew that Perez would be holding his hand tightly. She didn't believe there would be any bother at this boys' game, but there were so many people crammed into a small space, and she'd never been good in crowds. This afternoon, it would be even more scary. She was glad that she'd have their son home then.

Usually, Westray folk wouldn't have bothered with the Ba'. It was a Kirkwall tradition and not considered important by people from the outer islands. They preferred to spend Christmas Day at home. But this year must be different, because she started seeing people she recognized. There wouldn't have been a ferry, so perhaps a couple of the islanders had brought out their creel boats and offered a lift to Archie's special friends and relatives. A way of showing their support to his widow and sons. The first person she came across was Godfrey Lansdown, who *was* elderly, but definitely not infirm.

'I wouldn't have thought the Ba' would be your thing, Mr Lansdown.' Because the man was a birdwatcher, gentle and considered. Willow couldn't see that he'd take pleasure in such a rowdy spectacle.

'Since Edith died, I've felt the need to experience life to the full,' he said. 'I'm more aware of time slipping away. I tend to say yes rather than no these days to new opportunities. When Bill invited me, I took the opportunity to watch the game. Sometimes I rather surprise myself.'

In the distance she saw Nat Wilkinson, tall and awkward, centimetres above the rest of the crowd. He was alone. Perhaps his friend was over the crisis, or perhaps the Ba' had memories for Nat too.

Annie and Bill MacBride were there, taking a day off from the running of the hotel. They were holding hands in a shy, embarrassed way, like teenagers acknowledging their relationship for the first time. Willow didn't suppose they'd have spoken to Vaila yet about buying out Archie's share of the hotel. Bill might have been tempted to rush in, eager to start negotiations immediately, but Annie would be more cautious, more tactful.

She was about to speak to them, when she saw Vaila and the boys. She thought Perez would want to be with them, but he was talking to a woman she recognized as the head teacher from the grammar school, and he hadn't noticed them. He was still holding James's hand. Willow pushed her way through the crowd to join the Stout family.

Vaila looked exhausted, strained. Willow thought she could scarcely have slept since Archie had died. It was hard to picture her now working so hard on the farm. Even Iain seemed to tower above his mother. When she was standing with them, surrounded by the noise and the people, by all the fathers, Willow didn't know what to do, how to show support.

'This is very brave of you,' she said at last, and gave Vaila a hug.

'Ah well, this is Lawrie's last chance to be in with the boys and he's doing it for his father. Archie won the Ba' when he was a lad. Next year Lawrie will be sixteen and with the men, and it's hard to be up against those strong chaps. Iain could have joined in, right enough. There are boys younger than him in the team, but he had more sense, didn't you?' She stroked Iain's head. Lawrie stared out at the crowd.

'Well, brave of Lawrie too. It must be tough.'

'Will you stand with us?' Vaila looked up at her. The skin of her face seemed desperately thin, as if it could rip any moment to let the bone show through. 'That might stop other folk coming up to us. I can't stand their pity. Or their curiosity. It's just a drama to them.'

'Sure.'

'Lawrie's determined to play the game. I tried to talk him out of it, but he said it was for his father.' Vaila's voice was low and bleak. 'And we have to be here for him. The organizers want me to speak later. I wish today was over.'

'Are your parents here?' Willow thought the Angels might be better support than she could be.

'Oh yes. They'll be here, but I've told them to find a good spot to cheer my boy on. I can't stand people I know well to be near me. They fuss and I just feel like ranting and swearing at them. I don't want to upset them. Do you understand?'

'I think so.' Willow imagined Evelyn and Tom somewhere

in the crowd, watching their daughter and grandsons from a distance, banned from approaching. They'd be hurt already.

They stood for a moment in silence. Willow glimpsed the brightly coloured jacket of Rosalie Greeman, as the woman passed through the gathered supporters. Like an exotic bird flitting through a forest of green and brown, she'd appear suddenly and then was lost from view.

Vaila must have noticed too. 'Is that Rosalie?'

'Yes.'

'I'd like to speak to her, I think. Do you suppose she'll come over?'

'I suspect she might feel a little awkward about doing that.'

'Would you ask her?'

'Of course, if that's what you'd like.' Willow was surprised. It wasn't at all what she'd been expecting, but she was relieved too. If Rosalie would stay with Vaila, Willow would have the chance to work the crowd and see who else from Westray was here. She moved off in the direction of the patchwork jacket, and found Rosalie, standing alone, close to the doors of St Magnus Cathedral.

'You came,' Willow said. 'I didn't think you would.'

Rosalie gave a crooked little smile. 'Archie might not have been the love of my life, but he was a friend and I wanted to be here to say goodbye. Sometimes the ritual matters. It helps.'

'I'm not sure how much it's helping Vaila.'

'I saw she's here. She looks wrecked.'

'She'd like to see you.'

Rosalie raised an eyebrow in surprise. 'To have a row? Make a scene?'

'Honestly, I don't think it's anything like that. I think she wants to build bridges. She needs a pal.'

There was a moment's silence before Rosalie grinned. 'Imagine the gossip, when all the Westray folk see us together! It'll be worth chatting just to see their faces.'

'We'll go over then, shall we. Then I'll leave you to it.'

They pushed through the people to find Vaila. It was only fifteen minutes to the Ba' throw-up and every inch of the square and the surrounding streets was full. Apart from where Vaila and Iain were standing. Lawrie must have gone to find the rest of his team, and there was a space around Vaila and her younger son. It was, Willow thought, as if bereavement and grief were a kind of plague that other people believed might be catching.

Vaila saw them approaching. She and Rosalie stood staring at each other, and then almost simultaneously each held out her arms and they hugged. Willow moved quietly away.

She was looking for Perez and James, but they seemed swamped by the crowd, and she had no idea where to start. She got out her phone. Two missed calls from Perez, which she'd not heard because there was so much noise. He must be looking for her too. No point trying to contact him now – in the run-up to the start the noise was deafening. She wasn't sure they'd even hear the bells of the cathedral, which would set the game off.

The man who was doing the throw-up moved onto the cathedral steps. Willow didn't recognize him. He was thin and upright. He could, she thought, have been an army officer.

'Oh, that's a nice touch.' The words were spoken by a middle-aged woman she didn't know, whose mouth was so close to Willow's ear now, squashed by the crowd, that Willow heard the comment.

'Who is it?' She turned and shouted.

'Miles, George Riley's partner.'

Willow thought she should have realized. He was just as Perez had described him. He looked as drawn and grey as Vaila. The hands holding the heavy ba' were shaking. The woman was still talking. 'Usually, it's a star of the game, an old local who played lots of times in his youth. This is a recognition of all George did to record its traditions, and of his role as a teacher and mentor to our young people.'

'And an acknowledgement of the two as a couple, perhaps,' Willow said.

It was, as the woman had said, a nice touch.

'Aye. That too.'

There was a crackly PA system. Miles was handed a microphone. 'I'm here to represent George Alfred Riley. He should have been here in his own right. He loved this game, and he loved Orkney.'

There was a moment of silence as Miles waited for the cathedral bells to ring out the time. On the stroke of ten, he threw the ba' into the air and the boys surged forward, arms raised to have first touch. The game had begun.

Chapter Thirty-Seven

PEREZ COULDN'T HELP THINKING ABOUT BARBARA Johnson, holed up in the Kirkwall Hotel. She'd be grieving too. The hotel was some distance from where the Ba' was started, but he wondered if she'd hear the noise, the chanting. Her husband had been seen as the villain in the tale, a fraud and a cheat. Local people wouldn't mourn him as they'd mourned Archie and George. Even in death, it seemed, there was a hierarchy. Some were more worthy than others and that must make it hard. Everyone here had sympathy for Vaila and her boys; most for Miles. But he doubted that any of the spectators were giving Barbara a thought. It occurred to him that he should go and see her, once Willow had taken James home, in the break between the two games. Whatever her role in the murders, he hated to think of her alone in the bleak hotel room.

Then, as if his imagination had conjured the woman up, made her solid, he glimpsed Barbara Johnson through the crowd. He recognized her coat, an unusual dusty pink, the hood pulled over her head, although the day wasn't cold at all. It was a way perhaps of making herself anonymous. He wondered what she could be doing here, and if her presence threw into doubt the theories that he and Willow had dreamed up the night before.

He was about to ease his way through the jostling people to speak to her, when Lucy Martindale, the grammar school head teacher, pushed through the crowd towards him.

'Inspector, could I have a word? I know this isn't an ideal situation, but it is rather important.'

'Of course.'

It was quieter now outside the cathedral, where they were standing. James had run across to see Iain, his big friend, before the ba' was thrown. Willow had been there too, chatting to Vaila, but now there was no sign of her. Perez, scanning through the remaining people, thought they must all have followed the game through the lanes.

The action had moved slowly out of Kirk Green, and the crowd had followed, crammed into the narrow streets, where owners had fixed wooden planks known as Ba' barricades over the shop windows to prevent the glass from being damaged. It seemed that the uppies were winning. James would be disappointed. He was very much a doonie supporter.

Perez pulled his attention back to the teacher. 'How can I help?'

'Since you came into school to see me, I've been looking into George's work emails. I've come across a number of rather disturbing messages. It seems he wasn't quite the perfect teacher I'd imagined him to be.'

Perez listened carefully to Lucy's explanation. 'Can you send the messages across to me?'

He thought of Miles, upright, respectable, law-abiding. He wondered what the man would make of these revelations. Would it change the way he'd view his lover? Probably not. Miles had known all along that George was impulsive, a little entitled, overconfident. Perhaps he'd spun his evidence to Perez, protecting his lover's reputation as Barbara Johnson had fought to protect her husband's. What else might he do for his man? Surely, Perez thought, Miles wouldn't commit murder. But again, there was a worm of doubt. So many stories could be told around these killings, and he was no longer confident that he knew which was true.

He handed Lucy his card, so she had his email address.

'It's so upsetting,' she said, 'and of course I'll have to take action. I can't pretend that this didn't happen.'

Perez wanted to discuss these developments with Willow, but there was still no sign of her and James. Perez phoned her to find out exactly where she was, but there was no reply. Of course she wouldn't hear. There would be too much din close to the centre of the game. He wandered in the direction of the shouting and cheering, but he was more focused on the information given to him by Lucy, and by his glimpse of Barbara Johnson, than on his surroundings. He supposed George's emails provided the confirmation that they needed to close the investigation, but he couldn't allow himself to believe it. He felt no elation. No pride. At last though, perhaps they had their proof.

When Perez glimpsed Willow, she was on the edge of the mob, and she was talking to Miles. He saw her as a wild Viking woman, with her long hair tangled by the breeze, the strong features. The conversation seemed intense, intimate, and when he approached, he heard that she was inviting the man to spend the rest of the day with them in Harray.

Miles was refusing but was obviously pleased to be asked.

'Not today,' he said. 'Today, I'd be rather poor company, but another time.'

Perez felt a quick moment of relief. He couldn't *quite* trust the man.

Willow turned and saw Perez. 'Where's James?' A catch of anxiety in her throat.

'He came to join you and Vaila before the throw-up.'

'No!' Now she was almost crying. 'No, the last time I saw him, he was holding your hand.'

'He'll be with Vaila and Iain.' Perez kept his voice even. Willow always accused him of overreacting where the boy was concerned. 'Following the action. Cheering on the doonies.' But he'd recognized her fear and was struggling to breathe evenly. He'd never had a panic attack, but this must be close to it.

'I'll come with you,' Miles said, 'and help you to look for him.'

Perez wasn't sure he wanted this man's help. Not now. But he could hardly refuse. Not with Willow standing beside him, white and trembling, overcome too with a kind of terror.

It seemed that Miles had picked up on their anxiety and now his voice was brusque, demanding. 'What was he wearing?'

Willow described the jacket, the bonnet knitted by his Fair Isle grandmother with the puffin motif.

'That's unique, then.' Miles gave a tight little smile. 'I'll know him at once when I see him.' He strode off into the crowd.

Perez watched the man go, before turning to Willow. 'I should have held on to him, and not let him head off on his own. But you were only a few yards away. I thought it could do no harm.'

I was obsessed with this case, he thought. *I was glad that James had gone to find you, so I wouldn't have the responsibility of him. So I could plan what was needed to have this business over.*

Anxiety made his body tense and froze his mind. He couldn't think clearly and even his vision was blurred. He worried that he wouldn't see the boy with the blue down jacket and the hand-knitted hat. He wouldn't recognize his own son among all the other children, who were cheering and yelling. He thought the game was dangerous and riotous, and the police should have put a stop to it decades before. He should have gone with his instinct and called the whole thing off.

Willow put her arm into his. 'Not your fault.' Each word emphasized. 'But we have to find him.'

He turned to her. 'Could Vaila have him?' The question desperate and packed with meaning.

Willow shook her head. 'Maybe. But if she has, he'll be safe. I left Vaila with Rosalie and Iain.'

'I'm sure I saw Barbara,' he said, 'just after the throw-out, hiding in plain sight.'

That made Willow pause for a moment. 'Not playing the grieving widow then.'

They followed the crowd along the street. The game seemed stuck there, the houses tall on each side, pressing in on the boys. No sign of the ba'. The only indication of where it might be was a cloud of condensation over the players' heads. The weather might not be freezing now, but the boys were so hot and sweaty that they'd formed their own microclimate. They were a mess of bodies, of arms and legs, turning the group into one huge multi-limbed monster. Lawrie might be at the heart of the action, proving himself his father's son, but there was no way of distinguishing him from all the other players.

It was a giant rugby scrum with no rules, and between Perez and Willow came the crowd of spectators.

It would be impossible for the two of them to push their way through. From the upstairs windows of the buildings on each side of the road, people were watching and shouting. Nothing but noise on all sides, so there was no point phoning Vaila to see if James was with her. Even if she'd want to answer, she wouldn't hear. Perez's breathing had settled a little now and his vision had cleared. He couldn't see anyone from Westray. Perhaps Vaila, Iain and James had gone ahead of the players and were trapped on the other side of the melee.

He was wondering whether they should take one of the side streets, which would lead them beyond the jam of bodies, when one of the players broke away. The lad was small and wiry, and Perez didn't recognize him. He had the ba' in his arms and headed towards them, followed by the crowd. A doonie heading for the harbour. Perez pulled Willow into a doorway and out of harm's way.

Now, he thought, there was a chance of finding James. The crowd had thinned a little. People were more spread out as the boy sprinted ahead of them. Only the most active would be able to catch up. The players on both teams were chasing after the lad, but he was fast and fit. An athlete. This was probably his last year too in the boys' game and he wanted to make his mark. The spectators followed at a more leisurely pace. Though they hoped to be there to see the finish, this wasn't the main event. That would take place in the afternoon, with the men.

Perez and Willow waited for the spectators to pass. There was still no sign of Vaila and Iain, and Perez hadn't noticed

Lawrie in the tumbling mass of boys. Even Miles seemed to have disappeared.

This felt unreal again, a nightmare Alice in Wonderland world of strange creatures and vanishing characters, where nothing was quite as it seemed, where everything was shifting.

Perez stood for a moment to watch the action. The dark athlete might have been fast, but he wasn't strong and a muscular uppie lad had wrestled the ba' from him and was heading back up the street towards them. The uppie supporters started cheering. The progress of the game had changed again, and this was going better than they'd expected. Then Lawrie, a doonie, appeared out of the pack and snatched the ba' back. He turned, and head down he charged in the opposite direction, wrong-footing the opposing players. He was big, but he was fast too. He'd put clear space between himself and the following crowd.

Perez suspected that Lawrie was always going to win. He was always going to be the person who seized the ba' and ran with it towards the harbour. The committee and the other doonie boys might have planned it – *Let's give the lad his moment of glory, eh? In his father's memory* – or it might have happened on the day. Once Lawrie got the ba', nobody would have thought it right to challenge him. But maybe he'd got there on merit, because he was strong and swift, sprinting along the streets, quite alone now, the following crowd a little way off cheering him on. With his blond hair and muscular stature, he could have been a Viking hero, the subject of a saga.

Through the thinning crowd, far away, Perez thought he caught a glimpse of his son. A blue jacket and a knitted hat. Someone had hold of his hand and was leading him not towards the harbour where it seemed the game would end but away from it. They appeared to be running. Perez had the impression that the boy was being dragged against his will, stumbling. This wasn't what he'd expected at all.

'Vaila will have made her way to the water,' Willow said, 'to see Lawrie's moment of triumph. Perhaps she went straight there, knowing that this was how it would end.'

'No!' Perez was shouting. 'Look!'

Before Willow could answer, Perez had already set off in pursuit of the boy, through a series of lanes, pushing his way past the stragglers who were moving in the opposite direction, following the flow of play.

He lost sight of the boy almost immediately and wondered even if James had been there at all. All morning he'd been conjuring ghosts and monsters from his subconscious, twisting the facts to form more outlandish tales: first Barbara Johnson, then Miles Chambers and now his son. He turned a sharp corner, and in the distance, at the end of a residential street of grey terraced houses, he caught another glimpse of blue.

He'd stopped for a moment to catch his breath but started running again, his chest heaving. When he approached the end of the street, he saw he was in an area of the town unfamiliar to him. Everything was quiet. The noise of the Ba' seemed a long way off. The street was empty.

'Hey!' Perez shouted. 'Where are you?' Anger was making his head throb. He could feel a nerve pulsing in his neck.

He'd reached a cul-de-sac of small semi-detached homes, grey render and grey slate roofs. No sign of the boy or the adult with him. Now, Perez was doubting his vision again. He must have seen another child with a parent or grandparent, and they must have gone into one of the houses. *If* he had seen anyone at all. He'd have to go back to Willow and tell her that he'd made a mistake, and that James was still missing.

Then, as he moved closer, he saw a narrow footpath leading past one of the houses. It led away steeply, high walls on either side, a shortcut towards the harbour. He set off down it. And there they were, moving more slowly now, and Perez could make them out more clearly: James and Miles. Miles still had his back to Perez and hadn't seen him.

'Hey!' Perez bellowed again. 'Let him go! What the hell is going on here?'

Then the pair did stop and turn. The tall man and the small boy, still hand in hand, standing very close together because the path was so narrow, caught in a shaft of sunlight as the clouds parted briefly.

At that moment, Perez saw that James was laughing, giggling as he did when something had suddenly amused him.

'You're as red as a berry, Dad.' The boy shouted because Perez was still some distance away. 'You'd be no good at the Ba'.'

There was a sudden moment of relief, but Perez could still feel anger and adrenaline as stress in his body. His muscles tense and tight. He loped up to the couple and stood, fists clenched, face to face with Miles, and repeated the same question. But it was James who answered as though this was all some sort of joke.

'Miles thought we'd get to the water quicker this way. We wanted to be there at the end of the game. I knew the doonies would win and that's where they'd be. But I got a stitch, so we just had to wait and that slowed us down.'

Perez started to breathe again. He bent and took James in his arms.

'There's nothing worse than a stitch.' Miles's voice was serious and affectionate at the same time. Perez still had an irrational urge to hit him.

'Miles said you and Mum would be there too.'

'Mum *will* be there.' Perez kept his voice calm. 'But I wanted to find you. We were worried.' He looked over the boy's head and spoke to Miles. 'We didn't know what was happening.'

At last, Miles must have sensed something of Perez's fear, the fading anger. 'I couldn't tell you that I'd found him. You know that I don't have a mobile these days. And really, I thought this would be the quickest route to get to you. That's why we were running. I'm sorry.'

'No.' Perez smiled. But still he asked Miles to walk ahead of them, while he took James's hand. He wanted some space between them. 'Thanks for finding him.'

James, unaware of the anxiety he'd caused or the tension between the men, tugged Perez on, wanting to be there quicker, to see the end of the game. Perez made him wait for a moment while he texted Willow to say that the boy was safe and until he'd seen that the message had been read.

It seemed that Lawrie's progress to the finish line had been less straightforward than they'd expected, because he hadn't yet reached it. He'd been challenged by an uppie, a big lad with an incipient moustache who looked older than sixteen. There was a tussle for the ba'. None of the other players intervened. This was a combat between two individuals now.

Perez thought that if Barbara was back in her hotel room, she must surely be hearing the noise. If she'd had a room looking out at the harbour, she'd be able to watch the scene below her. Perhaps though she was still in the crowd, watching the finale play out.

He was distracted by the thought, and by the sight of some Westray folks at the front of what had become an audience, a semicircle of admiring people. Willow saw him before he noticed her. She rushed across the street to crouch and put her arms around her son.

Just as Willow joined them, Lawrie managed to get a grip on the ba'. He raced to the harbour wall. He stood for a moment, the ba' above his head, challenging an opponent to seize it at the last moment. Then, instead of hurling the ball into the Basin, he jumped with it, and other boys joined him. Every year, somehow one boy or man ended up there if the doonies won. A traditional end to the sport. Lawrie's head appeared above the water, lifted by the others, and the crowd cheered. This year, at least, there was no discussion about who was the winner.

Chapter Thirty-Eight

WILLOW COULD FEEL TEARS ON HER cheeks as she held out her arms to the boy. Tears of gratitude and relief, as if the emotion was so great that it had to spill out. She saw Lawrie leaping into the sea with the other boys, was aware of the splash that their entrance made, reaching even to where she was standing, the salty droplets on her cheek mixing with the tears. The sound of cheering that might have been waves crashing. Or thunder. Something inhuman at least. A monster roaring. But in this moment, none of that mattered.

'Miles found him,' Perez said. His voice sounded rather forced. It was as if he could hardly believe the boy had been found. 'He says they were on their way back to us.'

James was on the ground again, pulling his mother's arm, wanting to add his congratulations to Lawrie's family. Perez held Willow back, just for a moment.

'I'm going to end this now,' he said. 'I know we planned to wait until the afternoon, but this is the time, and we have all that we needed. Lucy Martindale confirmed it. Don't you agree?'

She thought for a couple of seconds, running the possibilities through her head, rational now that she was holding James's hand, not letting her eyes stray from him again.

'Yes,' she said. 'I agree.'

She watched the rest from a distance, looking over James's head. He was babbling about the adventure he'd had, how he was heading towards her and Vaila, but then there were too many people in the way, and he was too small to push through them, and there was the throw-up, and he wanted to see Lawrie win, so he'd kind of forgotten what he was doing and followed the crowd. Then he'd got a bit lost, and Miles had come and found him.

Willow was listening to him, and answered in the right places, saying how scary that must have been and how he'd been a brave peedie boy. She wondered if she should give the lecture about not going away with strangers, but this wasn't the right time, and anyway sometimes strangers weren't the most dangerous people. All the time though, she was watching intently everything that was happening across the road by the harbour.

The Westray folk were all there by the water now, and Willow saw that Miles had gone to join them. The boys' Ba' had finished earlier than it sometimes did, and the Kirkwall crowd were wandering away, to get something to eat or drink, or prepare for the men's throw-up at one o'clock. The big event. But for Westray people this had *been* the main event, and they'd gathered to congratulate Lawrie. Again, she saw Nat Wilkinson, hovering on the edge of the crowd, unsure whether he should be there at all. Rosalie Greeman brightly coloured, standing out from the crowd, laughing at some joke she'd been told by the person standing next to her. Godfrey Lansdown, still with his binoculars around his neck, his attention apparently distracted by some bird on the water.

Lawrie was climbing out of the harbour by a metal ladder built into the wall. The blond hair looked dark now that it was wet, oily, like a seal's fur. He was shivering. The air might be warmer than it had been the week before, but the water would still be freezing. James tugged her towards Lawrie, so he could congratulate the boy too. Vaila was there, holding a towel for him. The winner's jump into the sea was traditional and she'd come prepared. Bill and Annie MacBride, Tom and Evelyn Angel formed a semicircle around Lawrie as he pulled himself clear of the water. They clapped and he gave a shy grin.

'Your father would have been proud of you.' Tom Angel put his arm around his grandson, unbothered, it seemed, by the boy's wet body.

'Come away, man, and leave the lad alone.' Despite the words Evelyn's voice was affectionate. Proud. 'You'll get soaked.'

'We should go now.' Willow lifted James into her arms, so he couldn't resist her suggestion that they leave Kirkwall and head back to Harray. 'Let's get you home and find you some Christmas treats.' Because she didn't want James to see Jimmy Perez arrest his hero.

Chapter Thirty-Nine

THEY SAT IN THE INTERVIEW ROOM in the police station. Tom Angel was there as Lawrie's responsible adult. Vaila had said she couldn't face it. Perez thought she might have had her suspicions about Lawrie all along. Images of violence crawling into her head like worms. She'd have tried to push them away. Of course she would. She'd have believed that she was crazy with grief, that her imagination was thrown out of kilter. Who could believe that a son would kill his father? Then kill again to hide his tracks. In a place like Westray where nobody locked their door and where they left their keys in their cars. Where strangers were made welcome.

'This is a mistake, Jimmy.' Tom's words were firm and certain, breaking into Perez's thoughts.

But perhaps the grandfather had worried about Lawrie too. About the boy's temper. His obsession with violent computer games. His secret social media posts, that might occasionally have surfaced or been talked about by other kids in the community. Had one of the parents of the girls that Lawrie had bullied online shared their anxiety with Tom? Had he believed that when Lawrie left school, moved back to Westray and worked the farm, when he found a bonnie young island lass to wed and have his bairns, all would be well?

Lawrie said nothing.

Ellie was sitting next to Perez. She'd started the recording and given their names and the time. It was just past midday. In the market square, the crowds would already be gathering for the men's Ba'.

'I'm going to tell you what I think happened that night of the storm on Westray.' Perez hoped that the recording would pick up the sorrow in his voice, the kindness. He'd known Lawrie since he was a baby. Maybe the fiscal would mock him for that. But now, the sorrow might not be a bad thing; sympathy might help Lawrie to talk. Perez could use it to his advantage.

He leaned forward, his elbows on the table, so he was speaking directly to Lawrie. The other two adults might not have been in the room. 'George Riley came to Westray that day to work on his book, and to confront Tony Johnson about the theft of Magnus's research around the story stones, but he had another reason too. He wanted to talk to your father about some troubling events that had surfaced in school.' For the first time, Perez looked into Lawrie's eyes. The lad's face was red. Perhaps that was because of the exertion of the Ba' game, the chill of the water when he'd jumped into the harbour. But perhaps it was embarrassment. Awkwardness because he'd been found out. Shame. Perez hoped it was shame, that Lawrie was sufficiently human to feel wretched about what he'd done.

'George Riley was a pastoral care teacher. He enjoyed working with troubled youngsters. Students felt able to talk to him, when they'd never be able to confide in their parents. Because of that, he'd discovered that you'd been behaving inappropriately with some of the girls in school. A kind of grooming with the lasses in the hostel. Persuading them to take sexual images of themselves and send them to you, then threatening to make them public. A horrible kind of blackmail.' He paused for a moment and looked across at Lawrie. 'Did it make you feel strong? Powerful?'

Lawrie said nothing. He couldn't meet Perez's eyes.

'We won't use their names. They deserve a little privacy. But you know who they are. You've shared classes with them since you were thirteen. One of the lasses is self-harming. Another has just started being treated for depression. Both were too scared to tell their parents what was making them so miserable. Besides, they both came from the more remote islands where they couldn't always easily get home. And kids from those communities are expected to be tough. To survive. They were lonely and homesick, and you preyed on them.'

There was silence. Perez turned towards Tom Angel and spoke quietly adult to adult. 'George thought he'd be able to manage the situation himself. The head teacher only found out what had been going on after George's death, when she had access to his files. At least he kept decent records. I had a long discussion with her this morning.'

Angel was white with shock and disgust. It was as if he'd been slapped very hard in the face.

Now, Perez turned back to Lawrie. 'Mr Riley didn't follow proper procedures. Perhaps he was a little overconfident, a little arrogant, though I think he had your best interests at heart. He believed that, with the support of your family, he could help you to change. He persuaded the lasses that you had meant no harm, that you would never have spread those images. They probably had the impression that they were partly to blame for taking the photographs. Of course, he should have notified the head teacher and the police immediately. But he didn't want you branded as a sex offender at such an early age. It was a mistake, and it caused the deaths of three people. But you killed them, Lawrie. You have to take responsibility for that.'

There was silence in the room. The boy glared across the table at him. Perez continued in the same tone.

'Bullying at the grammar school isn't a new thing. I've talked to other people who suffered it to one degree or another. Especially those staying at the hostel. A bunch of kids away from home for long periods, trying to find their place in the system, it's hard.'

Lawrie stared at him. He remained silent.

'Unfortunately, Mr Riley couldn't always make things right.'

He hadn't helped Nat Wilkinson, for example, Perez thought. Or the lass who served me in the cafe next door to the gallery in Stromness and she wasn't even resident in the hostel. George had thought he could help both of them too. In Nat's case he'd made things worse. And when it came to the new head teacher, he'd believed that he knew best. That the rules around safeguarding didn't apply to him. The worst kind of arrogance.

'I understand what it's like to be staying away from home, an outsider, not fitting in.' Perez wondered if he could make out a flicker of recognition in the boy's face, but Lawrie turned away and when he looked back, his face was as blank and impassive as before.

'But that was the same for the girls you abused. They trusted you. They thought you cared about them, that they were special. I've seen the messages. You told them that you loved them.'

Perez waited for some response from the boy, but none came, and the detective continued:

'On the day that he died, your father met George at the ferry, and they talked. He wanted Archie to know what was going on at school and hoped that together they could help you to confront the behaviour. Maybe you'd have to leave the school. The situation had reached a point where the lasses' parents would have to be told, even though the girls hadn't wanted them to know. They'd be home over the holidays. The families might have wanted to press charges. It must have come as a terrible shock to your father.'

Perez imagined what that would be like: having to face the fact that a son had done something so unforgivable but knowing that in the end you would have to forgive him.

He continued the story, his words directed now as much to Tom Angel as to Lawrie.

'We know that throughout that day Archie was troubled. Rosalie Greeman thought it was an island matter that was haunting him, and so it was in a way. If news got out about what Lawrie had done, that would reflect on your family, but also on Westray. It's easy to lump folk together, for a place to get a bad name.'

Perez had suffered that at school too: off-island kids were considered such dweebs, so uncool. Stupid even.

It was time, Perez thought, to confront Lawrie with a direct question. 'When did your father discuss this with you?'

Lawrie stared back. 'He didna. There was nothing to discuss.' The answer was challenging and defensive at the same time. A teenager caught in a misdemeanour and trying to tough it out. But in this case the misdemeanour wasn't drinking underage or smoking a bit of weed. It was murder. Perez ignored the words and continued speaking.

'I think it was when the two of you were alone in Nistaben at lunchtime. Your mother and Iain were in Pierowall. Your mum was helping out with the old folk at the hotel's Christmas party and Iain was playing with a mate. That would have been a good time for a father-and-son chat.'

Silence in the room. Somewhere in the distance Perez caught the cheers of the Ba' spectators – the adult game was underway. They might be wondering why Vaila wasn't there to give her speech.

Perez lowered his voice a little. It was still sufficiently loud to be picked up by the recording equipment, but Lawrie and Tom would have to give their full attention to hear it.

'I knew Archie very well,' he said. 'When I was your age, Lawrie, he was more like a brother than a cousin. He had a temper on him. And a tongue. Man, he could cut you down to size just with his words. What did he say to you, Lawrie, to make you lose your temper? What did he threaten to do?'

This time there was a reaction. The boy's hands on the table clenched into white fists.

'Just tell me, Lawrie. I want to understand.' Repeating the lad's name, bringing him back to his family, letting him know he wasn't quite alone here.

'He said he'd send me away!' It came out as a cry of pain. 'He said I wasn't fit to stay in Westray. He said until I learned to behave, I could go and live with his relatives in Shetland.' A pause. 'In Fair Isle!'

As if Fair Isle was the end of the known universe, a kind of Van Diemen's Land in the North Sea for recalcitrant young men. In any other situation, Perez would have smiled. Even now, he saved the moment to share with Willow.

'What happened then?'

'He started ranting about Tony Johnson and the story stones, linking us all together. Like I was as bad as the guy who stole our history from my grandfather Magnus. Like I couldna be trusted. All I did was to have a laugh with those lasses. Not my fault if they fancied me. I didna force any of them.' But even as he was protesting, Perez could tell that wasn't true. Lawrie had felt both entitled and confused. He was a lonely lad with nothing but Internet porn to show him how to interact with unhappy young women and a macho swagger to cover the inability to find real friends.

'Your dad went out later and met up with Tony Johnson close to the Noltland dig. That's a long way from Nistaben. How did you get there? What was the plan? Because you must have had a plan.'

No response but a bull-headed stare, and a simmering anger. Perhaps the boy actually felt resentment at having to sit there, to be questioned like this when he should be celebrating his victory at the Ba'. Maybe he had so little understanding about what he had done.

Perez went on with the story. He might have been reading from one of James's picture books. His tone was the same.

'Your mother and Iain came back from Pierowall and you all had your tea together, then Archie went out. He'd arranged to meet Professor Johnson, hoping to challenge him about your grandfather's research, before heading to the bar for a drink with his pals. I've been wondering how you got to that end of the island. I'm sure you can drive. Most island kids learn to drive before it's legal on the mainland. But you had to wait until your mother had gone to Pierowall in her car and your father had already left in his. It occurred to me that you could have taken the tractor, but that might have been noticed. Who'd be out on a tractor at night at that time of the year? Then I realized. The quad bike. That was kept in the byre, and nobody would see you leave on that.'

Perez looked across the table at Lawrie. 'That was clever. Who would notice quad-bike tracks later after the storm and all that rain turning the island into one big bog?'

Lawrie said nothing, but Perez thought he'd liked that. He hadn't been called clever very often.

'How did you know that your father would be at Noltland?' Perhaps now, Perez decided, the boy would welcome the chance to show off.

And this time, Lawrie did talk. 'He told me he'd be there. When he was talking about Johnson and the argument they'd had, and how I was bringing disrepute on the community too. "The professor's demanded that I go and meet him. On a day like this! The cheek of it. I'll be there right enough, and I'll tell him what I think of him."'

Perez nodded. 'I think you got to Noltland just as your father had finished talking to Johnson. Archie would be in a foul mood, after the day he'd had, and then talking to that smarmy academic, who'd lied to him, trying to persuade him that Magnus had agreed to his work being stolen.'

Perez paused for a moment. 'Did you go there intending to kill your father?'

'No!' The sound came out like a roar. The boy's face was almost purple and his mouth wide open.

Perez waited for a moment before speaking and in the quiet, the boy's voice seemed to echo around the bare room.

'Then why don't you tell me exactly what happened?'

'I wanted to speak to him, to explain.' It was Lawrie's turn to tell a story, his version of events that he must have repeated over and over again in his bed in Nistaben and then in his room in the Kirkwall Hotel, an attempt to justify three men's deaths. He took a breath in an effort to appear calm and reasonable. Maybe an attempt to make Perez understand.

'My father went out. Iain was in his room on his screen, some fantasy computer game he was playing with his mates. My mother was clearing up the supper things. I said I'd go out to the byre, that there was something I needed to do. She hardly seemed to hear me. I wondered if Dad had talked to her about me, but she didn't seem angry. Not at me at least. Maybe something else had upset her, because she seemed kind of distracted. I didn't think she'd notice what I was doing.'

'You took the quad bike and headed out?'

'Yeah. I waited until my mother had left in the car. I got to Noltland before anything was happening. I was about to give up and go home. It was dark and cold, and I'd hidden the bike behind one of the dykes.'

Perez wondered if Lawrie had been glad that nothing was happening. Maybe he was having second thoughts about confronting his father. The boy continued:

'Then I saw them. Two torches heading towards me. There was an argument. The wind was so strong then that I couldn't hear what they were saying, but I could tell it was a row. I saw Johnson leaving Noltland and walking towards his car. He went right past me. I didn't think he'd seen me, but he must have done. I realized later that he must have waited and heard Dad and me arguing.' A pause. 'My father was just standing there.

It had started to rain, and yet he just stayed, watching me come towards him.'

So, Perez thought, Barbara had lied when she'd told them she'd seen Archie alive, running towards his car. A figure lit by a flash of lightning. She hadn't been quite sure that Johnson hadn't killed him, and it was the sort of dramatic tale she would make up. She'd been protecting her husband's reputation to the end.

'What happened then?'

'Dad had a torch in one hand, and he was looking at one of the story stones. He seemed kind of thoughtful. Perhaps he was thinking about his father. We all loved Magnus. I thought maybe he was in a mood to change his mind. About sending me away from Westray. If I promised not to do that sort of stuff again, he'd see that family's more important than anything.'

'You wanted him to forgive you?'

'Aye.' A pause. 'I guess that's what I wanted.' There was another silence. This time Perez didn't prompt him. He just waited for him to continue. For Lawrie to remember the words he'd already strung together.

'I didna shout,' the boy said. 'Not really. Only to be heard against the noise of the wind. I just wanted to explain. But he said that Mr Riley had sent through some of the photos I'd asked the lasses to take of themselves. That he could hardly bear to talk to me. He said I disgusted him.' Lawrie stopped again and stared across at Perez. Now his voice was hollow: 'He said that if I thought I'd ever inherit the farm, I was mistaken.'

Then Perez understood what had prompted the extreme violence. This was a lad who couldn't control his anger any more than his father had, who'd had his whole future mapped out for him – as a farmer, a husband, a father – and it had been ripped away. He'd thought his rightful inheritance had been stolen. In the end, Archie might have relented of course, but in the heat of that moment, with the wind blowing around them, Lawrie's future had crumbled.

'Your father was holding one of the story stones.'

'Aye, and the other was on the ground.'

'Then your father turned his back on you.'

'He shouldna have done that. He said he couldna bear to look at me.'

'And you picked up the other story stone and you hit him?'

'He shouldna have turned away.'

'I have to hear you say it, Lawrie. You hit him.'

'Aye, I hit him.' The words were clear and loud and defiant, but the beetroot-red face was streaming with tears.

Chapter Forty

Willow sat in the old manse with James. Although the day was milder, she banked up the fire. She felt the need for comfort. Her thoughts were with Perez. This would be one of the most difficult interviews he'd ever undertaken.

On the way home in the car, James had been lively, full of chatter about the Ba', fizzing with the reflected glory of Lawrie Stout's win.

'Lawrie did it, didn't he, Mummy? He won for the doonies.'
'Yes,' she'd said. 'He did.'

She wondered when he'd be old enough to understand what had happened in these days in the run-up to Christmas, and how she'd find the words to explain that just because boys were strong, they couldn't always do as they wished. He'd hear about it of course. The story would be everywhere. There'd be pieces all over the news, and earnest documentaries exploring the background to teenage violence, the role of social media in young people's lives, the easy accessibility of pornography. Maybe a drama, attempting to bring the murders to life. For a while, Westray would be invaded by the press. The family would be blamed.

Back home, James settled. He watched a film and built the small Lego kit he'd found in his stocking.

Willow prepared vegetables for the evening meal, but she was digging back into her memories wondering if there'd been anything that could have predicted Lawrie's behaviour. He'd been quiet, withdrawn, not as sharp as his brother, not as curious about the world away from Orkney, but helpful. He'd been kind to James. His parents might have had their problems, but they'd been good role models for their sons. The boys had always been loved and well cared for.

Then she remembered one evening in Nistaben. A party. Music and too much drinking. Archie had come up behind her and groped her. She'd shrugged it off at the time, not willing to make a fuss about Jimmy's best friend. Now the image stuck in her head.

Willow peeled Brussels sprouts and her thoughts turned to Vaila. How would she be coping with this? Would she be alone in that hotel room, with Iain, needing to hold things together for the younger son?

Her phoned pinged. A text from Perez.

We have a confession.

Chapter Forty-One

IN THE INTERVIEW ROOM IN THE police station, Perez was still asking questions, pinning down details.

'Were you sure your father was dead after you hit him? It didn't occur to you to fetch help?'

'I could tell he was dead.' Lawrie closed his eyes. 'I've lived on a farm all my life. I know death. I had the torch on my phone. I could see.' Perez wondered if he'd always have a picture in his head of his father's battered skull. The shards of bone. The blood. Would he wake up to it and see it before he went to sleep?

'His car was found outside the Pierowall Hotel. Did you move it from the golf course?'

Lawrie nodded. 'There was an old piece of tarp in the boot. I sat on that. I was kind of mucky. I was wearing gloves anyway because of the cold.'

So, Perez thought, *you were thinking clearly. Or did it feel like one of your computer games? Were you working out the moves as if you were playing, hoping to outsmart the competition, as you would on the screen?*

'Why did you shift the car?'

'I wanted to get home before anyone found him. If they saw the car at the golf club, they might start looking there.'

'What did you do with the tarp?'

'I took it back with me on the quad bike. It's hidden in a feed bag at the back of the barn. I was going to dump it off the pier, but I never got the chance.'

That would be the concrete evidence they'd been hoping for. Even if Lawrie changed his story now, they should have enough to convict him.

'And your bloodstained clothes?'

'They went in the washing machine. My mother had already put stuff ready to wash. I added my things and set off the machine. She was in such a state that night. I could tell she wouldn't notice.'

'Why did you take the other story stone away with you?' Perez hoped that the boy hadn't wanted to keep it as some sort of trophy. Or that he wasn't already planning another murder.

Lawrie just stared across the table and shrugged.

'You took it out with you when you came to Kirkwall. Why did you do that?'

This time Lawrie did speak. 'I thought you might search the house when we were gone. If you found it, you'd know that I was there that night.'

'So it was in that rucksack you took to your grandparents' house?'

I watched you carry it away with you.

Lawrie nodded.

At that point Perez called for a break. He sent a text to Willow and asked for coffee for Tom Angel and himself. Coke and a snack for Lawrie. He left Ellie in the interview room and sat for a moment in his office. To clear his head and to plan the rest of the interview, to work out again the timeline for the Maeshowe murder. He thought it would be less distressing for Lawrie to talk about Riley and Johnson. They weren't family. The confession might come more easily. Besides, the boy had already killed once by the time he came to murder them.

The duty sergeant popped his head round Perez's office door. He reported that the Ba' was over. Until it all happened again on New Year's Day. As if Perez would be as interested in the result as he was. It had taken three hours but the doonies had won the adult Ba' too. The officer was downcast because he was an uppie, and because it was Christmas Day and yet he was still here in the station. His wife was used to late festive dinners because he always watched the Ba', he said, but he had no idea when his shift would be over, and she was giving him grief. Hoping perhaps that Perez would show pity and send him home to his meal and his drams.

'This shouldn't take much longer.' Perez got to his feet and joined the sergeant at the door. He wanted to be home with his family too. He walked back into the interview room.

'Tell me about Mr Riley,' he said. They were sitting in the same places, in the small room with the high window looking out over the car park. The neon strip light fizzed occasionally, as if it might stop working altogether, and he had the start of a headache. Ellie had begun the recording again.

'Explain about that afternoon at Maeshowe.' In his mind, Perez was walking towards the burial chamber, the frozen grass crunching under his feet, stooping to get inside, waiting for the sunlight to recreate the mystery of the solstice.

Lawrie had clammed up again, jaws clamped shut, and Perez continued talking in his storyteller's voice.

'He wanted to talk to you, didn't he? About the stuff he'd found on your social media and the complaints from the girls at the hostel. It never occurred to him that you might have killed your father, or I'm sure he would have come to us first. He was obsessed with the history, and he thought that Professor Johnson had murdered your father.'

Perez wondered suddenly if that was true. George Riley had the confidence that came from an English public-school education and his fancy university.

'Or perhaps Mr Riley had an idea that you might be responsible for your father's death and thought he could persuade you to confess. Is that what happened?'

It would be in the character of the man, Perez thought. He believed the best in everyone, and maybe he was convinced that redemption was possible.

'No! It was nothing like that!' The boy's words came out as a shout.

Perez waited for a moment for Lawrie to say more, before continuing:

'So if he didn't know that you'd killed your father, Mr Riley still wanted to help. He believed that you were going through a really tough patch because your father had just died, and he wanted to help, to sort things out without it all blowing up into a nightmare for you, affecting your future. He was tight for time that day. He was just back from a conference, he had pantomime rehearsals, and he wanted to spend the afternoon with his partner. But he saw the clear sky and thought you'd enjoy the drama of Maeshowe, so he arranged to meet you there. One of his many kindnesses.'

Perez looked across at the boy, hoping again for a response, but none came.

'It took me a long time to work it out. The logistics, I mean. By then, you were staying in town in the Kirkwall Hotel. How could you get out to Maeshowe? You don't have many friends, do you? None that might help by arranging a lift. I could understand how you might escape from the hotel without your mother noticing. She was grieving, lost in a world of her own, and the doctor had given her something to dull the pain. Besides, Iain was playing games in the room next to hers. She heard him talking and she believed you were there, chatting with him, but he was talking to his gaming friends and not to you.'

Lawrie continued to stare into space.

'What did you tell Iain?' Perez asked, genuinely curious. 'Where did you tell him you were going?'

Now Lawrie did look directly at the detective. 'I told him I was meeting a lass,' he said. He gave a little smile that might have been a smirk, but that Perez hoped was almost wistful, as if Lawrie would have loved nothing better than having a girl to meet. Someone to care for and not to abuse. 'Iain said he'd cover for me if our mother asked where I was.'

Perez paused for a moment to clear his thoughts.

'You couldn't risk taking your mother's car – you were underage and without a licence – and a witness saw Mr Riley arrive in the car park alone, meaning he hadn't given you a lift. So how did you get there to meet him?'

He didn't expect Lawrie to answer the question and went on almost immediately. 'There's a bus stop opposite the Maeshowe car park and the same witness also saw the bus pull up there, and a passenger get out.'

This was why Belinda the dog-walker had called him at home on Christmas Eve.

'Someone got out,' she'd said in her loud, almost-drunk voice. 'I couldn't see who it was. There was nobody waiting at the stop, so that wasn't why the bus pulled over. No, I couldn't describe the person. I was driving back to town.'

But Perez didn't need to tell Lawrie that, and he knew they'd be able to track down the driver and any other passengers if they needed to. Someone would have recognized the boy. Orkney was that sort of place.

'Why don't you tell us what happened?' Perez repeated, his voice gentle again, almost fatherly.

Now, it seemed, Lawrie was prepared to speak.

'I thought he'd worked out that I'd killed Dad. And anyway, it was kind of his fault. If he hadn't interfered, if he hadn't talked to my father that day on the island, then I wouldn't have had to kill him.' The words spilled out, gushing like water from a pressure hose. He was a child again, making excuses for an action that could never be excused.

Perez looked across the table. 'You went to Maeshowe *intending* to kill Mr Riley. You had the second story stone with you. The one that your father had been holding.'

Now Lawrie sat upright, almost proud, as he spat out his bile. 'I thought if I used that to hit him, you'd believe that Westray history had something to do with the killings. I'm not as stupid as everyone thinks. You fell for it, didn't you? And anyway, what right did Riley have, with his fancy ways, living with his fancy man, coming to Orkney and telling me how to live my life?'

Sitting beside the boy, Tom Angel stared at Perez, horrified, still white and stony. In this moment, he saw his grandson as a monster, not as a child to be loved and protected.

'Why don't you talk me through it, Lawrie?' Perez's voice was as gentle as ever. 'Tell me what happened.'

'He was there waiting for me at the entrance to the chamber. He had a key, and he opened the gate. He went in first. You have to bend low to get in through the tunnel that leads into it. All the time he was talking. About the history of the place. An Orkney place. As if he knew everything there was to know about it, and he had to give me a lecture. As if I hadn't been born here. As if the islands didn't belong to me much more than to him. I was close behind him and just as he was going to put on the light inside, I hit him. He hadn't expected anything.'

'He was trying to be kind,' Perez said.

'When has kindness got a man anywhere?' Lawrie screamed out the words. It was if he was parroting them, that they were some kind of tenet of faith, learned from a twisted guru. Perez thought he'd probably stolen the phrase from one of his favourite manosphere Internet sites.

This time Perez didn't answer. He wanted to tell the boy that it was possible to be both kind and strong, but he knew that Lawrie wouldn't accept that. Not here and not yet. Besides, time was moving, and he wanted to be home. He needed a long bath to wash away the day and to spend time with his family.

'Why didn't you leave him where he was? Why shove him into one of the smaller chambers?'

'I don't know.' This time it came out as a mutter. 'I wanted to hide him away. I couldn't bear to see him.'

Maybe, Perez thought, *you couldn't bear what you'd done to him.* He hoped that was the case. That in that moment the boy had felt some revulsion, some guilt.

'And Tony Johnson? Why did he have to die?'

'He was a horrible man. He was trying to blackmail me.'

'He wanted you to give permission for him to use your grandfather's research?'

'Aye. Someone else coming to the islands to take what was ours.' Lawrie's voice was bitter, as if he was the victim here, as if again the killing was justified.

'I presume he saw you at Noltland that night when you killed your father.'

'I told you that already. He walked right past me after he'd had that row with my father.'

'And he saved up the information, knowing it might be useful, instead of coming to us and telling us what he knew.' Perez was talking almost to himself. He turned back to Lawrie.

'He phoned you on your hotel bedroom's telephone extension after your mother refused to discuss Magnus's research with him. He thought you could sign the letter, confirming the research was his. Magnus's grandson. Why did you arrange to meet him at the Stones of Stenness?'

'It seemed kind of appropriate.' The same bravado was coming out in Lawrie's words now. Tom Angel, still as marble, couldn't look at the boy.

'Did you get the bus again?'

'Aye, a later one. I waited until Iain was asleep.'

'And back into town?'

Lawrie nodded. 'The last bus back from Stenness. It was full of partygoers and drunks. I had my hood up all the way. I didn't think anyone would notice me.'

Perez thought this was all he needed. He couldn't stand this any more. He had the confession. The details could wait for the following day. The knife that had stabbed Johnson was probably Lawrie's. Used to cut twine on the farm, or gut fish when he was out on one of the creel boats. Now he was charged they could take the boy's DNA.

Outside it was black. The building was very quiet. Perez ended the interview for the recording and explained that Lawrie would be held in custody. They all stood up. Tom Angel seemed as relieved as he was that the thing was over. He couldn't look at his grandson. As they were leaving the room, Lawrie called after Perez:

'Uncle Jimmy. Will I be able to see Mum?' Now he was a boy again, waking up from a nightmare and crying out for his mother in the dark.

Chapter Forty-Two

VAILA WAS SITTING IN THE MORE comfortable of the interview rooms, the place where Perez had spoken to Barbara Johnson. That seemed like weeks ago. The duty officer had put her there when she'd turned up. He hadn't known what else to do with her. Vaila sat, curled up in one of the easy chairs, looking as small as a young girl. Or a frail old woman.

'Lawrie would like to see you,' Perez said.

She shook her head violently. 'I can't face him. Not yet. But I have to know, Jimmy. I have to know what's happened.'

'Lawrie has confessed,' Perez said, 'to killing Archie and the two others.'

She stared at him. Her eyes were wide. He couldn't tell what she was thinking. Perhaps it was too much for her to take in and she couldn't think at all.

'That's a good thing,' he went on. His voice was very quiet and gentle, and outside he could hear some drunk singing 'Flowers of Scotland'. 'It means there'll be no major trial. Nothing for the press to sink their teeth into and paw over.'

'You are sure that he's a killer, Jimmy? It's not some story he's made up in his head just to be famous?'

'I am quite sure.' A pause. 'Did he want to be famous?'

She shook her head. 'Not that. But maybe he wanted to be noticed more. Archie dragged the attention of everyone in a room towards him, and Iain was so quick and clever, and folk admired his musical talent so much. Lawrie was a good-looking lad and as strong as his father, but maybe he felt he was being overlooked.' Her eyes wandered around the room as if she'd only just noticed where she was. 'Why didn't you warn me, Jimmy, that you were going to arrest him?' The words came out as a cry, an accusation. 'Why do it there in front of everyone?'

'We suspected that Lawrie might be involved, but we didn't *know* until the game had started.' Perez thought this wasn't the time to go into details: the phone call from Belinda Thorne on Christmas Eve and then the conversation with Lawrie's head teacher. Vaila could have all the explanation she needed when the shock was less. Tom could take her through the interview and confession.

'Lawrie was never an easy boy,' Vaila said. 'He was always kind of stubborn. He struggled to make friends and I could never tell what he was thinking. But this! I spoke to my father while you took a break. Is it true, Jimmy? That he was getting the lasses at school to take crude photos of themselves, then blackmailing them? And all the porn he'd been watching. We never knew about that. Whatever Archie was like, he would have put a stop to that.'

Perez remembered an incident at a Westray party, soon after they'd moved to Orkney. He'd seen Archie, drunk, staggering up to Willow and trying to touch her breasts. Willow had dealt with it herself, hadn't even seen that Perez had noticed the incident. She'd never mentioned it to him, and he hadn't wanted to act the protector or to be seen to overreact, be thought prim and pompous. He'd even wondered briefly if Willow might have been flattered and had put Archie's behaviour down to a middle-aged man who'd never really grown up, pissed, acting out his adolescent fantasies. Nothing to spoil a friendship for. Now he felt angry with himself for letting it go. Had Lawrie been in the room too? Had he seen what had happened?

'Lawrie was always kind to James,' he said. 'Perhaps he found it easier to relate to younger children.'

'Was he?' Vaila's face brightened very briefly. 'Aye, he was, and he was no trouble in the school in Westray . . .' A pause. 'Maybe we should never have sent him out to the hostel. But *we* went away to the grammar school, and it did us no harm. Island kids grow up knowing that's how it'll likely be.'

'You can't blame yourselves.' Though of course Vaila would blame herself for as long as she lived.

'What will happen to him?'

'He's killed three people,' Perez said, because it wasn't only Vaila who had been bereaved, and the victims and their families deserved to be remembered too. 'He'll be away for a long time. But it's good that he's told us what happened. The court will take that into consideration. And his age.'

Vaila nodded, as if it was what she'd been expecting. 'I feel that I'm as guilty as he is. I should have known what he was doing. I could have saved two other men.'

'This wasn't your fault, Vaila,' Perez said again, but the words sounded hollow. They sat for a moment in silence. 'Will you see him now?'

He couldn't predict what her response might be.

She swung her legs round and got to her feet. 'Aye, I'll see him.' A pause. 'I suppose he's still my boy.'

Chapter Forty-Three

When Perez arrived home, the house was quiet. He sat for a moment in the car, putting himself in the right frame of mind to meet his family, and thought of the note that he'd left for Willow at the start of this, just before he'd rushed off to Westray in the middle of a storm. That felt an age ago. So much had changed since then. He'd lost his oldest friend, three men had died, and a screwed-up boy had been charged with murder. Perez felt himself unravelling, just as he had when he was stranded on Fair Isle and Fran had been killed in the middle of another violent storm, the blade of the knife caught in a flash of blue lightning. That image haunted him at times too. All this was too close to home, and memories were colliding. He wasn't sure he could face it any more. In the islands, everything was too close to home.

Then the door opened, and Willow came out to greet him. She must have heard the vehicle on the drive. She stood in the doorway, the light behind her. A familiar silhouette. He climbed out of the car, and they stood together.

'You okay, Jimmy?'

'Aye.' He was now.

'James is dozing in front of the telly. It'll be a nightmare to get him to bed when it's time, but he's shattered. Come away in. I'll get the dinner on.'

Perez went upstairs, showered and changed out of his work clothes, another attempt to switch his brain away from the job.

Then before he could get downstairs, the house was full of noise and laughter. James had realized that his father was home. He rushed up to greet him, buzzing with the events of the day. There were presents to open and a meal to eat, and that distracted James from his tales of Lawrie's heroism. Perez and Willow weren't sure how they'd tackle that subject. It certainly wasn't something to be discussed this evening.

Instead, they talked about what they might do the following day when Miles would come to visit. James, it seemed, had fallen for Miles too:

'He's very funny! And he can do magic tricks. He pulled a sweetie out of my ear.'

'Yes, he's a great guy.' Perez wondered if Miles would ever understand how reckless George had been, ignoring the rules around safeguarding, believing that he was some sort of knight in shining armour, charging in to rescue Lawrie from himself, and the two girls involved from future torment and abuse. But, Perez thought, Miles must have spent his career working with flawed characters and would have been clear-eyed about Riley. He'd known George's faults, but he loved him anyway.

The meal and the presents and the stories all took a long time, and for James, staying up so late was an adventure in itself.

At last, the boy went to bed. Despite the sugar and the excitement, he fell asleep immediately and the adults were left to themselves. They sat in front of the dying fire, Perez with a dram and Willow with camomile tea. Each staring at the embers, lost in their own thoughts.

Perez couldn't imagine what Vaila might be going through. He'd always thought that the worst thing in the world was to lose a child. But to have a child who had killed three people. Surely that would be more bitter.

'Do you think Vaila suspected that Lawrie was capable of murder?' Willow could have been reading his mind.

'I don't know. Maybe she had an itch of suspicion but didn't want to believe. She took the boys away from Westray as soon as she could. Perhaps she thought that was a way of keeping hold of Lawrie, of keeping people safe.'

'What would you do if you thought James had committed something so terrible?'

'He won't!' Perez was sure about that. 'We'll make sure he won't do anything of the sort.'

Willow didn't answer for a while. 'I'm not sure it's that easy. Vaila and Archie were good parents, in their own way. He grew up in a place that most people would consider idyllic. I never thought of Lawrie as being overly macho or unpleasant in any way at all.'

There was another period of silence. Then, because this seemed like a time of confession, he said: 'Earlier, sitting in the car, I wasn't sure I could do this any longer. It's too hard.'

He knew she'd understand what he meant by that – the case, working in a small community, policing people he knew.

He looked directly at her. 'I was thinking I'd resign.'

'And now?' she said.

He shrugged. 'Honestly? I don't think I'm fit for anything else. And someone has to do it, don't they? Somebody has to pick up the pieces when things fall apart.'

She smiled, as if it was the answer that she'd been expecting.

About the Author

David Hirst

Ann Cleeves is the multimillion-copy bestselling author behind three hit television series—*Shetland*, starring Douglas Henshall; *Vera*, starring Academy Award nominee Brenda Blethyn; and *The Long Call*, starring Ben Aldridge—all of which are watched and loved in the United States. All three are available on BritBox.

The first Shetland novel, *Raven Black*, won the Crime Writers' Association Gold Dagger for best crime novel, and Ann was awarded the CWA Diamond Dagger in 2017. She was awarded the OBE in 2022 for services to reading and libraries. Ann lives in the United Kingdom.

READ ALL OF
ANN CLEEVES

THE DETECTIVE MATTHEW VENN SERIES

THE SHETLAND ISLAND SERIES

THE VERA STANHOPE SERIES

  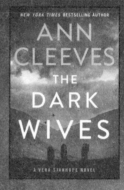

The Long Call	Raven Black	The Crow Trap
The Heron's Cry	White Nights	Telling Tales
The Raging Storm	Red Bones	Hidden Depths
	Blue Lightning	Silent Voices
	Dead Water	The Glass Room
	Thin Air	Harbour Street
	Cold Earth	The Moth Catcher
	Wild Fire	The Seagull
		The Darkest Evening
		The Rising Tide
		The Dark Wives

AVAILABLE WHEREVER BOOKS ARE SOLD

 MINOTAUR BOOKS